Rachel Grant

COVERT EVIDENCE

Janus Publishing

Copyright © 2015 Rachel Grant

All rights reserved.

ISBN-13: 978-1512097498
ISBN-10: 1512097497

Cover art and design by Naomi Ruth Raine

Copyediting by Linda Ingmanson

This book is a work of fiction. References to real people, events, establishments, organizations, or locations are intended only to provide a sense of authenticity, and are used fictitiously. All other characters, and all incidents and dialogue, are drawn from the author's imagination and are not to be construed as real.

All rights reserved.

No part of this book may be reproduced, scanned or distributed in any printed or electronic form without permission. Please do not participate in encouraging piracy of copyrighted materials in violation of the author's rights. Purchase only authorized editions.

This one is for Cael,

Because he goes to karate even when he's tired, has endured many character-building seasons in Little League, and is an excellent bow-hunter of gelatin-filled chocolate bunnies. Plus, he takes great care of Rikki Tikki Tabby.

CHAPTER ONE

Antalya, Turkey
August

MUSIC PULSED FROM the nightclub speakers several decibels above comfortable. Cressida stayed on the dance floor only because she'd promised her friend Suzanne she'd cut loose and have fun on her last night in Antalya before leaving the university-sponsored underwater excavation and heading east on a solo research trip. But her feet hurt along with her ears, and she had to leave for the airport in six short hours, making her regret her promise.

Suzanne was oblivious to Cressida's discomfort as she danced with three men at once. The locals really had a thing for leggy American blondes, and Suzanne had a matching appreciation for Turkish men.

Bumped into from behind, Cressida pitched forward, regaining her balance when a hand caught her shoulder before she slammed into another dancer. She turned to thank her rescuer, a smile on her face, but her stomach dropped when she met the familiar gaze.

Her reaction was instinctive. Her hand curled into a fist, and she swung out, slamming her knuckles into Todd Ganem's jaw with all the force she could muster from her five-foot-six frame. Caught by surprise, he stumbled back as his head snapped sideways.

The people around her froze as Todd teetered, then fell. She stepped over him, leaving the dance floor and gawking dancers. Her body flushed with adrenaline, or maybe she was going into shock.

What the hell is Todd Ganem doing in Turkey?

She made a beeline for the table where her group—graduate students from the underwater archaeology program at Florida State—sat, all with jaws agape and eyes wide. She came to a dead stop as she met the gaze of Dr. Patrick Hill. *Shit.* Dr. Hill, the head of the MacLeod-Hill Exploration Institute and the man she was counting on to fund her grant, had just seen her deck Todd. Could this get any worse?

She turned sharply, spotting an empty table far from Dr. Hill and the others. She needed a few minutes to regroup before facing them. She'd leave the bar and head to her overpriced hotel room right now if she could, but the translator had said he'd meet her here tonight, and she needed the translation for her trip into Eastern Anatolia.

She dropped into an empty chair, relieved to see Suzanne had followed her. She needed a friend right now. Decking Todd in front of Dr. Hill could well have just crushed her grant proposal—and she hadn't even written it yet. On the eve of embarking on the most important research trip of her academic career, the run-in with Todd could undermine everything she'd been working toward.

The sweltering night air seemed to rise another five degrees. She grabbed the bar menu from the table and fanned herself with it, taking a deep breath as she did so, willing herself to maintain a serene façade. She couldn't fall apart here, not in front of Dr. Hill. As soon as she had the translation, she'd go straight to her hotel room and indulge in a nice, private freak-out.

She and Todd had been together for ten months. Her souvenirs from their relationship included a blight on her academic record, the knowledge her advisor still didn't believe she was innocent, and a mug shot.

IAN WISHED HE could claim he saw the fist coming, but he didn't. He was as shocked by the punch as the man who received it. But then again, like the man who'd been hit, Ian had been distracted by the woman's cleavage and hadn't been paying attention to her hands.

She'd stepped over the man while cradling her fist, appearing somewhat dazed by the whole encounter, yet unapologetic and unafraid. If he were prone to hyperbole, he'd declare himself in love. As it was, he'd admit to being intrigued. Okay, and maybe in lust.

Medium height with long, straight, dark hair, a curvy build, and a deep summer tan, she was pretty enough, but until she'd taken the swing, her looks had been overshadowed by her tall blonde friend who now followed her to a table at the edge of the dance floor.

There was something hot about watching a woman unrepentantly deck a man and walk away without so much as a backward glance. She dropped into a chair and fanned herself with a menu, her skin glistening in the sweltering heat.

Sadly, he wasn't here to watch the woman. No. His job was never that enticing. He was waiting for the Kurdish rebel to show up, and he was getting damned impatient.

His partner on the op, Zack Barrow, was positioned closer to the dance floor and spoke to him through a hidden earpiece. "Fucking hot how she decked that guy and walked away. I think I'm in love."

Zack didn't have a problem with hyperbole. Typical rookie.

Ian lifted his drink to hide his barely moving lips and murmured, "She's a distraction we don't need." To everyone else in the bar, Ian was the bearded, hardened loner in the corner, drinking the night away in seclusion.

"It's not like anything else is happening here. Where the fuck is Hejan?"

"He swore to his God he'd make the drop tonight. He'll show."

"I don't trust him. He was a poor choice to turn—too much of a wild card."

Zack wasn't wrong—Hejan had always been high risk and never would have been Ian's first choice to double—but the Kurd was well connected and had something to atone for. Both traits made him an ideal spy. Hejan had come to him, which was always suspicious, but then, everything in Ian's line of work was suspicious. "He knows the game and the stakes. He'll show up."

The stunning blonde said something, and the brunette with the mean right hook offered a faint smile that didn't quite reach her large, wide eyes. In Ian's ear, Zack let out a low whistle. "Both women are hot."

"I don't give a shit if you want a threesome. We're not here to watch women." He said the words to Zack, but they were a reminder to himself as well.

"Hejan is wasting our time. Face it, Ian, he played you. He's probably making the drop somewhere else."

If Zack's statement were true, then months of careful work would come to nothing. This wasn't an acceptable outcome. Besides, Ian *knew* Hejan. "I've never been this far wrong about an informant before."

Zack chuckled. "The great Ian Boyd finally crashes and burns. I'm glad I'm here to see it."

"Fuck you," Ian said without heat.

"I bet Hejan can't lead us to the courier any more than I could."

There Zack was definitely wrong, but Hejan was Ian's asset, and Zack was only here tonight as backup. He knew minimum details.

"Keep your panties on. The night is young." But silently Ian acknowledged he was worried, and not just for the op. The Kurdish rebel carried a microchip several factions would kill for, and his tardiness was a very bad sign.

⊙

"HOW THE HELL did Todd even know I'd be at this nightclub?" Cressida asked.

Suzanne patted her hand. "Everyone on the excavation knew we were coming here tonight. Maybe Todd spoke to one of them. How did he leave the US, though? I thought they seized his passport when he was arraigned. Do you think it means he was acquitted?"

Cressida grimaced. "God, I hope not."

"Maybe you should have asked him before you took that swing," Suzanne said dryly.

"When I saw him, I didn't think. I just…reacted." She dropped her head in her hands. So much for appearing serene.

Suzanne stood and waved to the cocktail waitress. "We need a round of Tic Tac shooters. Stat."

"I'm not drinking," Cressida said. "I need to keep my guard up with Todd here. Shit. When Dr. Brenner finds out Todd is here, he's going to freak. He still doesn't believe I'm innocent." She'd have changed advisors if she could, but none of the other professors had wanted her either. Dr. Hill wasn't part of the department, though, and she knew him personally thanks to her internship with Naval History and Heritage Command the previous summer, making him her ace in the hole.

Until now.

"Everyone on the crew saw you deck Todd. It's obvious you aren't exactly chummy with him. You'll be fine."

Cressida massaged her temples. "Dr. Hill, who will have the

ultimate say on my grant proposal, witnessed me decking my felonious ex-boyfriend in a Turkish nightclub while I'm visiting on a student visa sponsored by the university and the MacLeod-Hill Exploration Institute." She flopped backward in her chair. "I'm totally screwed."

"Chill, Cress. You punched Todd. So what? We all wanted to deck him after the crap he pulled. So it happened in Antalya and not Tallahassee, no big deal. It was dumb of Todd to come here." She paused, and her brow furrowed. "Why the hell did he come here?"

Cressida leaned back in her chair, tilting her gaze to the ceiling. She'd give anything to be anywhere but in this nightclub right now.

This summer in Turkey should have been the perfect escape from the ugly events of spring. The project was ideal: excavation of an Iron Age shipwreck in the Mediterranean. Run by Dr. Brenner, her graduate advisor, it was her chance to win back his trust and that of the other students from her program. Best of all, Dr. Patrick Hill—the oceanographic explorer whose institute was the primary source of funding for the Iron Age shipwreck excavation—was here for a few weeks, giving her an opportunity to impress him before her proposal even landed on his desk.

Bottom line, Todd should be in jail for grand larceny right now, not in a nightclub in Antalya, Turkey, ruining her send-off as she left the project for a week to gather data for her grant proposal.

This research would form the foundation of her dissertation. It could make her reputation. Make her career. For a scholarship student who craved respect—and who'd nearly lost both thanks to Todd—this was her one chance to prove herself. Her one chance to *be* somebody.

But the rat bastard was here, ruining everything. Again. She curled her fingers into a fist, ignoring the pain the movement triggered in her sore hand.

The waitress arrived with their shots. "Your drinks were paid for by a guy at the bar."

"By the guy she punched?" Suzanne asked with a frown.

The waitress shook her head. "Not him." She nodded toward a cluster of people at the bar. "He's American. Green shirt, toward the end."

Cressida studied the group, surprised to see Dr. Hill had

moved to the bar and fit the description. Suzanne's eyes widened. "The one in the tan slacks? Tall, handsome, early forties?"

The waitress nodded.

A drink sent by the bigwig was unprecedented. But why? Was it a joke? A kiss-off because Cressida's chances of receiving the desperately needed grant were now nil?

Suzanne, clearly not freaking out about the situation in solidarity with Cressida, nodded to Dr. Hill and raised her glass in thanks. Dr. Hill's mouth curved in a slow smile. He raised his own glass in silent toast.

In that instant, Cressida's fears about Dr. Hill evaporated. "Suz, Dr. Hill just gave you *the look*."

Suzanne downed the shot in a single gulp, then met Cressida's gaze. "Yes. He did. I'm going for it."

"No way."

"Why not? His divorce went through months ago. I don't have a grant proposal under evaluation. I'll be defending next spring, and Dr. Hill and his foundation have nothing to do with my dissertation or research. Plus he's hot, and I've had a thing for him for years."

This was true, Suzanne had been unabashedly jealous when Cressida met him during her internship. "He's a bit older," she pointed out.

"Too old for *you*, sure. But I'm on the other side of thirty. Hill is only a year or two older than my ex."

Cressida gave Dr. Hill her own nod of thanks, then took a sip of her shooter. He tipped his head in acknowledgment, but his smile was entirely different from the one he'd given Suzanne. Good. Not just good. Perfect. She might survive this horrible evening after all. If only the translator would show up, she could head to her hotel room and get a few hours sleep before her early flight.

Suzanne stood. "I'm going to go talk to Patrick."

Cressida laughed. "He's *Patrick* now?"

"Well, if I'm considering having sex with him, I really shouldn't think of him as 'Dr. Hill' anymore."

Cressida smiled and shooed her with a wave. "Go. Hit on the world's foremost oceanographic explorer. Leave me all alone after what I've just been through."

"If he's upset you punched Todd, I might be able to convince him not to tank your grant."

"Well, in that case, give him a blowjob, and tell him I suggested it."

Suzanne winked at her. "The things I do for friendship." She crossed the bar with the confidence of a woman who always got what she wanted, and Cressida admired her self-assurance.

Alone at the table, she glanced around the noisy nightclub. It was a beautiful, sultry night in a hot, beguiling place. It was a shame that in this moment, it was the last place in the world she wanted to be.

She pulled out her cell phone. They were seven hours ahead of DC, meaning it was around three in the afternoon there. She tapped out a quick text to her friend Trina, telling her Todd was in Turkey and asking if she could find out if he'd been acquitted.

As she waited for a reply, she watched Suzanne and Dr. Hill—*Patrick*—on the dance floor. With Suzanne's entertainment for the night set, she would happily leave, but she still needed the translations.

"My uncle pulled strings to get me out of the US before the trial."

Cressida jerked her gaze up to see Todd on the other side of the table. She again curled her fingers into a fist. "I don't give a damn."

He shrugged. "I'm here because I have unfinished business. With you."

She jumped to her feet and planted both fists on the table. She enunciated each word carefully. "You do *not* have unfinished business with me. Our business ended the day you stole from the department."

"Excuse me, Miss Porter? Is this man bothering you?"

She turned to see Hejan, the translator. The wiry Kurd stood in a broad, menacing stance. Todd was bigger, but somehow Hejan managed to look meaner.

She smiled, grateful he'd arrived. He was late, but still his timing was perfect. Her conversation with Todd was decidedly over.

Todd let out an angry roar and slammed the table into her hip. Knocked sideways, she fell, landing hard on her side on the foul nightclub floor. Stunned by Todd's sudden violence, she was even more shocked when she twisted around to see he held her translator by the throat.

What the hell?

Todd was many rotten things, but he'd never been violent. In decking him, she'd been the one to cross that line. She surged to her feet, ignoring the pain in her hip, determined to intervene before Todd hurt Hejan. Strong arms grabbed her from behind, stopping her. "Let me go!" She struggled against the person who held her.

"Never get in the middle of a dog fight," the man said in a low tone that didn't disguise his American accent.

It was over in a flash. One moment, Todd's hands were wrapped around Hejan's neck, the next, Todd was being shoved toward the entrance by Hejan, who held a knife to his throat. Hejan ejected Todd from the club, then turned to face the packed room of frozen onlookers. The sharp tip caught the light as Hejan sheathed the blade in a practiced, unconscious motion. The shiny surface was clean and bloodless.

He hadn't hurt Todd, he'd just gotten rid of him. Shocking, but efficient.

She had trouble breathing as she took in how deftly and quickly Hejan had wielded the vicious blade. If she'd stepped in, she could have been seriously injured, or at the very least, she'd have thrown off Hejan's smooth timing.

The arms that had held her were gone, and she twisted to face the man who'd stopped her, but there was no one behind her. She scanned the faces of several men who sat alone or in groups, wondering which one had stopped her, but no one met her gaze. All eyes were on Hejan as he crossed the lounge to her side.

She almost wondered if she'd imagined it—the chokehold, the knife. It was crazy. "I'm sorry," she said to Hejan, knowing how vastly inadequate the words were.

The young Kurd shrugged like it was no big deal. The other patrons returned to their revelry. The world resumed spinning.

She didn't know what else to say. She reached for the table and pushed it back to line up with the others that ringed the dance floor. Hejan dropped into Suzanne's vacated chair at the same time Cressida resumed her seat. "I'd offer to buy you a drink," she said, "but you're Muslim."

He smiled. "I'll have a gazoz." He signaled to the waitress and ordered the local soda. Task completed, his gaze flicked down Cressida's side. "Are you okay?" he asked in a low, raspy voice she could barely hear under the loud music. Todd *had* hurt him.

"I'm fine," she lied even as her hip throbbed.

He reached into a thin satchel he wore slung across his chest, plucked out an envelope, and handed it to her. "A write-up of my translation and a digital recorder on which I recorded translations of the map in Kurdish, Turkish, Arabic, and Farsi so you can hear the pronunciation. Each language is in a separate file directory so you can easily play the place names for locals when they don't understand you."

"I've never considered using a digital recorder like that. I can see how that will be helpful. Thank you." It was brilliant, actually, but she worried how much it would cost her. "I must owe you for the recorder. They aren't cheap."

He waved her off. "The university provided it. You must return it when you come back next week, or they'll bill you for it."

She let out a small sigh of relief. She'd return it first thing because free was the only price she could afford. "Perfect."

Next, he slid a small card across the table. "My brother's phone number."

She tucked the card away, grateful for it. Hejan's brother, Berzan, had agreed to act as her guide and translator for the week. A guide was vital for this trip because southeastern Turkey—which bordered Iran, Iraq, and Syria, and was far more conservative than the western part of the country—could be considered unsafe for almost any American, especially now, with ongoing fighting with ISIS along sections of the Syrian border. Add to that the fact that she couldn't speak Kurdish, Turkish, or Arabic, was a woman traveling alone, and her trip was risky at best.

She'd spent the better part of six months planning this excursion—made thankfully cheaper because she was already in the country for the underwater excavation—and had no choice but to make the trip alone. At one point she'd planned to ask Todd to join her, but that ship had crashed, burned, and sunk. Of course, once she'd learned that he was a thief with shady Jordanian connections, she had to wonder if he'd had ulterior motives for being interested in studying ancient illicit trade routes in Kurdish territory.

IAN COULDN'T BELIEVE it. The woman with the mean right hook was the next link in Hejan's cell. He'd been ready to believe Hejan had only intervened because she needed help, but then Hejan handed her an envelope with a mark on the corner. The signal the envelope contained the microchip.

Hejan hadn't told Ian the courier would be unwitting, which meant this woman could well be a true conspirator who'd knowingly accepted the job of delivering the microchip to the leader of a Kurdish terrorist group. It rankled that he'd considered her attractive when it was possible she was a traitor.

"Are you certain she's American?" Zack asked through the earpiece.

"Her accent is American."

"That can be faked."

Ian studied her again. Turkey had a wide range of ethnic groups with an equally diverse set of physical attributes. The woman's dark hair and deep tan could easily pass for Middle Eastern. She bore a strong resemblance to the actress Natalie Portman, who, if he remembered correctly, was Israeli. But the way the woman moved, the way she talked, even the way she punched... Her mannerisms were all American. "Not under stress like that. She wasn't faking; she wanted to stop the fight. No way could she have hidden an accent."

Twenty feet away, the pretty traitor tucked the envelope into her purse. The packet stuck out of the small bag, easy picking for a brush drop.

Ian spoke softly into his drink. "Can't get a read on this. It's so...blatant."

"Get her picture so it can be run through the known associates database."

Ian rolled his eyes. He'd been at this far longer than Zack and didn't need to be told his job. *Rookies.* "Already sent it."

Hejan and the woman chatted for several more minutes, then she yawned and glanced at her watch. Hejan nodded and stood. She caught the eye of her blonde friend and waved.

The blonde smiled and returned her attention to the American man she'd cozied up to. It was odd that the blonde hadn't checked on the brunette after the fight.

The brunette wore a short, midnight-blue dress with a snug top cut low enough to reveal that impressive cleavage. She draped her purse over her shoulder just as a man walked by and bumped into her. The bag slipped and dropped to the floor.

She bent to retrieve it with reflexes that showed she hadn't had much to drink. While she bent over, Hejan got a prime view of her ass while Ian got a glimpse straight down her top. He corrected his initial assessment of her cleavage from impressive to downright spectacular, but a quick glance at Hejan revealed the man's gaze was fixed on the fallen purse, not the blatant display.

Yeah. Hejan had definitely passed her the chip, and now he was worried.

She slung the long purse strap across the opposite shoulder so it crossed her chest and wouldn't be easy to dislodge again, then she swept her long hair off her neck and twisted it in a knot that somehow managed to stay up without a fastener.

With her hair up, her high cheekbones became more prominent. She went from being simply pretty to…well, something more. Irrelevantly and involuntarily, he found himself wondering about her eye color.

Focus, dammit. The microchip is now in play.

Hejan and the woman headed for the exit, but not the main one, which emptied onto the busy Antalya street. No, they went through the hotel entrance. The woman had a hotel room?

Shit.

"Grab her drink and see if you can get a print," Ian instructed Zack. "I'll follow and get her room number."

She had a microchip that held information wanted by at least three countries and two terrorist networks. Ian couldn't lose her. If she managed to pass it up the line, then a terrorist organization would have access to the funding they needed to plan and implement a major strike. Ian's orders were clear: follow the chip, but if there was any chance he'd lose it, take out the carrier by whatever means necessary to stop the data from reaching the group leader.

His primary goal was to intercept the chip, identifying the group leader was secondary.

Hejan was playing a dangerous game, and unwitting or not, the woman was in it up to her beautiful unknown-color eyes.

Chapter Two

CRESSIDA LED HEJAN past the elegant flight of stairs in the center of the hotel lobby to her ground floor corridor. She hadn't planned on taking him to her room, but it had been hard to hear in the nightclub over the loud music, and she needed to go over the recordings and map with him, to make sure she understood both the translation and how to use the phrases he'd recorded for her.

Inside her hotel room, Hejan turned nervous. Very nervous. When she asked him what was wrong, he shrugged. "When you are east, especially near the border, never enter a bedroom with a man. It will get you in trouble."

Something in the way he spoke sent a chill up her spine.

He must have seen the fear in her eyes, because he paused and cocked his head, staring at her with uncharacteristic directness. In the several times they'd met over the last two weeks, he'd almost never looked her in the eye. He pulled a pendant from his neck and placed it over her head. "This will protect you. Wear it always. Promise you won't take it off."

Cressida lifted the necklace, still warm from Hejan's skin. The symbol was a Turkish evil eye, similar to the ones she'd seen in every tourist shop and outdoor market, but prettier, more elaborate. Not just blue-and-white glass but metal filigree holding polished, shaped glass. "It's beautiful." She started to take off the necklace. It was different and obviously special. "Hejan, I can't—"

He stopped her before she got the chain above her ears. "No. You need it. It will protect you. But keep it hidden. Next to your heart. Only show it to my brother."

She hesitated.

"I will be insulted if you refuse," he added.

Put that way, she didn't really have a choice. She was worried about this trip; a good luck charm might be the only thing that would put her mind at ease. She turned away from him and tucked the pendant between her breasts. With the long chain, it rested on her breastbone, hidden even with the low cut of the cocktail dress.

She led him to the couch and plucked the digital recorder from the envelope. They spent the next thirty minutes going over the recordings and digital file organization, making sure she knew how to use the recorder and could find the proper language when she needed it.

Task completed, she rubbed her tired eyes as Hejan folded his copy of the map he'd translated. The late night had caught up with her, and she was unable to stifle a wide yawn.

Hejan stood. "I'm sorry I was late, and now I'm keeping you up even later when you have an early flight."

"It's okay. I'm so thankful for your help and for arranging with your brother to be my guide."

Hejan frowned. "I forgot to tell you—there was a problem with Berzan's work schedule. He is trying to trade shifts so he can take you south toward Cizre tomorrow evening, as planned, but if he cannot, you won't be able to set out until Tuesday morning."

She tried to hide her disappointment. She'd just have to roll with it. She needed a guide, and Berzan was available and cheap, even if she had to wait a day. "Where does he work?"

"On the Lake Van ferry—"

There was a sharp pounding on the door. "Cress, open up! I *need* to talk to you."

Shit. Todd had found her hotel room. Could this night get any more ugly and complicated?

She was about tell him she would call security if he didn't leave, but Hejan slapped a hand over her mouth, shocking her with his quick, physical reaction. He pulled her back, away from the door. "No. Letting him know you are here will only add to your troubles—and mine."

She studied Hejan. He looked worried. Really worried. But then, he'd pulled a knife on Todd only...what, forty-five minutes ago? Was he afraid Todd had returned with the police?

She had no idea how the Turkish police worked. Just because no one in the nightclub had seemed to care didn't mean it wasn't a big deal. Hell, in the US, she was fairly certain bouncers would have detained Hejan until the cops arrived.

"You should go," Cressida whispered, nodding toward the sliding glass door that led to the patio by the pool. The hotel had been an extravagant expense, the only room in Antalya available at the last minute when her flight had been switched to six o'clock in the morning. That had forced her to take a room in the city because the water taxi from the island didn't run early enough for her to get to the airport on time. Now she was glad the resort had given her a room with poolside access.

"I can't leave, not with that man at the door," Hejan said. "He's dangerous."

"Todd isn't—"

Hejan merely touched his neck and looked at her pointedly, reminding her that Todd had shoved a table into her side.

Yeah, she didn't really know *what* Todd was capable of. Hard to believe she'd lived with him for months and had even thought herself in love with him.

"Go. Out the back," Hejan said. "Go to the airport."

She shook her head. "I should call the police."

"If you do, they may wish to detain you—and me—for questioning. You'll miss your flight."

Shit. Hejan had a point. She couldn't afford to reschedule, and Todd, of all people, knew that. He knew she'd gutted her savings for this trip and what it meant for her dissertation.

Hejan grabbed the digital recorder from the coffee table and shoved it into her hands. "Go. Now. To the airport."

She rubbed her eyes as Todd pounded on the door again. Hejan was right. Forget the expensive hotel room with the bed she hadn't even slept in. If she left now, she could avoid Todd and all the trouble he could bring crashing down on her. She needed to leave for the airport in a few hours anyway. It wasn't like she was going to get a ton of sleep. And with Todd at the door, she'd get zero sleep.

She padded silently into the bathroom and grabbed her bag of toiletries. Back in the main room she crammed it into her suitcase. She tucked her evening bag and digital recorder into her larger purse. She hadn't bothered to unpack anything else. She glanced down at the tight cocktail dress. Not exactly something she could wear in eastern Turkey without getting into trouble, but she'd have hours to change at the airport.

At the sliding glass door, she tugged at the secondary lock, a metal peg in the frame, but it was stuck. Hejan pushed on the door, taking the pressure off the peg, and plucked it from the hole. The door slid open without a revealing squeak. A low brick wall with a gate separated her private patio from the pool area.

Hejan unlatched the gate and held it open for her but didn't follow her through. She looked at him in question.

"I will deal with the man at the door."

She frowned. Hejan didn't even know who Todd was, let alone why he'd assaulted her. She thought of how quickly Hejan had produced the knife and couldn't suppress the small shudder that swept through her.

"No," she said. "Let's go."

Hejan shook his head. "Leave, Cressida. Now. You don't want to be here."

His eyes flattened and the congenial tone of voice disappeared. Had she imagined it? She'd hired Hejan as translator through the local university affiliated with the dig. It had been fortuitous that he was from Van and had a brother who could translate for her when she arrived. But she didn't know him. Was he the simple farm boy relocated to the big city, as he claimed?

Did it matter when she had a newly violent ex-boyfriend pounding on the door? She needed to get away. She would check in for her flight and wait behind security, where Todd couldn't reach her.

IAN TUCKED FARTHER back into the shadows of the pool area as the woman paused to talk to Hejan. Then, with her suitcase in one hand and a purse over her shoulder, she crossed the pool area at what appeared to be the maximum pace the tight cocktail dress and low heels allowed.

He whispered to Zack, "She's got her suitcase and is headed your way. Alone."

"Where's Hejan?"

"He stayed in her room." Ian crept along the pool perimeter, following at a distance. He pressed against a low wall as she paused to retrieve her key card to enter the hotel from the pool area. This time of night, the rear door was accessible only to hotel guests. Unfortunately, Ian hadn't been able to snag a key and would have to circle around.

"I see her," Zack said a moment after the woman entered the hotel.

Ian jumped the fence and entered the building through the nightclub. He skirted the busy dance floor and headed for the hotel lobby.

"She just stepped out to the front driveway."

Good. That meant the coast was clear for Ian to enter the lobby without being spotted.

Ian entered the opulent, brightly lit lobby. Through the glass door, he caught sight of the woman as she wheeled her bag to the front of the wide, circular drive.

"You want me to tail her from here?" Zack asked.

Ian hesitated. It could take her some time to get a taxi. "Wait with her. I need to talk to Hejan."

"Roger."

He turned to go to the woman's room but paused midstep when Zack said, "She's talking to the doorman." A moment later he added, "She slipped him some money. He's nodding and waving to one of the waiting cars."

Shit. Go after her or Hejan?

"The car is pulling up. What should I do?"

He had no choice. "Follow. Don't lose her."

"I won't."

Ian darted down the long interior hallway, then paused at the intersection with the wing where the woman's room was located. A quick glance revealed an empty, quiet corridor. He treaded silently on the expensive Turkish carpets and came to a dead stop when he reached her room.

Motherfucker. The door was ajar. A foot protruded through the opening.

"Zack. We have a problem. Do not, under any circumstance, lose sight of the woman."

"What's wrong?"

Ian pulled his Sig and shoved open the door. A man lay just inside the door in a pool of his own blood, glassy eyes fixed unseeing on the ceiling.

Chapter Three

"Her name is Cressida Porter. She's in Turkey on a student visa," Ian's boss, Stan Mott said, when Ian called him less than an hour later.

"Where is she now?"

"She went straight to the airport," Stan said.

"Is she flying to Van?"

"Yes. I've got Zack booked on the same flight."

"This is my op, Stan." Ian stifled a curse. It had been necessary for Zack to follow the woman while he stayed back and photographed and searched Hejan Duhoki's body, but Zack was backup on this. Hejan had been Ian's asset; no way would Zack take the lead.

"We need to tip off the Antalya police about Duhoki," Stan said.

"Not until her flight takes off," Ian said. "Even though Hejan was alive when she left, you know they'll detain her. We'll never get the next link in the cell if she doesn't go to Van." He paused. "Get me a seat on her flight. The seat next to hers, to be exact."

"You know I can't do that. She saw you at the club."

"She didn't see me."

"Zack said you held her back, during the fight. No way would she fail to notice you after that."

Ian silently cursed Zack. The rat. "She was focused on the fight. I retreated before she thought to look." He sighed and rubbed his chin. The beard would have to go, which was a shame. The extra-long beard helped him blend in in the Muslim world, and it was a shield against people noticing him. Supervisors had told him his face was too striking for covert ops, and he'd never go unnoticed, which was simple bullshit. His looks were nothing special in the Muslim world. But still, to get around that objection, he'd grown the beard and found it useful. "I'll shave and put on glasses. Even if she got a glimpse, she won't recognize me without the beard."

"Zack is ready to go."

"As backup. Zack's language skills are weak, and he reeks of newbie."

"Zack's been in-country for months, and he aced every simulation the Company put him through." Stan sighed. "But you're right about his Turkish. You're *sure* she has the microchip?"

"Hejan gave her an envelope marked in the corner, just like he promised. You and I both know whoever killed Hejan was probably after the microchip. Now they'll be after her."

"We should let the Turkish police nab her at the airport."

"We might get her—and the chip—but Hejan was adamant that the courier would lead us to the next link in the chain, who will take us to the leader. We can take apart the entire network with this op."

"Ian, you've been doing this too long to believe that fairy tale. It's *always* the next one up the chain."

Ian took a deep breath. He couldn't put into words how he knew it wasn't a bullshit lead. He just knew. From the moment he'd interviewed Hejan, he knew *this* was the informant, the man who would break everything open. Hejan was the real deal. All he said was, "This is it, Stan. She's the key, and with Hejan dead, she's the only lead we've got."

Stan clicked his tongue. "You're talking about using a civilian as bait."

"There's a good chance she's in on it. And we aren't the ones who put her at risk. Hejan did that when he gave her the microchip, and she accepted that risk when she took it from him. In a public place. In front of a hundred people. Get me a seat next to her on the plane. That will give me two hours to decide whose side she's on and act accordingly."

Stan sighed. "I'll see what I can do."

While Stan pulled strings, Ian took a long and involved Surveillance Detection Route back to his hotel so he could shave and prep for his role. Transformed, he then took another SDR, driving around Antalya, seemingly aimless. His role in the mission would have to be aborted if there was any sign he was being tailed.

Thankfully, after an hour and a half, he hadn't spotted any followers. He was clear to head to the airport. He pulled into the airport parking lot and called the intelligence officer who'd been gathering information on Cressida Porter. "What can you tell me?" Ian asked.

"She's here working on an underwater archaeology excavation funded in part by the Akdeniz University in Antalya, her graduate program at Florida State University, and the MacLeod-Hill Exploration Institute. One of our guys went out to the island where the crew for the underwater dig is living. Most were out—night on the town, just like Porter—but the professor running the dig was there. He's Porter's graduate advisor at FSU."

"Name?" Ian asked.

"Dr. Steven Brenner. One of those academic types who insists on being called 'doctor'—a real prig, according to our guy. He was none too pleased to be woken up early and questioned but eager to spill info on Porter. She's not his favorite student."

"Why's that?"

"A few months ago, another graduate student, Todros Ganem—goes by Todd—stole the university's new, state-of-the-art Lidar equipment. We're talking upwards of a few hundred thousand dollars, including drones for aerial survey. The equipment was recovered from his house, which Ganem shared with his girlfriend, Porter. He was arrested and implicated Porter in the theft, saying she needed Lidar drones for her dissertation research. Tallahassee PD arrested her, and she was facing serious time, but—and this is where it gets interesting—none other than US Attorney General Curt Dominick ordered the FBI to investigate, citing counterintelligence concerns. Sure enough, the FBI found evidence Ganem had sent out feelers to associates in Jordan prior to the theft. No word on whether he planned to use the drones to map sensitive locations on US soil, or if he simply wanted to sell them to finance his own research. Political motives haven't been ruled out. There was no connection to Porter's research, and the FBI found no evidence other than Ganem's word she was involved—he'd offered her up hoping to receive a reduced sentence. All charges against her were dropped. The university was forced to reinstate her."

"But Dr. Brenner doesn't believe she's innocent?"

"No. He thinks she asked Ganem to steal for her and, when he got caught, let him take the fall."

"What's the scoop on Ganem?"

"His parents immigrated to the US from Jordan the year before he was born. He has an uncle in Jordan who's high in the military. The uncle has made several inflammatory anti-American statements. It's possible the uncle or his cronies wanted the Lidar and drones for aerial reconnaissance of the Jordan/Syrian border."

"Where is Ganem now?"

"Also interesting—no one knows. He disappeared five or six weeks ago. Investigators think he's in Jordan with his uncle."

Ian frowned. "She decked a guy in the bar last night. Any chance that was Ganem?"

"Possible. We're trying to locate the blonde—Suzanne Davis—to confirm the man's identity."

"Why is Porter going to Van?"

"A research trip to gather data for a grant proposal. She wants to convince the private exploration institute—the one that's partially backing the shipwreck excavation—to fund a Lidar survey in southeastern Turkey to search for archaeological sites. She needs outside funding because FSU won't let her use their Lidar equipment after what happened with Ganem. According to Dr. Brenner, she resumed planning this trip the moment she was reinstated at the university."

Ian tapped the steering wheel. On one level, everything about Cressida Porter added up—she could be a squeaky-clean innocent grad student with poor taste in men—but throw the microchip into the equation, and nothing balanced.

"You should know," the intelligence officer added, "Dr. Brenner believes her research will take her closer to the border."

"Which border?"

"Southeastern Turkey."

Ian paused. "You mean Iran, Iraq, *and* Syria?"

"Yes."

"Holy fuck," Ian said.

"Yeah, I thought so too."

Ian had to admit, it was brazenly brilliant to use a woman—and an American woman at that—as courier. If he could pull off the academic angle, he'd have used the archaeologist cover himself years ago. Hell, covert reconnaissance missions with archaeologists likely predated T. E. Lawrence's survey of the Sinai Peninsula for British military intelligence a century ago, when the man was supposedly looking for evidence of the Exodus.

"What's her religious background?" Ian asked. "Are we dealing with a zealot?"

"We only know her mother's side, which is mixed Christian and Jewish. No word on if she's practicing either, so it seems unlikely she's an extremist with an agenda. Which leaves stupid as the only other reason she'd head into the region alone."

"The word crazy also comes to mind. And it's too early to rule out extremist, no matter how unlikely. Keep digging. Send what you find to my email." Call completed, Ian next dialed Stan. "What's the word on my flight?"

"By the time the airline agreed to cooperate, the passengers were already boarding and the seat next to hers was assigned. We had to pull yet more strings to ground the flight and rearrange seating."

"You got me in the seat next to her?"

"Yeah. They've switched planes, forcing a seating chart scramble. Do I need to remind you how much this is going to cost us? And I'm not talking money, I'm talking favors. I've burned through them all with this."

"It'll be worth it, Stan."

Stan sighed. "Your ticket is waiting at the VIP counter. Hurry your ass up, the new plane will start boarding soon. We can't hold the flight and don't have any favors left. This is a deep cover op, Ian. You're on your own once you board that jet."

"I know."

Chapter Four

CRESSIDA'S FRUSTRATION SIMMERED when they announced everyone had to disembark the jet on which they'd just embarked. She was tired and cranky and afraid the flight would be canceled. She grabbed her heavy suitcase from the overhead compartment and shuffled down the narrow aisle with the other passengers.

Nothing about this trip was going right. She was cursed. The universe was out to get her.

Stop being a narcissistic baby. This flight delay has nothing to do with me.

In the terminal, she made a beeline for the coffee stand next to the gate. She'd feel human with more caffeine in her system.

Coffee in hand, she settled into a seat. Exhaustion weighed on her like full diving gear. She'd actually fallen asleep underwater once. The hot Florida sun had beat down on the shallow water of the bathtub-warm Gulf of Mexico, and exhaustion mixed with heat had lulled her into closing her eyes, just to rest them for a moment...

She startled, realizing she'd done the same thing here. She rubbed her face and glanced around, trying to determine if she'd been out for more than a few seconds. Her eyes met those of a man sitting two aisles across from her.

She glanced away, uncomfortable to have met a stranger's gaze, even as her body flushed in an uncontrollable response to his sheer...*perfection*. How could a mere glance cause a physical reaction?

The scientist in her wanted to study the evolution of why eyes just that shape, capped by thick, dark brows, combined with those sharp cheekbones and that firm jawline with dimpled, squared chin, was such an appealing masculine combination. Why was his particular arrangement of features so harmonious? Why did she find more pleasure in looking at him than, say, the man sitting to his left? That man's nose was a tad wider, with cheeks that bore the marks of a losing battle with acne in adolescence. The man with acne scars wasn't unattractive. His face had a certain appeal, but it lacked the symmetry, the perfection of his neighbor. She doubted her heart would flutter after a chance meeting of gazes with him. Which was ridiculous, really.

She knew nothing about either man.

Her name sounded over the loudspeaker, dragging her tired brain away from musings on male beauty and surreptitious glances at the Adonis in the boarding area. She grabbed her bag and made her way to the counter, where the agent gave her a new seat assignment and boarding pass.

She returned to her seat and was disappointed to see the guy with the perfect face was gone. To occupy herself, she pulled out her cell phone. She'd shut it off hours ago to avoid Todd and now was tempted to turn it on again to check for messages, hoping to hear from Berzan. She wanted to know if he'd changed shifts so they could set out for Cizre tonight. Expecting to set out right away, she hadn't booked a hotel in Van and now was nervous about arriving in a remote foreign city without reservations. Anthony Bourdain, she was not.

Boarding began again, making the decision for her. She tucked the phone back into her purse, then lined up with the other passengers.

Inside the jet, she noted there were two seats on one side of the center aisle and three on the other, a different configuration from the first plane. That had to seriously mess up the seat assignments and explained the long delay. Cressida had been assigned a spot on the two-seat side, but there was a man sitting in her seat. And not just any man. It was the Adonis.

Panic swept through her. What if the ticket agent had screwed up and she'd been bumped from the flight by accident? How would she straighten this out when she couldn't speak the language? "Excuse me, there must be some mistake—"

The man met her gaze and flashed a warm smile. "My bad," he said in crisp American English, "I prefer the aisle—do you mind trading?"

She was too relieved to object. "No problem."

He stood and stepped into the aisle so she could get to the window seat. "Thanks. Can I help you with your bag?"

The cramped aisle and waiting passengers at her back had her practically pressed against him. It would be hard to lift her heavy wheeled carry-on over her head without hitting him with it. "Thank you," she said, then brushed past him into the row, leaving her bag for him to lift.

He dressed like a man traveling on business—dark slacks and a light button-down shirt that stretched tight over thick biceps when he lifted her suitcase above his head. She couldn't help but pause to admire the display.

He glanced down and caught her eye as he positioned the bag. His smile said he'd noticed her appreciative look. She flushed and settled into the window seat.

No. Men. She clearly had crap taste in that area, so the fact that she thought he was good-looking must mean he was a thief or a liar or had connections to anti-American activists in Jordan.

Or, if she was twice blessed, all three.

Adonis dropped into the aisle seat, knowing smile firmly in place. His gaze landed on her left hand. She couldn't help herself and peeked at his left hand too. No ring.

Not that she cared, because she wasn't interested. It didn't matter how attractive he was, with those pale gray eyes highlighted behind frameless, rectangular glasses, or the faint lines that creased his skin next to his eyes and mouth, telling her this was no young grad student but a man.

She was so *tired* of grad students.

He offered his hand. "John Baker."

"Cr-rista." She stumbled, employing a fake name on impulse. She'd promised her friends she'd be careful, and giving her real name to a total stranger was definitely *not* safe behavior. "Crista Portman."

The man cocked his head. "That's funny, because I was just thinking you look like—"

"Natalie Portman. Yes. I've been told that." She affected a casual shrug. "We aren't related." She'd been hearing about her resemblance to the actress since her braces came off when she was fifteen, which was why she'd co-opted the woman's last name. "And thank you. I consider it a compliment." She was always flattered when someone made the comparison, because she was nowhere near as pretty as the *Black Swan* actress.

The man held her hand a beat too long, and her heart rate picked up—her reaction had more to do with that handsome face than with her impulsive lie. Plus he smelled good. Shaving cream and soap combined with a musky scent that made her want to breathe deep and relax. But maybe that was due more to her utter exhaustion than to the attractiveness of her seatmate.

"Is your final destination Van?" he asked.

She pulled her hand from his. "I don't know you, Mr. Baker, and I don't share my travel plans with strangers."

His grin deepened as if he relished a challenge. "Call me John. And I understand your caution. A woman traveling alone can't be too careful. What brings you to Turkey?"

She should grab her book and end the conversation right here and now, but...she didn't want to. After a hellishly long night and having to face an ex she'd hoped never to see again, it was refreshing to meet a handsome stranger. Maybe it was the simple fact that he came from her country but had nothing to do with the insular world of underwater archaeology that made him appealing. He knew nothing about her relationship with Todd and the fallout from his lies.

It hit her, all at once, that in addition to being upset by Todd's arrival, she was also homesick. She'd been in Turkey for eight weeks and was tired of the struggle to get around when she didn't speak the language, and heading east, the difficulty would only get worse. John Baker...he spoke her language.

"What brings *you* to Turkey, John?"

He flashed a smile and winked. "Business."

An announcement was made in Turkish, Arabic, and at least two other languages she didn't recognize. The seat belt light turned on. Cressida adjusted her belt and stowed her purse—plucking out a book and tucking it in the seat pocket in case she decided to end the conversation. Flight prep completed, she leaned back in her seat and said, "What sort of business?"

"I work in private security—my client—a tech company I'm not at liberty to name—is sending me to Van to make security arrangements for an upcoming meeting between company executives and officials from all over the Middle East."

Security. She knew a few men in that field. His muscular build made sense, as did his polish and charm.

The jet pushed back from the gate. She let out a breath she hadn't realized she'd been holding. After months of planning, saving, and stress, she was finally on her way to Eastern Anatolia on an insane quest to find an ancient aqueduct that would make or break her academic career.

Chapter Five

IAN LEANED FORWARD and plucked Cressida's—or rather, *Crista's*—book from the seat pocket. "*Serçe Limani: An Eleventh-Century Shipwreck,*" he said, reading the title. "A relaxing beach read?"

She smiled. She had a beautiful smile—full, engaging, warm, with perfect white teeth on display. This surprised him, but then he hadn't seen her smile like this in the bar last night.

"Research," she answered.

"Research for what?" he pressed. She was determined to be taciturn, but engaging with people who didn't want to be engaged was his specialty. And he could do it in six languages.

"For my dissertation," she said with a hint of pride in her voice.

"What are you studying?"

"Underwater archaeology. Specifically, illicit trade routes through Turkey, Iraq, Iran, and Syria, as observed by mapping shipwrecks in the Mediterranean and the utilization of Byzantine-era aqueducts and cisterns. It's part of a larger evaluation of trade in the Middle East but my focus is primarily on the illicit routes that may have led to the downfall of civilizations."

Ian smiled. Her desire to be reticent was overwhelmed by her desire to impress him. She had a strong need for male approval. This was going to be easy.

And, in all honesty, he *was* impressed.

He flipped through the book, which appeared to be a lengthy academic paper. He glanced again at the cover. "INA?"

"Institute of Nautical Archaeology—it's part of Texas A&M University."

"Is that where you're a student?"

"No. I'm a grad student at Florida State."

"Gainesville?" he asked, knowing he was wrong and wondering if she would bother to correct him. After all, she didn't want to talk to him.

"Tallahassee."

He suppressed a grin. He was in, and they hadn't even reached cruising altitude yet. "Right. Good football team. The Seminoles."

She nodded. All at once she seemed to realize she'd told him too much. She gently took her book from his hands, opened it to her bookmark, and settled back in her seat.

He'd give her a few minutes. Let her get lulled by the fact that he wasn't pressuring her to talk. But he couldn't give her too long. He intended to have dinner plans with her before they landed.

He pulled out his own book—written in Arabic—and settled back to read. With his peripheral vision, he saw her eyes widen when she took in his reading material. She hadn't asked him for details on his work or where he was from, and now he'd laid the bait to make her curious. Hopefully, the same insecurity that made her want to impress him would go into overdrive now that she knew he was no dummy.

He glanced sideways at her and tossed her an absent smile, the look of a man engrossed in his reading. She smiled back and resumed her own reading, a light flush on her smooth, tanned cheeks.

She really was lovely. How had he missed the slant to her eyes last night? Brown but flecked with amber and framed by long, elegant lashes, her eyes were downright mesmerizing up close.

Prior to this job with the Company, he'd served in the Army with Delta Force, working covert ops for the military. In all his years of undercover work, he'd never slept with a target for his job. It had never been necessary and, technically, couldn't be required. But he'd always known there might come a time when sex would be a logical action to maintain cover.

In short, for his country, he was a willing soldier, but that didn't mean his body was a mindless patriot and, given the types of women he'd dealt with on covert ops, more often than not, sex wasn't a tool in his arsenal.

Could he take one for Team USA if this mission required it?

He had no doubt he could muster the necessary patriotism.

TWENTY MINUTES AFTER takeoff, the flight attendant arrived with the beverage cart. Cressida ordered coffee, but John touched her hand and said, "Let me buy you a drink as thanks for trading seats with me."

She shook her head. "It's still early, and I'm short on sleep. One drink and I'd go down for the count."

After they both had coffee and the flight attendant had moved on, John said, "You'll have to let me take you out in Van, then."

She frowned.

"You don't like that I'm being so forward," he said.

"I'm surprised by it. You don't know me. I could be married. Or have a boyfriend. Or I could be gay. Or crazy. Or any of a dozen other things."

"I know you aren't married." He glanced at her left hand and raised a brow.

"Too easy. I'm an underwater archaeologist. I've been diving on a shipwreck twice a day for the last two months. The married crew members don't wear rings so they won't lose them in the Med, and after eight weeks, there's no tan line or cheater imprint."

"Yes, but no married woman in her right mind would fly into Eastern Anatolia alone without a wedding band."

Her mouth snapped closed. "Okay. So I'm not married. But I could have a boyfriend. Or be a lesbian."

He shook his head. "Definitely not a lesbian. *That* was obvious right away."

She felt her face flush. Okay, so he'd caught her admiring his muscles. But, damn, he had a nice body. No harm in looking. "And the boyfriend?" she asked, feeling like a glutton for punishment.

"Well, if you have one, then I have an hour and a half to determine if it's serious and I should back off." His voice dropped so low she could barely hear him over the whine of the jet engine. "So, is there a boyfriend?"

It wouldn't hurt to flirt a bit, would it? Her ego was still sore from Todd's betrayal. They'd supposedly been in love, yet he'd implicated her in a felony to save his ass. "No. No boyfriend."

Definitely no boyfriend.

◉

IAN'S LACK OF success in securing a date—or at least a phone number—by the time they landed in Van had him on the ropes but not defeated. She'd responded in all the right ways, but he hadn't closed the deal.

The woman was an interesting mixture of cautious and rash. She'd been sloppy in giving a fake name when her real one had been broadcast over the loudspeaker in the boarding area, but earned kudos for being aware she should be protective of her identity and destination.

That clumsy fake name argued for innocence. A player would have been aware her name had been announced in the crowded terminal. Only an innocent would think no one would notice.

"Because we Americans need to stick together," he said, holding out his business card. "Call me if you need anything."

She thanked him and tucked the card into her purse.

"If you decide you'd like company, my evenings will be free," he added.

She smiled. "I'll keep that in mind."

As long as she stayed in Van, tailing would be easy. He'd identify her hotel and get a room there as well. Tonight they'd find themselves at the same restaurant, and he would continue to wine and dine her. He'd planted a bug in her book and could safely hang back in the airport. He wouldn't lose her unless she was on to him, in which case he had far bigger problems.

Inside the terminal, she paused to scan the arrivals area. She frowned, clearly disconcerted at not seeing…whoever she'd hoped to see. She faced Ian and pasted on a false smile and said goodbye, then headed to an information desk. He hung back, cell phone pressed to his ear, and watched her with his peripheral vision. He listened via the bug, which transmitted directly to his phone, as she asked about hotels in Van.

Tourism was rare in Eastern Anatolia, which meant she wouldn't have trouble booking a room in one of the nicer hotels. The man at the desk recommended an old hotel near the lakeshore. Ian called and booked a room before the clerk finished translating the options to Cressida. He headed to the taxi line.

Several minutes later, she emerged from the terminal and he smiled and raised an eyebrow while nodding toward the half-dozen people who separated them in the growing line. "We could share a ride?" he offered.

"We might be going in different directions," she said with a sexy, crooked smile.

"Do you think I care?"

Her pretty eyes flashed with amusement. "Thank you." She left her spot in the line. The moment she stepped out, Zack and two others stepped in behind her.

"Only if you promise to join me for dinner," Ian added before she slid into the line at his side.

She glanced at the ever-growing line. "Seriously?" she asked.

"Yep. Dinner. I know a great local spot. No one makes better *içli köfte* in Van. You'll love it."

She shook her head in exasperation. "I guess I don't have a choice."

He laughed. "You sound so thrilled."

"Maybe this is better?" She placed a hand on his chest. "Thank you, John. I'd be delighted to have dinner with you." Her voice was a soft, sexy rasp.

Damn. She was good at turning on the sexy.

Maybe too good.

Chapter Six

CRESSIDA PURSED HER lips as she considered her wardrobe options. She was meeting John in the lobby in ten minutes and everything she'd packed except the blue cocktail dress—which wasn't an option in a region in which she'd need to wear a headscarf more often than not—was bland. Her clothes were perfect for a woman who didn't want to be noticed.

But she wanted John to *see* her. Hell, she sort of wanted to see John. All of him. And she didn't really mean the *sort of* part.

Apparently, taking a nap after her long, brutal night had woken her reckless side.

She dressed in beige slacks and a blue cotton button-down shirt, then made a face at her boring reflection. She'd been foolish to agree to dinner. She should be playing it safe. John Baker didn't exude safe.

With a deep breath, she left the security of her hotel room, grateful for the five hours of sleep that had restored her humanity, even if it meant she hadn't made it out to explore the city. At least she'd be sharper than she'd been on the flight.

As if. Just looking at him made her tongue-tied.

She stepped out of the elevator into the lobby and scanned the room. No sign of John.

She felt a familiar ache in her belly. She'd been stood up before. It was a bleak, worthless feeling when a date didn't bother to show. She'd give him five minutes, then she was out of here. She had her pride. And she could take smug satisfaction in knowing he couldn't track her down to apologize, should he want to. He didn't know her real name.

Two minutes into her small grace period, he stepped into the lobby, and her mind went blank. Holy crap. He was even better looking than she remembered. How was that possible? Surely he'd made a deal with Hades or something, because no mere mortal had the right to be that hot.

He crossed the wide, open floor to her side, his eyes crinkling behind his glasses as he smiled. "Sorry I'm late. I was delayed by a call from my boss."

This was a first in Cressida's world. She didn't think any of the men she'd dated knew the definition of the word "sorry" let alone would employ it in a sentence. Yet this man dropped it when he was only two minutes late. She liked that. Probably more than she should. "Oh? Is it past six? I hadn't realized."

He laughed. "Liar. You're a scuba diver. Timing is everything to you. A minute too long at the wrong depth is trouble in your world. It spills over into your daily life, and you're punctual to the minute, I bet."

She frowned, but not in displeasure. He'd pretty much nailed her with that assessment. "How do you figure?"

"You check your watch constantly." He touched the spot between her brows. "And you get an adorable wrinkle here, when you are delayed—like when the cab was stuck too long at an intersection." He leaned closer to her and whispered in her ear, "It makes a man wonder if you time everything."

Her entire body flooded with heat at the innuendo. As if that wasn't enough, his lips brushed her ear. "Lavender," he murmured. "Nice."

She shivered. She should be put off, but that recklessness that had been eager for this dinner now considered skipping the meal all together. She might need to thank Suzanne for throwing a box of condoms in her suitcase when it hadn't occurred to Cressida she might want them.

She was here to gather information for her dissertation, she reminded herself, which would start when she spoke with Berzan after he got off work this evening. No sex with John Baker, no matter how well this date went.

She cleared her throat. "Thank you."

He pulled back. "Hungry?"

"Starving," she said truthfully. She'd had only a paltry pastry this morning at the airport and had woken from her long nap feeling ravenous.

He held out an arm. "The restaurant I mentioned is only a few blocks away. You up for a walk?"

"Absolutely." She took his arm, enjoying the feel of his firm bicep and the crisp, soapy smell of his skin. The sultry evening air enveloped her in a warm embrace.

They reached the restaurant, a small, cozy space she would

never have guessed was a restaurant from the tiny sign and storefront. Inside it smelled heavenly, roasting meat, spices, and flatbread. The savory scents reminded her just how hungry she was. They were seated quickly, and John conversed with the host in Turkish, who nodded and smiled and then disappeared into the kitchen.

"The food here is more Kurdish than Turkish, so I ordered some samples for you to try. Hope you aren't feeling homesick for a burger and fries."

She shook her head. "No. I'm game to try new things. It all smells wonderful."

"They don't usually serve alcohol here, but the owner has a few bottles of wine he keeps handy for non-Muslim friends. They have a nice Italian wine that goes well with the lamb *köfte*."

She cocked her head, impressed that he was considered a friend by the proprietor. "Do you come to Van often?"

He shrugged. "Now and again."

A man came to their table and greeted John warmly. John introduced Cressida, startling her when the fake name was the only word she'd understood. *Damn.* She should probably tell him the truth. She held out her hand to the proprietor, but the man smiled and crossed his arms.

"He offers no offense. He's devout and can't touch a woman who is not part of his family after washing, before prayer. And the *Mu'adhin* is about to deliver the *Adhan* for *Maghrib*."

Cressida nodded and smiled. "I understand. It's nice meeting you."

The man beamed and spoke rapidly to John before nodding to her and leaving.

"It'll be hard for me if I don't have a translator, won't it?"

John nodded. "Not many speak English here. You haven't arranged for a translator?"

"I did, but he's working right now, so we haven't connected. I'm hoping to hear from him tonight, after he gets off work." She leaned forward. "It's a shame you'll be busy with your job, or I'd offer you the money I was going to pay Berzan."

"Berzan?" he asked.

"He's the brother of a man I hired in Antalya for some translation work."

John's eyes flattened, but the look passed so quickly she almost wondered if she imagined the cold, hard look. But the chill that trickled up her spine said it had happened.

The waiter arrived with the bottle of wine followed rapidly by the tray of samples John had ordered, and the unsettled feeling passed.

As she tried each item, John explained the dish, warning her before she sampled the raw meatballs—the Turkish version of steak tartare—in case she was likely to react to the dish.

The waiter returned, and John ordered more food based on her preferences, then taught her the names of the dishes she'd enjoyed the most. Heat infused her as she faced him across the intimate table and sipped her wine. How far should she let this go?

"Tell me about your research," John said. "What do you hope to find in Van?"

"I won't be staying in Van. I'm heading south."

"South? There isn't much south of here. Except Syria."

She pressed her lips closed and wondered how much she should tell him. "There's a lot of real estate between Van and the border."

"And you expect to find…?"

"Nothing during this trip." That was mostly true. "I'm just here to line up contacts. Pave the way for conducting a Lidar survey of an area where I hope to find things next year."

He raised an eyebrow. The simple gesture was infused with sexuality. "Lidar? What's that?"

"It's a type of remote sensing. With Lidar, you measure distance by illuminating a target with the laser. The reflected light is analyzed. It was developed in the '60s, but the technology has really improved. The applications for archaeology expand every year. With a Lidar survey, I'll be able to find cisterns and underground aqueducts that were lost over a thousand years ago—ones I believe were an important part of illicit trade routes."

"You're talking about the Silk Road?"

"I'm talking about a Silk Road *bypass*."

John sat back in his chair. He looked impressed. "That would be something."

She leaned forward, warming to the subject, which, after all, had been her obsession for months. "I think dyes, precious metals, gems, spices—you name it—were traded using underground passages. With Lidar mapping, I can find those cisterns and aqueducts and prove my theories."

"You really think there are hidden tunnels in the Eastern

Anatolia hills?" His tone was skeptical.

"Have you ever heard of the Gadara Aqueduct?"

John shook his head.

"It was Roman, built to supply water to the city of Gadara in modern-day Jordan. It's the longest known tunnel from antiquity. Construction began around AD 90 or 100, and it took a hundred years to build. The underground sections are sixty-six miles long. The tunnel is about two meters tall and one and a half meters wide."

"Yes. But people know about it. *You* know about it. Nothing that big could remain hidden for two thousand years."

She grinned. "That's where you're wrong. Gadara was discovered in 2004. By an archaeologist."

That handsome mouth curled into a sexy smile, and his eyes lit with warmth that said he didn't mind being told point-blank he was wrong. "Seriously?"

"Yep."

"What makes you think there's something like that here?"

Cressida leaned back. No one knew the complete answer to that question. Most of her fellow students were good people. Friends. But that didn't mean they wouldn't try to beat her to making such a significant discovery by submitting grant proposals of their own. She took a sip of wine. Tonight it would remain her secret. "Tell me about your work, John. What are you doing in Van?"

He laughed. "Touché." He lifted his glass in a toast to her and took a drink. "As for what I'm doing in Van, right now, I'm having dinner with a beautiful woman."

Heat pooled low in her belly. This first date was going awfully well. But numbering it implied there could be more. And there couldn't. Wouldn't. She was here to work.

What made this date special was its singularity. This was a one-time fantasy come to life. A no-strings, one-night-only, once-in-a-lifetime fling with a hot man in Turkey.

Anything more than that was just asking for trouble.

◉

IAN ALMOST WISHED the date were real. If it were, he wouldn't hesitate to act on the ready invitation in her eyes. Lulled by the food, dim lighting, and fine wine, she had transformed from the timid American he'd met on the plane into a sultry siren.

Her reluctance to reveal too much about herself had faded as she warmed to her subject, but what surprised him even more was how much he—Ian, not the prick John he pretended to be—was turned on by her.

But he couldn't let his dick do the thinking, especially since she hinted she had a lead on ancient tunnels in the Kurdish region of Turkey. If such tunnels existed, the information would be valuable.

Turkey had many security issues, the least of which were bordering unstable regimes like Syria, Iraq, and Iran. The real concern for the government was the country's Kurdish population. Years of government-sanctioned second-class treatment of Turkish Kurds, whose very language was forbidden, had created a large discontent population. The recent alliance between the Turkish government and the local Kurdish population due to the threat from ISIS in Syria and Iraq wasn't enough to make up for decades of repression. The Kurds remained uneasy, untrusting, and not all factions were on board with the alliance.

The restaurant they were eating in was owned by a local Kurd who'd once whispered—in Kurdish—his frustration with the ongoing harassment by Turkish military officers who acted as the governing authority in the region. The very fact that Ian was fluent in the forbidden language made finding Kurdish allies in this part of the country easy. The hard part was letting them know he spoke their language when everyone was a potential informant.

Smugglers' tunnels in the region could be a game changer. The *Partiya Karkerên Kurdistan,* or PKK, was only the largest and most well-known rebel group. Hejan's group was smaller, was not allied with the Turkish government, had designs on becoming the leading separatist group in the region, and had a history of using terrorist tactics to make it happen.

After learning the focus of her study, one thing was clear to Ian. It was no fluke that Cressida had been selected as courier. She might be unwitting, but somehow, her research had nabbed the attention of Hejan's group. Given that, as tempting as Cressida was, sex with her could screw up the mission. For starters, if she was in bed with him, she could hardly be out passing off the microchip.

After dinner, Ian placed a hand on the small of her back as they strolled down the narrow street. If this were a real date, he wouldn't hesitate to duck into a covered doorway with her so he could slide his hand lower, pull her against him, and taste her.

Damn, she smells good.

But this was a date between Crista Portman and John Baker. John couldn't get laid when Ian had work to do.

The street was quiet as they walked the blocks to the hotel. Neither Ian nor John entwined fingers with hers, no matter how natural such an action might have felt. John wouldn't start something he couldn't finish, and Ian wasn't invited to play at all.

Inside the hotel, they crossed the lobby to the lift. She paused and met his gaze before hitting the button for her floor. He smiled as he again inhaled her sexy scent. From her pause, he figured she'd hoped he'd invite her to his room, but with his silence, she'd caved and would lead him to hers.

She'd left the cautious woman on the airplane, apparently.

They reached her floor, and he followed without a word. At her door, she paused and met his gaze, one eyebrow raised in question.

This was the moment when John, if he existed, would pull her close and taste that mouth. He'd run his tongue along the full upper lip that had fascinated him from the first time he saw her—right before she decked a man.

He was hard and ready. Ian would have trouble walking away if John kissed her. "I'm afraid the evening ends here, Crista."

Her brows flattened in confusion, not anger, but with the right pressure, he could push her in that direction and debated which reaction would suit his needs.

"I'm sorry," she said in a soft voice, "did I misread you all evening?"

He let out a sigh. "You didn't misread, I miscalculated. Tomorrow will be a busy day, and I need to be sharp. I'm still adjusting to the time zone—I flew into Antalya from DC yesterday morning. Much as I would love to continue this evening, I need to sleep. Alone."

A nice guy would ask if he could see her again. John *was* a nice guy, but Ian, not so much. And right now, Ian was calling the shots, because Ian was the one with a job to do. He leaned in and kissed her forehead, a brotherly peck. Insulting, really, after how much John had hit on her. "Have a good night," he said and headed to the elevator. He turned and met her gaze, then stepped into the lift.

Chapter Seven

What the hell just happened?

Cressida stood outside her door in stunned silence as John stepped into the elevator. The door slid closed behind him, and still she stood there. She breathed into her hand. Her breath might be a bit garlicky, but he'd eaten the same damn food. Shock dissipated as she remembered the avuncular kiss. Anger surged past confusion. *What an ass.*

She'd made such a fool of herself. She unlocked her room with quick, angry movements, jerked the handle down, and shoved open the door. What was *wrong* with her? How the hell did she meet these guys?

Tired and has a long day tomorrow, my ass.

She was baffled as to why he'd bolt after the blatant signals he'd sent all evening. She hadn't misread him, dammit.

Had he been telling the truth? Was she just being petulant because she was hot and bothered and unsatisfied? He'd given her his card. She could call and ask him point-blank what his deal was.

She dug around for the card in her purse and found her phone instead. A glance at the screen, and she groaned. The voice mail messages she'd ignored when she sent Berzan a text with the name of her hotel earlier had since doubled in number. She scanned the list of missed calls. None were from Berzan's number. Odds were the messages were either from or about Todd. She didn't want to deal with Todd right now.

Why the hell not? She was already in a bad mood. May as well get it over with.

But the first message wasn't from Todd. Nor were the next several. They were all from Suzanne, who sounded upset but wouldn't say why.

Dr. Hill had probably had sex with her and scrammed. And while she wanted to judge Dr. Hill badly for it, she was feeling a little perturbed that at least Suzanne had gotten laid. She couldn't deal with Suzanne's post-hookup emotional trauma on top of her lack of hookup trauma.

Of course, she'd have to *care* to feel trauma, and she definitely didn't care about John Baker and his lame-ass excuse for bolting.

The next message was from Trina, who was concerned after receiving Cressida's text about Todd. As she'd expected, there was no message from Berzan.

She frowned at the phone. Call Trina or leave the line open in case Berzan called? As she stared at the smooth face, the phone vibrated with an incoming text. Relief flooded her. It was from Berzan.

> *Sorry for the delay. Hejan said he explained. We can set out tomorrow morning. If you meet me at the ferry dock at the end of my shift at 2100, we can discuss our itinerary. I have already arranged lodging in some of the smaller villages.*

She glanced at her watch. It was only eight thirty—or twenty thirty—more proof her date had ended pathetically early. Just enough time to meet Berzan. She replied to his text that she'd be at the dock then tucked the phone into her purse. She'd call Trina later.

It was for the best that things hadn't worked out with John. She was here to work, and meeting Berzan was a thousand times more important than getting laid.

◎

IAN'S HOTEL ROOM was one floor up, directly above Cressida's. He entered his room and nodded to Zack, who lounged in the corner chair with a tumbler half-filled with an amber liquid cradled in his hand. "Interesting shit, that stuff she told you about tunnels in Kurdistan," he said.

Ian nodded and approached the dresser where Zack had left the bottle of scotch. Glenlivet. A brand to make a good Scot proud. Not that he knew where in Scotland his ancestors were from, or if he had any kin there now, but he liked to think he did, liked to believe he had greater familial connections on this earth than the woman who'd birthed and named him.

A drink would dampen his reflexes, and he needed to stay on guard. He poured a splash of scotch into a glass. A taste. That was all he could have. He tossed it back, and his belly warmed instantly. The placebo effect eased knots in his shoulders he hadn't even felt until that moment.

He itched for another splash. Another burn. The bottle called to him. But the small taste was all he could have.

Story of his life.

He could view, and at times even sample, the pleasures other men took for granted, but the comforts of American life weren't for him. He'd given his life over to his country, and lived—and deep down believed he'd someday die—for that service. When he finished a job, he moved to the next one, never pausing to enjoy the very liberty he sacrificed for.

He replaced the stopper and turned to face the balcony, avoiding Zack's interested gaze for the moment. Ian had known Zack was listening to every moment of his "date" with Cressida. It was necessary and expedient that his backup on this op be fully informed. But that didn't mean he liked it. The idea of Cressida's vulnerable flirtation being witnessed, even mocked, by another agent left a bitter taste in his mouth that even the scotch couldn't burn away.

Lake Van glistened in the darkness beyond the window. Something about this sleepy, underdeveloped part of Turkey called to him, but was another pleasure he could sample but never fully enjoy.

As was the woman he would tail for the next few days.

If he were Hindu, he'd wonder who he'd pissed off in a previous life to find himself in this situation. But he wasn't Hindu. He wasn't Muslim. He was a secular warrior in the midst of a holy war, and his primary goal was to protect his country from being targeted or drawn into the battle.

"So, what's the deal? You think she's part of Hejan's cell, or is she being used?"

Ian kept his back toward Zack. "I think she's being used." But his opinion changed nothing. Not when there was no way to be certain.

A soft buzz sounded. He turned to see Zack's feet hit the floor with a thump as he pulled out his cell phone. The screen flashed. "Looks like it's time to find out. Cressida is on the move."

"Where is Sabal?"

"On the street, ready to follow her on foot or in a car," Zack said.

"Good. I'll lag behind him. Finish searching her room while she's out."

"I should follow and let you conduct the search. She's never seen me. If she spots you, she'll spook."

While Zack's argument was logical, there was no way in hell Ian would let him take over. It was Ian's job to follow the microchip and identify the courier. No one else's.

THE MAN AT the front desk only spoke a few words of English. Cressida smiled and pulled out the digital recorder Hejan had given her. Folder one held all the basic phrases. She looked up the file number on the crib sheet and played words that translated to "how do I get to," then said "ferry dock" in English. She added, "boat" in Turkish, because that word—thanks to weeks of living on an island and riding a water taxi into Antalya on a regular basis—she knew.

The man's face lit up. He pulled out a street map and circled the hotel location and pointed to the long spit, then inked in a thick line for the route she should follow. It wasn't far from the hotel at all, just in the opposite direction from the restaurant she'd walked to with John.

She said thank you in Turkish and stepped outside. The night had cooled somewhat, and she took a deep breath of the fresh air that wafted from the vast lake. A brisk walk was definitely better than stewing in her hotel room.

She walked along the water, finally reaching the spit. The area was wide and open, making her feel safe in spite of being a stranger in a strange land.

Her mother's crap taste in men had resulted in a childhood of feeling unsafe in her own home. At the age of thirteen, Cressida had gone to her local community center and taken every self-defense course they offered. Over the years, she'd taken classes in a half-dozen different martial arts—she and her mother had never lived in one neighborhood long enough for her to move up in belts—but she'd achieved enough proficiency to kick a guy in the balls without hesitation. Well, kicking in the balls was the one thing her various sensei and sifus had discouraged, but she'd never been interested in winning tournaments.

Those years of lessons gave her the courage to walk boldly down the pier in spite of the gathering darkness and her unfamiliarity with the area, but deep down she wondered if she'd used poor judgment in walking alone at night. But surely Berzan wouldn't have asked her to meet him if it were a problem?

A few men loitered on the long pier, but they paid no attention to her as she passed. There wasn't a ferry at the end, but the boat was probably running late, meaning she was in no hurry to reach the dock.

Two-thirds of the distance down the brick walkway, she stopped at an empty bench and sat. A glance at her watch said it was one minute after nine. If the boat didn't turn up soon, she'd ask one of the men she'd passed about the schedule, but for now she was content to sit and enjoy the quiet night in a part of the world she'd dreamed of visiting ever since she deciphered the map key.

Water lapped against the lakeshore, a soft rippling sound that soothed nerves still raw from rejection. How stupid was she to go out on a date with a stranger when she should have been working?

Nothing good ever came from getting involved. It only brought heartache. And sometimes felony charges.

◉

IAN FOLLOWED CRESSIDA at a distance, cursing the quiet night that forced him to hang back so far. The hound, Sabal, was in front of him, keeping a closer tab on her. He was local and blended better than Ian could, especially now that Ian had lost the beard.

Cressida parked herself on a bench as Ian's phone vibrated. He took the call from Zack.

"She brought a lot of papers," Zack said. "Photocopies, mostly, but some are maps and scholarly looking reports. A few satellite photos—really nice definition—with different lines drawn on the image. As expected, the reports are all about shipping and land routes from the Middle East into Asia."

"Photograph the maps and satellite pictures," Ian said as he watched her rise from the bench and move closer to the train platform at the end of the pier.

"Doing what I can. But there are a lot. It'd be easier to just take them."

"No. We aren't done with her, and that would tip her off. Leave no trace."

"Shit! Someone's at the door."

Alarm shot through him. "Get the hell out. The balcony. Now." The call cut off. Ian cursed. What the fuck was going on?

Behind him, the ground rumbled. A moment later, a whistle sounded. The train from Iran was arriving.

Shit.

The courier had to be on the train. How the fuck did he not realize that when he saw where Cressida was headed?

Because she'd asked the clerk about the ferry, not the train.

The ferry was just visible in the distance on the lake. Between the noise and hubbub of passengers transferring from train to ferry, there would be plenty of opportunity for chaos.

Cressida walked along the edge of the grassy median that separated the brick walkway from the train tracks until she reached the break in the fence where the train passengers would disembark. She leaned a hip against the back of the last bench on the spit, her gaze fixed on the incoming train.

After the abrupt end to his call with Zack, he had a bad feeling about this drop. It didn't matter that the port was well lit with vapor lamps glowing brightly every few hundred feet. It didn't matter that she was in a public place that would soon be filled with people.

In his line of work, crowds could be more dangerous than deserted alleys.

He reminded himself Cressida Porter was a means to an end. He'd been working toward this moment for months, and nothing less than capturing a terrorist leader hung in the balance.

He nodded to the hound, signaling that he should move in, and Ian wished he had a dozen more hounds on this rabbit, but for this op, he only had Sabal, who would follow Cressida after she made the drop.

Ian would follow the microchip.

A man approached her from behind, blocking Ian's view. He stiffened, until it was clear the man was just curious about the out-of-place Western woman.

Ian met Sabal's gaze. He rubbed a hand across his beard, the signal a brush drop had not occurred.

Slowly, the smelly diesel train rolled down the long spit and came to a halt with a piercing squeal, capturing Cressida's attention as she cringed and covered her ears.

Masked by the noise of the train, a man darted out from the tracks in front of the train and made a beeline for Cressida. He yanked her purse from her hip, but she wore it over her shoulder and across her chest, and her neck caught in the strap. The wail of the brakes ended after Cressida's shrieks began.

Pulled from the bench she'd been leaning against, she grabbed her bag, caught in a tug-of-war with the would-be mugger. He moved behind her, so the strap would dig into her throat and yanked harder, breaking her grip. Her head snapped back.

Ian darted toward her, but disembarking passengers spilled from the train, blocking him.

Her scream cut off, and from the glimpse he saw between the press of bodies, the strap was choking her. Ten people deep behind her, Ian was stuck, moving against the flow of traffic. The solitary hound was closer.

The mugger dragged her backward until she tripped and hit the ground. She landed on her back, and the purse slipped free of her neck. Her screams resumed. The people who'd just disembarked and witnessed the violent mugging now backed away, giving her assailant room to flee.

The mugger darted across the tracks in front of the train, heading toward the terminal building. He disappeared behind the train. Cressida shot to her feet, and the foolish woman *chased* her mugger—a man who had nearly strangled her. Sabal was on the other side of the shocked crowd, not close enough to stop Cressida or the fleeing assailant.

Ian dived through onlookers, breaking a path through the disembarked passengers. He followed Cressida across the tracks. She turned right and ran up the spit parallel to the train.

He chased her, while she chased the mugger, who darted into an open passenger car. *Shit.*

Ian prayed Sabal was ready to intercept if the mugger exited on the other side of the train. He dug in for more speed, closing the distance between him and Cressida. But he wasn't fast enough.

She turned and followed her mugger onto the train, then let out a horrific scream.

Chapter Eight

A SCREAM ERUPTED from Cressida's throat as pain ripped along her scalp. With a hard yank on her hair, the man she'd slammed into when she swung full bore into the open passenger car pulled her across the aisle, then tossed her down the steps on the other side. She tumbled out the door, landing on the sharp gravel.

The man exited the train car by leaping over her, then ran full bore down the empty tracks that paralleled the train. She staggered to her feet. She couldn't let him get away with her passport.

An arm gripped her from behind and spun her around. She shoved at whoever had grabbed her, determined to chase down her mugger and reclaim her purse, but the man's grip tightened, and he flashed a vicious-looking knife in front of her nose. Her gaze traveled from knife to the man's face, and she met the predatory eyes of a complete stranger.

The air in her lungs whooshed out of her. She couldn't scream. She couldn't move. A paralytic nightmare come true.

I'm going to die. Here. Now.

Her body quaked. She couldn't breathe. She was deaf to all sound but the pounding of her heart.

The man shook as if he chuckled. His mouth moved. As the hand with the knife swept out, she dropped, throwing herself into the jagged gravel. Sound resumed. She could breathe again. But terror still held her in a fierce grip.

She rolled to escape her assailant. The sharp rocks sliced her shirt and cut her arms. She swept out her leg, catching her attacker in the shins, and he stumbled forward, knife arcing toward her.

From nowhere, a man crashed into her assailant, knocking him to the ground and dislodging the knife, which landed inches from Cressida's eye.

The man who'd tackled the thug moved fast—a blur of violence. Her attacker hit the hard gravel just feet away, and her rescuer pounced, pounding the downed man's face with several rapid punches.

In shock—and amazement—she realized her savior was John. *How had he...?*

Her attacker's head fell back, the man unconscious. John's gaze darted around. Feral eyes met hers, and she scooted back, pulling herself into a ball at the base of the train. Who was this man who'd just beaten the crap out of a knife-wielding thug? How did John find her? Why was he even here?

John Baker now terrified her as much as the knife had.

His gaze turned to search the spit, where her original mugger had fled. He released the unconscious man and stood. Another man ran to his side and asked John a question in Turkish. John's gaze flitted from Cressida to the direction the mugger had gone. He answered in rapid Turkish of his own, and then the newcomer ran off in that direction.

"Sabal is going to see if he can get your purse back," John said, reaching out a hand to pull her to her feet.

Cressida ignored the hand and didn't say a word. She just wrapped herself in a tighter ball.

He crouched down in front of her. "Are you hurt?"

She was too numb or maybe too terrified to know if she'd been injured. She squeezed her knees to her chest and gave a short jerk of her head in answer.

"Crista, I'm here to help you." His voice was soft, cajoling.

She met his gaze. Clear gray eyes stared into hers with a degree of concern that touched her vulnerable, terrified core.

She wanted to believe him, but he didn't add up. He'd spent the entire flight trying to learn her travel plans, then pumped her for information about her research at dinner, only to dump her in her hotel room with nary a good-night kiss after seeming to want nothing more than a tryst with her. Now, slightly more than a half hour after he'd claimed to be exhausted and jet-lagged, he was here, just in time to save her.

She squelched a gut-level needy response to his worried gaze and glared at him. "Go away."

The compelling concern disappeared as his eyes flattened. "Um, why not try 'thank you for saving my ass'?"

She wasn't taking any of his bullshit. "What are you doing here?"

"I told you, I'm in private security. Some of the VIPs who are coming to Van for the high-level meeting will be arriving by train. I came here to check the security of the facility. Clearly, it sucks."

"This time of night?"

"Yes."

"After you gave me the brush-off because you need to sleep."

He sighed. "I had no plans to come here tonight. I told you the truth. When I got to my hotel room, I received a message from my client expressing security concerns about the inbound train. I decided to check it tonight so that tomorrow night—if I could convince you to have dinner with me again—I wouldn't have to cut our evening short because I need to work."

His claim that he'd planned to ask her out again caused an annoying girlish flutter. Could she *be* more pathetic? She wouldn't even be in Van tomorrow night. "Who's your client?"

"I'm not at liberty to say."

"Who's the guy who just ran after my mugger?"

"Sabal. He works for me."

"I saw him. Earlier. When I was waiting for Berzan. But I didn't see *you*." The implications of that stole her breath. *John had me followed by someone I wouldn't recognize.*

The man on the ground next to her groaned. John kicked him in the head, and the groans stopped.

The violent act was so casual. So chilling. And yet it was directed at the man who'd pulled a knife on her, so she could hardly condemn John for it.

He took her hand and pulled her to her feet, then tugged her toward him as though he might hug her. She resisted.

"I'm not the bad guy, Crista. I called Sabal—he's one of our local contractors—to meet me here. He arrived first. I walked up just as the train arrived. I saw you, but given how I screwed up tonight, I was afraid to let you know I was here, so I hung back. When I heard the ruckus on the platform and saw you were being mugged, I was shocked and tried to get to you, but couldn't. I'm sorry I didn't stop the attack." He looked down. "If I hadn't screwed up earlier, this never would've happened. We'd be in bed right now. Together."

Don't give in.

"I'm sorry. I was stupid and never should have left you like that." He touched her cheek, tracing downward along the column of her throat, lightly touching her raw skin, which had been abraded by the strap of her purse. His jaw tightened as he studied what she imagined must be an ugly welt across her neck.

His gaze and touch said he cared.

She glanced away, ashamed of the suspicion she'd felt. What was wrong with her? Like there was some vast conspiracy in Van that involved *her*? Narcissistic much?

John had beaten the crap out of an armed man to save her. It was as simple as that. She glanced at her attacker and shuddered when she again saw the eight-inch knife. She shook her head to clear it. "Thank you. I think you saved my life."

He placed a finger under her chin and raised her face. She met his gaze. His eyes were clear and earnest and warm. "You're welcome." His fingers caressed her cheek. "I do this for a living, you know—assess threats, provide personal security. The first rule—never fight or chase down a mugger."

She wanted to look down, but his hand prevented it. "I guess that was pretty stupid. But he got my money. My passport." Panic shot through her as she mentally inventoried her purse. "My phone. Christ, John, what am I going to do?"

He pulled her against him, wrapping her in a warm hug. One hand cradled the back of her head and pressed her to his chest; the other stroked her back. "I can help you."

"The nearest US Consulate is in Adana. I can't afford to go all the way to Adana."

"Where are you headed from here? Back to your underwater dig, or back to the US?"

"Back to the dig in Antalya."

"With a police report, you should be able to fly back on your return ticket. You can deal with the passport in Antalya."

"But my research—it will take me close to the border with Syria. There are so many checkpoints…"

"I work security. I know people. I'll see what I can do."

His words and the embrace were exactly what she needed, offering strength, courage, and hope. She absorbed what he offered, grateful beyond words for this man's skill and incredible timing.

Footsteps approached, and he gently released her. Sabal, the man who'd pursued her mugger, stood before them. John spoke to him in Turkish. Sabal responded and shook his head in a sharp negative. She supposed it was too much to hope he'd be able to recover her purse so quickly.

They exchanged more words she couldn't understand, then Sabal approached her attacker. He lifted the man's head by the hair and turned his face side to side, as though inspecting him.

With an arm around her shoulder, John led her away from the train. "Wait. Shouldn't we stay and talk to the police?"

"Sabal will handle it."

"Don't I need to make a statement?"

"Sabal will tell them everything. We'll go to your hotel room, get you cleaned up, then go to the police station."

She glanced down at her clothes. Her top was filthy and her slacks torn—a big slice ran down her hip. The situation felt surreal. The mugging. The knife. John coming to her rescue. She was freaked out by everything, but the loss of her passport and cash was her first concern. Trina could probably wire money to get her through the next few days, but she hated the fact that she'd have to hit up a friend for financial help.

Trina wasn't going to believe this story.

Cressida stopped short. "Wait. Sabal is going to talk to the police?" She sounded dense, she knew, but it had taken her that long to put the implications together. A violent mugging could do that to a person, apparently. "He's going to tell them what happened?"

"Yes."

She looked down. Damn. Time to fess up. "He needs to know—my name isn't Crista. It's Cressida. Cressida Porter."

John raised a sardonic eyebrow and flashed a teasing smile. "Fake name? I guess I really *did* come on strong on the flight."

She grimaced. "All my friends have hounded me about being careful on this trip. It seemed like the right thing at the time, but I regretted the lie at dinner."

He shrugged. "I understand. Security is my business. But you should know a fake name isn't much protection, not unless you have fake ID to back it up." He paused. "Cressida." His low tone made it sound as if he were tasting the syllables, and the heat in his eyes said he liked the flavor. "Shakespeare? *Troilus and Cressida?*"

She experienced a slight frisson. The man could speak and read Turkish, and he knew the title of one of Shakespeare's lesser-known tragicomedies. She was impressed. "I'm actually named for the car—Toyota Cressida—you know, conception story and all that."

"Is it okay if I make a joke here, or is it a sensitive subject?"

"Have at it."

"Good thing it wasn't a Unimog."

She laughed. "Good one. Usually people say Gremlin." She

leaned into him, shocked to feel so comfortable, when just minutes ago she'd been full of distrust. Even terror.

He glanced around the long spit, which had gradually emptied as people transferred from ferry to train and train to ferry. "You used a fake name, and yet you went out alone after sunset?"

"I figured Berzan wouldn't have said to meet him here if it wasn't safe." She glanced around. "Wait. Berzan. He was supposed to be coming in on the ferry."

John nodded toward the dock. "The ferry has already unloaded."

But there was no young Kurdish man looking for her. Unease slid through her. "Where is he?"

"Berzan is your translator's brother?"

"Yes."

"I hate to say it, but it appears Berzan lured you out here and mugged you."

His words stunned her to the core. "You think Berzan was my *mugger?*"

John shrugged. "Or the guy with the knife."

She came to a dead stop. "I lied to you about my name to stay *safe*, then made plans to meet with an armed mugger?" But it was worse than that. *Hejan.* "What does this mean about my translator? He was *helping* me. I trusted him." Had he really done the translations she'd paid for? Were the phrases on the digital recorder to be trusted?

Sonofabitch. The digital recorder! It was inside her purse.

Had Hejan set her up? Why would he do such a thing?

CHAPTER NINE

IAN HAD FUCKED up his mission. His one job was to go after the mugger. Stupid, foolish, fatal mistake to have taken on the man with the knife.

Primary objective: Don't lose the fucking microchip. And he'd failed. Cressida—no matter how sexy or innocent—became expendable the moment the chip left her possession.

He knew that. Better than anyone.

But he'd been blind to the mugger's escape at the sight of her struggling against an armed assailant. Something in him snapped, and he'd FUBARed the mission.

They walked silently back to the hotel. She battled panic at the loss of her purse, but from his perspective, it was better that she'd lost everything instead of just the microchip. Without her money, phone, and passport, she needed him, and he was ready to be her knight in shining fucking armor. Which was necessary, thanks to his massive lapse in protocol.

He'd stopped to save a woman who could well be complicit, and in so doing had lost a chip a terrorist organization had killed for once already.

Worse, Sabal hadn't been able to raise Zack on the phone, nor had Ian. He had no clue what they'd find when they got to the hotel. All he knew was he couldn't let Cressida out of his sight.

What did it mean that Hejan had told her the guide—*his brother*—was named Berzan? The name was a signal intended for Ian. He needed to know everything she knew about her supposed guide. It was his only hope of picking up the trail to the chip.

He'd already sent Cressida's cell phone number to Stan. If the mugger still had the phone on him—and if he was a complete fool—they might find him when the phone pinged cell towers. He'd receive a text if they got a lock on "Berzan's" location.

Ian was good at his job and prided himself on his tradecraft. He'd been based in Ankara for the last two years. Before that, he'd been in Bahrain. During his time in the Middle East, he'd recruited a record number of spies. But if they didn't get anything from Cressida's phone, then this was the fuckup of all fuckups and could end his association with the Company. This kind of disaster didn't just get a covert case officer fired, it could get him killed.

Beside him, Cressida was anxious. Rattled. Scared. He'd ruthlessly broken through her caution and distrust both on the jet and again next to the train. He had to remain ruthless in his dealings with her. He couldn't let himself be swayed by pretty, innocent eyes. But he had to do it while playing the mild-mannered prick John Baker.

Jesus, he'd wanted to screw her brains out earlier—and not because he was playing her. In his personal rulebook, kissing, even sex for the job were fine, but honest desire, when there was doubt about her loyalty? It bothered him that he even felt it.

He'd screwed up the mission because of that desire. Because of her.

She was an unknown risk, and until he had the microchip, he had to control her. The fact that her tradecraft sucked argued against her being a spy. As it was, the team in Ankara had gathered more intel on her background, which he'd read this afternoon while she napped.

He knew about the blank space on her birth certificate where a father's name should be. Now he had another piece: Cressida Porter knew the make and model of the car in which she was conceived, but not the name of her biological father.

Dubious paternity was one thing they had in common.

He draped an arm around her shoulders, and she leaned into him. Good. She was already relying on him.

The facts of her life were simple and sad. Her pregnant mother had been tossed out by disapproving parents at the tender age of fifteen. It appeared Cressida had never met her maternal grandparents, who lived in a wealthy, gated community outside Baltimore.

When Cressida was born, the hospital sent the bill for the uninsured labor and delivery to her grandparents, but they refused to pay it. Both mother and child were minors, and when threatened with court and public shaming, the Porters quietly paid the bill, then paid their daughter, Sarah, to move across the country with their granddaughter. Monthly payments halted on Sarah's eighteenth birthday.

With cold parents like that, it was no wonder Sarah had gotten knocked up at such a young age. But life in California wasn't much better for baby Cressida. The police visited her home often due to Sarah's loud, violent fights with her various boyfriends. Cressida received her own bruises, and CPS intervened a few times, culminating in a stint in foster care before she ran back to her mother's house.

In spite of all this, according to school records, Cressida had been a brilliant student. She graduated near the top of her high school class and received a full scholarship to Berkeley. She turned Cal's graduate school down in favor of the underwater archaeology program at Florida State.

Nothing in her background added up to someone who'd become disillusioned with her country and joined a terrorist group, but he still had questions.

No doubt Cressida's childhood had been the stuff of nightmares, but her struggle wasn't the sort that generated anti-American sentiment. No. Her background was a breeding ground for depression, low self-esteem, and abusive boyfriends of her own.

International terrorism wasn't on the long list of side effects, let alone the short one.

But he couldn't ignore the boyfriend with Jordanian ties who'd stolen Lidar equipment and implicated her in the theft. Now, here she was in Eastern Anatolia, hoping to use Lidar to find ancient smuggler tunnels.

As Ian escorted her through the lobby of the old hotel, he slid his hand down her spine, settling on the small of her back. That Lidar theft nagged at him. Had she fooled everyone?

Was Ian simply another dupe to a sexy spy with exceptional acting skills?

THE HOTEL CLERK'S eyes widened when Cressida entered the lobby all torn and dirty. He spoke rapidly to John, who answered in Turkish, explaining, she assumed, her mugging. After a moment, the man produced a new key to her room and slid it across the counter. To John, she said, "Thank you. I don't know how I would have explained the situation without your help."

His jaw tightened as he touched her cheek, his thumb lightly tracing what she suspected was a raised welt. She had to look like hell, which matched how she felt. "We'll just have to make sure you don't go anywhere without me from here on out," he said.

The idea of him feeling even slightly protective of her made her pathetic heart beat a little faster. "That's impossible. I have research, and you have work—"

"I'll clear it with my boss. You need an escort, and I'm volunteering."

She didn't understand him. One moment he could be *too* nice, *too* accommodating. Then she'd get a hint of…something… A darker nature, maybe. Or a dangerous vibe. Whatever it was lurked deep, telling her that Mr. Affable wasn't necessarily the real John. And if she were being honest, she was more attracted to the man he hid than the one he presented. It appeared she'd inherited her mother's poor sense of self-preservation.

There was more to it, though. She couldn't meet his gaze without returning to the moment he'd swooped in and saved her. The knife still loomed large in her mind. She could so easily imagine it finishing the arc and slicing into her.

John had fought with a brutality that in any other circumstance would horrify her. The dangerous vibe wasn't in her imagination. That was the real man, buried under that amiable demeanor. And he'd unleashed that ferocity to save *her*.

She was no stranger to violence. She'd witnessed her mother take blows and had received a few herself when she was younger. Never, not once in the darkest times of her childhood, had anyone been there to help her when she needed it. His presence and action had fulfilled a long-buried childish dream of rescue.

Then there had been that moment right after he'd knocked out her assailant, when he'd looked at her with an intense, concerned expression that spoke to her core. He was a stranger, yet he'd looked at her like she was something to be treasured, protected. She'd felt as precious as an ancient, gilded vase inscribed with secrets of the past.

She'd waited her whole life to see that look on a man's face.

There was something seriously wrong with her if she could flip from terror to lust to distrust in the flash of a second, but it had happened as they stood next to the train, and now here she was, leading him to her hotel room, hoping more than anything that once they were alone, he'd kiss her.

A kiss could make her forget the terror. Forget her lost passport and money. Forget her stupidity. She wanted, more than anything, to forget. Just for a moment.

Todd had ruined her last night in Antalya, and now she'd been mugged in Van. In true Turkish fashion, she wondered if she were cursed. Without thinking, her fingers strayed to the evil eye pendant, which hadn't protected her. But then again, John had come to her rescue, so maybe it had.

She thought of a way to thank John for his services, proving she was as foolish as her mother, a woman whose sexual history was a textbook of don'ts.

"You okay?" John asked.

She stepped into the tiny elevator, realizing she was dazed, and it showed. "Fine. Sorry. Just…shaken up, I guess." She leaned against the back wall, tucking herself into the corner.

He hit the button, then faced her, stepping so close she was warmed by the heat of his skin. His eyes were hot with desire. "I very much want to kiss you right now."

Her heart kicked up a notch. *Maybe wishes do come true.* "What's stopping you?"

He rubbed his thumb over her bottom lip. Her heart no longer merely raced; it pounded with the force of a bass beat. "We're both coming down from adrenaline, and your judgment is clouded by gratitude."

The heat that had begun to unfurl low in her belly retreated. "You're turning me down. Again." She couldn't hide the hurt in her voice.

"No. I'm giving you a chance to back out while I'm still able to listen to my conscience."

That delicious heat returned. She placed a hand on his chest and felt the truth—his heart beat as rapidly as hers. "To hell with your conscience."

The elevator door opened on her floor. Before he could turn, she leaned up and brushed her lips over his. His mouth didn't respond, but his eyes flared with hunger. He stood frozen before her, blocking the exit, his thoughts unreadable but his desire unmistakable.

The elevator doors closed. "We missed my floor," she said. Her voice was a dry rasp.

"Who needs a conscience?" His mouth descended to hers. She opened to let his tongue inside—hot, arousing, exactly the stress reliever she needed.

She slid her hands up his chest and around his neck. He pressed into her, pinning her in the corner. His tongue delved deeper, a firm sensuous caress that lit a fire in her center. He tasted sweet, hot. Perfect.

John Baker was nothing like any man she'd dated. For starters, he was pure alpha in the way he spoke, moved, and beat the crap out of armed thugs. Not to mention he was tall, muscular, and fluent in multiple languages. Brawn and brains happened to be her very favorite combination, and the confidence in his kiss turned her into a puddle of want. She gave as much as she took, reveling in the sweet heat.

He lifted his head, releasing her mouth. She opened her eyes. His gaze burned with arousal that likely mirrored her own. Behind him, the elevator doors slid open. She'd been so caught up in the kiss, she'd forgotten they were in a public elevator.

His broad chest blocked her view, she shifted to glance around him and caught sight of a couple. The woman wore a dark chador. Her eyes were wide with shock.

John cleared his throat and stepped back.

She glanced at the control panel. They'd overshot her floor. "Going down?" she asked.

The couple took a step back and shook their heads. The man said something in Turkish or Farsi, which she interpreted as, "We'll catch the next one." The door slid closed again.

Cressida hit the button for her floor, met John's gaze, and licked her lips. "I am definitely going down."

He laughed—full, loud, sexy—and she felt a rush.

Jumping into bed with him was crazy, but right now, in her freaked-out vulnerable state, crazy might be what she needed.

The elevator stopped again at her floor; this time they exited. When they reached her room, she pulled the key from her pocket and glanced over her shoulder at John. "Can we order wine from room—"

John pushed her aside, out of the doorway. A gun appeared in his hand. "Get down."

"What—"

"The lock is broken." His voice pitched low.

She glanced at the handle. Fear took her breath. A crowbar or some other tool had snapped the mechanism.

Nagging doubts returned to the forefront. John had been on her flight. He was in the same hotel, he'd been on the train platform when she was mugged, and now, he was here. With a gun.

John—not the elusive Berzan—was the only common denominator.

She stared in horror at the man with the gun trained on the door. A moment ago, he'd kissed her silly. But she'd regained her wits and did the only smart thing—what she should have done by the train—she kicked him in the back of the knee, then ran for the stairs at the end of the corridor.

Chapter Ten

MOTHERFUCKINGSONOFAWHORE. She'd caught him off guard, and Ian went down. He bumped the door, shoving it open, forcing him to throw himself to the side, out of the line of fire.

He tucked himself against the wall as Cressida bolted down the hall. He wanted to follow her, but his six would be exposed if he did. He jumped to his feet and kicked the door wide. A quick scan. No one.

She'd almost reached the stairwell. No time to search—he had to go after her. He couldn't lose her like he lost the damn chip. He sprinted down the corridor and shouted, "Cressida! Wait!"

She shoved the door open and disappeared. *Shit!* Whoever had broken into her room was just as likely to be waiting in the stairwell, but chasing her down with his gun out would only freak her out more. He holstered his weapon at the small of his back. The action could be the biggest mistake he'd made all day, and given his fuckup by the train, that was saying something.

He launched himself into the stairwell. She'd reached the landing below and was rounding the corner. He leapt down and caught her waist, pulling her down. He rolled to take the brunt of the fall.

His back hit the wall. His arm held her trapped, pressed against him. With his free hand, he covered her mouth, cutting off a piercing, echoing scream. "Quiet! I'm not the enemy—"

She bit him. It hurt like a bitch, but he didn't release her.

"Dammit, Cressida. I'm trying to help you."

Eyes wild with fear, she pressed her teeth deeper into his flesh.

He sucked in a sharp breath, praying she wasn't desperate enough to break skin. "I might need that hand to beat the crap out of the next asshole with a knife who attacks you."

Her jaw eased but didn't release him.

"Please, Cress. Whoever was in your room could still be there. You're vulnerable."

Her teeth unclenched.

"Don't scream. Please." He lifted his hand from her mouth.

Her eyes were hard, cold, and unflinching.

He'd kissed her to play her, to see how far she was willing to go, but like a damn rookie, he'd gotten caught in the heat. In the end, the kiss was real, and it had taken a world of effort to stay in character.

This is a job. She is a job. Forget the other crap and do your fucking job.

"Why did you run?" he asked.

"I don't know why I was mugged or why my room was broken into. Yet I know you were on the plane. You have a room in my hotel. You appeared by the train right after I was mugged. And you have a gun—yet I never saw you claim a bag at the airport. Which means either they let you take it on the plane, or you got it here. Who *are* you?"

"I told you. I'm a security consultant. The gun is part of my job."

"Bullshit. I'm not an idiot. I can do math, and you don't add up."

He smiled, but with a grim bent. This would be easier if she were a fool. "Dumb luck got me a seat next to you on the plane. I'm a single man, and you're a beautiful woman. I spend more of my time in the Middle East than I do on US soil, and you were like a taste of home. So I'm guilty of being homesick and probably superficial." He stroked her cheek as the fear in her eyes slowly receded. "I was on the pier by the train platform for my job, for which I carry a gun, which I checked through a security service and picked up before heading to the taxi line. You must not have seen it." A lie, but she likely didn't know Turkish gun-check procedures, and he wasn't about to tell her he'd stored more than one gun and a few other necessary items in Van last month when he scouted the area for this mission.

"I have high-end clients who need protection," he continued, "so I have permission to carry concealed throughout the Muslim world. Local governments want my clients' business."

"If it's not somehow connected to you, then why was I robbed?"

His hold on her loosened—but interestingly, she didn't take the opportunity to break away. They must present quite a picture, lying on the hard floor of the landing between hotel floors. He rose and pulled her to her feet beside him. "Let's go to your room and see what we find."

He could still see hesitation in her eyes. He'd lost her tenuous trust, but she *wanted* to believe him, which was half the battle.

How to play her? Another kiss?

No. Too soon. Too heavy-handed.

He took a deep breath. He had only one option, but it required putting his trust in her. If he was wrong, if she was a part of Hejan's cell, then he was signing his death warrant. He reached behind his back, slowly, and pulled his Sig. Holding the top of the gun with the barrel pointed down, he pressed the grip into her hands.

She looked at him questioningly. Guarded.

"Have you ever handled a gun?" he asked.

She nodded.

"Good. Keep it. We're going to go up to my room. I'll grab another gun, then we'll search your room." He hoped to hell that if Zack waited in his room, he was listening and would vacate immediately.

She studied the gun in her hands. "No safety?"

"No. The safety is the long pull for the first shot."

She met his gaze. "Thank you. And I'm sorry I kicked you. And bit you."

He shrugged. "You've good instincts for self-preservation. It appears you might need them." That was an understatement.

As they headed up the stairs to his room, he pulled out his cell and speed-dialed Sabal, but the hound didn't answer. Shit. He needed to know what Sabal had learned from the guy with the knife. She'd want to report the break in to the police and would no doubt question why Sabal hadn't delivered her assailant to local authorities as promised.

His hotel room was blessedly empty and undisturbed. He retrieved his backup weapon, and together they returned to her third-floor room. At her broken door, he pulled his gun and nodded to her, indicating she should mimic his movements. They flanked the door, but he entered first, well aware she was at his back with a loaded gun.

If she wanted to take him out, this was her moment.

She didn't shoot him.

He released his pent-up breath and quickly searched her room, equally relieved when some unknown intruder didn't shoot him either. Not shot twice in the same minute. Maybe his luck was changing.

Her room had been thoroughly tossed. Papers were spread everywhere, and her bed had been stripped.

He dropped onto the bare mattress. "You can't stay here," he said. "It's not safe."

"I'd love to leave, but I have nowhere to go. I don't have money or ID. At least this hotel already ran my credit card. With the lock broken, they should give me another room."

He waved his hand to indicate the mess. "Someone obviously wants something from you. Did they get it?"

Her face showed nothing but fear and bewilderment. "I don't know. I'm nobody. I don't have anything anyone could possibly want."

He believed her, which surprised him. "Don't forget the man with the knife. It wasn't a simple mugging. This was all planned."

"You're scaring me. Worse than I already am. I have no idea what's going on or why."

"You *should* be scared. Listen, my company has a safe house in the area. I'm taking you there."

She stiffened. "Shouldn't I go to the police?"

"We'll stop at the police station on the way." He wasn't sure if his words were a lie. He might be able to take her to the police, but he needed to talk to Zack first. Or Sabal. He needed to know what the hell was going on. Then he'd know what to do with Cressida.

"If I go to a safe house with you, won't it look like I disappeared?"

Dammit. He'd hoped she wouldn't catch that implication right away. "For your safety. Yes."

She studied the gun in her hand, as if weighing it. He had a feeling the heft of the gun equaled the amount of trust she had in him. "I need to go to the police and call my friend Trina. People need to know where I am. I'd be a fool to take off with a stranger and disappear."

He stepped toward her. John needed to turn on the charm, but she was so skittish, he could easily overplay his role. He lifted her chin with his forefinger, bringing her gaze to his. "I work in security, Cressida. This is what I *do*. Something strange is going on, and you are at the center of it. I'll figure out why, but to do that, I need you to let me protect you."

Her gaze darted around her trashed hotel room. She sucked in a sharp breath and, he suspected, stifled a sob. "I'm here to work.

I need to gather data for my grant proposal. For my dissertation. I've worked my whole life for this trip. I spent every penny I have just to get here. There must be some sort of mistake. Whoever is behind this must have me confused with someone else. I'll go to the police. Clarify that I'm nobody. Maybe this"—she waved her arm to encompass her trashed hotel room—"will stop, once whoever did it realizes they've targeted the wrong person, and then I can do the work I came here to do."

Her voice held a new edge of desperation. She wasn't ready to accept that her plans to search for ancient tunnels had been derailed. There would be no expedition south, no Lidar survey. Given that this was the focus of her studies, he imagined this meant there would be no PhD.

He could tell her Hejan was dead so she'd know this wasn't some random mistake. But she was too busy grappling with denial. The truth could break her—and deepen her well-founded suspicions of him.

His only option was to abduct her. It would be for her own safety, but she'd never believe that.

JOHN HAD EXPLAINED they were taking an SDR—Surveillance Detection Route, he clarified—to the police station, which was why they twisted around on the narrow streets of Van for at least forty-five minutes. Cressida fought nausea as they took sharp, quick turns. This had to be the strangest, most awful twenty-four hours of her life.

She was riding in a car—*when did he rent a car?*—with a man who appeared to know the city as if it were his hometown, who had at least one too many coincidences as far as she was concerned, and who carried a gun. She was a fool for getting in the vehicle, but she hadn't felt like she had a choice. The concierge didn't speak her language and, according to John, wasn't eager to give her another hotel room after she'd broken her first one. He said he wouldn't give her a new room until after the police report had been filed, so she'd packed her bag and gotten in the car with John.

He'd saved her at the train station. And he let her keep the gun.

That means he's one of the good guys, right?

A nighttime view of the streets of Van would normally excite her, but today she'd been attacked on every level that mattered: financially, academically, and physically.

The map Hejan had translated for her had been taken. Without it, heading east toward Iran was useless. She had no landmarks to match up terrain, and no historical data to cross-reference. She rolled her shoulders, a feeble attempt to shake off the tension that had gathered there. That area had been a long shot anyway.

Her best lead was still south, near Cizre, close to the Syrian border. *That* map had been in English from the start, and she'd stared at it until the image was imprinted upon her brain. She'd left the map in Tallahassee on purpose. Bringing it to Turkey would have been risky—she didn't trust her fellow grad students, who all wanted in on her potential discovery.

Had the thief been after her prized map? If so, score one point for paranoia.

She couldn't believe one of her fellow grad students was behind this, but who else would have a motive? The historic tunnel—if it existed—was destined to make headlines. Maybe it wouldn't make her household-name famous, but she'd be known in archaeological circles, certainly.

But she still clung to the theory that this was all some horrific mistake. It had to be.

The roads were busier in the heart of the downtown area, even at this time of night. Cars drove erratically, not overly concerned with traffic laws. In spite of the fact that John was a skilled driver, she was tense from the unexpected movements of the other vehicles.

"Shouldn't we be there by now? I mean, Van isn't *that* big."

"I think we're being followed."

She jolted upright. "What?"

"Relax. Don't draw attention."

"Relax. Right." She tugged on her seat belt to make sure it was secure. "Which car?"

"Third one behind us. Blue Opel Astra sedan."

She started to turn, and he dropped a hand on her knee. "Don't look—you present a target." He flipped down the visor on her side and opened the mirror flap. "Use the mirror."

She adjusted the visor until she could see the car. The Astra just looked like any other car. She couldn't see inside the dark vehicle. "How long have they been following?"

"Since the hotel. He was farther back for a while. He moved

up after I took a few quick turns. He doesn't want to lose us."

"How are we going to lose him?"

"Simple."

Without warning, John twisted the wheel and wove through oncoming vehicles. Cressida held her breath against a scream. She was going to die. In a violent car accident. And if she survived, she was going to kill John.

"Hold on," he said, his voice calm and even as he threaded the needle between an oncoming bus and a man on a scooter.

Back in the proper lane, he took a sharp right, down a tight alley, and they wove between carts and garbage, finally coming out the other side. He zipped into a gap in the speeding traffic, and they were off, heading in the opposite direction from where they'd started.

"Did you see what happened to the car following us?"

She pressed a fist to her racing heart. "I assume they died in a fiery collision with the bus."

"No. He couldn't make the turn and ran off the road. Tail gone." He sounded so smug and satisfied.

She slumped down in her seat. Slowly—very slowly—her heart rate returned to something resembling normal. The city disappeared behind them as dwellings spread out. "Where are we?"

"On the road to Kurubaş."

She bolted upright again. She'd studied enough maps of the area to know that was a small town south of Van. "What? I thought we were going to the police. In *Van.*"

"I changed my mind."

The nagging fears and doubts that she'd been trying to ignore surged to the surface. Her breathing became shallow as the full import of her situation sank in. Her body flashed into full-blown panic, no passing Go, no two-hundred-dollar payday. She was in deep shit. And it was her own stupid fault for trusting John Baker. "You." She gasped for breath. "Are." Another heave. "Abducting." She hiccupped at the end of that word before choking out, "Me."

She grasped at the door handle. She could throw herself out of the vehicle. But the door was locked, and in the moment it took for her to fumble with the mechanism, he'd sped up. Diving from the vehicle would maim or kill her.

His hand landed on her knee. "No, Cressida, I'm protecting

you."

"Get your fucking hand off me."

He lifted his hand. "Sorry. It's just—you're panicking."

She sucked in another gasping breath. "Don't you think I know that?"

The car slowed. He pulled onto the narrow shoulder and stopped. She reached for the door handle.

Stupid. She should have grabbed the gun, which she'd set on the floor at her feet.

Instead, he grabbed it, but he didn't point it at her. He released the clip, which fell into his lap, rendering it useless as anything but a club.

She grappled for the door handle again. He reached for her, but his hand stopped short. "Cressida, I'm not abducting you. I'm protecting you. You can't flee. You don't know the language. You don't even know where we are."

She froze. John was right; she couldn't flee. Her suitcase was in the backseat, and they were stopped on a road in the middle of nowhere in freaking Eastern Anatolia. She curled her fingers around the handle but didn't pull it. "You aren't abducting me. Right." She met his gaze. His jaw was tense, but his eyes...they said something else. "And if I open this door and get out of the car, what will you do? Will you grab me? Pull the other gun and threaten me?"

"I'll try to talk you out of it, but I won't stop you." His voice was low, almost pleading. "My company has a safe house on the outskirts of Kurubaş. I'm taking you there. We can regroup. Figure out what to do."

"We? As in you and me, or you and Sabal?"

He leaned back against the driver's seat and closed his eyes. "I don't know what happened to Sabal. I can't reach him. That worries me."

"He was supposed to take the guy with the knife to the police. He was going to file a report for me..." Her voice trailed off. If Sabal hadn't gone to the police, then no one knew she'd been mugged. No one—except Berzan, who might not even exist—even knew the name of her hotel. Not that it mattered since she wasn't there anymore, but she hadn't called Trina yet, or Suzanne.

No one who cares if I live or die knows where I am.

She was a cipher. Invisible. If she disappeared, no one would have the slightest clue where to start looking.

"You weren't safe at the hotel. I *had* to get you out of there."

"Why didn't you take me to the police?"

His hands curled into fists. "Remember the phone call I made while you packed?"

She nodded. She'd shamelessly eavesdropped, but he'd spoken in Turkish. For all she knew, he'd called his wife and said good night to his kids.

Where the hell did that thought come from? She had no doubt John was hiding things from her, but she had no reason to think a wife and kids were among them. And even less of a reason to feel a tinge of pain at the mere idea.

She was seriously whacked. Abducted for five minutes and already suffering from Stockholm syndrome? She was an overachiever in the psychoses department.

And nice to know her track record for picking the worst men imaginable remained unbroken.

"I was talking to my boss—reporting what had happened. He did a little checking, and apparently, there's a warrant out for your arrest in Antalya. A man was murdered in your hotel room last night."

Chapter Eleven

As far as lies went, it wasn't a bad one. Especially since it was damn close to the truth. Ian congratulated himself for coming up with it and thereby securing her cooperation, because he couldn't take the catch in her voice when she'd panicked.

Except now she let out a choked shriek, which was sort of worse, actually. "Todd or Hejan?" she asked, her voice cracking on the second name.

"What?"

"Was the d-d-dead man Todd Ganem or"—she struggled for breath—"Hejan Duhoki?"

"The second one. Duhoki. Who is Todd Ganem?"

She shocked him by flopping against his chest. Apparently, her need for comfort was greater than her fear of him. Ian wrapped his arms around her and stroked her back, telling himself it was what John would do, but knowing he held her because he wanted to, not because it was his damn role.

"Okay, forget Ganem. Who is Hejan Duhoki?" His quick lie was even better than he'd hoped. He could question her, *finally*.

"My translator."

"You mean the guy who set you up with Berzan, the mugger?"

"We don't *know* Berzan was my mugger." She pulled away from his chest and swept back a lock of long dark hair, tucking it behind her ear. "I barely knew him, but his death must be my fault.

"How so?"

"My last night in Antalya... Jesus, was that just *yesterday?*" She rubbed her temples. "Please. Let's continue on to the safe house. I can tell you on the way. I need a bed."

He nodded and put the car in gear. "What happened yesterday in Antalya?"

She got her emotions under control enough to tell him about Ganem showing up first at the bar, then her hotel room door. She briefly described Ganem's arrest, followed by her own, and the fact that Ganem had fled the US with the aid of his powerful uncle in Jordan.

He pulled into the carport of the safe house. The neighborhood—old, run-down, and largely abandoned after the 2011 earthquake—was quiet.

The house itself was little better than a shack; half of it looked to be on the verge of collapse, but the support beams were solid, making it the ideal hideaway.

"Is this where you take all your clients?" Her tone was skeptical.

He laughed. "No. This is a fallback position, in case something goes wrong, and we need to hide the CEO of Microsoft. No one would ever think to look here."

"Is the CEO of Microsoft your client?"

"No, random example."

He stared at her, trying to decide his next move. Too risky to leave her in the car while he checked out the house. No choice but to enter together. He kissed her, a brief press of his lips to hers. "Please don't shoot me," he said and dropped the Sig and magazine into her lap, then pulled out his own pistol.

◉

CRESSIDA FOLLOWED JOHN into the run-down house, hardly able to believe the place was habitable and longing for either of the two hotel rooms she'd paid for in the last two nights. The interior was as dilapidated as the exterior, but the tidy rooms smelled of cleanser.

Even as she willingly followed the man who may have abducted her into the house—although the fact that he gave her back the gun argued against abduction—she wondered if her trip could possibly be salvaged. Her academic career had ridden on success here, and her universe, her essence, everything she'd worked for since she was seventeen years old had been entirely based on academic success and the respect it could bring.

She would never be rich, but she'd have a career that made her happy, because she knew from her mother's example that happiness wasn't to be found in relationships. Now, with a Master's degree under her belt and well on her way to a PhD, she was still the bastard who craved acceptance and respect. A shrink would have a field day inside her brain.

But everything had changed in the last few hours. This wasn't about academics anymore. She had reason to believe her life was in danger. And she didn't know if John Baker was her savior or her warden.

Fight him, or work with him?

Run or stay?

The US Embassy was too far away. Even the nearest consulate was several hours by car. If she had a car. Or could get through the checkpoints without ID.

She was exhausted but strangely wired. Maybe she could figure out what to do if she had a cup of coffee. Coffee fixed everything. She made a beeline for the kitchen.

"What are you doing?" John asked.

"I need coffee."

"You don't need coffee. It's almost midnight after a hellish day. You need sleep."

She turned and glared at him. "You may be my warden, but you aren't my mother. I can have coffee at midnight if I want to, dammit."

He shrugged. "There's some Nescafé in the cupboard."

She hated instant coffee, but it would have to do. In minutes she had a warm bowl-shaped mug cradled in her hands. She lifted it to her mouth and breathed in the aroma.

When she was a little girl, she'd get up early to join her mother in the kitchen for alone time. If a man lived with them, he inevitably slept late, because Sarah Porter was never in long-term relationships with men who worked regular, daytime hours. The smell of coffee brought back those moments—one-on-one time with the only person in her world who mattered and a slice of happiness for an attention-starved girl.

Sarah was a smart woman. Her fatal flaw was the need for the love and affection she'd never received from her own parents. A fatal flaw Cressida shared with her mother, but triggered by different circumstances. Cressida was all about the daddy issues.

At best, the adult men who'd populated Cressida's childhood were takers—selfish pricks who preyed on her mother's weaknesses. The three worst had been predators, emotionally or physically abusive. One, Two, and Three had needed to dominate and control.

During the reign of Two, Cressida had done a stint in foster care, but she'd worried about her mother, fearing Two's violence would escalate without Cressida there to protect her. Cressida snitched a gun from her foster family's arsenal, and ran home. The end result was Two moved out—in a hurry—and Cressida was no stranger to pulling a gun on a man. Now the question was, could she pull the trigger?

"Where did you go just now?" John asked, breaking the spell cast by the scent of hot coffee and bitter memories.

She took a sip. The brew had a richer flavor than she'd expected. She met John's gaze over the mug. "I was wondering if I could shoot you."

He cocked his head; one corner of his mouth crooked in a faint smile. "What did you decide?"

"I haven't yet."

He stepped toward her. "Can we start over? Or at least go back to where we were after I saved you at the train?"

"You mean when I was terrified of you?" She shrugged. "Sure."

"No. I mean when you looked at me like I'm Superman."

"I can't do that." She pushed off the counter and entered the tiny living room. "So, what's the plan from here? We threaten each other, then form an uneasy alliance, or should we skip the drama and you let me go?"

He touched her arm, and she turned to face him.

"I think," he said, "we'll go with the threatening and alliance thing if those are the only options. It's not safe for you on your own."

She felt every millimeter of his hand on her bare arm, and the tempo of her heartbeat increased. She didn't trust him. But his touch wasn't harsh or violent. And in her mind, she saw his face in that moment beside the train. And later, in the elevator. She shivered at the memory of his hot kiss.

He didn't scare her. Far from it. John Baker turned her on. And *that* scared her.

She glanced around the living room. "Tell me something that will help me trust you." She set her mug on a low end table. "What is this place?"

"This area was hard hit during the 2011 earthquake. The neighborhood was abandoned. They've only just gotten electricity back. The locals were more than eager to sell my company several houses in the area."

She glanced at the canted wall that separated the living room from the kitchen. "What sort of idiot company would pay for this wreck? Who do you work for?" Christ, why hadn't she asked him that already? What was *wrong* with her?

He glanced at her sideways. "I guess you never read my card. I work for a company called Raptor."

Shock filtered through her. "*Raptor?*"

"You've heard of them?"

Relief fluttered through her. John worked for Raptor. Trina's boyfriend, Keith, was the CEO, and the private security firm had provided protection for her and Trina last summer in DC. She *knew* Raptor. For the first time since the crazy had started, the tension in her belly eased a fraction. She could call Trina, who could get the scoop on John from Keith. "My close friend Trina is shacked up with your CEO."

Surprise flashed in John's eyes. "Keith Hatcher?" he said.

She nodded. "Yes. I was living with Trina when they started dating a year ago." She paused as the full meaning sank in. This ramshackle house was *owned* by Raptor.

She felt light. Relieved. "That changes everything. I lived with Trina because I was in DC for an internship at Naval History and Heritage Command. My boss was Mara Garrett—the US Attorney General's wife. She and Curt are friends with Raptor's owner. I've met him too." She stopped abruptly and waited for John to fill in more than a name. What if he'd said he worked for Raptor because it was a convenient lie in the face of her obvious suspicion?

Chapter Twelve

Trina Sorensen leaned against her kitchen counter in her apartment in the heart of Washington, DC, and stared at the screen of her cell phone, willing it to ring. It had been over twenty-four hours since Cressida had sent the text about Todd's sudden appearance in Antalya, and five hours since Curt called to say the body of a murdered Turkish man had been found in Cressida's hotel room. Trina had left messages and texted Cressida several times but had received no response.

Authorities in Antalya had confirmed Cressida had caught her flight to Van, but by the time they'd located her hotel, it appeared she'd fled. The night clerk had informed the police that Cressida had returned to the hotel in torn clothing and sporting welts on her arms and neck. She claimed she'd been mugged. He also said she'd been accompanied by an American man who he thought was a guest of the hotel, but he wasn't certain.

As far as anyone could tell, Cressida and the American had disappeared.

Was the American Todd Ganem?

After everything Todd put her through, Cressida wouldn't be in his company unless she was under duress.

Warm arms surrounded Trina, and she released her phone as she leaned back against Keith's chest. She closed her eyes and took a deep, shuddering breath. "If Cressida's okay, she'd have replied to one of my texts by now."

"She was mugged. She lost her phone."

"But what about before she was mugged? Why didn't she text me then?"

He stroked her hair. "For all we know, her battery died."

She turned in his arms and hugged him. "I appreciate that you want to make me feel better, but we both know this is serious, and I need you to be honest with me about the situation instead of trying to humor me."

"I'm not—" He stopped. After a long moment, he cradled her

face and brushed his lips across hers. "Okay. I'm sorry. I'm being protective, which is not what you need right now."

"Thank you." She gently nudged him away so she could pace. She was anxious and needed to move. "We need to get everyone together. Curt, Mara, Lee, Erica, Alec, Isabel. Maybe we can *do* something. Curt can get us updates from the State Department. Maybe Lee can hack her phone and find out where she is. Alec can use his senate connections...I don't know, for *something.*" She twirled to face Keith. "Don't you have a Raptor team working with the Kurds in northern Iraq? How long would it take for them to get to Van?"

Keith looked sheepish. "They're, um, gearing up now."

She pursed her lips. "And you didn't tell me this because...?"

"I didn't want you to know how worried I am. I figured you were afraid enough already."

She gave him a short nod. Okay. Those protective instincts again. Unnecessary, but awfully sweet. *Once.* "When will they reach Van?" she asked.

"The car line at the border is a nightmare, especially with heightened security due to ISIS. It will be faster for them to fly and land on the NATO airfield in Batman."

"How far is Batman from Van?"

"Roughly two hundred miles."

She tried to quash the disappointment. "They won't reach Van until sometime tomorrow, then."

"They'll find her. My guys are the best. You know that."

"Who's on the team?"

"Mostly ex-Special Forces guys you don't know. But Sean Logan was working a security detail in Greece and is en route to Istanbul now. He'll meet up with the team either in Batman or Van."

Those words, more than any others gave Trina hope. Sean knew Cressida. More important, Cressida knew Sean. Cressida didn't trust easily, but she knew Sean was safe.

◉

IAN WOULD BE sweating if his cover with Raptor wasn't fully backstopped. He knew enough about the private security company to get through this conversation. But the fact that Cressida knew Keith Hatcher personally was a problem.

Ian had never met Hatcher and didn't even know if the man

had been briefed on the false credentials Raptor provided Ian and a few other Company men. It had been set up thanks to connections between the deputy director of the CIA and Alec Ravissant, not long after Ravissant bought Raptor. The "embassy employee" cover was weak with overuse in the Middle East, and so Ian—or rather John—had bona fides from a real security company with international contracts and operatives stationed in several countries in the region.

But Ian had fucked up yet again. He'd told Cressida he'd flown in from DC yesterday—which was where Raptor's home office was located, where Hatcher lived and worked—he couldn't admit he'd never met the man who'd taken over as CEO when Ravissant won a seat in the US Senate last November. The company was big overall, yes, but not the DC office. And if Cressida's friend was Hatcher's girlfriend, she probably knew that.

Plus there was the reminder she'd worked for the wife of the US Attorney General. Could that be why she'd been selected to carry the chip? Or were they back to the possibility she was a traitor who'd cozied up to the AG's wife?

Thank God he wouldn't be the guy who informed Curt Dominick his wife needed to be questioned. As it was, this little wrinkle meant the head of the CIA would question Dominick. Unwitting or not, Cressida Porter had carried data for a terrorist cell. Her connections in DC would suffer fallout.

"You know Rav," he said casually, using Alec Ravissant's nickname. "What are the odds?"

She studied him, suspicion in her gaze. "Given that I worked for NHHC and lived with Trina Sorensen last summer—and given what happened to her—pretty low, actually."

Her pointed look caused his brain to race. Shit. What happened to Sorensen? He'd been in Istanbul, chasing down Chechen rebels who were trying to link up with al-Qaeda, but the way she looked at him made him think a Raptor employee should know the details. If it involved Trina Sorensen, then it must have to do with Hatcher, not Ravissant. All at once it came to him—the CIA *had* briefed him, since it related to his cover. "You were living with Dr. Sorensen when the explosion took out Hatcher's home?" There were more details that came to him, but everything the CIA had learned after the explosion was classified, and Ian doubted even Cressida knew who was really behind the attempt on her roommate's life.

Her features relaxed, telling him he'd said the right thing. "It was terrifying. She was assigned a Raptor bodyguard after that, and I even stayed at Alec's estate in Maryland for a few days while things were sorted out."

Hell and damn, this couldn't get any worse. Sorensen had been assigned a bodyguard? Shit. Cressida would expect him to know the guy. There was no way he could bluff his way out of this. For a moment, he considered telling her the truth. Would she laugh in his face if he told her he was a CIA case officer?

Shit. He *couldn't* break cover. Not until he knew exactly why Hejan had chosen her. "I don't know the details—I was working on a security assignment here in Turkey most of last summer." It was always good to stay as close to the truth as possible. "My language skills keep me in the Middle East about ninety percent of the time." He dropped onto the sofa.

The tightness in her jaw had eased. She cleared her throat. "I'd like to call Trina. I need to tell someone where I am—and who I'm with." She waved her arm to indicate the room. "I'm scared because no one knows where I am."

At least she hadn't said she was terrified of *him*. Progress. But unfortunately, Trina was the last person she could call, not until he was certain Hatcher would confirm his employment without hesitation. If he looked up Ian's human resources file, he'd find the necessary documentation, but if he answered without bothering to check, he'd raise more questions for Cressida than Ian could safely deal with right now.

He frowned apologetically. "No cell phone coverage out here. We're too far from the town. The earthquake took out the secondary cell tower. It has yet to be fixed."

Her brow furrowed. "Can I see your phone?"

He plucked it from his pocket and handed it to her. He hadn't lied about cell coverage, but he had no clue how he was going to put her off when they were in antenna range.

She raised an eyebrow as the screen woke with a request for his passcode.

He told her the number without hesitation. As promised, the phone had no reception. Her shoulders relaxed as she handed him back his phone.

She flopped down on a chair in the living room. "So what do we do about Hejan? I need to tell the police what I know. If Todd—" Her voice cut out, and he knew she'd unhappily connected those dots. She shook her head. "No. Todd was many crappy things, but I can't believe he's a murderer."

Ian moved to the chair in front of her and leaned toward her with his forearms resting on his thighs. He took her hands in his. They were cold and trembled a bit. "We need to figure out our next step. You walk into a police station right now and they'll take you into custody, and I might not be able to help you." This was mostly a lie. Ian could vouch for the fact that Hejan had been alive when Cressida left her hotel room, and Stan had passed that information up the line. The police wanted her as a witness, not for murder.

Her shaking fingers closed around his. A gesture of trust. He was such a shit to scare her this way.

"Thank you. It seems like every decision I make—chase my mugger, stay at the hotel, go to the police—is wrong somehow." She leaned forward and brushed her lips over his. A soft, fleeting warmth before she pulled back. Full stop retreat.

He smiled. "There's another decision I'd rethink. If I were you, I'd do this." He kissed her, slipping his tongue between her lips.

She responded with a low groan deep in her throat as she stroked his invading tongue with her own, garnering a physical reaction from him that had nothing to do with why he'd pursued the kiss but everything to do with why he didn't want it to end.

He took her face between his hands and pulled her forward, urging her to his lap as his mouth caressed hers with an intensity that surprised even him.

Damn, but she turned him on.

She complied with his silent plea and settled onto his lap. At last, he had Cressida's sweet, perfect body in his arms, her ass pressed against an erection that belied his mercenary kiss. His mouth left hers so he could nuzzle below her ear and slide down her smooth skin to nip at the hollow of her collarbone. He wanted to taste all of her, to feel her nude body against his, to make her come hard and fast against his mouth and then again when he was inside her.

He wanted to enjoy the slide of her inner thighs against his hips as he thrust into her, to make her cry out his name as he brought her to orgasm.

The rush of heat was fast and furious. Logic disappeared in the wake of overwhelming want. From the way she kissed, the way she attacked the buttons on his shirt, she'd been hit by the same raw need. His arms tightened around her, then he stood, lifting her. This would be better if they moved to the bedroom.

But he hadn't even taken a step when she pushed at his chest and said, "John, is that smoke?"

He shook his head, uncertain if she'd made a joke about the heat between them and feeling strangely irked she'd called him John. A second later, he smelled it.

Shit. He set her on her feet and pulled his gun. *Of all the dumbass things to do.* He'd gotten fucking distracted, and now their "safe" house was on fire.

CHAPTER THIRTEEN

THIS WAS NOT happening. It couldn't be real. Cressida was trapped in a nightmare. It wasn't possible that Todd had appeared in Antalya; Hejan had been murdered; she'd been robbed (twice); possibly abducted (in spite of being foolish enough to want to jump in the sack with the man, she still wasn't sure); and now black smoke poured from under the front door of the ramshackle hideaway.

Her gaze darted around. The side door to the carport was their best exit. She took a step toward the door, but John caught the back pocket of her jeans, stopping her.

"Not yet," he said and nudged her backward. He scooped up the small rug she'd been standing on and dropped it against the base of the door, partially stemming the waves of smoke. Next he shoved the couch backward and slammed the heel of his boot into the floor, which gave way under the quick pressure of the blow. He knelt over the hole and tossed splinters of wood aside, then plucked a backpack from the hidden recess.

With the bag slung over his shoulder, he turned and caught her shocked gaze. "Firm believer in the Boy Scout motto," he said, then strode past her toward the side door. She followed, plucking her gun from the kitchen counter on the way.

He paused by the exit. "We go together." He nodded toward the gun in her hand. "Can you shoot if you have to?"

She nodded, tightening her grip on the weapon.

"I'll unlock the car with the remote the moment we open the door. The driver's door is closer. Dive in and crawl across to the passenger seat. I'll follow and provide cover fire if need be."

He did *not* just use the words "cover fire" in a sentence. She just stared at him, her mind caught on that one phrase and unable to move forward.

He stroked her cheek. "You'll do fine, Cress. I believe in you." Then he kissed her, a quick hard kiss that broke her mental paralysis.

She took a deep breath and nodded. "On three?" she asked, because wasn't that what people said in these situations?

A smile lit his eyes. "On three." He then whispered the count in her ear.

He shoved the door open, and she sprang forward. In seconds, she was inside the car and crawling across the gearshift, John right behind her. Thankfully there'd been no need for cover fire.

The engine started instantly. She hadn't even twisted into her seat before they lurched backward down the short driveway, then, with a sharp turn, launched forward down the bumpy, pitted road.

She grappled for the seat belt as her head bounced against the roof. Finally settled in the seat with a fastened belt, she found her voice. "Is anyone following us?"

"No. But if the purpose was to smoke us out, they know we only have two choices once we hit the main road."

"Which are?"

"Return to Van, or head west. There's a NATO base in Batman."

She glanced out the window. The night was pure inky black. No streetlights. No city lights. No car lights ahead or behind. Complete darkness, all around. "Which way are we going?"

"To Batman. You'll be safe on the base."

THIS TIME, CRESSIDA didn't protest and say she needed to gather research for her grant proposal. Being smoked out of the safe house appeared to have woken her to the seriousness of the situation. Or maybe it was learning Hejan had been murdered in her hotel room. Ian didn't particularly care which had gotten through to her, he was just glad she was cooperating.

"How far is it to Batman?" she finally asked.

"About three hundred kilometers."

"Can you translate that to hours?"

"Four and a half, maybe five. This time of night, we should get through the checkpoint quickly."

"How will we get through? I don't have my passport."

"Hopefully I can talk our way through. If not, bribery."

She slid down in her seat and murmured, "I can't believe I've sunk to bribery."

"You won't do the bribing, I will. And only if it seems necessary."

Ian drove in silence as he considered the situation. He'd set up the house near Kurubaş just a few weeks before, when Hejan had told him the microchip was destined for the Van region. Given the number of dwellings abandoned due to the earthquake, it had been an easy task to find a place that would suit his needs. At the time, he'd given himself twenty-to-one odds he'd need it, and fifty-to-one he'd need the apartment he'd outfitted in Siirt.

Because the Kurubaş house wasn't an official asset, he'd told only one person the location, but thankfully, he'd told no one about the Siirt hideaway.

He just prayed they'd get to Siirt safely so he could stop running and call Stan. Because it appeared CIA rookie Zack Barrow—the only person who knew the location of the house on the outskirts of Kurubaş—was working for the wrong side.

Chapter Fourteen

AS ZACK KNEW he would, Ian was taking the girl to Batman. Zack had read Ian's playbook and knew every move he'd make between Van and Batman. Admittedly, Zack had been surprised when Ian informed him of the remote safe house, but all the better to run him down in a place where he'd feel secure. Too bad Ian had plucked the wire from Cressida's back pocket after smoke poured into his little hidey-hole. Zack found the listening device in the charred Turkish rug Ian had dumped in front of the door.

Finding it meant Ian suspected Zack, but then, Zack had never taken Ian for a dumb case officer, just a complacent one. Although the hideaway near Kurubaş didn't argue for complacence. Ian was supposedly a decent poker player, but Zack knew every one of his tells.

The fact that Ian suspected Zack didn't change the game. It just upped the stakes.

"Why aren't we chasing them?" Todd Ganem asked from the passenger seat of the old British Land Rover. "You're letting Cressida get away."

Zack sighed. He was tired of dealing with Ganem's inflated ego and foolish questions. The archaeologist's loyalty remained unclear, but he'd been useful in drawing Cressida out of the hotel with a text message. That Hejan had given Todd's cell phone number to Cressida and told her it belonged to her supposed guide had come as a surprise. Hejan had believed to his dying breath that Ganem was his ally. A fact Zack would do well to remember.

"You can't chase in a Rover. But don't worry, they're going right where we want them. And by the time they get there, Ian Boyd will be the most wanted man in Turkey." Zack put the Rover in gear and pulled onto the road. They'd follow at a distance. There'd be plenty of time to catch up when they reached the checkpoint. "It's time for the Company's favorite bastard to get burned."

NOT SURPRISINGLY, THE checkpoint was quiet at two in the morning. The sleepy military guard requested their IDs with rote attention. Ian launched into his story of being mugged on their honeymoon in a mix of broken Turkish and English.

The Turkish soldier nodded for him to pull over to the side of the road. Without papers, a perfunctory examination of the vehicle was required.

He'd told Cressida they were pretending to be newlyweds visiting his ancestral villages. She stood by him next to the car, gripping his hand and leaning her head on his shoulder like a tired, besotted bride who'd just suffered an ordeal. That she could convey it all without speaking a word of Turkish impressed him. But then, she *had* been through an ordeal.

He brushed his lips across hers and suffered a pang that his life could never allow for a honeymoon with a woman like Cressida. He'd never considered himself a 'til-death-do-us-part type of guy, so it was a rare moment when he entertained such regrets. He'd decided years ago to share his twisted path with no one. He certainly wouldn't punish a woman he cared about with a life of espionage.

The soldier asked him to open the trunk. He shined his flashlight on Ian's suitcase—the one he'd carried on the flight and which contained only the innocuous contents needed for a business trip—Cressida's suitcase and the backpack he'd grabbed in Kurubaş were tucked in the footwell of the backseat, and not likely to be examined in this token search. As a precaution, both guns were hidden under the driver's seat. John Baker was licensed to carry in Turkey, but their plea of no papers meant he couldn't prove it.

The soldier said he'd need to inspect the bag before they could be on their way. Ian hesitated, then decided not to attempt a bribe. The soldier seemed honest and showed no sign of intending to halt their journey. Ian plucked the suitcase from the trunk and handed it to the soldier.

The man nodded and carried the bag toward an inspection table.

Ian draped his arm around Cressida again and pressed another kiss to her temple. "We're almost done, love." That he whispered the endearment so only she could hear it blurred the lines between fiction and reality, but to her, he was John. Reality was far from twenty-twenty.

Several feet away, the guard unzipped the bag and began rifling through the contents. The man lifted a burner phone from the bag. "Your phone is ringing," he said in Turkish.

Then Ian heard the ring. Old-fashioned—like a rotary dial phone from the seventies. But even creepier than hearing a phone that should be silent ring was knowing the phone should have been shut off completely.

He shouted a warning to the guard even as he tightened his arm around Cressida's waist and pushed her toward the cover of the low ditch that lined the road. He pulled her against him and rolled to take the brunt of the impact. He finished a rotation, planting her beneath him to protect her from the coming explosion.

A massive boom rent the air.

Heat seared his exposed neck, and debris rained on his back. Sharp, hot granules moved with the speed of bullets and burned through his shirt.

Cressida groaned, a gurgle that sounded as if he'd knocked the wind out of her.

Pain sliced across his upper back as hot metal lit on his shoulder blade.

There must have been a bigger explosive in the suitcase than what would have fit inside the phone. The phone was just the trigger. But then, Zack had plenty of time to rig it while Ian enjoyed his dinner with Cressida.

He grunted and rose to his knees, dislodging the burning metal. He grabbed Cressida and dragged her to her feet as he stood. "Get in the car!" His own words were lost to the ringing in his ears.

She nodded and ran for the vehicle. He slid into the driver's seat as she took her place on the passenger side. In seconds, they were back on the road, driving forward into the burning Eastern Anatolia night.

Chapter Fifteen

IT SEEMED LIKE John had been driving forever, but logic told Cressida it had been less than an hour since the explosion that must have killed the Turkish soldier. She wanted to think the explosion had nothing to do with her, but she wasn't naïve enough to believe the comforting lie.

Not anymore.

People didn't blow up because of mistaken identity. People weren't murdered in hotel rooms because of academic rivalry. No one could want the information she'd found on underground aqueducts that badly.

John's theory, that the explosive was planted when the car was parked in the carport of the house near Kurubaş, made sense. It also explained the ease of their escape, even why they were smoked out to begin with.

Every time she thought about the soldier, she had trouble breathing. Was she to blame?

She couldn't imagine why, or how, or what it had to do with her. Yet deep down she knew it was her fault. She cleared her throat and said, "The explosion—it will be all over the news. It will be labeled a terrorist attack, won't it?"

"Yes. And that's what it was."

"How could it be? I'm so confused."

"There is something you don't know about Hejan Duhoki."

She stiffened. He must have learned something when he called his boss at Raptor. "Something I need to know…and you're just telling me now?"

"I didn't say you need to know, just that you *don't* know."

"Goddammit! I have a right to know about Hejan!" She gritted her teeth. "Tell me *everything* you know."

"I'm shocked you haven't guessed."

"Guessed what? That you're an asshole keeping secrets?"

"Hejan Duhoki was an integral part of a terrorist network."

"No." Cressida's voice was firm. She was in full denial, even after everything she'd witnessed, everything she knew to be true.

"Yes," Ian said, sparing her no sympathy. He was too tired and in too much pain from the burns on his back to treat her with kid gloves. "He's a known terrorist and was being watched." Ian had to play this carefully. She still didn't know who he was, and the Raptor cover could still hold up if he didn't reveal too much. But *how* he revealed what he'd held back was going to be tricky.

A glance in her direction showed she'd fixed him with a tight-lipped stare. He faced the dark road in front of him. His shoulder burned. He'd only slept for four of the last forty-eight hours. And his assigned backup on this op was no mere traitor, he'd just deliberately killed a Turkish soldier in a way that would cast suspicion directly on Ian, while the woman at the center of it all wanted answers he couldn't give.

He'd come to one inescapable conclusion: Zack must have monitored the checkpoint from a distance and had set off the bomb in such a way as to alert Ian—ensuring he and Cressida survived the blast. But to what end?

"What does any of this have to do with me?" Cressida said. "Hejan was a translator, not a"—her voice cut out, and she took in a breath—"terrorist. The university recommended him. He was a nice guy. He helped me when Todd showed up."

"Turkish authorities believe Hejan did the translation work for you because you were coming here, and he had something that needed delivering."

"I had something? You mean, *that's* why my purse was stolen? My room searched? Why the hell didn't you tell me this before?"

Ian grimaced. He deserved every bit of her anger. "Because I wasn't sure you weren't involved. What did Hejan give you?"

"A map I paid him to translate," she said with lessening heat. "He also recorded Kurdish and Turkish phrases for me on a digital recorder. He included specialized words and phrases an archaeologist searching for a lost aqueduct would need."

"A digital recorder. USB?"

"Yes. It had a USB plug."

"Those are storage drives too."

"Sure. They're backup drives, but I didn't need that, because I didn't bring my computer."

"But that doesn't mean Hejan didn't save files on it."

She leaned her head back against the seat with a wince. "I suppose. The recorder only lists audio files on the display. Because I never plugged it into a computer, I have no idea if there were non-audio files. You should have told me this when you first abducted me."

He smiled at her accusation. "I never abducted you. I took you to a safer place."

"A safer place—you mean the one with the smoke, or the roadside stop that blew up?"

"Touché. So...it appears one of my associates is playing for the wrong team. The house near Kurubaş was supposed to be safe."

"The wrong team." She paused. "You mean Keith has an operative who's a traitor? We need to call him! I—"

Ian rolled down the window and chucked his cell phone out into the darkness before she could make a move for the phone.

"What is *wrong* with you? I *know* Keith. I know his home number—because I used to *live* there. If there's anyone I know we can trust, it's Keith Hatcher."

Time to lay the lies on thick. He could throw a few truths in for good measure. "First, that phone was compromised. My associate has the number. I should have tossed it right after the explosion—I wasn't thinking. Second, do you really think Keith Hatcher will listen to you when you tell him one of his employees is a traitor? You, a person who was arrested for grand larceny a few months ago? Your only proof of innocence was the fact that you have friends in high places.

"Do you really think Hatcher will listen to you above a trusted employee who has likely already informed him that you were in on the grand larceny theft with your ex-boyfriend all along? You can bet your ass that he's already told Hatcher you met up with your supposed ex and a known terrorist in Antalya. Tell me, Cressida, how are you going to convince him when everything points to you?"

Chapter Sixteen

Cressida closed her eyes, as if that would block out John's words. She rolled down the window and breathed the cool night air. Inky darkness shrouded the world a few feet beyond the car, hiding snow-covered peaks in the distance. She took a deep breath. The crisp, cool air indicated they'd risen in elevation since they were on the shores of Lake Van.

She glanced sideways at John. His features were no less handsome in profile as his intent gaze studied the road ahead.

Who is he?

Did it even matter? Right now, he was her only option. She might fail with him, but she'd definitely fail without him.

She cleared her throat. "I *do* think I can convince Keith. Trina's a good friend. So is Mara Garrett—the attorney general's wife—and Erica Kesling. I mean, Scott," she corrected, not caring that John probably had no clue who she was talking about. In this moment of isolation and fear, she needed him to understand how important her friends were to her. They'd stood by her through the Todd fiasco, when her grad school friends—except Suzanne—had been ready to believe the worst.

So it stung to hear John say Keith wouldn't believe her. Because if those friends didn't trust her, she had no one. She shook her head against the wandering thoughts and said to the man sharing her small space in the universe, "Trina will believe me. Keith will listen to her."

"I wish it were that simple, Cress." John's voice was softer, more sympathetic. "But some awful stuff has gone down, and you can bet your ass your reputation is being trashed right now. Mine too. Until we have a better grasp of what's going on, we're on our own."

She hadn't really considered what helping her had cost John. For all she knew, Keith was ready to fire him. He'd saved her life—two, three times?—in the last several hours. Her clothing was dirty and torn after the roadside explosion, but she hadn't been injured. Or killed.

She reached up and touched John's cheek. Middle-of-the-night shadow abraded her fingers. She'd thought him handsome on the flight and had alternated between attraction and distrust every moment since.

She traced his jaw, enjoying the feel of his skin, remembering the kiss in the elevator, and then in Kurubaş. "I'm sorry," she said. "I'll tell Keith you're one of the good guys."

His hand dropped to her knee as he kept his gaze on the road. "Don't worry about me. I can take it." His fingers squeezed softly. "But right now, I'm exhausted. I have another place we can go to. No one knows about this one. It *will* be safe. I promise. Once we're there, I'll catch a few hours of rack time. Then we'll continue to Batman."

"Sounds good as long as there's a bed."

"Yes. One. It's a studio apartment."

Heat coiled in her belly. They'd share the bed, certainly. The only question was if they'd do anything other than sleep. It would be oh so easy to give in to the intense attraction. And after everything that had happened, making love with the man who'd saved her life repeatedly seemed more than inevitable. It might even be essential.

⬢

DAWN HAD BROKEN across the steppe by the time Ian leaned against the door of the small studio apartment and let out a deep sigh of relief. Cressida dropped onto the bed, then flopped backward. She looked damn sexy splayed out like that, but that probably wasn't her intent. Still, he could enjoy the view.

He grabbed a bottle of water from the small fridge he'd stocked weeks ago and cracked it open. Chilled water had never tasted so good.

"Don't bogart that bottle," Cressida said. Her T-shirt rode up, exposing her flat belly. He was tempted to pour the water on her skin, then lap it from the pool.

He took a step toward her, intending to do just that. The attraction was mutual, and they'd both earned a break and physical release. Sure, he needed sleep, but it could wait. He stopped, remembering that when they'd kissed in Kurubaş, she called him John, which bothered him. She'd been kissing John while Ian kissed Cressida.

He didn't want her as part of the job. He wanted *her*. And he'd be damned before he had sex with a woman he genuinely wanted while using John as an alias.

Of course, he'd never be able to tell her his real name or the real reason he'd ended up next to her on that flight. His job didn't work that way. His *life* didn't work that way, and being a covert operative was the only life for him. He wouldn't do anything—*ever*—to jeopardize that. Not even fall in love.

Not that he could fall in love with Cressida—attraction, hell yeah. But love wasn't possible. Not for him. She was part of a classified op and would never learn the truth. She'd be filed away at Langley. Another completed mission. The end.

Telling her his real name would compromise the mission, his job, his life. He couldn't have sex with her, not unless he was John.

He handed her the bottle. She scooted up, still on her back but now leaning on a bent elbow, and took the half-full bottle. She emptied it in one long drink. "Do you have ibuprofen in that backpack?" she asked.

"Yes." He dug into the bag and grabbed the painkiller.

She squinted at the Turkish label. "You sure this is ibuprofen?"

He nodded.

"How good is your Turkish? You sounded convincingly bad at the checkpoint."

"I can imitate broken Turkish with a bad accent or speak flawless Turkish when need be."

"How? Your American accent is also perfect—generic, almost regionless. Except for one point at dinner, when you used the word 'pop' instead of soda."

"My Midwest background slips through sometimes."

"Are you from Illinois?"

"Good guess." It was also a correct guess, but he'd have told her she was right no matter what she said.

"How does a boy from Illinois develop a flawless Turkish accent?"

"I have a good ear."

She raised an eyebrow. "C'mon, we're talking Turkish. Plus you speak Arabic. And Kurdish. Farsi too? They can't be easy languages to learn, let alone master."

It wasn't like hiding the truth mattered. She'd never find John Baker because he didn't exist. "I grew up in Chicago, in an area that has a large Turkish and Arab population. Most of the Arabs I knew growing up were Palestinian, but our next-door neighbors were Turkish on one side and Egyptian on the other. In the Turkish family, three generations lived in a tiny two-bedroom apartment. A boy my age was part of the third generation. He was my best friend. I practically lived in his noisy, crowded apartment." She didn't need to know why Altan's apartment was preferable to his own.

"I picked up the language. When *Babaanne*—my friend, Altan's, grandmother—overheard me talking with Altan in Turkish, she decided to teach me to read and write it. Later, in college, I majored in Middle Eastern studies and took classes in several other languages of the region. My Arabic is good but not flawless. My Farsi is passing."

"And you took your language skills and Middle Eastern studies degree and got a job in private security?" Her eyes conveyed her skepticism.

Was she finally connecting those nagging dots?

"Actually, I joined the Army first. Served with Delta Force. The GI bill paid for my college education, post Army. Between my language skills, military experience, and understanding of the Middle East, private security was a logical choice."

She seemed to accept that, and he wondered why he'd been so frank. He didn't have to mention Delta, but he'd wanted to. He was proud of his service, and he supposed he wanted to impress her. Stupid when this could go nowhere. "I'm going to take a shower. Get some rest."

She nodded even as her eyes drifted closed. She had to be more exhausted than he was. He, at least, was trained for this.

In the shower, his shoulder burned under the hot spray. Pain surged across the exposed nerves. He quickly adjusted the temperature to cold. He sucked in a sharp breath and leaned his forehead against the cool tile wall and waited for the burn to recede to a low throb.

The cold spray helped his shoulder, but the rest of his body shivered. Between the throbbing in his shoulder and the icy water, thoughts of screwing Cressida evaporated, which was a bonus, he supposed.

Except he liked thinking about screwing Cressida. It was a hell of a lot more fun than thinking about how far south this mission had gone.

What was Zack's game here? Was he herding them toward Batman or the consulate in Adana? If so, they were the last places Ian could take her. The fact that she was still alive meant Zack needed her for something, but what?

He soaped his body, wiping the grime of the explosion from his skin. Cressida's skin was also dirty from the blast. She'd need a good deal of soap, which would slide down those slender hips and that firm, round ass, in ribbons of white suds, conforming to her curves.

Her full breasts would be perfect handfuls. He imagined the texture of her aroused nipples on his tongue. He washed his hair, allowing the cold spray to hit his face. The frigid water and his burned shoulder could no longer compete with his erection.

"Need any help?"

He turned to the sound of Cressida's voice, wiping the water from his eyes. She'd pulled back the curtain and stood—beautifully, magnificently—naked just outside the narrow stall.

"Holy fuck," he muttered, taking in her perfect body. Smooth skin, round, high breasts with dusty-pink nipples that made him salivate. That slender waist, and those sexy, curved hips. But most of all, he was caught by the gorgeous grin she wore as her beautiful brown eyes widened at the sight of his ready erection.

"Why yes, I think you do," she added, her voice low and husky, which made his cock twitch. She pushed the curtain wider and stepped into the spray, then jumped in reaction to the cold. "What the *hell?*"

He slammed the water off with the side of his fist, then grabbed her before she could flee the shower stall. He nudged her back to the tile wall, and she squealed at the cold. Then he kissed her while his chilled, wet skin met her warm, perfect body. His erection pressed against her belly as his tongue slid inside her mouth. He thrust forward with his hips, enjoying the feel of her soft, smooth skin against the underside of his hard cock.

She tasted so damn sweet. His tongue entwined with hers in a hot, hurried dance. His balls tightened. He couldn't get enough. Taste enough. Feel enough. With his hands under her ass, he lifted her, allowing his cock to slide between her thighs and press against her clit.

She broke the kiss, rocking her head back against the tile as she let out a soft moan.

"You like that?" he asked. He thrust his hips. His cock slid across her clit, then stopped with the tip at her opening. She was slick, hot. Ready.

He stroked her with his thumb while he teased her swollen opening with his eager cock. Silky wet heat enveloped him. He'd gone from fantasy to reality so damn fast, he almost wasn't certain this was real.

She let out a very real moan, and he remembered one of reality's greater drawbacks. "Dammit. We need a condom."

With one arm, she gripped his good shoulder. She kissed him again and pressed her hot core against the tip of his penis. "No problem." She panted as he pulled back to slide the tip over her clitoris again. "I had some in my suitcase." She flashed a cunning, satisfied grin. In her free hand, she waved the square foil wrapper, identifiable in any country.

He wouldn't have sex with her, not without birth control, not when she didn't know his name. But they *did* have condoms. And she was naked. In his arms. What did names matter anyway? "Ian" was just the Gaelic version of "John" after all.

"You're sure?" he asked against her lips.

"Shut up and put your cock in me." She ripped open the wrapper with her teeth.

Still supporting her, he pulled back so she could sheathe his erection. He groaned as the condom unrolled and she stroked his cock.

His mouth caught hers, and he held her against the wall, tasting, stroking. She released his thick erection, and her hands slid up his chest as she kissed him back. She sucked on his tongue as he thrust into her mouth. He lifted her higher, positioning his cock between her hot thighs, pressing against her vagina. The tip just grazing the edge.

One thrust, and he'd be in deep.

She whimpered at the torment, and he chuckled. Her hands stroked his delts, shifted to cradle his neck, then slid over his shoulders to his back.

White-hot pain sliced through him. He jolted backward, unable to stop himself. Her warm fingers had rubbed his raw, burned flesh.

Chapter Seventeen

"I'M SORRY!" CRESSIDA stared in shock as John's face lost all trace of color. She'd hurt him. She knew he'd been scraped when they tumbled on the rocks, and now she wondered if he'd been hurt worse than that. He hadn't said a word. There'd been no blood on his shirt, but then it had been dark, and she hadn't really looked.

"You were hurt in the blast, weren't you?"

"I'm fine. Just give me a moment."

Thinking back, she realized that when she'd pulled back the shower curtain, his head and shoulders had been coated in shampoo. Whatever hurt him so badly, she hadn't seen it. And then there was the frigid water. Maybe the apartment *did* have hot running water, but he'd chosen cold for a reason.

He still held her. She wiggled against him. "Put me down. We'll finish this later."

"No. I'm fine."

She cupped his face and kissed him, then pulled back. He was still erect and seemed to mean it when he said he wanted to continue, but she was more worried than aroused now. "Put me down and turn around. Let me see."

She gasped when she saw the burn. No wonder it hadn't bled. On his left shoulder blade, a strip of skin one inch wide and three inches long had burned, blistered, and popped. "Holy shit. That must hurt like hell."

"I've been able to ignore it. Except when it's touched or hit by hot water."

"Why didn't you tell me?" She gingerly probed the healthy skin around the burn, exploring the reddened, puckered edge.

"That bad?"

"Worse. It's a second-degree burn—nearly third. You should have told me." She felt terrible realizing he'd finally been cooling the burn and she'd interrupted.

"We needed to get here as fast as possible. No time to fuss."

Guilt swamped her. "You got this protecting me. I was under

you while debris rained down."

He turned in the small shower stall to face her and cupped her chin. "This is what I do, Cress."

The way he said it triggered a tide of emotion. The last thing she needed was to start thinking there could be more here than sex. More than comfort between two people who'd been through something together.

He touched the evil eye pendant that rested against her breastbone. "Beautiful pendant—much higher quality than the usual tourist offerings. But I don't think it's helped us much."

She let out a distressed laugh. "Yeah. Total juju fail." Unease settled through her. It was odd to stand naked in the shower with him while he studied a charm given to her by a dead man. A terrorist. Who'd been murdered in her hotel room.

She'd lost her mind. She never should have stepped into John's shower. But she'd wanted a mindless escape, to return to the moment when he'd kissed her and they'd been ready to move the action to the bedroom except thick black smoke had interrupted them.

She stepped back, out of the shower. "I should bandage your shoulder. Does this place have a first aid kit?"

"Yes." He unrolled the condom and dropped it in the trash, then flashed her a smile. "I hope you have more of those."

Heat gathered in her belly at his mention of their unfinished business. "I do."

He brushed his lips across hers in a quick, warm kiss. "Good."

She grabbed a towel from the shelf and thrust it into his hands. "Cover up before I forget you need a nurse and not to play doctor."

He grinned. "You first."

"I'm going to take a quick shower. When I get out, I expect to find you naked—but only from the waist up—and belly down on the bed."

"Yes, ma'am."

She turned on the water, grateful for the hot spray. She'd felt a sudden chill at the idea of how close they'd both come to getting blown up and needed the heat of the shower to wash away both the grime of the explosion and the fear.

The room was a sea of steam by the time she emerged. She toweled off, then ran her fingers through her hair to detangle it. Her brush was in her suitcase in the main room. She'd thought to bring a condom into the bathroom, but not a brush. Yeah, well, priorities. She had them.

She stepped out of the bathroom. As ordered, John was stretched out on the bed. His feet were at the head while his cheek rested on a pillow at the foot. He'd turned on the TV to CNN International and had positioned himself to watch on his belly, and then fell asleep during her lengthy shower.

Damn. Could she fail him any more? She'd promised to tend his wound and instead took a shower and had a pity party while he waited. Now he was finally resting, and cleaning the burn would wake him.

He'd laid first aid items out on the dresser. She grabbed saline solution and cotton swabs. On the TV, images of the aftermath of the explosion at the checkpoint filled the screen. She knew the explosion would be news but was surprised to see it on the international channel. She hit the volume button so she could hear the British newscaster's voice-over.

John stirred as she dabbed at the burn with the solution, but he didn't wake. The information on the news was as expected. Speculation of a terrorist attack. A Kurdish separatist group named as the likely perpetrators with additional speculation that it could be a new branch of ISIS.

Wound clean, she broke the seal on the antibiotic ointment and applied it to his skin. John woke fully, a soft smile on his handsome face when he shifted his sleepy head to meet her gaze. "How long have I been out?"

"Only ten or fifteen minutes." She finished spreading the cream and pulled out a gauze bandage. "How's the pain?"

"I took a painkiller. Non-prescription, but still, stronger here than we have in the US. So not bad."

She smiled. "I'm glad." She ripped off strips of tape and secured the gauze. "You hungry?"

"Starving. There's some canned food in the cupboards."

"Sounds delicious."

He laughed, then his eyes lit with heat. He plucked at the towel she wore around her torso. "You didn't get dressed."

She shrugged.

On the TV, footage of a Turkish official making a statement condemning the attack was interrupted. The image flipped back to the anchor desk. "We have a startling development in the Turkish bombing investigation."

John's focus was on the TV as he said, "We can get groceries after we both sleep for a few hours."

She nodded, more focused, like him, on the TV. "What do you think is going on?"

"We received an anonymous tip," the anchor said, "that a suspect in the bombing is actually a CIA operative who allegedly turned double agent."

Shock made air whoosh from Cressida's lungs. "Your associate is CIA? I thought he worked for Raptor."

The reporter continued, "With two anonymous sources confirming the information, CNN has decided to disclose the man's identity, because he's armed and dangerous and may have already killed one Turkish soldier."

John lunged for the TV. A picture flashed across the screen. Cressida caught a glimpse just before John hit the power button and the image disappeared.

The picture hadn't been of some man she'd never seen. No. The picture had been a snapshot of a bearded John Baker.

Chapter Eighteen

Ian stood in front of the TV, frozen. Shocked. Stunned. Rocked to his core. Never in all his years as a covert operative had he ever imagined what this moment could or would feel like. He'd been burned. His life's work gone in an instant.

He'd been labeled a terrorist. A double agent. A traitor. Bile rose in his throat.

Every faction would now be gunning for him. Shoot to kill.

And if that wasn't bad enough, he had Cressida to deal with. Turning off the TV had been a stupid mistake. It hadn't prevented her from seeing his picture and hearing the lies, but it had stopped him from finding out what had been disclosed.

Cressida pummeled his good shoulder, demanding answers. He brushed her aside and hit the power button on the TV.

"—Ian Boyd is considered armed and dangerous," the news anchor said as another picture of him appeared on the screen, this one from when he was in the Army and beardless.

Shit. He was well and truly cooked.

"Boyd has been an employee of the United States Central Intelligence Agency for the last five years. Prior to that, he served in the military. He received several medals for his service and served as an operator with the US Army's secretive tier-one counterterrorism unit popularly known as Delta Force."

"They left out my years in college," he murmured. "You'd think they'd be all over my Middle Eastern studies degree."

Cressida glared at him. She was afraid, but he gave her credit for not showing it. She grabbed clean clothes from her suitcase and marched into the bathroom.

The layout of the small room came to mind. *Crap!* There was a window to the courtyard behind the ground floor apartment. He tried the knob. Locked. "I'm not a double agent, Cressida. Zack is. Open the door. We need to talk."

"I'm getting dressed."

"And I've seen you naked. So open up."

"No."

"Then step back, because I'm busting the door down." He kicked the knob. The frame splintered, and the door swung wide.

Cressida's head and shoulders were through the high window. She was halfway to freedom but struggled to get her knee up so she could straddle the ledge.

"Sonofabitch. I don't need this," he muttered as he grabbed her hips. She kicked backward, but he cinched his arms tight, preventing her from hurting him as he dragged her back through the window. "Cool it. I'm not going to hurt you."

She twisted in his arms and pounded on his chest. When that failed, she landed a blow on the bandage.

Pain exploded. White light flashed behind his eyes. He dropped her and staggered backward. She landed on her ass at his feet. Her eyes were wide, round, and full of nut-grinding fear.

He struggled to breathe as his nerve endings flamed. He slumped down against the doorframe. Cold sweat gathered at his hairline. He faced her across the short stretch of floor. "Don't. Do that. Again."

"You lied to me."

"Of course I did." Pain receded by slow millimeters.

"You don't even feel bad about it."

"No. Why should I? I was doing my job. For Uncle Sam." He shrugged and added, "You lied about your name."

"Yeah, but I'm not a traitor."

"Then explain why the first time I saw you, you were hanging out with a terrorist."

Her eyes widened. "You were there?"

"Of course."

She dropped her head back against the wall and stared up at the ceiling. "Am I your mission?"

"Yes."

"Why?"

"There's a microchip with information vital to Hejan's group. He gave it to you. My mission was to follow the chip."

She lowered her chin, meeting his gaze. "How do you know Hejan gave me anything?"

"Hejan had turned against his group. He was gathering intelligence for me. For the CIA."

She fixed him with a glare. "If you're a double agent, I won't shed a tear when you're caught and killed."

For a cat with her paw caught in a trap, she was awfully bold. And equally likely to bite him. "Do I need to sleep with one eye open?"

"Yes."

"You can't beat me, Cressida. I'm not just CIA. I'm Delta. I've run ops. I've killed for my country. A few hours ago, a man died while I protected you. I could have saved him. I chose you. So keep in mind that a wisp of a young scholar won't get the best of me, no matter how beautiful. No matter how much I want to fuck you."

Her eyes widened at his blatant declaration. "Was your plan to screw me so I'd be lulled into submission? Was this some sort of twisted James Bond thing?"

"I hit on you on the flight and at dinner for the job. The kiss in the elevator was also on Company time. But the rest has been because I'm a man and find you attractive. So shoot me."

"I intend to."

He laughed at that, his gaze scanning her from head to toe. "I've never slept with anyone who didn't know my real name."

"What, do you want a medal? And you didn't seem to hesitate in the shower."

He shrugged and leaned his head back against the doorjamb. "A beautiful, naked woman who I very much want to fuck stepped into the shower with me. I've never claimed to be noble. If you hadn't touched the burn, I'd have slid deep inside you and would have enjoyed every hot thrust. You would have too."

Her pupils dilated. In spite of everything, his words aroused her. Hell, him too. Raw honesty was a heretofore unknown turn-on. The way her cheeks flushed with desire every time he said he wanted to fuck her just made him want to keep saying it. "I didn't plan to seduce you. Hell. *I'm* not the one who brought the condoms. But I still want to fuck you. Very much."

She cleared her throat. He loved the way she did that and wanted to keep making her throat dry with desire. It was the only thing that sounded remotely good in a world where he'd just lost everything that mattered to him.

"Who are you working for?" she asked in a husky voice.

"Up until about ten minutes ago, the CIA. Now, apparently, I'm a free agent."

"Al-Qaeda? Kurdish separatists?" She paused and sucked in a sharp breath. "ISIS?"

He sighed. She was determined to steer this conversation in non-titillating directions. "Hejan was a Kurdish separatist. I was his case officer. His manager."

"The story you told, about how you learned Turkish, was that true?"

"Yes. And I did grow up in Chicago." What could he say to gain her trust? It was going to be a long-ass journey to the consulate if she fought him the entire way. "Like yours, my mom was a single mother. And like you, I don't know my father's name. But I can do you one better. My dad was *a* john. My mom's sick joke was to name me after him. Ian is John in Gaelic. So my preferred alias isn't just a convenient common name."

He kept all emotion out of his voice as he told her that. Hell, he'd *never* told anyone that. Not even Altan, his best friend and next-door neighbor who'd known exactly how his mother earned the money to pay for her ever-increasing addictions.

"Where is your mother now?" she asked.

Ian shrugged. "Don't know. Don't give a damn." He lifted his chin at the condemnation in her eyes. "Don't judge me, Cressida. She doesn't deserve my consideration."

Those beautiful brown eyes cast downward. "I'm sorry," she said, with a slight catch in her voice.

He gave a short, sharp nod and swallowed the lump in his throat. He could go days, weeks even, without thinking of his mother and preferred it that way.

He slowly rose to his feet, reaching out a hand to pull her up. Not surprisingly, she refused his help but stood anyway. "Microwaved canned beans are waiting for us. And now that you know who—and what—I am, it's time you tell me everything Hejan told you. Zack drove us to ground instead of killing us for a reason. My guess is you know something or have something he wants. Did Hejan give you anything besides the digital recorder?"

◉

IT TOOK ALL Cressida's willpower to keep her face blank and not touch the evil eye pendant. She didn't trust John—*dammit, Ian*—not by a long shot. She'd tell him about the pendant only if she decided she could trust him.

Ian's question clicked everything into place. Aside from the digital recorder and the translated map—which had been taken from her hotel room in Van—the only other item Hejan had given her was the pendant. He'd given it to her in private and had been particularly tense about it. The pendant was important. But why? What made it special?

Maybe when John—*crap, Ian*—was asleep, she'd be able to check it out.

She ate her beans and told him about Hejan. What else could she do? She couldn't run. He'd stop her before she made it to the door. She was entirely dependent upon him.

Stupid of her to choose to seduce him rather than grab his money and gun and run while he was in the shower. Such a fool. Had she ever trusted a man worthy of the sentiment?

Since she was seventeen and harbored a shameful crush on Three, she'd traveled a straight path to destruction with the men she wanted. She crossed her arms over her chest and sat back against the head of the bed. "Can we watch the news? I want to know if they mention me."

"It doesn't matter. You're stuck with me either way." His voice had hardened. Ian had a different voice and manner than John. Ian was harsh. Suspicious. Angry.

She had her own anger where he was concerned. "You could have stopped me, you know. When I left the hotel last night to meet Berzan, I still had the digital recorder. I'd have given it to you. You could have prevented all of this from happening." The accusation burned in her throat. "You probably could have saved Hejan too."

"My job wasn't to save Hejan."

She shivered at the way he said that. "What was your job?"

"My job was to follow you, witness the drop, and follow the next link in the chain to the top."

"I was bait."

He cocked his head. "In a manner of speaking, yes."

"When you put a worm on a hook and dangle it in front of a hungry fish, it's bait."

"Not always."

"When does bait want to be pierced with barbs and eaten?"

His gaze narrowed. "When it's a lure, with hidden barbs, embedded, part of a beautiful, vicious design. I had no idea what you were, Cressida. I still don't."

"I'm not a fucking lure."

His smile was slow and sent the wrong kind of shiver up her spine. "You're certainly alluring."

Or maybe it was the right kind. All she knew was she felt things she didn't want to. "Fuck you."

"Is that an offer? I accept." His eyes swept her from head to toe. "You are so damn hot, not even frigid water could keep me down."

His words pissed her off—and turned her on in the most twisted way. For once, she knew he spoke the truth. He'd screw her without regret if she just gave him the green light.

Hot, erotic memories of the shower flooded her. If he'd just moved his hard cock a few millimeters, she'd have pressed down, and he'd have been deep inside her. One deep thrust and her whole body would have been gripped with pleasure. What was *wrong* with her?

She was sick. Depraved. And likely held the land-speed record for Stockholm syndrome.

"Think about it," he said in a deep, seductive tone. The polished businessman she'd met on the flight was long gone. This man was all rough edges and rumbly voice. Carnal. Primal. A warrior.

His hard body was pure sculpted muscle. If she'd ever in her life wanted a no-strings-attached fling, Ian Boyd would be the type of man she'd want. Alpha to his very core with a body worthy of a master artist.

However, sex with Ian Boyd had far more than strings. It had ropes. Handcuffs. Possibly even treason attached. "Pass, thanks."

He leaned into her and rubbed his thumb across her bottom lip. "Your eyes are so expressive. You have a hard time hiding what you're thinking. And for a moment there, you were remembering how it felt—how *I* felt, against you. In the shower. And you want to finish what you started."

That was no magic trick. He'd probably been thinking the same thing.

She brushed his hand aside and stood, then crossed the room and turned on the TV. She returned to the bed and sat cross-legged, trying to block him out as she watched the news.

He settled beside her, reminding her that no matter how she felt about him, they'd be sharing a bed. They both needed sleep, desperately, and he clearly wasn't about to make the gentlemanly offer and take the floor. Frankly, she didn't gaze at the floor with longing either.

The news was all about Ian. He groused and complained about

the inaccuracies and cursed bitterly at the characterization. When a hastily pulled together interview was announced and a man in uniform appeared on the screen, Ian went silent. She had a feeling he held his breath.

"Who is that?"

"Shhh," he said, waving her off.

On the TV, the CNN anchor said, "We've just received a clip of a statement made by Lt. Col. Harrison Makefield. Makefield was accused double agent Ian Boyd's commander when Boyd was a Delta Force operator."

The anchor's voice cut off, and the recorded statement began. "I've known Boyd for over a dozen years. There is no doubt in my mind he's innocent of the crimes he is accused of. Someone in the CIA"—a bleep covered the next word—"up, and they've hung a good man out to dry. I've never had a finer, more patriotic soldier under my command. I will stake my reputation—my entire career—on his innocence."

Ian leaned back against the headboard, a soft smile on his face. Much more like the smiles she'd seen from John than anything Ian had displayed. "Thank you, Harry." He touched his fingers to his brow in a salute. "He's a fine man."

His change in demeanor was…captivating. The harsh edges were still there, but part of the anxiety left him. He laughed at some of the more outrageous accusations. He smiled.

Ian Boyd's real smile was devastating. As John, there'd been an obsequiousness that carried through to his smile. But Ian… Ian bowed to no one, least of all a foolish archaeologist who'd managed to embroil herself in an international incident.

What if he really was what he claimed? An agent, one of the good guys, who'd been burned by the real traitor?

"The fact that Zack Barrow hasn't been mentioned means his cover's intact," Ian said. "My guess is he's pulling the strings. He's the only person who knew about the safe house."

She glanced sideways at him. "He had to know he'd be your first suspect when the house started to burn. So why did he light the fire?"

"He knew I'd be so busy reacting—trying to get you to safety—that he'd have time to pull this stunt, blowing my cover before I could inform Ankara. No way can I call Ankara now. If we'd gone straight to Batman, instead of stopping here, I'd be in custody now—and likely wouldn't survive the night. Hell, he probably planned to show up at the NATO base and take you off their hands—with my boss's blessing. You'd have trusted him after learning I was the double agent." Ian paused, his gaze fixed on the TV, which showed footage of the burning checkpoint. "He must've rigged the explosive while we were at dinner."

"Do you think he was nearby during the explosion?"

Ian nodded. "A cell phone is an easy remote, but he had to be watching, to know the soldier had the bag and we were clear. He knew the ring would alert me, that I'd protect you."

She shuddered at the idea that someone could blithely detonate a bomb knowing it was in an innocent soldier's grasp. But that's what terrorists and traitors did. Then there was Ian, who'd protected her and would sport scars for the rest of his life because of it. "Why did he kill the soldier?"

Ian fixed her with a stare. "It was the first shot fired in the next holy war. A Turkish soldier targeted by the CIA." He waved his hand at the screen. "You can see what a big deal it is, as our governments alternately point fingers, then scramble to show unity."

She gathered the loose bedspread into her fist, wondering how she'd gotten caught up in something so outrageous. So horrific. She'd thought things were bad when Todd claimed she'd stolen university equipment, but that was a scuffle on a playground compared to this. "Was Zack behind the mugging?"

"I think so. He had the guy with the knife in position to prevent me from following the mugger." Ian frowned. "He knew I couldn't leave you, even if it meant letting the data get away."

"What's on the USB drive that's so important?"

"Two things that I know of: bank information that will allow Hejan's group to retrieve millions of dollars set aside to fund international bombings, sabotage, and radical violence; and a list of Americans who fund terrorism."

Chapter Nineteen

CRESSIDA'S GORGEOUS MOCHA-and-amber eyes went wide with shock. "Americans funding terrorism," she said flatly. "I know it happens. But I can't understand it."

"That's because you aren't greedy." It was one of the things about her that appealed to him—her motivation appeared to be academic achievement, not financial gain. "Nor are you a religious zealot."

She clutched her evil eye pendant. "No. I'm just a fool."

"Stop being so hard on yourself. Hejan used you." He wanted to savor the flavor of that innocence on his tongue. In his line of work, he never encountered innocence. "My first guess as to why Zack turned is he was hired by someone whose name is on that list. There are a number of people who support terrorism because they benefit from the military industrial complex. A country living in fear is a country willing to spend on their military."

"You aren't saying our government...?"

"Not necessarily. We can't rule out the possibility there are military personnel on the list, but I'm talking about the CEOs of companies like Raptor. I'm talking about gun and airplane manufacturers."

She reared back. "No way is Keith Hatcher funding terrorism."

"Relax. It was just an example you'd understand. No one suspects Raptor—not anymore. Alec Ravissant is solid. He checked out on all levels and so did Hatcher. But the previous owner...well, let's just say he was guilty of far more than he was convicted of. The rumors of biological weapons were true."

"How do you know?"

"Sorry, it's classified."

She dropped the pendant and crossed her arms. "I'm trying to trust you, Ian. I'm trying to understand."

He sighed. Did the secrets matter anymore when they had to work together to get out of this country and survive? "I assisted the Department of Justice on that case, working the Middle

Eastern angle. Yes, I found a connection, and that's all I can say."

She nodded and flopped back against the headboard. She'd dressed quickly in the bathroom, right before her escape attempt. She hadn't put on a bra, and her nipples showed clearly through the thin fabric of her shirt in the cool, air-conditioned room.

His cock thickened as he enjoyed the view, even though it was doubtful they'd ever return to the sort of truce that included recreational sex. Too bad, since, with Ian's cover blown and being wanted for the murder of the checkpoint guard, they couldn't seek refuge at the NATO base in Batman. They had a much longer route to safety now and would be spending several days together. Her bold invasion of his shower had awakened his libido with a vengeance.

They watched the news for another hour, mostly a repeat of what they'd already heard. Sabal was never mentioned. Neither was Zack. Nor was Cressida. Ian was a traitor. The news—or lack thereof—in a nutshell.

His old CO was ready to go to bat for him, as were a few of his Delta buddies. The CIA had gone mute, which was standard protocol. The director made a cursory statement about this being an ongoing investigation, confirmed Ian was employed by the agency, but did not say in what capacity. The director did add that outing a covert agent's identity was a felony punishable by up to ten years in prison and a fifty thousand dollar fine. He went on to describe the death of Richard Welch in Greece in 1975—the result of the man's affiliation with the CIA being outed, and reminded reporters of the Valerie Plame debacle.

Ian was left feeling exactly as he was supposed to: wondering if the CIA had burned him, or if Zack had, and if it was Zack, would the CIA stand by Ian or hang him out to dry?

Zack had had hours to convince the powers that be of Ian's guilt, while Ian had…nothing. No way to prove he hadn't killed the guard. Not even Cressida was convinced of his innocence.

She lay on her back on the bed next to him, one hand tucked beneath the pillow and eyes closed. He didn't believe for a moment she was asleep. She wasn't that good at deception. Not with him, anyway.

He took the opportunity to study her. The spectacular body splayed before him in light cotton shirt and jeans. Her dark lashes were startlingly long against tan cheeks. The delicate arch of her eyebrows, her full lips, and the gentle curve of her chin were such a harmonious blend, he could stare at her for hours. A strange notion. He'd never had time for such a simple pleasure before.

They'd reached an uneasy truce, but she'd made it clear she considered herself his prisoner. When they left this apartment, she'd turn him in at the first opportunity, thinking she was doing the right thing as an American patriot.

He would die. And odds were she would too.

Somehow, he had to save her from herself and get her out of this damn country.

SLEEP CAME FITFULLY for Cressida. It didn't help that she shared a bed with a man she alternately feared and wanted. A man who was so big and muscular, he took up more than half of the double bed.

A man who might be a terrorist. A man who was holding her prisoner.

A man who'd saved her life. More than once.

A man who made her forget the insane situation with one touch of his deft fingers.

She twisted under the covers and studied him, wondering how deeply he slept. She wanted to check out the pendant. Could there be a microchip inside?

Hejan had been adamant that she never take it off. Even as he set her up for this awful journey, he'd been warning her. But of what?

Ian's short dark hair stuck up on one side. His features were softened with sleep, his mouth less foreboding when not accompanied by a suspicious stare. Firm, square chin with a slight cleft below soft lips, the feel of which haunted her every time she closed her eyes. Sharp cheekbones, thick dark brows—they all combined to make a handsome face that would have caught her eye anytime, anywhere.

Even in the air-conditioned room, sweat gathered at his hairline in sleep. It glistened in the bright daylight that seeped through the blinds. She imagined running her tongue across his collarbone, tasting the salt on his skin. She licked her lips, then let out a silent sigh at her foolishness.

She scooted to the edge of the bed. She'd go to the bathroom and check out the pendant. Careful not to wake her sleeping guard, she placed one foot on the floor.

A hand latched on to her wrist with an iron grip. "Where do you think you're going?" His voice didn't even sound sleepy.

"To pee. Is that allowed?"

"With the door open, sure."

"I don't think our relationship has progressed to the peeing-with-the-door-open stage."

"Fine, then I'll stand outside the door and listen."

"You're a bastard. You know that, right?"

He shrugged. "So are you."

"Yeah. Aren't we a pair?" She stood and crossed to the bathroom. True to his word, he followed.

"I don't know what you're worried about. The door doesn't even close after you smashed the handle."

"I'm not worried. Just cautious."

Inside the bathroom, she studied the pendant.

"I don't hear anything."

"Back off. You're giving me shy bladder syndrome."

He laughed.

In disgust, she dropped the pendant back under her top, took care of business, then returned to the bed. She'd learned nothing about the pendant, except that it looked solid at a quick glance—no obvious hidden chamber. Hard to imagine it could be something terrorists desperately wanted.

Wired, she couldn't close her eyes, let alone relax enough to fall asleep. She shifted positions. Right side. Then left. Nothing was comfortable.

"You need an orgasm," Ian said, his voice breaking the tense silence.

She snorted. "You must have been an awful teenager. Always telling girls 'we could die tomorrow,' in an attempt to get in their pants."

He chuckled. "Come to think of it, we *could* die tomorrow, but I didn't mean it that way. I meant you're wound tight. An orgasm would relax you. You can take care of it yourself. Or, I could help."

"That's very magnanimous of you."

"I'm a giving sort of guy. I can make you come with my mouth or fingers. No penetration. Nothing in it for me."

How sick was she to be tempted by his indifferent offer? It didn't help that the idea of making him hot, then leaving him empty held a certain spiteful appeal. She flipped over on her belly.

"No, but thanks." Silence descended. The air conditioner clicked on. The unit had a high-pitched whirr that scraped at her already taut nerves. Finally she said, "What happens next, Ian?"

"We head west."

"We aren't going to Batman?"

"No. Batman is where Zack will expect me to go, and any soldier—NATO or otherwise—who believes I'm a traitor will take a shot at me before stopping to ask questions. I've got an unwritten shoot-to-kill on my head. Possibly even a written one. NATO is out."

"Why west?"

"Because the countries to the east will kill a CIA agent even faster than a NATO soldier will kill a traitor, and to the south is a heavily patrolled and closed border with a country embroiled in a vicious civil war. We'll head to the Med. Maybe we'll catch a container ship to Venice."

"Why Venice?"

"Because it's not in Turkey, where I am currently wanted for killing a Turkish soldier."

"And from Venice? Where do we go from there?"

He shrugged. "First we have to get to Venice."

"Do you speak Italian?"

He said something, soft, low, a gravelly texture in his voice she'd only heard when they were in the shower. Desire ripped through her with lightning speed. She had no clue what he'd said but had a feeling it was explicit and involved her.

"You aren't going to ask me what I said?" She could hear laughter in his voice.

"I think I can guess."

He said more in the same low voice. Soft, sexy words that knit a seductive spell.

"What gives, Boyd? You're hitting on me more now than when you were playing the role of John Baker. Yet I have the distinct feeling you don't like me."

The bed shifted as he rolled to his side. They were face-to-face in the shadowy room. "I never said I don't like you. Besides, it was Baker's job to win your trust, but he didn't trust you. He thought you were smart. Sexy. But he had a lot of questions. He had to maintain a degree of professional distance. *I* on the other hand—"

"What, no more third person?"

"John Baker is a role. I am Ian." His fingertip traced her lips.

"I had the same suspicions as Baker, but my secret is out, and I've been able to question you directly when Baker couldn't. My doubts are gone. Professional distance is no longer possible or required."

"So your attitude toward sex now is 'why not'?"

"Pretty much. We're stuck together." The finger tracing her lip slipped inside her mouth, a slight strategic advance followed by a quick retreat. "I'm still hot from your shower invasion. I want to fuck you, very much. I want to make you come, make you call out my name in that sexy throaty voice you have when you're turned on. Sex would release tension and pass the time. Win-win."

"I wanted sex with nice-guy John Baker. I'm not interested in Ian Boyd." This was an outright lie. She'd been interested in John Baker, sure. But Ian Boyd? He turned her on in the most disturbing way. And she feared he knew it.

She realized now that Ian, not John, had been the man who gazed at her with stark concern in his eyes after the assault by the train. For a moment, a brief flash of time, Cressida had *mattered* to Ian Boyd. And after twenty-eight years of craving a look like that, she wanted to matter again to the man who'd given her the first taste.

"You're lying, Cressida. You want me as much as I want you."

"Physically, sure. But that doesn't mean I'll act on it." She paused. She had no pride left to lose, may as well admit the truth. "I've got an abysmal track record with men. Every time I've trusted my judgment, I've gotten burned. And with you, I'm completely at a loss. If you're a double agent, and I stay with you, I'm dead. If I take off on my own, then Zack or whoever blew up the soldier will find me. Lose-lose."

His finger left her lips, traced her cheekbone, then strayed to her hairline. The touch was gentle, sweet, and, surprisingly, lacked persuasion. "I don't think there's anything I can say to convince you you're safe with me. But will you accept you're *safer* with me? We need to work together if we're both going to get out of Turkey alive."

She nodded. She'd given this a lot of thought. "I won't run from you, and I won't try to turn you in."

He shifted closer and kissed her forehead. "Good. Get some sleep, Cress. Every hour after this one could be worse than the ones that came before."

"Well, aren't you a little ball of sunshine?" she said with a grimace.

He chuckled. "I've promised myself I won't lie to you anymore. Ever. That includes giving you my honest take on our situation. And frankly, it isn't good. In fact, we could die tomorrow, so if you want to get laid, now's the time."

She let out a soft laugh and rolled over. They both needed sleep if they were going to survive the upcoming difficult hours.

Chapter Twenty

ERICA SCOTT TWISTED her key in the old lock on the front door of Building One in the Washington Navy Yard. At eight p.m. on a weeknight, no one was around, which was her purpose for dropping in at the office after business hours. Her boss, a man who bore the impressive title of Underwater Archaeologist for the US Navy, was long gone and therefore wouldn't pepper her with questions due to his constant need for attention. She'd have quit her job at the NHHC two years ago, if she didn't have designs on the man's job.

She nodded to the portrait of Lincoln in the front hall as she did every time she entered the building and climbed the stairs to her office, a large room that overlooked the Anacostia River. The wiring in the building might be sketchy, cold drafts made the office uncomfortable in the winter, and over time she'd become a believer in the tales that the building was haunted, but damn, she had a view, even at this late hour, as lights sparkled off the dark flow of the river.

She dropped the résumé files she'd brought home on her desk. In two months, the Navy planned to bring up a sunken US submarine from the Strait of Juan de Fuca, and her boss had been urging her to oversee the excavation. Diving would be done primarily by Navy divers assisted by the laughably named SCRU—Submerged Cultural Resources Unit—of the National Park Service, but the project would require several deep-water dives to ensure the historic vessel wouldn't be destroyed during retrieval, and Erica had yet to tell her boss she couldn't dive because she was eleven weeks pregnant.

She planned to suggest her assistant, Undine Gray, for the job, but knew the boss man would insist they come up with a short list of candidates from the résumé files. He had a thing for Undine and would resist sending her off for two months. But Undine had grown understandably uncomfortable around him, which was one of the reasons Erica wanted to send her.

Undine, Trina, Mara, and her former intern, Cressida, had taught Erica what it was like to have friends again after the painful loss of everyone who'd mattered to her years before. Of course, one reason she'd bonded so quickly with Cressida might have something to do with her being an intern. Erica couldn't even *say* the word intern without smiling.

Now Cressida was in trouble, and she would do anything to help her, which was why she'd come to the office after hours. A CIA operative had been outed in Eastern Turkey—in the very area Cressida had gone to research. Erica was here to search the service records for references to Ian Boyd. She had better access to Navy files than Army, but Delta Force and SEALs often worked together. That overlap could lead to interesting tidbits. She and Mara had agreed the computer records request should come from Erica's computer, not Mara's, given that Mara was married to the attorney general.

She'd just accessed the database and had typed in Boyd's name when her phone rang, causing her to jump. No one but Lee, Mara, and Trina knew she'd gone to the office at this hour.

Caller ID rarely worked on the office phones. It had to be Lee, checking on her. The stick had turned blue two weeks ago, and they'd yet to tell anyone the news. Right now it was their little secret, and Lee was adorably giddy about the whole thing. Erica didn't know if she was ready to be a mom—thankfully, she had several months to get used to the idea—but Lee, he was beyond ready to be a dad. She rubbed her belly as she reached for the phone. This was one lucky baby, to have Lee Scott for a father.

"Erica Scott," she said as greeting. She was still surprised by how much she liked sharing his name, liked the way it bound them together. Kind of a shock considering how long she'd put off marrying him, but that wasn't because she didn't love him and want to spend the rest of her life with him. It was the exact opposite. She'd loved him too much to marry him before she was certain she wanted to have children. He'd always been clear he wanted children, and she couldn't doom him to childlessness because she was afraid of motherhood.

"Ms. Scott, I'm with the CIA. We have some questions for you about your former intern, Cressida Porter."

She jolted. Had her computer search alerted them? If so, that was awfully fast. "Um, sure?" The man hadn't even given her a name, but she supposed with the CIA that was to be expected.

"I will be at your office in five minutes."

"No," Erica said firmly. "I'll go to Langley." No way in hell would she take anyone's word they were with the CIA. The only way to confirm their credentials was to meet inside their lair.

"Fine. We'll expect you within the hour."

After she hung up she sent Trina a text: *Late night confab needed after I meet with boys at Langley. Your place or mine?*

A minute later, Trina replied: *Keith's office. Raptor has files. Bring Lee.*

The "Raptor has files" part of her message was hopeful. It meant, thanks to his Raptor cover, they had access to information on Ian Boyd. They were gathering everything they could on Boyd. It was time to find out if he was friend or foe.

IAN DECIDED IT would be safest to leave the studio apartment an hour before dawn. He restocked the backpack with supplies while Cressida dressed. She stepped out of the bathroom with a scarf draped over her hair. "Is this how it's supposed to go?" she asked as she fussed with the ends of the cotton cloth.

He stood and took the ends, rearranging the drape so it covered her gorgeous brown hair without signifying any particular religious group. He stared into her eyes, all at once thinking Muslims were crazy to want to hide something so beautiful. His hands dropped from the scarf to her hips. He didn't know why he continued to touch her, and searched for a reason. Testing her timid trust? Surely he had an agenda. His life was *always* driven by agenda.

But right now, it appeared his agenda was to kiss Cressida Porter, for no other reason than that he couldn't resist.

He kissed her softly at first, giving her the opportunity to refuse. When she didn't, he deepened the kiss. His tongue slipped between her lips and explored both her mouth and response. Ian Boyd kissed Cressida Porter for the very first time.

Her response differed from her wild, wanton seduction in the shower. Her tongue slid against his, not promising a hot, fast fuck, but offering something far more pleasurable, far more intense. Far more arousing.

In alarm, he lifted his head, breaking the kiss. He held Cressida against his chest as he rested his chin on her covered head. Eyes closed, he caught his breath. Was he developing…*feelings* for her?

He felt responsible for her, sure. That was understandable. He might even like her. And he appreciated her intelligence, even enjoyed her company. But feelings, caring, emotional attachment, those were dangerous. He might not be John anymore, but she was still a mission. An assignment. Without her, he couldn't prove his innocence. He'd forever be known as a traitor. That was unacceptable.

Emotional involvement with Cressida Porter was a dipshit idea.

"That was...*interesting*," Cressida said. She leaned back and met his gaze, her eyes filled with confusion.

Yeah. Welcome to the club. He gently pushed away from her. "Ready to go?"

Her eyes narrowed. "Goddamn typical man..." she grumbled good-naturedly as she turned and grabbed her suitcase.

He couldn't resist objecting. "*Typical?* I assure you, I'm anything but."

She glanced over her shoulder, her mouth twisted in a wry smile. "You're a braggart who avoids any hint of emotion. *Typical.*"

She had him there. He plucked a wad of cash in three different currencies from his backpack and handed it to her. "If we get separated, you'll need this."

Her jaw snapped closed, and all hint of humor left her.

"If anyone recognizes me, I want you to run—as far from me as possible. Head to the US Consulate in Adana. If you can't get to the consulate, then go to the press. The more public you are, the safer you'll be. Got it?"

"Yes."

"Good." It hardly mattered what would happen to him. The important part was getting Cressida to safety.

CRESSIDA GRUMBLED WITH frustration when Ian insisted she choose which of her belongings were the most important and transfer them into a smaller backpack. The rest would stay behind in the studio apartment in Siirt. She was tempted to leave a note with her papers, but what would she say? *Help, I've been abducted by a spy who is trying to protect me, and everything he's done to help me has only put him in worse danger. He might not be the bad guy. But I'm not sure. So only save me if you can do so without harming him.*

Leaving a note proved impossible, though, when he went

through all the items she left behind, ensuring nothing important was missed. His mouth quirked in a smile as he plucked the box of condoms from the suitcase and deliberately tucked it into her backpack.

His smile combined with the action sparked a flash fire in her center. Damn traitorous body. She cleared her throat and said, "What will happen to my stuff?"

"Nothing until the landlord shows up when the rent is due next month."

Well, a month from now would hardly help her anyway. She mulled what she knew as her body cooled. She'd decided to trust him, but her trust remained fragile. She again debated telling him about the pendant.

Once he had what he wanted, he might abandon her. He'd made it clear the microchip was his mission, not protecting her.

She didn't have to decide now. She could tell him later. Or never.

Never was probably a good idea.

With her belongings transferred, she said good-bye to her notes. To her plans. This was the end of her academic glory before it had even begun, because there was no way in hell she'd turn in that grant proposal now. She would never find the tunnel.

If she survived and escaped, nothing could convince her to return to this place where she'd been used as a courier for terrorists.

She followed Ian to the apartment building's garage, where he led her to an Eastern European motocross-type bike and handed her a helmet. At least now the backpack made sense. No way could she carry a suitcase on that thing, and the saddlebags were only big enough to hold his backpack. "Where did this come from?" she asked.

"I bought it when I set up the apartment. It's always good to have backup transportation, especially agile vehicles. Bikes and horses are the only way to get around here off-road."

Cressida took a step back. "Wait. Off-road?"

"There are military checkpoints in every direction. Off-road, we can avoid them."

She blanched. Going overland? In this terrain? Was he insane? "I can't," she said. Her reaction was visceral. She felt as if a brick wall stood between her and the bike. She couldn't take a step toward it.

Ian placed a hand on her shoulder, gently nudging her forward. Toward that invisible wall. "You can." His voice dropped to a soft, soothing tone. "You will."

"I'm scared. I've never liked motorcycles."

He pulled the scarf from her head and stuffed it into her backpack, then slid the shiny black helmet in its place. "Wear my leather. It will protect you. And I'll take it easy. I promise."

Leather in the summer sun would be unbearable during the heat of the day, but she understood he was sacrificing his skin for hers. Again.

His lips brushed against hers, then he buckled the strap under her chin. "You can do this, Cress."

Did she have a choice? *No.*

She broke through her mental wall and mounted the bike. "Please tell me you're good at driving these things."

He grinned and donned his own helmet. "Honey, have you ever seen a James Bond movie? Don't you know spies are good at everything?"

The cocky statement made her laugh, and a small amount of her tension dissipated.

He climbed in front of her and kick-started the scary bike, and in moments they were tearing across an open oil field, heading south into the Eastern Anatolian hills.

THE OVERLAND RIDE was bone crunching and miserable. Cressida clung to Ian's back, her hands tightening in time with each jolt. He'd have bruises from her grip to match the ones on his ass from slamming into the seat so often.

A mental image of kissing bruises in the same location on Cressida's body distracted him as he chose a bad line over a rocky outcrop and paid for it with a hard landing. Behind him, Cressida let out a stifled grunt.

She hated this. And likely hated him. But what could he do? His job wasn't good for making positive long-term impressions.

Except, he no longer had a job.

He pulled up behind a high rocky outcrop, this one tucked next to a steep hill, and shut off the engine. They were a hundred kilometers from nowhere and hidden on three sides by the rocky cliffs. After hours of riding, they could rest. Eat. Talk.

"Why are we stopping?"

"Water," he said simply, climbing from the bike and plucking a bottle from the saddlebag.

She followed suit but struggled with the helmet buckle. With the flick of his thumb, he released the sticky clasp. "Thanks." After taking a long drink, she asked, "Have you decided where we're headed yet, besides west?"

He'd given it a lot of thought while riding. It wouldn't be easy to get passage on a container ship, and Cressida hadn't been burned. She could seek help from US authorities. "You're going to the consulate in Adana."

"Isn't that like a gazillion kilometers from here?"

He smiled. "It's about ten hours by road."

She shuddered slightly, gazing across the rugged terrain. "But we aren't riding on roads."

"Yeah. It'll take two days. Three at most. For now, we're heading to a friend's, near Gercüş."

She stiffened. "Do spies really have friends?"

"I'm a person, so yes, I have friends. And I'm a covert operative—a case officer. My job is to recruit spies—like Hejan. Technically, I'm not a spy."

"A case officer? What does that mean?"

"I look for people—people with access to other people or organizations, like, for example, al-Qaeda, who may be interested in providing information to the US. I recruit them. They're the spies, and I manage them."

"That doesn't sound nearly as sexy as being a spy."

He shrugged. "True spies aren't usually sexy. They're greedy, disloyal bastards, or they're out for revenge. Or they're trying to play me—they want me to think I have an inside man, when they're feeding me shitty intel."

"Then why do you work with them—the ones who are trying to play you?"

"Because I can feed them equally shitty intel."

"What kind was Hejan?"

"He was hard to pin down. He was a volunteer—usually they're the squirrelly ones. The volunteers put out feelers, say they've had a change of heart, they want to work for the good guys. We can't ignore them. If they're for real, they can be vital. Like the guy who helped us nail Anwar al-Awlaki."

"Was Hejan for real?"

"I'd been working him for about ten months. I thought he was legitimate. He had good motive for his change of heart. He told me his job was to pass a microchip to someone who would then pass it to a courier, who would then deliver it to his organization's leader. He promised me a direct line to the big guy, who we've been trying to identify for three years. But he also told me the info on the microchip wasn't the usual deal. This package was big. And because of that, a special pigeon would make the delivery—you."

"I didn't know—"

"Yeah. I believe that now." Ian kicked a rock and watched it skitter across the uneven ground. "Hejan said not to lose you. He said even if I thought the delivery was made, to stick with you." He frowned. "I had no intention of following that advice. My primary objective was the data." Ian had spent hours considering Hejan's wording. His guess was Hejan had played both sides very carefully. His compatriots had sent Hejan to Ian—wanting him to pretend to double—but Hejan had fooled the members of his cell and really had turned. He'd given Cressida more than she knew. Which was why Ian wanted her to remember exactly what Hejan had translated for her. *What* was on that map?

Hejan's associates had likely killed him when they realized he'd betrayed them for real. And they probably knew Cressida was their only hope for recovering whatever information he'd passed along.

Ian reached for his helmet. "We need to hit the road again."

She grimaced. "If only there *were* a road."

"Another hour, and we'll stop for the day. I promise."

IN THE EARLY afternoon, they reached Ian's friend's house on the edge of a small village near the larger town of Gercüş. The house was a ramshackle structure built of flat stones stacked high with intermittent concrete bricks and the occasional wooden plank. It was the only house in the area that was wired for electricity, and even had a satellite dish. A cow and her young calf grazed in the front yard, making Cressida smile.

How could you not trust a man with a calf in the yard?

She climbed from the bike, sore all the way to her marrow. It had been hot as hell under the thick leather, and she suspected the temperature neared a hundred Fahrenheit as they crossed the hilly, dry terrain. In spite of her discomfort, she couldn't help but notice this part of Turkey, with snowcapped peaks in the distance, was even more beautiful than she'd imagined.

Beauty or not, she'd give anything for a five-star hotel with Jacuzzi tub, but eyeing the house, she'd settle for hot and cold running water. Ian unlatched a low gate, and she followed him through the side yard to the back door, where he knocked softly. The door was opened a moment later by a portly elderly man. "John Baker, I've been expecting you." The man offered a polite bow, then stepped aside to permit their entry.

"Rajab, thank you," Ian said in English.

"I suppose I should call you Ian now," Rajab said, then turned to Cressida. "This must be the young lady they mentioned on the news. Welcome to my home." He bowed his head politely but made no move to shake hands, so Cressida murmured a greeting with her own slight bow. "You are more lovely than your pictures on the TV."

"They have her picture? Has a name been released?"

"They said your companion is Cressida Porter." He led them up a narrow staircase. "You have big troubles, my friend." They entered a tiny living area adjacent to the kitchen. There he turned on a flat-screen TV with the flick of a button.

Cressida smiled, realizing this man's TV was bigger and better than her own, crushing several assumptions she'd made based on the dilapidated exterior of the house. The man turned to her with a questioning look. "English only?"

She nodded.

He changed to CNN International. "They first mentioned you about an hour ago. They say you are an archaeology student and may have been abducted by Ian. Either that or you are his accomplice."

"That would never hold up," Ian said. "A full accounting of my time in Turkey will prove I didn't lay eyes on Cressida until three nights ago."

"The news doesn't care about what is either true or provable. They only care to be the first to say whatever it is." Rajab's voice was almost jovial.

"Can we stay here for the night, Rajab? We'll leave at dawn tomorrow. We just need food, fuel, and rest."

"Yes. Yes. Of course. But tell me, where will you go?"

Ian just shook his head.

Rajab shrugged. "Come. I will show you to your room."

With heartfelt thanks, Ian and Cressida made their way up another narrow flight of stairs. The room was tiny, but it had a bed, which to Cressida was all that mattered. After showing them the bathroom—no hot tub, but a tiny shower with hot running water—Rajab left them alone.

Ian touched her cheek, a gesture she'd grown accustomed to and recognized as an impulse he couldn't seem to control. Not that she wanted him to. "Rest. I need to talk to Rajab. Alone."

"I thought we were done with secrets?"

"No, I'm CIA. I'll always have secrets. I only promised no more lies."

She frowned. "I want to know more about Hejan." It had been impossible to talk as they rode across the steppe.

He covered her mouth and shook his head. "Not here," he whispered.

"But Rajab is your friend."

"Yes. And he's a zealot separatist who's offering his room in hopes of gleaning information for his cause. I'd give him a three on a scale of one to ten for how much to trust him. But that's good, because I wouldn't give anyone else more than a one or a two right now."

"What would you rate me?"

He smiled and ran a hand down her side. "Sweetheart, you're a ten, all the way."

She rolled her eyes even while feeling a flash of heat at the compliment. "I meant in trust."

"I trust you."

She wondered if that meant she was a five or higher, but he didn't seem interested in quantifying. "Does Zack know Rajab?"

"No. I've been working this region for a long time. Zack was assigned to assist me just for this case. He's a rookie; Ankara is his first posting. He doesn't speak Kurdish. He has no idea who my contacts are out here, nor the depth of my knowledge of this region."

"What about your boss? Does he know?"

"I never report contacts unless they become assets. Rajab isn't an asset. A good field agent always has a backup plan."

"And Rajab is your backup plan?"

"One of many. Now, take a shower if you want. Then come down for dinner."

She nodded, and he kissed her, the gentle peck of a couple's temporary good-bye. Strange that it should feel so natural.

Chapter Twenty-One

DINNER WITH RAJAB consisted of Kurdish meats rolled in flat bread. Even though the hour was still early, Cressida was exhausted from the slow, bouncing, hot, uncomfortable ride. After the meal, she went up to the bedroom to rest, alone. She managed to doze, but only fitfully. She felt nervous without Ian by her side.

Strange, since yesterday she'd alternated between wanting him and wanting to flee from him.

She had a wicked bad case of Stockholm syndrome and feared her taste in men was more like her mother's than she'd ever imagined.

Except Ian was nothing like any man she had ever known.

Unbidden and unwelcome, Three came to mind. The worst of the predators, Three had taught her an important lesson when she was seventeen years old: scumbags like him were ruled by their egos and dicks. Three sought to prove he was the super-alpha by seducing the daughter and the mother, knowing full well it would destroy them both.

And he'd almost succeeded.

She wondered if Zack was like Three. What caused a man to turn against his country? No doubt money was involved, but there had to be more. Ian was the seasoned operative, while Zack was the rookie, but currently, the rookie had the upper hand.

If Zack were anything like Three, he'd be jacking off while watching CNN right now.

She rolled over, hating that she'd let Three back into her thoughts. If there was one memory she wished to erase, it was her final confrontation with him.

Better to think about Ian instead. He was on the opposite end of the spectrum, a man who didn't need to prove he was alpha. He just *was*. It was in his essence, an integral part of him. His strength was her compass, compelling her to follow his direction. She didn't wonder why she'd Stockholmed so quickly; she only marveled that she'd been able to challenge him at all.

The old mattress dipped under his weight, and she couldn't stop herself from sliding backward, toward him. His arm wrapped around her belly and pulled her snug against his chest. He'd stripped to his underwear, and his warm bare thighs tucked up under hers. Spooning with him was comforting after the craziness of the last two days. Too comforting, when she should be keeping her guard up.

She scooted forward. "Too hot," she said, which was a lie. The evening had cooled considerably.

He chuckled. "You were bolder yesterday."

She rolled over to face him. "You were John yesterday."

"I prefer being Ian—especially when I'm in bed with a beautiful woman."

"See now, there's John—ever ready with the complimentary line."

"No. I find you sexy and beautiful, whereas John saw you as a job. John will say anything, because he *has* to be likable. Frankly, I think he's a smug prick."

"Whereas Ian is darker and dangerous." *And so very alpha.*

"I'm former Delta Force and a covert operative. John was a glorified security guard."

She laughed. John didn't get any respect from Ian. His face was cast in shadows, but there was enough light to see the desire in his eyes. "What happens tomorrow, Ian?"

He shook his head and pressed a finger to her lips. "Not here."

He'd been speaking so freely about his alter ego, she'd forgotten his concerns about Rajab. "If the walls have ears, then there is no way in hell you're getting laid."

He laughed. "I know. It would be stupid—too distracting. But, damn, I want to fuck you."

Every time he said those words, heat unfurled in her center. The phrase was coarse and hard—pure Ian—and for that reason, she found it sexy as hell. She suspected he knew it.

He leaned close and whispered in her ear, "Sleep, Cress. This may be the last bed we have for a while. Enjoy the luxury while you can."

IAN WOKE ABRUPTLY two hours before dawn. A tingling in the back of his neck told him it was time to go. *Now.*

He'd been in the business too long to ignore the feeling and nudged Cressida awake. "We're leaving," he said in a whisper. "Now. Through the window."

She shook her head, sleepy and confused. And frigging gorgeous and tousled, but this wasn't the time to notice that. "But we're three stories up," she whispered.

"Rock wall. The flat stones have plenty of hand- and footholds."

Her eyes widened in alarm. He hoped to hell her work meant she had done some climbing and was up to the challenge, because this climb had to be completed quickly. And without a safety line.

He pulled on his clothes, shoes, and backpack as Cressida did the same. They'd slept with the window open, so there was no need to pray for silent hinges. Ian had scouted the window when Rajab first presented the room, just in case, and knew there was an exterior lip that jutted out beneath the window, marking the base of the third floor. They could position themselves on the plank before descending.

He climbed onto the ledge first, then scooted to the side, so Cressida could climb out. She straddled the opening, then froze. Gripping the open frame, he placed his other hand on her thigh. "You can do this, Cress." She had to. He couldn't leave her here, and they sure as hell couldn't stay.

A soft thump sounded inside the house, and Cressida's chin jerked in alarm. *Shit.*

It was the nudge she needed, and she slipped out the window and onto the ledge with the speed and stealth of a cat. Thank God. And Allah. And Yahweh. And Vishnu. And hell, throw in Zeus and Odin for good measure.

The wall was wide enough for a side-by-side descent. Ian planted both hands and one foot, then prodded lower for another perch. Repeating the process for each hand- and foothold, he descended several feet, while Cressida climbed down on a parallel track. The burn on his shoulder ached from the abrading backpack, but the pain couldn't compete with the adrenaline that pumped through his system.

He neared the second-floor lip, and a glance to the right showed Cressida was stuck a few feet above him. Her hands were shaking, badly, as her right foot searched for a toehold.

The irregular surface of the wall made it impossible to see where to plant feet—she had to feel for it—but she prodded the wall dangerously close to a second-floor window.

Ian traversed to her side. Her shaking was even worse up close. "You've got this."

A thump sounded through the window near Cressida's shoe. Whoever had entered Rajab's house was on the stairs—headed for their bedroom with the open window.

They had maybe fifteen seconds to get off the wall and onto the dirt bike. "Bigger steps, Cress. We've got to go."

She nodded as sweat rolled down her neck. She shifted her weight to just her fingertips so she could prod even lower with her foot. Finally she found a cleft that could hold her, and she moved her other foot, then her hands, now in rapid, smooth choreography.

Ian followed suit, and five feet from the ground, he jumped, then planted his feet and opened his arms wide and whispered, "Jump."

She leapt out from the wall without looking, even though she was a full eight feet up. Ian caught her, marveling that she'd trusted him without hesitation.

If they didn't need to get the hell away, he'd have kissed her—in thanks for the trust, in gratitude for her quick and safe extraction—but that would have to wait for a time when a kiss wouldn't get them caught or killed. With her hand in his, he ran toward the barn where he'd parked the bike, just as he heard a shout from the third-floor window.

He rounded the side into the barn and came face-to-face with Rajab. His friend lifted a gun and pointed it at Cressida.

"Thank you, my friend, for escaping the house. It is difficult to wash blood from the wood floor."

CRESSIDA STILL HADN'T stopped shaking from clambering down the rock wall. She felt dizzy at the sight of the gun and more than a little nauseated.

"Give me the microchip," Rajab said.

She shook her head. "I don't have it." The pendant was hidden beneath her shirt, but she felt it, sticking to her skin thanks to the sweat that had pooled between her breasts during the terrifying climb.

"Well then, I will just have to kill you and then take my time searching you. Every...little...crevice." The last was said with such a repugnant leer. Shit, this guy had necrophiliac fantasies...and he wanted to play them out on *her*.

"You kill her, Rajab, and no one will ever find the chip. Hejan told her where it is. She's the only one who knows where to find it." Ian made the statement with such authority, even Cressida believed him for a second.

Rajab wasn't nearly so trusting. "What is the American word you are so fond of, Ian? Bullshit?"

Ian took a step closer to Rajab, tucking her behind him. "If you so much as touch her, I will slice you open and piss on you as you bleed out." His voice was low and menacing.

Rajab flinched, and Ian sprang. He kicked Rajab's hand, dislodging the gun, and then landed a blow on the man's throat. Rajab went down. Ian went after him and landed another blow to the head, but Rajab managed to get a hand on Ian's throat.

"Get his gun, Cress," Ian croaked.

She was already scrambling after it. It slid across the hard-packed dirt floor toward the barn opening. She plucked the weapon from the dirt. Behind her, inside the barn, a sickening cracking sound was followed by a soft grunt.

"The guy in the house will be here any moment," Ian said.

A noise in the darkness beyond the barn alerted her, and Cressida turned as she raised the gun. A man charged toward her.

"He's here," she said and pulled the trigger.

Chapter Twenty-Two

THE CRACK OF the bullet split the silent morning. Ian's gaze jerked from Rajab's lifeless form to Cressida, who held the gun clasped between wildly shaking hands. She was still standing. Presumably, whomever she had shot at was not.

He plucked his own gun from the holster at the small of his back. With weapon raised to the ceiling, he approached her slowly so as not to rattle her. Who knew how she'd react? He pitched his voice low and adopted a soothing tone. "Is he down?"

She nodded without looking away from the dark morning into which she'd fired.

Ian scanned the shadows, seeing a lump on the ground ten meters away. "Rajab is dead. I'm going to check out the other. I need you to cover me. Can you do that?"

She nodded again, and light from the crescent moon revealed wide, scared eyes. But they weren't wild. Not losing-her-shit-crazy eyes. Good.

"We'll approach him slowly. Together."

"He was coming straight at me, Ian. I didn't think...I...I didn't mean to..."

"You did good, Cress. I'd have done the same thing." He *had* done the same thing when he snapped Rajab's neck.

They reached the second man. Ian pointed his gun down at the body and prodded the mass with his foot. The guy wasn't twitching.

The silvery moonlight splayed across the man's head and shoulders.

Holy shit. Neck shot. She'd severed his carotid artery with one clean bullet. A one-in-a-million hit.

More stunning, though, the man she'd shot was Sabal.

Ian took a step back. Rattled.

He'd guessed but still hadn't wanted to believe Sabal was in league with Zack. Sonofabitch. Sabal. Rajab. Cressida was right. Spies didn't have friends. Even spies who weren't really spies but case officers.

Cressida gasped, and the gun slipped from her slack fingers. Ian caught it, before it could hit the ground. "Careful. This sucker has a hair trigger after the first pull." He uncocked the Sig.

"Ohmygod. I—I was aiming for his belly."

"You were shaking." He wanted to take her into his arms and comfort her, but there wasn't time. He needed to search the body and get the hell out of here. There could be more coming. Hell, there could be another one in the house.

The gunshot had ensured everyone in the tiny village was now awake. The only question left was, would they descend on them with pitchforks, or would they ignore the sound as another skirmish in the ongoing unrest between Kurds and Turks?

"Hold together just a few minutes more. I'm going to search him and finish searching Rajab, then we're out of here." He pressed the gun back into her hands, hating that he had to do it while she was falling apart, but they needed to work together to get out of here in one piece, and he was counting on the inner strength he'd witnessed repeatedly to hold her together.

She sucked in a deep breath, then gave him a short nod. "Okay." She raised the gun, pointing it outward, into the surrounding darkness, and said, "Search him."

Damn, she was amazing.

Not surprisingly, Sabal had nothing in his pockets. Ian was painfully tempted to return to Rajab's house and search all three crooked floors. But his gut said they didn't have time.

He plucked the gun from Sabal's hand and checked the magazine. He rammed the clip back in place and flicked the safety. After a quick glance at Cressida, he continued searching the body. "He was armed and ready to fire. He probably never dreamed you'd shoot. The fact that you didn't hesitate saved your life." And mine, he silently added. If Cressida had been shot, Ian might well have been too stunned to react and save himself. He'd never doubted his ability to do his job before, but he didn't have a stellar track record for doing the right thing when it came to Cressida Porter.

It appeared he'd found his Achilles heel.

Back in the barn, he finished searching Rajab. Coldly, methodically, he ran his hands through his pockets. Trying to forget the fact he'd considered this man a friend. That he'd just killed him.

He checked his watch. Five minutes since the shot. They'd pushed their luck to the limit. Time to get the hell out of the village.

He was tempted to take Rajab's car, but it was too identifiable and would limit them to the roads. It was back on the bike for them. At least he'd managed to fill both the tank and the spare gas can strapped to the back. They had enough fuel to ride for hours.

Cressida waited until the bike was out and engine revving before she tucked away her gun and donned the helmet. She was moving like a regular operative, and damn he was impressed.

They set out over the wicked, rocky hills, the loud engine announcing their exit as surely as the bullet had heralded their presence. Minutes later, they were back on the steppe, waking only sheep and goats as they crossed the uneven ground.

◉

THEY STOPPED JUST after dawn, having traveled several miles in the wrong direction, away from Adana. Ian parked the motorcycle in the lee of a hill and shut off the engine. "We'll stop here and rest for a few hours."

Every muscle ached as Cressida swung her leg over the bike to dismount. "You sure this is safe?" she asked.

"Nowhere is safe. This is better than every other option."

She rubbed her eyes, which ached from the strain of trying to see the rough ground ahead as they barreled through the dark night.

"The river we've been skirting, it's the Tigris, right?"

He nodded as he plucked his backpack from the saddlebag. "What can you tell me about this area?"

She shrugged. "Not much. My research into the terrestrial archaeology of Turkey is relatively recent. My specialty is underwater."

His brows lowered. "Yeah. I was wondering about that. What the hell is an underwater archaeologist doing studying the landlocked borders of Turkey?"

She really didn't want to get into the hows and whys with him. She'd had enough trouble with the dissertation committee. "Trade routes on land are a strong influence on the water routes. And the illicit routes even more so." She plopped down onto the hard ground with a water bottle in hand and leaned against the slope of the hill. "If you can find where the secret route meets sea, you'll find the smugglers' ships. The pirates. It's all connected."

Ian shrugged. "That's no different from the modern drug trade—a water route is no good if you can't sneak the drugs on shore or over the border."

"Exactly."

He dropped down beside her. She held out the water bottle, and he took a long drink. He set the bottle down, then pulled a gun from his backpack and checked the load. Satisfied with his inspection, he held it out to her.

She hesitated. It was the gun she'd used to kill Sabal.

"I want it by your hand whenever we aren't riding," he said.

She took the weapon. "It's so sweet the way you keep giving me guns. Most men start with flowers."

He smiled.

She studied the killing tool. Had it killed others, or just Sabal? "I recognized him. The man I killed. He was Sabal. You introduced us by the train platform."

He nodded. "He would have killed you without hesitation. He and Rajab seemed to believe you have the microchip. They would have killed and gutted us both, to be certain neither of us swallowed it. That's what Rajab meant about the blood, why he wanted us in the barn, not the house."

She shuddered. She knew he was telling her this so she could accept what she'd done. And she did. At least, right now her plan was to save the freak-out over killing Sabal for later. Right now she needed to stay focused so she could protect the microchip.

The one Ian didn't know she had. Or probably had.

She couldn't let terrorists get the microchip.

Ian's mission was now hers.

Again, she considered telling him, and again, she wondered if he'd take the chip and leave her to her own devices. Getting the microchip out of the country would be far easier without her weighing him down.

She didn't think he'd be so callous, but why take the chance? The pendant was safe with her for now.

Ian pulled a bag of trail mix from his pack and offered it to her. She shook her head. A hard knot had formed in her belly when she killed a man, and she had no intention of eating again this month.

"You need to eat," he said firmly.

"I think I'll vomit if I eat."

He put an arm around her, pulling her snug against him, then lay back onto the hillside, his chest her cushion against the hard ground. "We'll rest first, then you have to eat."

She nodded. He was right, but she was glad he didn't insist she eat now. "This is so not what I imagined when I planned this trip," she muttered as she listened to his beating heart.

He chuckled. "Strange, because this is how my trips to Eastern Turkey usually go."

"Bull."

He laughed fully and threaded his fingers through her hair. It felt heavenly after wearing the tight helmet for what had to be a million bumps. "There's been a fight or two. Okay, four. But I haven't killed anyone since I was in Delta."

"I don't...get it. Why did Rajab help us at all? Why feed us and give us a room?"

"He wasn't in charge. He had to get in touch with his boss and await orders. His job was to keep us there until his organization could send someone. I took a chance, believing his separatist group wasn't affiliated with Hejan's, but clearly I was wrong." Ian looked up, his gaze becoming a thousand-mile stare that probably didn't take in the deep blue of the sky.

He stroked her back. "I won't lose sleep over killing Rajab. He betrayed us. I knew it was a possibility, but I'd hoped..." He sighed. "My worry is he probably told his contact we're on a bike, going overland. Which means heading west overland is out. And we probably need to ditch the bike. It's too loud and visible every time the land flattens out."

"So what do we do?"

"I don't know."

The words were so flat. So bare. It hadn't occurred to her Ian had run out of options, out of backup plans.

An idea formed. She gripped the pendant as a frisson ran through her. She knew in her gut this was the right move. She leaned up on an elbow and kissed him—the first time she'd initiated a kiss since she learned his real name. "Ian, if you had information on a tunnel—one that might even cross under the Syrian border—could you use that information to get the Turkish government to help us?"

CRESSIDA HAD IAN'S full attention. "What do you mean?"

"I should probably tell you more about *why* I came to Eastern Turkey. As you mentioned, it's a little odd for an underwater archaeologist to write a dissertation on terrestrial archaeology. It all started with a map."

"A map?" Ian's gaze strayed to her backpack. "A map you have with you?"

"Sort of." She paused, her gaze dropping to his chest.

It hit him in the gut, the realization that Cressida had been holding out on him. He stiffened and pushed back, separating his body from hers. He tried to get a grip on his temper, reminding himself she'd had a hell of a lot of reasons to hold back.

The awful truth was, against all the rules of spydom, he'd started to care about her. And the idea that she still didn't trust him was a kick in the balls.

He'd sat down to play Texas Hold'em, but the game had switched to blackjack. He *hated* blackjack. There was no bluffing and the opponent was the house. Blackjack was for the devil.

Texas Hold'em was a covert operative's game. In Hold'em, the shared cards leveled the field, while the hidden ones gave the game meaning. You never played the cards, you played the person across the table.

But with Cressida, he wasn't sure who his opponent was, or why they were in opposition. All he could see when he looked at her was a woman who made him want something he'd never had. He was the bastard son of a cold-hearted whore. Never loved. Never valued—at least, not until he'd become an asset to his country. A status he'd now lost. Yet he looked at Cressida and imagined—even wanted—the impossible.

While his world had shifted on its axis, nothing had changed for her. When this was all over, odds were she'd hate him with every fiber of her being. And he could hardly blame her.

He pushed past the pain in his chest and asked, "What map?"

With her heel, she scraped an arc in the thin layer of dirt that coated the rocky ground. "I probably shouldn't have photographed it with my personal camera... My job was to photograph and catalogue everything in the cabinet—so I wasn't totally cheating. It's just...a few of the maps intrigued me. So I took pictures of them with my own camera, without telling anyone."

"I'm lost here, Cressida."

She continued in the same distracted manner. "It wasn't until later, when I noticed the signature, that I realized that particular map was special."

"What map?" He took pride in the way he kept his voice even when he was dying the death of a thousand cuts inside.

She pursed her lips, then sighed, finally meeting his gaze with clear, focused eyes. "Last summer, when I interned at NHHC, I was given the chore of cataloging the contents of an old armored file cabinet. The cabinet had been labeled as top secret sometime after World War II and then forgotten. It'd floated from cubicle to cubicle for as long as anyone could remember. Trina was the last one to house it. Mara decided enough was enough and got permission for me to catalogue the contents."

"You were authorized?" Ian asked. This could become an important point later if Mara Garrett's ass were on the line.

"Yes. It was approved by the top brass."

Good. The attorney general's wife hadn't screwed up royally there. "So what's the deal with the map? How old is it?" *And why the hell is it important now?* But he kept his impatience at bay. Barely.

"My best guess is the map was drawn in 1914—a few months before World War I broke out."

"And who created the map?"

She looked down. No longer willing to meet his gaze. "An archaeologist."

"Dammit, Cressida, stop being coy. I need to know what the big deal is."

"T. E. Lawrence." She sucked in a long slow breath, then blurted in plain English. "The map I found was drawn by Lawrence of Arabia."

CHAPTER TWENTY-THREE

CRESSIDA'S HEART POUNDED with the admission. She'd never told anyone that detail. Not even Suzanne. And she'd always felt like crap for keeping that little tidbit back. It was just that, when one finds a map drawn by T. E. Lawrence pinpointing a heretofore unknown Roman aqueduct, and one needed a stellar subject for one's dissertation, what was the lucky grad student to do?

If she found the aqueduct, she'd give full credit for the find to T. E. Lawrence. The man deserved it, along with all the other accolades that had come his way during his short life. It wasn't like she planned to steal his glory. She just wanted to be the first person to *re*-locate the aqueduct. She still had to do the groundwork. She'd spent months poring over satellite images, coming up with a Lidar protocol that was most likely to not only find the Lawrence aqueduct, but others as well. She suspected there were more.

"Prior to being a brilliant military strategist for the Brits in Arabia, T. E. Lawrence was an archaeologist who worked in northern Syria. His work included forays into the Ottoman Empire before the Empire's demise."

"Stop," Ian said in a harsh, clipped tone. "Beating. Around. The fucking bush. What was on T. E. Lawrence's map?"

She winced. She supposed that was exactly what she'd been doing. It was just difficult to finally tell someone everything. "He found an ancient Roman aqueduct. A tunnel that could well be over fifty miles long, and there's a chance it passes under the Turkish/Syrian border."

Ian stared at her in silence for a long moment, his face unreadable. Then his eyes flattened and he surged to his feet. "*Sonofamotherfuckingbitch!* You're telling me this *now?*"

She rubbed her eyes and tried to digest his hostility. She hadn't thought he could be angrier than he'd been in Siirt, but this was much worse. She suspected that if she doused herself in gasoline, he'd offer her a match. "Ian, you're the first person I've *ever* told about T. E. Lawrence's find."

He kicked a rock, sending it skittering across the rugged ground. "You beautiful fool. Don't you get it? They *know. That's* why you were chosen to be the mule. You were about to embark upon an expedition deep into Eastern Anatolia to find the most valuable tunnel since…*fuck*. I don't know…*ever*. And you tell me this now? *Me*. The only person in the *entire country* who is helping you."

She jumped to her own feet and stared him down. "Get your head out of your ass and listen up. I didn't tell *anyone* about that map. No one. So Hejan couldn't have known what I was about to do or why. And you can drop the outrage that I didn't trust you enough to tell you, because I don't trust ANYONE!"

It was true. How on earth could she trust anyone, when everyone—even her own mother—let her down? Hell, *especially* her mother. No one, *ever*, had loved her enough to put her first. So she'd never put anyone else first. It was simple math.

She grabbed her backpack and shoved the water bottle and gun back inside.

"What do you think you're doing?"

"I'm done resting. You can come with me or not, your choice."

"You aren't calling the shots here, sweetheart. It's going to get damn hot in the next hour. We aren't going to walk fifty miles in the worst heat of the day. So sit your ass back down. You aren't escaping me now that I know *why* you're so valuable."

He might be right about the heat, but his choice of words rankled. They were back to the vocabulary of kidnapping. He considered her his prisoner. Screw that. One thing she did know about Ian at this point—probably the only thing she knew—was that he would never hurt her.

She backed away from him, slowly. "You're wrong. I'm not valuable to anyone. Certainly not to Zack—how could he possibly know about the tunnel? No one knows."

"He knows." Ian spoke with such certainty.

"I didn't tell my advisor or Suzanne, or Mara, Trina, or Erica. Hell, I didn't even tell Todd, when I lived with him and we were supposedly in love—"

She stopped abruptly as her own words hit her.

She dropped her backpack, which landed on the ground with a

dull thunk. "Oh. Shit. Todd." Her stomach burned, and she wondered why this realization hurt so much. She'd faced and accepted Todd's betrayal months ago. She'd boxed him up and put him where he could never hurt her again.

Except, he just had. What a lovely, double-edged sword he wielded.

She paced in a tight circle. "Shit. Shit. Shit." She sucked in a gasping breath. "It must have been Todd." She could barely breathe as the connections came together, a mental assault, so many betrayals.

Ian grabbed her shoulders, halting her frenetic pacing. "Tell me everything. Everything about Todd. Everything about the map."

She cleared her throat against the pain that had lodged there. "Todd and I started dating right before I went to DC for my internship. I really liked him. He was different. Really smart, for starters. His parents were immigrants from Jordan, which he'd visited a lot along with Saudi Arabia, Egypt, and Syria, before the civil war started. He was exotic. Well traveled. Fascinating. But his parents put a lot of pressure on him, being an only child and first-generation American."

"Jordanian immigrants named their son 'Todd'?"

"His real name is Todros." She glanced at him askance. "But I'm guessing you already know that."

He nodded. "Checking to see if you knew."

"Yeah. I knew my boyfriend's frigging name."

Ian raised a brow, a silent reminder that she'd been ready to jump into bed with him the first night—when they both were using aliases.

"We lived together," she said flatly.

Did his hand clench into a fist at that? Was it possible James Bond was jealous?

Don't flatter yourself.

"My DC internship was...amazing. I mean, it was cool to be working for Mara Garrett *and* Erica Scott." She cocked her head. "I'm guessing you know who Erica Scott is."

He nodded. "Better known as Erica Kesling."

"The wedding was last spring." She paced the small strip of ground between Ian and the bike. "I lived with Trina, and we really clicked. Between Trina, Erica, and Mara, they're hella connected. I got to go to fundraising parties at the Smithsonian and National Geographic. They even took me along to a political schmooze fest for Alec Ravissant at Dr. Patrick Hill's Annapolis mansion."

"Dr. Hill, the oceanographer?"

"Yes. The head of the MacLeod-Hill Exploration Institute. His organization is a large source of funding for the shipwreck excavation I was working on in Antalya. He's tight with my advisor, so going to a party at his house was a pretty big deal. Such a big deal I invited Todd to go to the party with me," she said, returning to the reason for the tangent in her explanation. "He flew up for the weekend so he could go."

"So you were pretty serious already?" Had Ian's voice turned flat? No. She was imagining things.

"Not then. We'd only just started dating. Suzanne said later—after he was arrested—she thought he'd originally asked me out *because* of my internship—he knew I'd get to meet Dr. Hill and wanted an in." She didn't bother to say how much Suzanne's suspicion had hurt—the idea that Todd's interest in her had stemmed from his ambition. "But I liked him, and I thought he liked me. I didn't want to go to the garden party as a fifth wheel, tagging along with the high-profile couples. I didn't think Curt Dominick would appreciate hanging out at a political event with a lowly intern." She smiled, thinking of Trina. "It was right before Trina met Keith, and at the time she had the hots for Dr. Hill's assistant. Some jackass whose name I forget...but I knew she'd be busy at the party pursuing that guy, so I invited Todd." She let out a humorless laugh. "I was wrong about Todd *and* Curt. Todd was so busy sucking up, he ditched me, and I spent the afternoon playing pool with Mara, Curt, and Lee.

"When we left the party, I thought Todd would be pissed because I hadn't hung out with him, and he was worried I was mad for the same reason. Trina had left with Keith—and had her own man issues to deal with—but really, I'd had a great time. Todd had a great time. We'd both been invited to join Dr. Hill on his next submarine mapping demonstration he was setting up for Erica's benefit. Hill really wants his institute to be locked tight with the Navy's underwater archaeology program..."

"Get to the point about Todros Ganem and how he's involved." There was no mistaking the hostility in Ian's voice.

She glared at him. "After that weekend, things shifted between Todd and me. It was a good weekend for us, relationship-wise. We became more serious."

Yeah, his jaw was definitely clenching. So maybe the spy felt something for her after all. "The next two weeks were insane. Keith's townhouse blew up. Alec Ravissant assigned Sean Logan to act as Trina's bodyguard. Eventually, I was moved to Alec's house. The bomber was identified right before I flew back to Tallahassee. It had been so crazy, I hadn't set up a place to live. I stayed with Suzanne while I apartment-hunted. I couldn't find anything that wasn't a craphole and was frustrated. Todd suggested I move in with him. It was early in the relationship, but I figured what the hell, I needed a place. And"—she fixed Ian with a glare—"I *liked* him. A lot. I figured my luck had changed, and I'd finally found a good guy."

Her breath hitched. Things really had started off great with Todd. She'd forced herself to forget that last spring but couldn't deny it now. "That Thanksgiving, he flew home to visit his parents in Delaware. I hadn't met them yet, and he wanted to prepare them for his non-Middle Eastern, non-Muslim girlfriend. I was pretty much their worst nightmare, and we talked about making a joint visit over winter break, after he'd softened them up.

"I stayed in Tallahassee over the holiday weekend and, with nothing to do, decided to study the maps I'd photographed over the summer. It had been such a busy semester, I hadn't had time to even look at them until that point." She paused. "It was just a cursory examination. Nothing about the particular map stood out. It wasn't like T. E. Lawrence had labeled it 'Eastern Turkey' or anything. There was no scale. It was just a sketch map. Matching his hand-drawn lines to the terrain without a scale was...a challenge. It wasn't until I realized that what I thought was a label was actually the mapmaker's signature that things got interesting. A quick Google search on T. E. Lawrence, and I was pretty sure the map I'd photographed back in DC was a genuine Lawrence of Arabia original. The signature looked good, and why would anyone forge his signature on a map that had been filed away and forgotten?"

From Ian's fixed gaze and intent eyes, she knew she had his rapt attention. "After that, I researched T.E. and learned he worked at Carchemish, on the Euphrates River in northern Syria in 1911 and again in 1914. Once I had Carchemish as a starting point, I was able to narrow my search, and eventually matched the map to the area west of Cizre, east of Nusaybin. Historic maps generally ignored that area, so it wasn't easy. T.E.'s notes indicated an archaeological site, but not just any site, an underground Roman aqueduct. My guess is it was a Roman effort to route water from the Tigris, and I think it originates near the current village of Kefshenne and goes south from there, filling in the dry stretch of land between the Tigris and Euphrates."

She glanced to the southeast. Somewhere in the distance beyond the near hills, the river flowed. "I suspect T.E. mapped it right before World War I broke out. In 1914, he went on a mapping expedition on the Sinai Peninsula after Carchemish—but the expedition was really cover for British Intelligence, who wanted reconnaissance of the area—and he must have explored the area near Cizre either before or after that excursion. Most, if not all, of his maps from that period went to the British War Department. A stamp on the back indicated the map had been property of the British Naval Attaché, and I know they regularly trade information with the NHHC. Basically, I think the Attaché gave it to the US Navy anywhere from sixty to eighty years ago, and it was filed away with intelligence gathered during both World War I and World War II, and forgotten."

Ian had been silent for a long time. But she didn't doubt he was keeping up with the story.

"So, back to Todd. He returned from Thanksgiving, and I debated whether or not I should tell him what I'd found. I mean, I'd just been handed an amazing subject for dissertation research—except, it wasn't underwater. I had to work my ass off to sell the topic to my advisor, using the trade routes angle— without mentioning Lawrence."

"If you'd told him about the Lawrence connection, would he have approved it without question?"

"Probably. Maybe." Cressida rubbed her arms, feeling chilled as she admitted to the one thing she felt guilty about. "I didn't mention the map or Lawrence, because academia can be cutthroat. I worried my advisor would...try to steal my lead. Take my glory. It wouldn't be the first time that happened to a graduate student." She bit her bottom lip. "But the hardest part was not telling Todd. He was desperate—really, really desperate—for a dissertation topic. He squeaked by on his MA. It was well written and hit all the right notes, but in the end, his underwater survey of a Sint Maarten bay turned up nothing. He'd hoped to find the hull of a Spanish naval vessel sunk by the Dutch in a 1630s battle, but he got nada. If he didn't come up with something better for the PhD, he'd be done academically. And his parents were pissed that he was pursuing academic underwater archaeology and not computer science."

"Do you think he would have stolen your project?"

"He didn't have the power to steal it—not like a professor could—but he certainly would have wanted in on it. Equal billing. I knew him well enough to know he'd take over. It would've become *his*. I've been pushed around by enough men in my life to know I didn't want to open that door with Todd. But there is enough research involved to feed a dozen dissertations, and I would have happily shared—after I found the site and got full sole finder's credit."

She shook her head as guilt stabbed at her. "Todd didn't know why I'd fixated on Roman aqueducts in Eastern Anatolia, but he must have guessed something had triggered my sudden shift in research." She resumed pacing. "If he found out, it would explain a lot, actually. He could have hacked my computer the weekend I went to visit my mom. I usually bring my computer, but Mom insisted I unplug. She told me in no uncertain terms to leave my work at home or don't bother visiting. It must have been too much for Todd to resist, being home alone with my laptop."

She closed her eyes, imagining how Todd must have felt when he discovered her secret. "A few days after I returned, he broke into the department and stole the Lidar. Looking at it now, my guess is he wanted to cut me out. He probably had some insane notion of heading out here on his own and finding the site before I could. With his Jordanian family, he would certainly have had an easier time arranging the trip."

"More likely he intended to sell the equipment to his Jordanian relatives."

"Yeah. I heard the FBI found emails on his hard drive that indicated he was trying to sell the equipment. I was told he wasn't anti-American or pro-Jordanian. He just wanted money. When he was caught, he implicated me. I was stunned. I'd been in love with him, and he claimed I'd put him up to the task of stealing hundreds of thousands of dollars' worth of equipment from the department I'd devoted my life to." She met Ian's hard gaze. "It appears the fact that I didn't trust Todd is what set him off. It might even be what set this entire horrid fiasco in motion."

She took a deep breath as she digested her own words. "He may have promised his uncle or Hejan's group he'd find the tunnel in exchange for getting him out of the US. It could explain why he's in Turkey."

She looked out over the landscape, toward the Syrian border. She guessed they were forty or fifty miles away. "To me, it's an archaeological site. A rare find that could launch my career, establish me as an expert in something." She frowned. "But I wonder if Todd saw modern implications."

Chapter Twenty-Four

IAN HAD KNOWN the potential for illicit purposes when she first described ancient tunnels, but the proximity to an international border changed everything. The fact that it could be a route into a NATO country from volatile Syria—and vice versa—well, the implications were huge. And horrifying if the knowledge got into the wrong hands.

"My plan for this trip was a scouting mission," Cressida said. "To see if Lidar could be effective for survey. The Gadara Aqueduct was built by digging a series of well-like vertical shafts—called qanats—every twenty to two hundred meters, then workers tunneled between the shafts. The shafts were later filled in, but archaeologists have found over three hundred entrances so far. Lawrence marked two qanat entrances on the map, but there must be more. He indicated the tunnel was several miles long."

"What does Todros know?" Ian refused to call the sonofabitch Todd. Todd was Cressida's boyfriend. A man she'd been in love with. Whereas Todros Ganem was a traitor with Jordanian ties who might have given terrorists the coordinates to a smugglers' tunnel. "Does he have the map?"

"If he found Lawrence's map on my computer, he won't have everything he needs. I cut the key from the jpeg file and buried it on my hard disk. Just the map wouldn't tell him a thing. My guess is he found my composite map—one I'd drawn as I was trying to narrow down the location."

"Where is your composite map?" He looked at her bag. "Do you have it?"

She pointed to her temple. "It's in here. I created it. I know every contour line. So I didn't bring it. I didn't trust the other grad students. After the fallout with Todd, some of them turned on me. And they all wanted to know what my lead was. So I left the map behind in Tallahassee."

"So Todros knows the general area of where to look, but not the exact coordinates?"

"*I* don't even know the exact coordinates. I calculated the accuracy of my map to be within five kilometers. That isn't a huge area for a pedestrian survey if you know what you're doing."

"And Todros knows what he's doing."

"Yes. He teaches survey courses to the undergrads." She paused. "Taught. He taught survey courses." Her gaze dropped, preventing Ian from seeing her pain at Todros's actions.

Todros had lived with Cressida. She'd loved him, yet the motherfucker had betrayed her. For what? Academic glory? Revenge? Or was there a political ideology behind it all? Had he seen the potential of the tunnel and wanted to exploit it? What drove a man to betray a woman like Cressida? To betray his country? Because sure as hell the moment Ganem popped the lock on the anthropology department door, he'd made his choice.

Why had he shown up in Antalya when he did? And where was he now?

Ian wished he could see Cressida's composite map. "Why didn't you bring a computer?"

"I was warned traveling to Eastern Anatolia with sophisticated mapping software and data would be a bad idea."

She took a step toward him, then stopped. "Ian, I know you're mad I didn't tell you, but you need to understand, this has been my secret, and mine alone, for months. I had no idea *anyone* had seen my composite map. I honestly didn't think it was relevant to what was going on. I'm sorry—" She stopped and took a deep breath. "I haven't told anyone. Not my best friend. Not my mother. Not my advisor. I didn't even tell the man I lived with. It never even occurred to me it was something *you* needed to know."

Put that way, it was hard for Ian to hold it against her. But he tried. He was developing feelings for her—which was flat out forbidden in his world—while in Cressida's world, Ian was just another mistake on a long list of them.

She'd kissed Ian once. Not that he was counting...except apparently he was...

All he really knew was his life was forever changed thanks to this screwed-up mission, and Cressida Porter had managed to steal a piece of him he hadn't known was up for grabs. "You can find an entrance to the tunnel?"

She bit her bottom lip. "Maybe. But I doubt we'll be able to open it, not without tools and a team of workers. My goal for this trip was just to locate it. Then use Lidar next year to map the length."

As a poker player, Ian didn't like the odds. But at this point, he had no other hand to play. "We're ditching the bike. We'll rest during the heat of the day and start walking in the late afternoon. For lack of a better plan, we'll head to your tunnel." He patted the ground next to him. "We may as well rest in the shade while we can." He refused to acknowledge the reason he urged her to his side was because he wanted to be next to her.

He had a feeling he'd never recover from meeting Cressida. He wasn't sure he even wanted to.

WALKING SOUTH WAS far more pleasant than the bumpy motorcycle ride, except Ian missed the press of Cressida's thighs and the feel of her hands on his hips. When they rode, every bump and bounce was a reminder that she was with him. That they were alive.

And in spite of everything, he was pretty damn grateful to be alive.

The burn had ached less on the motorcycle, as his pack had been tucked in a saddlebag, but walking forced him to wear the forty-pound pack crammed with weapons and survival gear, and even though Cressida had tripled the layers of gauze, there was no avoiding the rub of pack on wound.

But the pain was yet another sign he was alive, so he accepted it without complaint.

It was half-past dark, and they'd covered at least ten rugged miles when Ian saw a campfire lit in the distance. They finally drew close enough for him to discern the camp configuration. He stopped and held a hand out to halt Cressida.

"What...?"

"Sweetheart, would you like something other than trail mix for dinner tonight?"

Her brows drew together. "That depends. Is that a friend of yours?"

"Nope. Never met them before in my life. They're Kurdish nomads. Shepherds. You'll never meet kinder, more giving people. Best of all, they won't have phones, TV, radio, or computers. They won't have seen our pictures on the news. Given we've got about forty miles of walking ahead of us and need to refresh our supplies, I think we'd be wise to accept any charity they offer."

She smiled, and her shoulders relaxed a bit. "So what's our story?"

"It's doubtful they speak English, so you don't have to worry about memorizing a role. Odds are they're Sunni Muslims. We'll say we're married and on vacation." He cut a glance her way. "We'll go with the honeymoon cover again. Everyone's a sap for newlyweds."

As they walked, he took her hand and threaded his fingers through hers. "This is how they would expect American newlyweds to walk."

Her fingers tightened around his. "They wouldn't be bothered by the public display of affection?"

"Hand-holding is common in the Arab world. Men hold men's hands here as a sign of friendship. While a man holding a woman's hand isn't as common, we're Americans, and even Kurdish nomads are familiar with Americans and our relaxed social mores. If we want to sell them on the fact that we're married, we need to look like what they'd expect to see."

She halted midstride, their entwined fingers forcing him to stop too. "So, you mean I can do this in front of our potential Kurdish hosts?" Cressida released his hand and slid her arms around his neck, then planted her lips on his. Her tongue invaded his mouth. Sweet, hot, and sexy as hell.

He cradled her face between his hands and slid his tongue over hers. This. He needed this. She gave him a taste of everything he'd given up for his career. Everything he could never have.

He ended the kiss before he completely forgot himself. If all went well with the nomads, not only would they have all night, they'd even have a bed.

"So is that a yes?" Cressida asked.

He shook his head, trying to remember what the hell they were talking about. Oh yeah, PDAs in the nomad camp. He cleared his throat. "Um. No. That would be a bad idea. In fact, you'll probably be expected to hang out with the women and keep your hair covered."

There'd been no need for her to wear her headscarf so far, but she'd kept it with her and pulled it out of the pack now and draped it over her hair. Ian arranged it into the proper drape.

Her wide mocha eyes caught the moonlight, and he held in a breath to even out the gut-clenching awareness that this was no ordinary attraction.

He took her hand and continued toward the campfire that beckoned. "I'll tell them we're here to visit my motherland—my mom was an ethnic Kurd. We ran out of gas when I got it in my head that it would be fun to go off road and explore. You'll pout and show you're annoyed with me for insisting on the dangerous adventure."

They walked in companionable silence, the light of the fire growing brighter with each step. "So my handsome new husband led me astray on our rental bike. We were on our way to meet your cousins on our honeymoon to fulfill your granny's dying wish."

"I like that. Nice attention to detail, without being too elaborate."

"Why did I agree to fulfill your granny's wish on my one and only honeymoon?"

"I promised you a five-star hotel in Istanbul. And a Turkish bath. And to satisfy you in every way."

Her breath hitched. "That would do it." She squeezed his hand as they drew nearer the camp. "So. Am I mad at you for our predicament, or too infatuated to care?"

"With me as your husband? Infatuated. Obviously."

He glanced sideways and caught her eye roll.

"I'm pretty sure it's your fault," he added. "You wanted to go off-road."

"Please. A woman who wants a five-star hotel and sex isn't going to beg to ride off-road on terrain likely to make you a soprano."

"Sweetheart, there's no need to worry in that department."

"I'll be the judge of that."

"I can't wait."

Her throaty chuckle sent a jolt of desire straight to his groin. In the midst of the most messed-up op ever, he was...*enjoying himself.* Huh. That was a first.

They approached the camp. Ian cradled her hand in both of his as he hailed the nomadic shepherds in their language and said a silent prayer that these people were exactly who they appeared to be.

He was sick to death of surprises and betrayal.

Chapter Twenty-Five

CRESSIDA'S HEART POUNDED as they entered the camp. It was late. Dark. Four men sat around the fire. One held a drum, another a sitar—or something like it, Cressida wasn't sure—and the soft music came to an abrupt stop when Ian hailed them.

She had no clue what Ian said, but his manner was congenial—very John, if she were to analyze him—and his tone upbeat. The men smiled and ate his John act up. Cressida was whisked off to join the women. As far as she could tell, this was a group of four or five families. The cluster of tents was more permanent than an overnight camp, but, as Ian had said, no electricity. No modern conveniences.

The women spoke rapidly, and Cressida couldn't understand a word. But a plate of food was set before her, and after hours of walking, her appetite had returned. She thanked the women profusely for the warm, spicy meal. A few of the dishes were similar to foods she had tried in Van when she had dinner with John—a lifetime ago.

After the meal, the women presented her with a basin of heated water, and she realized they were offering her a bath. A cloth soaked with perfumed water was the most heavenly thing she'd ever smelled—until she was handed a homemade bar of soap with inclusions that looked like flower petals and herbs. Never in her life had she enjoyed the spicy, warm scent of soap as much as she did at that moment.

The women left her alone with hot water and the most precious bar of soap in the world, which she used to scrub her skin and work lather through her hair. When the women returned, they dressed her in a peasant blouse and skirt. Embroidered in the local custom, the cloth had to be valuable, and she protested. But the women didn't understand, and she didn't want to insult them. So she donned the clothing, tying the laces across the bodice. The cotton garments were clean, soft, and comfortable.

Fed, clean, and clothed, she was led to another tent—this one slightly farther from the others, and from their knowing glances and occasional giggles, she had a feeling she and Ian were being given special accommodations because they were on their honeymoon.

Unlike the goat-hair tent where she'd been fed and bathed, her new tent had tapestry walls. The main piece of furniture in the square room was a futon-like pallet. Beside it sat a low table surrounded by pillows. The floors were covered with elaborately woven kilims.

Beautiful and exotic on a normal occasion, after days on the run, the tent represented paradise. And she'd be sharing it with her…*husband*. They had stopped running, even if only for one night.

Now it was time for *her* to stop running and take what she wanted. It was time to pause and enjoy a moment of pleasure with Ian. After all, they could die tomorrow.

The women left her, and she sat on the pillows by the table and poured herself a cup of tea. Ian would join her soon. Her body heated at the thought of acting on the sexual current that had pushed her toward him from the moment she met his gaze across a crowded airport terminal. Of finally reaching the release that had coiled in her since they'd almost made love in the shower in Siirt.

She sipped her tea and waited.

And waited.

The tea turned cold. The music outside the tent continued. An hour passed. She stretched out on the futon. Her eyes felt heavy, and she couldn't keep them open.

The music stopped sometime while she dozed. She woke up to silence and wondered where Ian was.

He wasn't coming.

Maybe he'd left her. Maybe he'd tucked her safely away with these people she couldn't communicate with. Maybe he was *gone*. He'd abandoned her…

Hurt and fear rocked her to the core.

How humiliating to be abandoned by her fake husband on her fake honeymoon, right before they were about to do some very real consummating.

The canvas curtain door shifted, and Ian entered the tent. Relief flooded her but didn't eclipse the fear of abandonment that had struck with shocking speed. "Damn you!" she growled as she launched herself at him. She grabbed his shirt and pulled him to her, pressing against the chest she'd feared she'd never get to touch again.

"Did you miss me?" he asked.

She released his shirt. "No. Why would I?"

He smiled a devilish, carnal smile. "Because you want me."

"Maybe I did, before you left me alone—*for hours.*"

He moved closer. "I was ingratiating myself with our host." He shrugged. "Working. Protecting your ass." He smiled and reached for the named body part.

She stepped out of his reach. "The music ended a while ago."

"Ten minutes isn't a while. And I took a walk." His voice lowered. "So I could get you something."

She eyed the hand he'd tucked behind his back, as if he reached for his pistol. What kind of game was he playing? "I already have a gun."

His smile deepened as he produced a fistful of wildflowers. "For you."

She sucked in a sharp breath. A ragged bunch of flowers had never looked prettier. She took them from him and held them to her face, breathing in their fresh scent. "You were picking wildflowers?"

He nodded. "I can't wine and dine you, but I could at least get you flowers."

In the middle of this crazy, scary nightmare, Ian had gone off into the night to gather flowers? She clutched the handful of blossoms even tighter in her fist.

He took a step toward her. "I'm used to being alone. It's how I've always been. Now, my world has exploded. I've been burned. Yet all I want is you. I don't want to be alone when I can be with you."

Cressida's breath caught.

"Sooooo…you want to finish what you started in Siirt?" he asked.

She laughed at his quick emotional retreat and set the flowers on the table. She planted herself before him. "You didn't need the flowers. All you had to do was step inside the tent."

He stroked her cheek. "Yeah, but I wanted to see you smile when I gave you the flowers. Because your smile is the most beautiful thing I've ever seen."

IAN CAUGHT CRESSIDA up against him and took in her sexy, sweet scent. They were safe, and would remain so for at least a day. During this respite, he planned to explore Cressida Porter. Thoroughly.

She slid her hands around his neck. "Tell me one thing, Ian. One thing to make me believe in you."

"In Antalya, I wanted to break cover when I realized you were Hejan's pigeon. Something about you…struck me. I didn't want you caught up in this mess. But all I could do was hold you back when the fight broke out, to keep you from getting hurt."

Her eyes widened. "That was you?"

"Yes."

Her voice turned husky. "If I'd met you that night…things might have gone differently."

He shook his head. "You would have met John."

"That's too bad, then," she whispered in a throaty voice, "because I'm not interested in John. I want Ian."

"John isn't here. Poor bastard was killed in an apartment in Siirt." Ian's heart pounded, and he wondered why. This was just a joining of bodies. A respite. One he desperately wanted, but not vital.

Yet somehow, this moment *felt* vital. Like he was baring his soul, not just his body. It was crazy, but still, he felt it, the pounding heart, the windup of increasing tension. He was coiled tight, ready to spring. Ready to touch. Taste. Own.

Cressida reached for his shirt and pulled it up, over his head. She purred softly and stroked his pecs and biceps. He couldn't help but flex and flash a smile. "Yours. All yours."

"What do you want in return?"

He tugged at the ties on her peasant blouse. "You. All of you."

"You aren't asking much."

"I'm giving everything and asking for the same."

"Okay, then."

He undid the bow above her breasts to open the embroidered top. She didn't wear a bra, so the split blouse exposed her high, round breasts and nipples waiting to be tasted. He cradled her breasts, rubbing his thumbs across the tight peaks, while his lips trailed down her neck, across her soft cleavage, finally stopping to suck one nipple into his mouth, then the other.

Her fingers threaded through his hair as she let out soft panting breaths. He raised his head and kissed her deeply. They had all night, and he intended to enjoy every minute.

Starting with tasting all of her. He pulled the blouse over her head and tossed it aside, then dropped to his knees. His hands skimmed her flat belly, then tugged down the full skirt that hid the part of her he ached for. From her scent, he knew she was aroused and ready. A sweetness that was pure, sexy Cressida. He almost felt a buzz as all the blood in his body surged to his cock. Lightheaded and hard, he reached for her sexy lace panties and slid them down her smooth thighs.

"You're beautiful," he said with all the reverence he felt.

"You already know you're getting laid. You don't need to lay it on so thick."

He sat back on his heels and looked up at her. She was serious. More than serious. She was…self-conscious. How could she be? She was perfect. Stunning. Every fantasy he'd ever had—on steroids.

He stroked between her thighs, touching the slick heat he couldn't wait to taste. She let out a soft moan, but he sensed she was still nervous, not relaxed enough to enjoy the invasion of his tongue. "I'm telling you the truth. You're beautiful. Perfect. Sexy." He stood and took her hand, leading it to his thick cock trapped in his now very uncomfortable jeans. "See what you do to me?"

"Even a perfect Delta Force spy will get hard when presented with a naked woman."

"Not like this—"

She pressed her fingers to his lips. "Just shut up and kiss me."

"Yes, ma'am," he said and followed orders. He opened his mouth and explored hers with his tongue, groaning at the sweet taste of her. Even more arousing was her response. Sexy heat and soft sounds. The mewing noise she made in the back of her throat only made him harder. "Touch me," he said against her lips.

Her hands slid down his bare chest and cupped his erection through his jeans. Why was he still wearing jeans? He murmured hot promises in her ear, what he intended to do to her, but mostly, how he intended to make her feel.

She purred and sucked on his tongue as she opened the buttons of his fly. Then her soft hand pulled him free and stroked the length of him, while her other hand shifted to cradle his balls. Intense pleasure pulled a low growl from his throat.

She pushed him toward the pallet and he realized he was not the one in charge of this encounter. Cressida had always been in charge. And now she was proving it. She could do anything. Demand anything. And he'd give it to her. Hell, he'd probably even break cover if she asked.

She'd bewitched him with her amazing mix of innocence and sexy. And he was ready to finally have a taste. He pulled back from her touch and nudged her to the bed. "No. *I'm* seducing *you*." He followed her onto the low futon. "And you're going to scream my name—my real name—before I enter you."

"Who are you again?" she asked and let out a naughty laugh.

He narrowed his gaze. "You'll pay for that, missy." He placed his hand between her thighs, sliding his fingers along her slick opening and stopping on her clit. Humor left her as she let out a soft pant. "Ian," she said.

"More," he demanded.

"Ian Boyd."

"What do you want?"

"I want Ian Boyd." She sucked in a sharp breath as his finger flicked across her clit. "Inside me." He stroked again. "Now."

He smiled. Damn, Cressida Porter was the hottest, sexiest thing he'd ever seen. He scooted lower and slid his tongue over her clit. She bucked upward, against his mouth. He licked her soft folds, savoring the sweetness and slick peach texture, as he pressed his tongue inside her.

She groaned and clenched against him. He could come just from the taste, the feel of her pleasure. This was Cressida, splayed out before him. The woman he'd seen from afar and wanted to protect. The woman he'd discounted. The woman who'd turned his world upside down.

According to his orders and training, he should have gone after the microchip and left her unprotected by the train. But he'd stayed with Cressida and let his target slip away. Wanton. Scared. Beautiful. Cressida had ruined his mission, and all he wanted was to lose himself inside her sweet heat and forget the bullshit mission from hell.

Forget that his life as he knew it was over. Forget that his cover was blown. That he'd been betrayed by two men he'd considered friends.

He nudged her thighs wider and licked again. He grazed her swollen clit with his teeth, and she bucked against him. He purred with his own satisfaction and slipped his tongue inside her, repeatedly. So hot. So wet. So ready.

He stood and kicked off his shoes and finally shucked his jeans. He was barely naked before she reached out and stroked his cock and made a soft sound of want. He met her gaze. Those big, brown eyes were wide open and full of hunger. "Open your mouth."

She did, without hesitation, and he slid inside. *Damn* that felt good. Better than anything he'd ever felt before in his life.

Ever since she'd stepped into his shower in Siirt, he'd wanted this. Her. He'd wanted until his balls ached. And the reality was even better than he'd imagined.

She rocked back, then sucked him in, deeper than before, opening her throat. The woman was a suck goddess. She wrapped her hand around the base and stroked as she controlled the slide of his cock in and out of her hot mouth. She swirled her tongue around the tip, then let him go. "Condoms," she demanded.

He turned and grabbed the box from her backpack. He sheathed himself, then spread her thighs wide and stroked her clit with the tip of his cock.

"Yes. That. Now."

He slid inside her with one smooth stroke. She closed around him, so tight the pressure and friction was enough to make him forget his own name. He stopped, seated to the hilt, and took her breast into his mouth.

"Ian," she said with a pant.

He grinned and pulled out, thrusting faster, harder, the second time. "More."

"Ian Boyd," she said. "Ian Boyd."

"What do you want, Cressida?" His lips trailed up her neck and he nipped at her ear.

"You. Ian. This. Ian. All of you."

He braced himself on one hand and slid the other between their bodies to stroke her clit. "How about this? Do you want this?"

"Yessssss."

He laughed. He stroked. He fucked. And through it all, she cradled him, tightening on his cock as she edged closer to orgasm. He kissed her neck, her breasts, her mouth. And he thrust, pumping into her, feeling so damn good with every deep slide.

Beneath him, she arced her back and let out a shuddering gasp. "Ian. *Yesss*. Ian." His name was melodic on her tongue. *EEEeee-an*. She came. And she came. His body coiled tight, his own orgasm building to a blinding intensity. He crested, and thrust into her as he came hard. Long. Intense. He growled with his release as he came inside her sweet, tight body.

Spent, he grabbed her around the waist and rolled to his side, keeping her against him, still deep within her perfect body. He kissed her, his tongue delving into her mouth in a thorough exploration that expressed more than words how much he enjoyed being inside her.

As his heartbeat slowed, he lifted his head and looked into her eyes. Beautiful. Brown. And right now, sexy and satiated.

His heart tripped. This was no mindless sex romp. He cared about her. To prevent himself from saying something foolish, he took her breast into his mouth and sucked. He blew cool breath over the wet peak and watched as her nipple tightened. Then he played with her other breast.

When was the last time he'd shared an intimate moment—beyond sex?

His life in the Army had been dangerous, and he hadn't invited relationships. And his life in the Middle East, a secret life, had made intimacy impossible. But Cressida knew exactly what he was, who he was. He didn't have to hold back from her. He could trust her.

This could be real. He, Ian Boyd, wanted for murder and espionage in the Middle East, was having a quiet, thoroughly enjoyable postcoital moment, because he trusted someone. The evil eye pendant rested between her breasts, and he found it sexy that it was the only thing she wore. With his tongue, he traced the chain down the valley.

At last, he was eye to eye with the necklace and stopped. The pendant was like a million others, but...different.

And he'd seen this particular evil eye pendant before.

He jolted upright, leaving the heat of her body as he scrambled to stand. *"Motherfucking shit balls."* He turned and kicked the low table. The flowers scattered, littering the kilims that covered the dirt floor. "Were you *ever* planning to tell me you got the pendant from Hejan?"

Chapter Twenty-Six

CRESSIDA BOLTED UPRIGHT, Ian's sudden violence a shock after the tenderness in his touch. Now she felt exposed to be naked while he cursed and looked like he wanted to kick the table again.

She grabbed the blanket and rolled over to pull it from underneath her body and cover herself.

"Well?" he demanded. "Why didn't you tell me?" He slammed a hand into the tent's thick center pole.

She jumped.

He faced her with his hands curled into fists.

She wrapped the blanket tightly around her and scooted backward. "Stop trying to scare me."

"I'm not *trying* to do anything. I'm *asking* why the fuck you didn't tell me about the necklace."

"Because when I first realized the pendant was important, I didn't know if I could trust you."

"That was two and a half days ago. Why didn't you tell me when you told me about the map?"

"I considered it, but couldn't trust you wouldn't take the pendant and leave me."

For some reason, that seemed to take his breath away. He just stared at her. Mute. Finally he said, "Well, I'm glad to know trust isn't a prerequisite for sex for you."

Her belly did a slight flip at the hurt in his tone. She had no choice but to go on the attack. "Oh, like you trust *me*. If it's okay for you to screw me without trust, then I don't see why I can't do the same."

His jaw snapped closed, and she felt bitter satisfaction at pointing out his gross double standard, until he said, "Well, that's where we're different. Because I trusted you." He jerked on his jeans and headed for the tent flap. He paused in the opening but didn't turn to face her. "If you try to run, Cressida, know that the nomads will never help or protect you. You are here with a bed and a tent thanks to *me*. I'm your only hope and protection."

With stiff shoulders, he left, and she sat reeling over the fact that she'd hurt him. Deeply.

She looked at the damn necklace. He must have seen it on Hejan. It was just common enough that it had required a close inspection to realize it was actually a unique piece.

What had Hejan intended when he gave it to her without instructions beyond *"never take it off"*? He'd said it would protect her, but all it had given her was grief.

And now it had driven a wedge between her and Ian, just when things had gotten very promising. She dropped the pendant. No. The evil eye hadn't driven the wedge. She had. She hadn't trusted Ian. Had, in fact, kept a vital secret from him, refusing to tell him she may hold the key to clearing his name.

No wonder he hated her. And from the look on his face when he pulled on his clothes, she had no doubt he hated her. She flopped back on the sleeping pallet, pulling the blanket tightly around her as she tried to hold back tears. The sweat from their lovemaking hadn't even dried.

She wanted to blame this miserable feeling on her lousy taste in men, her horrible track record, but she had a feeling this one was all on her. Ian had lied to her, sure, but it was his job…and his job was far more important than anything *she'd* ever done. Hell, it was only US national security hanging in the balance.

Ian was one of the good guys. And everything he'd done for her… Well, he hadn't known she still had the microchip, so the only possible reason for him to stick by her was because she was an innocent in the crossfire. That made him far better, in fact, the very *best* guy she'd ever known or was likely to meet.

And she'd just fucked up. Big-time.

She wiped her eyes. She would not cry. She was so far beyond crying, and this wasn't even close to the worst thing that she'd had to deal with since arriving in Van.

She grabbed the cleanest shirt she had left from her backpack and slipped it on. Then she gathered the flowers that had scattered across the floor. Purple, pink, blue, and orange, the small blossoms were bright and cheerful in the dim oil-lantern-lit tent. She could identify only two among the dozen different types—the scarlet and blue pimpernels, which were closed buds inside the shadowy tent. Pimpernels, she knew, only opened when the sun shined.

As a freshman in high school, she'd devoured the novel *The*

Scarlet Pimpernel, and her troubled romantic soul had planted the scarlet variety in a planter box on the tiny balcony of her one-bedroom third-floor apartment she shared with her mom. Just as the seeds began to sprout, her mother's boyfriend—unnumbered because he didn't count among the predators—dropped the terracotta bin off the balcony to make room for his pot plants.

Cressida had retaliated by throwing the pot plants over the railing and paid for it with a broken arm. She never attempted gardening again.

Until this moment, she'd only seen the bloom in pictures. But now she held one in her hand.

Had Ian recognized the flower or read the book? The story, about a British baronet with a secret identity—the Scarlet Pimpernel—who smuggled French aristocrats out of France during the height of the Reign of Terror, had been her first romance novel. The first time she'd fallen in love with a fictional man.

And now, here she was on the run with a covert operative in Eastern Turkey who was trying to smuggle her out of the country, and he'd given her pimpernels right before making love to her in a Kurdish nomad tent. She suspected her heartache was due to realizing she was falling in love with the enigmatic spy, but he would never forgive her for holding out on him.

IAN CURSED HIMSELF as he marched on the cold steppe. Could he be more pathetic? Storming off? He should go back, take the necklace, and break it open. Find out what treat Hejan had placed inside. But he'd left to gather his emotions first.

He would never, ever hurt Cressida, but that didn't mean he didn't fear for the table and other objects in the tent. He was a man used to taking out anger and frustration in the gym on punching bags. Right now he needed an outlet, and all he could do was walk.

He reached the narrow stream where he'd gathered wildflowers earlier, disgusted with himself for giving in to the ridiculous impulse to treat Cressida as anything other than a mission. He should just have fucked her without the sappy gesture. It had been a stupid, wasted effort for a cold woman.

Except, nothing about Cressida was cold. And nothing about her made him feel cold. Quite the opposite. Being with her made him feel alive, to the degree that he hadn't realized how dead he'd felt before.

But fuck it. The microchip was back in play, and he had a job to do. There was no room for sappy craptastic emotion. He needed to figure out how to get himself and Cressida out of Turkey and back to the US with the microchip—*which, holy hell, she'd had all-fucking-along*—and get it into the hands of the CIA, where the information could do some good.

That chip was his ticket out of being branded a traitor and executed. If he handed it over at Langley, there would be no question about his loyalties. With his cover blown, he could never again work as a covert operative, but there were other options— ones available to him again thanks to the microchip. No one understood the situation in Turkey better than he did. He could stay on with the company as an analyst. Plus, he liked the idea of not being executed. A lot.

It was time to get his head out of his ass, face Cressida, and take the goddamn chip. He returned to the tent, braced, almost expecting to find her gone. But there she was in the dimly lit shelter, sitting up on the bed where they'd just made love, clutching the flowers he'd given her. She looked forlorn, but he'd be damned before he fell for that one.

Cressida Porter was a mission, nothing more. He'd screw the hell out of her—he had no problem playing the emotionless fuck game—if that was what she wanted, but any ridiculous thoughts of something more between them were long gone.

For a moment—a stupid, fanciful moment—he'd thought a relationship between them might be possible. His life with the CIA was over. The old rules were gone. But now he had his mission back, bringing the old rules with it. It didn't matter that Cressida didn't trust him, that for her it had just been a fuck, because for him, that was all it could ever be.

"One question, *sweetheart*." He couldn't help but put a hard-edged emphasis on the endearment. "Did you ever plan to tell me? Or were you just going to continue letting me risk my ass to save yours, when I had no idea you held the key to our salvation?"

"I don't know." She shrugged. "Maybe? We'll never really know." She dropped the flowers on the table and pulled the pendant from under her T-shirt. "How did you know this was Hejan's?"

"I saw him wearing it. More than once. The filigree work

makes it unique." And now, he realized, Hejan had wanted him to see it.

How long had Hejan planned this? Clever bastard. He had to know he was going to die.

"You saw it in the shower. You didn't notice it then."

"I was distracted then." He did not want to think about how she'd looked in the shower, her perfect breasts slick with water. He held out his hand.

She sighed and lifted the chain from her neck and handed it to him. He held it near his eye and stepped closer to the oil lamp hanging from a hook on a wooden beam.

There. A hairline seam on the back.

She pursed her lips. "So you really think the plans to the Death Star are inside?"

"Cute." He ran his thumbnail along the seam. He might be able to open it with a thin blade.

She stood and stepped up behind him, standing close so she could look over his shoulder at the pendant. He stiffened. He could smell their earlier lovemaking on her and didn't like the reaction it stirred in him. She touched his shoulder. He shook her off and stepped away.

She caught her breath, and that small hitch of hurt stabbed at him. "Ian, I'm not a spy. I'm a grad student who hired a guy to do some translation work. That's it. This—what's going on—isn't my world. This isn't my life. I don't know who to trust. The only constant in my world right now is the North Star. It's the only thing that's exactly what it should be, doing its job and giving me direction. But even that can be hidden in cloud cover. Then I'm lost."

She tapped at the evil eye. "Until we fought in the bathroom in Siirt, I thought it was just a necklace given to me by a superstitious man before I took off on a risky trip to an unknown place. He gave it to me after I'd had a nasty run-in with an ex-boyfriend who shouldn't even be in Turkey. I accepted the necklace because... *hell, why not?* I needed something to ward off evil." Her voice cracked. "But all that damn pendant did was bring it on. And for the record, I've been wrong about every other man in my life, so why should you be any different? You lie for a living, after all."

"I lie for the good guys, Cress."

"How am I supposed to know that?"

He knew it was a fair question, but still, it rankled. "Maybe because you've gotten to know me? Hell, you were willing to fuck me. It seems like that should mean something."

"Well, I've screwed other men who I found out were liars after the fact. I've learned I can't trust my instincts."

Ian put the pendant around his neck. He was beat, and it was too dark in here to try to crack open the back with a knife. He might damage the chip. "I'm going to bed." He stripped down to his boxer briefs and slipped under the covers.

Cressida stood by the oil lamp, staring at him.

"Blow out the lamp and get in bed."

She rubbed her eyes and looked like she wanted to continue talking. But he was done talking, done hearing the hows and whys of her distrust. He rolled to his side, presenting his back to her, and pulled up the blankets.

Behind him, he heard her soft breath. The dim light flickered, then vanished, casting the tent in deep darkness. She climbed into the bed, but he didn't feel even a smidgen of heat. She was keeping her distance.

In spite of everything—including the fact that he'd gotten off not an hour before—just the thought of her in his bed triggered an erection. Biological reaction. That was all.

He lay there, breathing slowly, willing the hard-on to go the fuck away. Slowly, the tightness eased, and eventually, sleep came.

Chapter Twenty-Seven

IAN SLEPT FOR six solid hours. Cressida wasn't in the bed when he woke. He was usually a light sleeper; just her climbing from the pallet should've woken him. But damn, he'd been tired, and for the first time in days, he'd been as safe as possible, housed by kind strangers who knew nothing of their situation.

She wasn't in the tent, which caused a moment of panic. He reached for the pendant. It still circled his neck. If she'd managed to escape, at least she hadn't taken his ticket to salvation with her. He quickly pulled on his clothes and stepped out of the tent. If Cressida had fled, he'd track her down.

But she hadn't. She crouched over a metal basin flanked by two other women, hand-washing clothes. She'd dressed in the Kurdish skirt and blouse he'd eagerly stripped from her the night before, and he felt his cock thicken at the memory. He could see her garments—and some of his—hanging on the clothesline, drying in the bright morning sun.

The women chattered in a language she couldn't understand, and she worked silently, scrubbing what appeared to be a child's dress without lifting her gaze.

She was so fucking lovely, perched next to the washbasin. Her headscarf had fallen, exposing her beautiful long dark hair, which glistened in the morning sun. Finally she glanced up and caught his stare. She flashed a tentative smile.

If they really were newlyweds, he'd scoop her up, throw her over his shoulder, and carry her into the tent, where he'd do nothing but make love to her all day and all night. But the newlywed cover was just another lie in a life built on deception.

Having ascertained she was present and accounted for, he crossed the camp to pay respects to their hosts. Several of the men were off with the flock, but the elder had remained in camp, sitting regally under the shade of the goat-hair tent that was his primary domain.

At his invitation, Ian sat down with the man for a cup of tea. A while later, Ian saw Cressida return to the tent they'd been given, and he excused himself from the elder's company. In the tent, he cornered Cressida, who appeared flustered in the light of day.

"What's the plan, Ian?"

"We rest here for another day. Regroup. Then we're going to find the entrance to your tunnel."

"We won't be able to open it. It's not like we could *use* it."

"I know. Just finding it is valuable intel."

"And after we find it—*if* we find it—how do we get out of Turkey?"

"With the tunnel location in our back pocket, I think I can convince the CIA to send an exfil team—and we won't need to mention we have the chip until we're safe in the US. Last month, I set up another safe house, in Cizre. After we find the tunnel, we'll go there. Then I'll get in touch with my boss."

Her gaze flicked toward the bed, and he was tempted to suggest they fully play out their newlywed roles, but didn't. She'd see right through him and know how much he wanted her, instead of taking his words as a smart-ass proposition from a hardened covert operative.

He plucked the pendant from his neck. "It's time to see what this thing holds."

"You think it's more than a chip?"

"I hope so." He pulled a knife from his backpack and wedged the small blade into the seam. A gentle tap, and the back split open. Inside, he found the chip, a thin sliver of metal-coated plastic—it was the internal memory card from a USB drive. He closed his eyes against the flood of relief. Then, with a deep breath, he lifted the card and saw a folded scrap of paper. *Cressida* was written on it in Hejan's neat scrawl.

Hejan had left her a note?

The woman in question reached for it, but he shook his head and plucked it from the small compartment in the pendant. "It's for me," she protested.

He carefully unfolded the paper and smiled. "And for me." He showed her his name—*John*—written below the fold. He scanned the contents, which were written in Turkish.

"What does it say?"

"What we've already figured out. Todros Ganem was brought to Turkey to find the tunnel for Hejan's organization. When Todros couldn't find it, he said you could. Because of that, you were chosen to be the mule." But there was more, and the last bit of info in Hejan's note caused Ian's nostrils to flare and his vision to blur.

He set the paper, chip, and pendant on the low table and took a step toward her. Her eyes widened, and she stepped back. Her reaction pissed him off.

She cleared her throat. "Why do you insist on calling him Todros? No one calls him Todros. He's Todd."

"Todd Ganem was your boyfriend. You lived with him. Screwed him. Loved him. Todros Ganem is a thief, a traitor, and part of a terrorist cell. Todros is his Jordanian name, and I don't want you to forget where his loyalties lie."

She retreated another step but came up against the tent pole he'd been corralling her toward. She stopped and lifted her chin. "I know exactly what Todd is."

"Todros. Call him Todros."

She drew in a sharp breath. "You're *jealous*?"

He planted himself before her. "Of course I'm jealous. He had all of you. Including your heart. Because of Todros, you couldn't trust *me*. You didn't tell me about the pendant. I'd happily shoot the motherfucker in the balls."

She shrugged. "Get in line."

"Do you still have feelings for Todros?"

Her eyes narrowed. "You asshole. Do you honestly think I'd make love with you if I had feelings for another man?"

"We didn't make love. We fucked. That's all. And yes, I do think you'd fuck me, if it's part of your game plan."

"I don't *have* a game plan! I'm just a stupid academic caught up in something I don't understand."

His vision was hazy as he zeroed in on the source of his anger. "I think you do have a plan. I think you didn't tell me about the pendant because you were waiting to give it to your real partner."

"What the hell are you talking about, Ian?"

"Hejan said he hopes you met up with Todros in Van. If not, you need to call the number Hejan gave you again. It's Todd's number."

"I don't understand. The only number Hejan gave me was Berzan's." Her eyes widened as the color drained from her face. "The text I got—the one telling me to go to the ferry dock—was from *Todd*?"

"Don't act so surprised."

She pushed against his chest. "Back off."

"Why? Are things not going according to the plan you set up with Ganem?"

"No! Because you're freaking me out!" She shoved at his chest again. "You're what, six foot two? Two hundred pounds of muscle? I'm five six and couldn't take you in a thumb wrestle. So back. The fuck. Off."

"Are you working with Todros?"

Fear faded as her eyes flashed with anger. "No! I hate the bastard. Dammit, Ian, I want you! I'm falling in love with *you*! You stupid, blind, jealous oaf!"

His heart squeezed. *Love?* Not possible. He didn't elicit that sort of emotion in others and had a hard time believing her after she'd held out on him.

But still, she looked so beautiful in her rage. He wanted to pull her against him, plant his mouth on hers, then toss her on the bed and make love to her until they both forgot everything but each other.

What was stopping him?

He wanted her. She wanted him. It was that simple.

He caught her by the hips and scooped her up, lifting her while pulling up the wide skirt, freeing her legs to wrap around his hips. Her hot center pressed snug against his instant erection as he slipped his tongue between her lips. Her mouth opened, and she sucked on his tongue with the same urgency he felt.

She tugged at his fly. He shifted to the bed and set her down, yanking down his zipper as he dropped to his knees between her thighs. She rolled to the side and grabbed a condom from the box he'd left next to the pallet, ripping it open as he freed himself from his briefs. He tugged down her underwear as she rolled the latex over his cock. Sheathed, he slid deep inside her. She felt so right, like her body was his home.

She groaned in pleasure. He covered her mouth with his. Their hosts might not understand English, but hot, hard sex had a universal language of its own. He pumped into her, each stroke taking him to the edge of orgasm far too fast. She panted, and he reached between them to stroke her clitoris. The pants became a purr.

She sucked on his tongue while rocking her hips against him. Shit. He was going to come. He increased the pressure with his thumb, and she let out a low throaty noise and clenched tight around him signaling he was cleared for takeoff. He continued stroking in time to his thrusts as he soared, no longer tethered to anything but the sound of her continuing orgasm.

He kissed her deeply as he rode the wave back down. Cressida's eyes fluttered open. She cupped his cheeks between her hands and kissed him, giving with the same intensity she took.

The look in her eyes told him everything he wanted to know. She really was falling in love with him. And dammit all to hell, his face probably said the same damn thing.

He and Cressida were alike in so many ways. Fatherless. Survivors. He could fall in love with this woman who had the brains and drive to overcome being dealt a hand as pathetic as his own.

Her lack of trust was no longer the issue. He could forgive her for that—hell he understood her reasons. But they had a new problem, one that made a relationship between them a risk he couldn't afford. With the microchip in hand, the old rules were back in play.

He was a covert operative. A soldier. He'd accepted long ago his life would be solitary. He didn't allow himself to feel. To care. Because caring made him vulnerable.

Caring gave the enemy leverage.

Yet he cared about Cressida. More than he should. More than he could. And with the microchip in play again, putting her safety first wasn't an option.

Chapter Twenty-Eight

THE INTENSITY IN Ian's eyes rocked Cressida to the core. He looked at her like he had when he comforted her next to the train. With protectiveness. With fierce caring.

If Todd had ever once looked at her in this way, she'd have told him everything in a heartbeat and invited him to join her in the research. But Todd had never gone all in, which was what she'd been desperate for, the one thing she still needed. Someone who cared about her enough to put her first.

In an instant, the look on Ian's face vanished.

He pushed off her, sliding out of her body. He pulled down the full skirt, as if seeing her splayed out before him was indecent. He removed the condom and tucked himself back in his pants and said, "Thanks. But that changes nothing," as he zipped his fly.

The words hurt like a blow to the gut—or heart. She knew how to roll with blows but found she was unable to roll with this one. She sat on the pallet, frozen. In shock.

Ian turned and lifted the door flap.

His hasty retreat told her more than his cruel words had and broke the paralysis that held her mute. "*Bullshit.* It changes everything. That's why you're fleeing."

His back stiffened. The flap dropped from his fingers, falling closed in front of him. He stood, staring at the canvas, posture so straight he looked like he'd rejoined the Army.

"I saw the way you looked at me."

"Sweetheart, let's get one thing straight. What you saw on my face wasn't anything but a guy who just got laid and liked it. I've made no secret of the fact that I want you. Hell, I want you so bad, my teeth hurt." Slowly, he turned and faced her. "Give me five minutes, and I'll be ready to go again. But it will never be anything more than sex for me. I don't do relationships. Understand?"

She had no clue who he was now. He showed no hint of John. Or Ian. This was a new incarnation, and he made Ian's harder edges look like cotton candy. She wanted so much to call bullshit again. She believed in her gut there was something else going on here, but when had she ever been right about a man?

"You're an asshole. Got it." She rose from the bed, grabbed her backpack, and started shoving all her belongings inside. Whoever he was, he wasn't worthy of the foolish feelings she'd been developing for him.

"What are you doing?"

"I might have issues when it comes to men and relationships, but even *I* know I deserve better than this. I'm out. I'm walking to the nearest village. I'll turn myself in." She couldn't take clothing from these kind people, and she didn't want to spend one more minute in Ian's company, so she yanked off the peasant blouse and skirt, not caring that she bared herself before him when she'd already been stripped emotionally. She pulled on a T-shirt and reached for her jeans. Stupid of her to have washed her other pair of Levis. Now she'd have to carry wet clothing.

Ian plucked her pack from the ground, securing it like a hostage. "I can't let you take off on your own."

That he still thought he could order her around triggered another burst of anger. "I won't be on my own. I'm going to find my partner. *Todd.*"

It happened so fast, she didn't even have time to blink. One moment she was zipping up her jeans, and the next she was flat on her back on the pallet, pinned under Ian, his eyes blazing with anger. "Are you working with Todros?"

◉

CRESSIDA POUNDED AGAINST his chest, but he didn't feel the blows in the wake of the kick to the nuts she'd delivered with nothing but words.

"Jesus, don't you understand sarcasm? How can you possibly believe I'd work with the man who lured me out for a violent mugging? What is *wrong* with you?"

What is wrong with me?

How about that he wanted her more than air, and just hearing her say the name Todd caused a blinding burst of jealousy? Or maybe he'd been warped by years as a covert operative forced to keep emotions at bay? But most of all, he figured he was broken by the need to gouge a hole in his heart before she got too deeply inside, because it was the only way he could do his job.

They needed an emotional firewall if he was going to complete this mission.

He pushed up to his knees, straddling her, and rubbed a hand across his face. Cressida was right; he was an asshole. But he couldn't change that. Wouldn't apologize. Wouldn't do one thing to ease the rift he'd created, no matter how much he wanted to. He couldn't be the operative he needed to be if he allowed himself to care. He couldn't have her. He couldn't fall in love. Not now. Not ever.

"Finish packing," he said. "I'm going to pay respects to our hosts, then we're leaving."

"I'm not going anywhere with you."

"You're sure as hell not going anywhere without me. You can hate me all you want, but all roads out of Turkey go through me."

"WHERE ARE WE going?" Cressida asked for the dozenth time in the hour since they'd left the nomad camp. She was pretty damn sick of his silence and kept asking herself why she'd stayed with him. But she knew the answer to that one: without him, she'd probably die.

"Same plan as before. We're going to see if T. E. Lawrence really did find a Roman aqueduct in 1914."

She glanced askance at him but stopped after only getting a glimpse of his chin. That sexy, stubbled chin that she'd nibbled on while they'd made—no. *Had sex.* Hot. Intense. But only sex. Because Ian claimed he didn't do emotions. Well, except jealousy. That was one emotion he had no problem exhibiting. "As I've told you several times in the last hour, we're going the wrong direction."

"It was important the nomads see us head in this direction. We'll go south after dark."

"We'll need to cross the Tigris at some point."

He snorted. "I'm former Delta Force. I can get us across the river."

Why did cocky have to look so good on him?

"So what are the odds we'll be able to find this tunnel entrance?" he asked.

She shoved her various irritations aside. She'd made the decision to stay with him, and they had to work together. "Lawrence's map indicated a crumbling stone house was extant over the first tunnel entrance he found, but he capped that one, and there is no way you and I could lift the capstone. He found another entrance to the south. My guess is five hundred meters, but without a scale it's hard to be sure. If we find both, we'll know we have the tunnel. There's even a chance—if we had the proper tools—we could open the second entrance. If the stone house is still there, finding the tunnel will be easy. If I'm wrong, we'll never find it in this landscape. Not without Lidar."

"Does Todros know about the stone house?"

She caught the edge in his voice as he called Todd by his Jordanian name. His jealousy hinted at feelings he denied having. Was she deluding herself? Hearing only what she wanted to hear? She'd be better off listening to his words. Like the ones he'd said right after sliding from her body.

She shook her head to wipe the memory of his callous rejection from her mind. He'd made the rules clear. He hadn't rejected her body. Just her heart.

"Cressida?"

Right. He'd asked a question. She'd gone to DC for Erica and Lee's wedding at the peak of cherry blossom time—in early April. While there, she'd popped into NHHC and studied the map key again. That was when she realized Lawrence had marked the stone house ruins and deciphered his notes on the subject. But Todd had been arrested in March, before her DC trip. "No. At least I don't think so. I didn't zero in on the location of the house myself until over a month after he was arrested."

"This could get rough. We're heading toward the Syrian border, which is heavily patrolled these days, and refugees overrun some sections—but mostly that's to the west. If Todros and Zack are looking for the tunnel, we're heading straight for them. If I could tuck you away someplace safe, I would, but I need you to find the tunnel."

I need you. Words she'd waited her whole life to hear. Hell, words she'd hoped to hear from *him*. But not in the context she'd have liked. He didn't say he wanted her. He didn't even say he liked her. No. She could lead him to the tunnel and nothing more.

She shrugged. "So it gets rough. It's not like I have anything else to do today." She felt his gaze but didn't look up. She had trouble looking at him and not searching for signs he'd lied in the tent. "I know Hejan said they chose me to be the mule because Todd told them I could find the tunnel, but I don't see what the benefit was for them. Why me?"

"The usual courier either joined ISIS or was killed by them. Hejan wasn't certain. All I know is he hadn't surfaced in months. You were the perfect replacement, really. Out here, they could easily kill you after they had the chip and the tunnel location. There would have been far fewer questions if you'd died here, so close to the Syrian border."

She shivered. That part might still come true.

"I will do what I can to protect you, Cressida." The words were softly spoken and carried emotion he couldn't hide. "But first and foremost, my mission is to get the data to the CIA, FBI, or US Army. The intel is more important than you. More important than me. If it comes down to a choice between saving you or delivering the microchip, I *must* choose the chip. And you must do the same."

She nodded. What was one life versus thousands? The microchip would give a terrorist group access to enough money to finance a major strike.

Was this the sort of choice Ian had to make often? Was this where his harder edges came from? Was this why his face had said one thing after they made love, but his mouth said another? Because he needed to be prepared to choose the microchip over her? If this was the sort of thing he faced on a regular basis, then his life must suck. So he'd hurt her feelings. Boo-fucking-hoo.

She kept her face forward and back stiff as she cleared her throat. "Is that what you're afraid of? Because if so, you needn't be. I understand. I get the stakes. I know how important I am versus the data on the microchip—which is to say, not at all."

She studied the landscape ahead, refusing to look at the man to her right. "I know how volatile the Middle East is, and I know ISIS and al-Qaeda and probably a dozen other groups would like to bring that volatility to US soil. I would never expect you to put my safety first, not when there's so much at stake."

Next to her, Ian made a soft sound low in his throat.

His hand found hers; he intertwined their fingers. She came to a dead stop, forcing him to halt or let her go. He turned, and finally she met his gaze.

His jaw tightened. There was an inferno of banked emotion in his gray eyes.

All at once, he dropped her hand and resumed walking. "Don't start getting ideas. You know the rules."

Chapter Twenty-Nine

IT WAS WELL past midnight when they stopped for the night after crossing the Tigris River, which had been easy, just as Ian had promised. Dams built in the last century meant the Tigris was no longer the raging river of the ancient world, making it easy to find a shallow, wide stretch to wade across.

They continued for another mile south of the river before finding a spot that was remote yet sheltered. "We'll camp in the lee of the hill," Ian said, "and refill our water bottles from the oxbow lake."

Cressida stared at the hard ground without enthusiasm. After walking for over eight hours, she just might be tired enough to sleep on the wafer-thin camping mat with only an emergency blanket for warmth and her backpack as pillow, but she doubted it.

Ian stepped away to empty his bladder, leaving her to prepare dinner—which would be beef jerky, with trail mix for dessert. He had tablets in his pack to purify the lake water. She had to marvel at the supplies to be found in his backpack, the ten essentials, plus weaponry. She pulled out the sleeping mat and set it aside—wishing he'd thought to pack two—then rifled through the bag to find the purification tablets and thin Mylar blanket. Instead, her fingers landed on something smooth and rectangular.

The deep thudding of her heart pulsed down her arm, extending to the hand that clutched the object. She slowly pulled it out of the pack, trying to get a grip on her emotions, unsure what she was feeling. Hope? Fear? Anger?

Her breath caught when the dim moonlight glinted off the flat screen.

Ian has a cell phone.

Anger. Definitely anger.

Anger at him, but also at herself, because really, *of course* he had a phone. Stupid of her not to realize days ago. One may have blown up, and he may have tossed another out the window, but a

Boy Scout who had cash, food, the ten essentials, and a stockpile of weapons would certainly have another phone.

She could have called Trina days ago, when they were holed up in Siirt. Trina would have gotten Keith to send a Raptor team in to extract them. Raptor operatives wouldn't shoot to kill, not with Cressida standing in front of Ian, blocking the shot.

She would be back in the US by now. *Safe*. Not on the run in a country where she didn't speak the language. Not stuck with a heartless spy who'd helped get her into this situation but hadn't once let her make a decision about how to get out of it.

She hit the power button, and the screen lit. They were probably out of range now, but still, she could hope. Her heart pounded as she waited for the antenna bars to appear. But none came.

She turned off the phone. Tomorrow, when they neared the aqueduct, they'd pass within a mile of a decent-size village. Odds were there'd be an antenna.

"We've been out of antenna range since we left Rajab's house."

Cressida startled, causing the phone to pop out of her hands. It bobbled in the air, but she caught it. She shuddered, imagining missing and watching their salvation hit a rock and shattering. She turned to glare at Ian. "You complete and utter bastard!" Her eyes burned with the intensity of her outrage. "I could have gotten us out of Turkey before we even went to Rajab's if you'd let me use the phone."

"I couldn't let you call your friend before I was burned, because I wasn't certain Keith Hatcher would confirm my Raptor credentials. And after… I couldn't trust you wouldn't turn me in."

"So you dragged me to your 'friend's' house—trusting someone who *did* turn you in, who was ready to kill us both. Because of you, I had to kill a man." Her voice shook on the last sentence. She'd tried to push Sabal out of her mind as they fled. What had the sex been about if not escaping the horror by taking a moment of pleasure?

But now all she could see was Sabal's glassy eyes.

Ian reached for the phone, but she snatched it to her chest. "Mine!" The word echoed when it hit the rocky hillside.

"I was just going to turn it off—to conserve the battery. Searching for antennas is a quick way to drain a phone, and we don't have a solar charger."

She hated how calm he sounded. Reasonable, when her whole

body shook with emotion. "I already turned it off." She crammed the phone into her sports bra.

He laughed. "Honey, I'm not exactly afraid to go there."

Their first argument in the nomad camp came back to her. "Yeah, nice to know trust isn't a prerequisite for sex with *you*. You screwed me, then had the gall to feign outrage over *my* lack of trust, when you *still* hadn't told me you had a goddamned phone!"

"We were out of range. The phone was nothing but a fragile paperweight."

"You still could have *told* me. Maybe if you'd shown me one ounce of trust, I could have trusted *you*." She spun on her heel. She couldn't look at him as anger and hurt burned from the inside. She wanted to take the damn phone and walk all night until she caught a cell signal, but she wasn't that stupid.

If she wanted to survive, she was stuck with the rotten, jealous, untrusting bastard. She struck out anyway, needing distance to cool her temper. She hadn't gone ten steps when his fingers snaked around her bicep. "You can't go off alone."

She yanked her arm from his grip. "Give me some credit—for once. I'm not stupid. I just need to get away from you so I don't do something I might regret."

He stepped back, perhaps realizing she meant it. Honestly, she was afraid of the violence she felt charging through her. Bad enough she'd decked Todd. She hardly knew who she was anymore.

Ian cleared his throat. "Don't go far."

She nodded stiffly and marched toward the oxbow below the hill. When she reached the thicker grass that lined the bank, she dropped to her bottom and pulled her knees to her chest, just like she'd done when she was younger and desperately needed a hug.

Back then, when all hell broke loose at home, her mother was the one who needed comfort and aid. Even when the violence had been directed at Cressida, she'd been the one to coach her mother through the lies they had to tell in the emergency room to avoid another stint in foster care.

She couldn't let her mother see her tears, because that inevitably sent Sarah into a guilt spiral that triggered depression. But all Cressida had wanted was for her mother to hold her, to love her, to let her express her hurt and anger without it being eclipsed by Sarah's drama.

Eventually, Cressida had stopped crying, because the price was too high. But now she thought of Hejan, who was dead—murdered—and Sabal, whom she'd shot in the neck. She'd *killed* a man. Her eyes burned with tears, and for the first time in over a decade, she didn't fight them. She tightened her arms around her legs as her body shook with the sobs.

Somewhere out on the dark steppe was Todd, a man she had lived with and loved, but who'd betrayed her and had set in motion the sequence of events that had led her to this moment. And tomorrow, a terrorist or a spy may well find and kill her. Kill Ian.

When she was a teenager, she couldn't call for help because telling the world what she faced at home meant foster care and leaving her mother vulnerable. She felt now the same helplessness she'd felt then. The same outrage. When she'd faced down Three, she'd promised herself she was done being helpless.

She cried for the person she used to be, who was surely gone now, and the person she'd become, who might not live to see the mother she loved and resented.

She heard footsteps behind her. *Damn him.* He couldn't even let her have a shred of dignity. She swiped at her eyes but didn't turn to face him. "Go away."

He said nothing, but the sound of his steps came closer. Finally, he was at her back, and he dropped down. His thighs slid alongside hers as his arms wrapped around her. He pulled her back snug against his chest, cradling her.

"I'm not crying about the damn phone. Or you, for that matter." She sniffled and wanted to push away from him, but couldn't find it in her to reject the hug she'd needed since she was thirteen years old.

His lips brushed her temple. "I know."

"This isn't about you at all."

"Shhh," he said.

"I'm not weak, you know."

"Honey, you're the strongest person I know. And if anyone has earned the right to cry, it's you. So cry. I'm not here to stop you. I'm here to hold you. We can sit here as long as you need." And then, Boy Scout that he was, he handed her a bandana, which he must have had tucked away in some pocket of his backpack full of wonders.

CRESSIDA FELL ASLEEP in Ian's arms. His back and shoulders cramped as he sat next to the small, quiet lake holding a beautiful woman while looking up at a magnificent starry sky. For another man, this might be a romantic moment, but not for Ian Boyd. No, his first and only moonlit lakeside snuggle with a woman he wanted with every beat of his sorry heart happened deep in Kurdish territory when they were on the run for their lives, and the woman had just spent an hour crying because she'd reached her limit. Or maybe she'd cried because Ian was an ass.

He frowned at a pinprick of light that slowly moved across the night sky. A satellite. A conduit for communication. A connection to the outside world.

Yeah, she'd probably cried because Ian was a jealous, judgmental, pigheaded ass.

He lost the satellite in the mass of stars that defined the Milky Way. With no light on the ground and the moon but a silvery crescent, the night sky was as magnificent as he'd ever seen it. As magnificent as Cressida pushing past her fear to escape Rajab's house. As magnificent as when she stood up to him in Siirt when she had every reason to believe he was a traitor.

As magnificent as when she made love with him in a nomad tent.

Easy to feel insignificant when staring up at the vast, unfolding universe, but really, he felt more insignificant facing Cressida. He should have told her about the phone in Siirt, the moment his cover was blown. He'd been reeling, and it never crossed his mind to put his life in her hands. Yet, without her knowledge or consent, her life had been in his since she boarded the plane in Antalya.

By the time they reached his apartment in Siirt, she'd been assaulted, robbed, kidnapped—by him, no less—and had witnessed a bombing that killed one man and could have killed her. It was no wonder she'd freaked out when she learned he worked for the CIA and everything he'd told her was a lie.

And he'd never even attempted to make it easy on her. He'd pushed her, determined to find out if she was part of Hejan's cell or not. Maybe, if he'd just tried trusting her, they could have had a romantic lakeside tryst in the US. There was a cabin in West Virginia he'd visited once when he'd been on leave right before heading south for training at the Farm. The cabin had been situated on a private lake surrounded by acres of woods, and the thought of taking Cressida there and making love to her in the sunlight on the low bank made him hard.

But to be fair, all thoughts of making love to Cressida—anytime, anywhere—made him hard. And someday, if they made it out of Turkey alive, he intended to do everything he could to convince her to give him…what? A few days? A week? A month?

He'd told her the truth when he said he didn't do relationships. Temporary was all he could offer.

He'd never considered a future that didn't include the CIA. He'd never really imagined living in the US and using his talents in a less dangerous pursuit. And he sure as hell had never allowed himself to imagine sharing his life with a woman he loved.

He'd always figured love wasn't in his genes. Hell, a boy who couldn't even muster love for his own mother certainly couldn't love someone else. But here he was, holding a woman who'd admitted she was falling in love with him and her words had triggered a scary, elated thrill.

For the first time in his life, he believed he *could* love someone. And from the blow to the nuts he'd felt just glimpsing the hostility in her eyes, he had a feeling that person was Cressida Porter. He'd been a fool to think creating a rift between them would somehow stop him from actually caring. He hadn't gouged out his heart; he'd just made a bigger hole for her to slip through.

He'd lived by one simple rule as a covert operative: the mission above all else. He couldn't change the rule, so it was time to change the mission.

THE SUN WAS high and bright when Cressida woke with a start. She'd fallen asleep in Ian's arms, and sometime later, he'd woken her and they'd moved to sleep against the protected hillside. She sat up and searched for her spy, spotting his dark hair in the sea of green grass by the lake. He sat, staring at the water, where he'd held her as she cried a dozen years' worth of tears.

The lake glistened in the morning light, and Ian glowed in its reflection. *Shit.* Judging from the way her heart went all pitter-pattery, last night's crying jag hadn't cured her infatuation. If anything, the way he'd held her had made it worse.

She wiped her eyes—crusty from crying, naturally—and could only imagine what a horror she presented. She'd braided her hair before leaving the nomad camp, but the tie had loosened, and snarled strands poked out all along the pathetic plait.

She stood and brushed off her clothes, then stepped around a rocky outcrop to take care of business in private. Hard to be sexy when camping while on the run from terrorists and double agents. At least she'd done enough terrestrial fieldwork to be comfortable roughing it. She smiled, thinking of how Trina would be horrified. The historian wasn't a fan of camping and would never have cut it as an archaeologist.

Cressida returned to where she'd slept and frowned to see Ian approaching. The sun was at his back, leaving his face in shadow, but from the set of his shoulders, she had a feeling he wasn't in a cheery mood.

Yeah, well, that made two of them.

She wanted a shower, a cup of coffee, and eggs Benedict for breakfast, but she'd be willing to trade the first two for the third. At this point, might even trade Ian for eggs Benedict. That way, she could keep the coffee.

He approached like a Terminator, his gaze never shifting left or right until he stood before her.

"I'm—"

Before she could say another word, he cradled her face between his large, rough hands, and his mouth covered hers. His tongue stroked hers in a deep, wild kiss that woke far more than her libido.

His hands slid into her loosely bound hair, pressing her tightly against him as he plundered her mouth. Need pulsed from her center, and she gripped his shirt, as much to keep herself upright as to prevent him from retreating after decimating her protective walls and stealing her breathless response.

This was *Ian*. The man who'd brought her flowers before making love to her. He was different, all semblance of control and holding back gone. He kissed like a starving man at an all-you-can-eat buffet. He nibbled. He teased her tongue into his mouth and sucked on it in a way that could make her believe she was the only thing in the world he'd ever wanted.

He groaned and ended the kiss, taking in a sharp breath, then he leaned his forehead against hers. "Change in plans. Forget the tunnel. I'm taking you to the nearest cell tower. I want you to call your friend with Raptor connections. We're getting you the hell out of Turkey."

She tightened her grip on his shirt. "What about you? Will you come with me?"

He frowned, and she knew exactly what he was about to say.

Behind her, a man cleared his throat and said, "Wow, Ian. I never guessed you had it in you to play an asset so well. But don't worry, you needn't keep up the pretense with Ms. Porter any longer."

Ian grabbed her hips and shoved her behind him, shielding her from the man who stood ten feet away, sporting a nasty smirk. But even more disturbing than the smirk was the gun he pointed directly at Ian's chest.

Chapter Thirty

COLD CALM SETTLED in Ian's gut as he stared down the bore of Zack's gun. He couldn't think about Cressida being in danger. He focused instead on the fact that Zack hadn't shot them at the first opportunity.

Zack needs us alive.

Ian had game here, and Zack was a rookie player.

"Did she tell you the location of the tunnel yet?" Zack asked.

Typical cheap ploy: divide and conquer. After everything they'd been through, Cressida would never believe Ian had been playing her. Or, rather, she already knew *when* he'd been playing her.

He tightened his fingers on her hips, keeping her behind him. Damn him for kissing her. A foolish act in broad daylight after they'd been in the same location for hours. Especially when they were closing in on the tunnel. He'd failed Covert Operations 101.

His gun was in the holster at the small of his back. Cressida could grab it. He didn't dare rock backward to press the weapon against her hips. Zack would notice. Zack was many things, but dumb wasn't one of them.

"I need to see your hands, Ms. Porter."

"Screw you. If you wanted us dead, you'd have shot us already," she said.

Ian smiled. Cressida was new to the game, but she caught on quickly, and every little rebellion that let Zack know he may have a gun but wasn't in control would chip away at his focus until Ian could make a move.

Zack was an analyst first. He'd completed his training for covert ops but didn't have Ian's military background. The fool was in over his head, and Ian intended to drown the sonofabitch who'd burned him.

"Hands up, or I'll shoot Ian in the balls."

"Do it. I'm done with him anyway." Ian's heart rate shot up as Cressida stepped out from behind him. At least it rattled Zack to have more than one target to cover—which told him Zack didn't have anyone covering his six. Or if he did, he didn't trust his partner. One of the hazards of being a traitor.

Cressida stepped farther from Ian, visible only in his peripheral vision to his left. She let out a soft, cunning laugh. "Ian may have been using me, but I don't really give a fuck, because *I* was using *him*."

At that, both Zack and Ian turned to her. She grinned, and her shoulders lifted in a delicate shrug. "What? You didn't think I saw you in the bar in Antalya—both of you? Jesus, I was there to pick up a microchip. You think I'm so stupid I didn't lay eyes on the man who 'protected' me by holding me back from a knife fight? God. Your egos." She rolled her eyes. "And then when you magically appeared next to me on the flight, and in my hotel... I'm working on a damn PhD, and you think I'm too stupid to pick up on these things?"

She thrust her chest out and took a step toward Ian. "But then, you were too distracted by these, weren't you?" She squeezed her breasts. "I hate to break it to you, Ian, but these babies aren't my best asset." She pointed to her temple and lowered her voice to a throaty whisper. "It's what's up here that matters, and I've got more going on up there than both of you combined." She licked her bottom lip, slowly. "I mean, look at me. I don't even speak the language but I got you to deliver me here, where my real partner, Todd, can't be far away." She puckered her lips in a sexy pout and added, "And I even got laid."

She turned to Zack. "You see, Zack, I'll do *anything* to get what I want. I'll even do any*one*." She took a step toward him. "It looks like Ian is no longer of use to me."

Ian's gut burned. She was playing Zack. He knew she was playing Zack. But her act...was flawless. This woman was cunning. Beautiful. Even her voice was different, as if everything he'd seen before had been a role and now he saw who she really was.

No. This was the act. The woman who'd cried in his arms last night—that was the real Cressida.

"Don't take another step closer," Zack said.

"Fine. But don't you think we should take away Ian's gun and tie him up? Because he's looking pretty pissed right now, and I, for one, am not keen on the idea of him shooting me or breaking my neck like he did Rajab."

"You want me to let you take his gun? How stupid do you think I am?"

She laughed. "You really don't want me to answer that."

Zack's shoulders stiffened. Good. One way or another, Cressida was throwing off his game. "Cressida, you're going to take his gun, but this is how it's going to go down." Zack stepped toward her. He met Ian's gaze and slowly smiled, then shifted his gun from Ian's gut to Cressida's head.

Ian couldn't stop his nostrils from flaring or hands from clenching into fists. Zack's smile widened. "You put on a pretty show, Ms. Porter, but Ian isn't buying it. And neither am I."

She'd stiffened the moment Zack's gun changed targets, but Ian was still impressed by her outward calm. He only saw her profile, not her eyes, but her voice remained low and confident. "I don't give a shit if Ian doesn't believe it. What he doesn't know—what you don't know—is I've been dealing with assholes like him my whole life. He sees me as a fuck, a fun entertainment, not a threat. A naïve little girl to manipulate and control. I learned how to play men like him when I was thirteen." A harsh edge entered her voice. "I even come when they screw me."

Cressida inched to the side as she spoke, widening the distance between herself and Ian. Zack's gaze and pistol followed her.

"I know what you're doing, Porter," Zack said. "It won't work." But Zack didn't realize how much she'd skewed his angle on Ian, or he'd order her to step in line.

She shrugged. "If you know anything about me, you know I'll do anything to survive. Even fuck a scumbag traitor."

Zack glanced at Ian, his gaze narrowing—probably as he realized Ian had inched closer. He whipped the gun in Ian's direction again. "Not another step, Boyd." To Cressida, Zack said. "You've already fucked a traitor. Haven't you seen the news?"

"I don't really give a damn which one of you is the traitor. I just want to find the tunnel and go home."

It was clear Zack was torn between watching Cressida advance versus keeping an eye on Ian. He had to believe Ian was the bigger threat, but Cressida wasn't to be ignored.

"I know exactly what gets your rocks off, Zack." She turned, catching Ian's gaze. Her eyes were cold and hard. "Ian was the big man in Ankara, but now he's been burned, and look who has the gun." Her voice lowered even more as she took a step toward him. "Wait until you see the rage on his face when I blow you while he watches."

At her words, fury surged up Ian's esophagus. The shock of emotion forced out a primal grunt as he held his muscles in check. He wanted to rip Zack's head off for threatening Cressida and was pissed as hell at her for attempting this tactic.

She flashed Ian a cold smile, let out a purr-like growl of her own, and took another step closer to Zack, bringing her within arm's reach of the traitor. "Want to know a secret? I'm turned on by the idea of fucking with Ian's head like that. After the way he's treated me, he has it coming." She reached down and brushed her hand over Zack's fly. "Glad I'm not alone."

Zack's gun wobbled at her brief touch but remained pointed at Ian. She laughed and stroked him again, less tentative the second time.

Zack's gaze remained fastened on Ian—and Ian did nothing to hide his rage. Cressida was right. Seeing Ian destroyed was what fed Zack's ego and clouded his judgment. If she could play her part, he could play his. "I'll kill him," Ian said through clenched teeth.

Satisfaction flared in Zack's eyes. Cressida flicked open the top button of his fly. His grip on the gun tightened until his knuckles turned white. "On your knees, then," he ordered.

She dropped, slowly.

Ian held back an eruption that could rival Vesuvius. He *would* kill him.

His vision hazed when she slipped her fingers inside Zack's pants and made a throaty sound he'd heard her make only twice before.

All at once, Zack let out a grunt and doubled over. Ian lunged for Zack at the same time Cressida surged upward, grabbing his head with both hands and kneeing him in the face as he dropped. Zack pulled the trigger, but the shot went wild as his head snapped back and he flopped to the ground.

Ian slammed into him. The gun flew from Zack's hand. Blood poured from his nose. Ian grabbed him by the throat.

From the agony that contorted Zack's features, Ian figured Cressida had twisted his nuts into a figure eight before she broke his nose.

Standing above Zack now, she delivered a swift kick to his crotch. Ian released Zack's throat, allowing him to curl into a ball like a potato bug. She squatted down and wiped her hand on the scrubby grass. Her face revealed the revulsion she'd been holding back. As she rose, she covered her mouth with the back of her hand as if she were trying not to heave. "I promised myself I'd never do that again."

Again?

Later, Ian would explore that statement. Right now he had to deal with Zack. He stood and kicked Zack in the head. Once. Twice. The tension in Zack's body eased and his body uncurled. Ian lifted the traitor by the shirt and pulled back for a punch when Cressida stopped him with a hand on his arm. "I think he's out."

Ian released him. Zack's head hit the ground with a hard thunk. "If I ever see you touch another man's junk again, I will shoot the bastard."

"It's okay with me if you shoot him. But don't kill him. We need him to clear your name."

He wanted to kiss her in thanks for her chillingly good performance, but Zack could have accomplices who would strike the moment Ian attempted something so stupid. Instead, he pulled his weapon and turned in a slow circle, searching the landscape for threats.

She was right about not killing Zack, and given that the man was unconscious, it would be straight-up murder. His gaze landed again on the double agent who'd ordered Cressida to her knees before him. He'd never been so tempted to commit homicide in his life. "We need to tie him up," he said.

She grabbed a paracord bracelet tied to Ian's backpack and unraveled the thin rope. They traded jobs. Ian bound Zack's hands and feet, while Cressida stood guard. He searched Zack's pockets, finding car keys and a cell phone, but nothing else. He shut off the phone—no point in broadcasting their location if they caught a flicker of a signal—and said, "He must have parked a distance away, or we'd have heard him."

"What's the plan?"

He sat back on his heels, staring at Zack's prostrate form. Cressida was his mission now. Her safety came first. Zack's arrival changed nothing. In fact, the idea of handing Zack to a team of Raptor operatives held enormous appeal. Without Zack in the picture, he might be able to complete the other mission, after Cressida was safe. He had the microchip. There was still a chance the courier would show up and he could force the man to lead him to his terrorist group's ultimate leader.

"We'll find Zack's vehicle and drive southeast. There should be a tower in the village that's about six klicks from here. Then we'll wait for the cavalry, I guess."

Chapter Thirty-One

ZACK'S VEHICLE TURNED out to be an old British Land Rover with plenty of room to store a trussed-up Zack in the back between a large jack, a toolbox, and a wealth of camping supplies. Ian found zip ties in the toolbox and replaced the paracord that bound Zack with the thin strips of plastic, cinching his wrists and ankles tight to the same rear-seat mount and his neck to a different mount, limiting his movement and ensuring he would be very uncomfortable when he returned to consciousness.

They'd driven for about thirty minutes when Cressida powered up Ian's phone and a single flickering bar appeared. The rush of emotion at seeing the little flashing graphic made her suck in a sharp breath. Ian pulled to the side of the narrow dirt track that served as a road. He glanced at the back of the truck and held a finger to his lips. They had no clue what they were going to do with Zack, so for now, if he was conscious, they couldn't discuss their plans.

With a nod, Ian indicated she should grab her backpack and climb out. He did the same. After locking the truck, he pulled the distributor cap from the Rover, effectively disabling it.

"Are we leaving him?"

"I hope not, but I'm not taking any chances. Never assume we'll return to any location. Always be prepared to run." He paused and studied the landscape. "We need a place to lay low to make the call. This area is too open. Zack probably has people in the area."

"How far is the village?"

"About two kilometers. We might get lucky and find an old barn or other abandoned structure on the outskirts."

Luck was with them, for a change. After walking for ten minutes, Cressida spotted an ancient-looking stone shed nestled against a hillside across the dirt road. Overgrown with vines and built with the same type of stones as the bedrock, the structure blended into the landscape from the side, but a rusted metal roof gave it away.

Broken planks of wood—remnants of a door—half covered the entrance. When they slipped inside, Cressida was thankful to be out of view from the road that led into the village, even if it meant hanging out in a crumbling shed that smelled of rats and rotting grasses.

She pulled out the phone and met Ian's gaze. "You ready? There's a chance Trina's phone is being monitored." In all likelihood, Lee had secured the line, knowing Trina was the first person Cressida would call, but they had to be prepared for anything.

Ian's gaze was intense, carrying the weight of a thousand unspoken words. He pressed down on the cell phone. She stiffened, tightening her grip on it. She'd twist his balls too before she let him take the phone from her.

He shook his head, and one corner of his mouth curved in a sad way. "I'm not going to stop you, Cress. I was moving it so it wouldn't be between us when I do this." He pulled her against him and stroked her hair, his large hand holding her head to his chest. His lips landed on her temple. "You were amazing and saved us both. When we're far away from here, I want you to tell me what you meant by 'again.'"

She had no intention of ever telling anyone the story of Three. Especially not Ian Boyd.

He lifted her chin and pressed a kiss on her lips. "Call Trina."

She nodded and entered Trina's number. With every touch of the screen, her heart rate jumped. By the time she pressed the phone to her ear to wait for the call to connect, her pulse raced fast enough to power a small city.

TRINA'S FACE FLUSHED and her belly flipped when Caller ID indicated an overseas call. She nodded to Keith, who speed-dialed Lee on the landline as soon as she hit the answer button. "If this isn't Cressida, I'm hanging up," she said in a shaking voice.

There was a long pause, a delay caused by the international call, before she heard Cressida's clear voice. "Treen, it's me."

Her eyes teared at the sound of Cressida's voice, and she flopped into a chair at the kitchen table. "Ohmygod! Sweetie! We've been scared to death. Where are you?"

"I'm okay. For now. But I need help."

Keith frowned as he murmured something to Lee, and Trina remembered her script. As much as she wanted to talk to Cressida and make sure she was okay, they didn't have that luxury. She had to assume every second of conversation could be the last. "Cress, Sean is looking for you. Right now, he and a Raptor team are in Cizre. Can you write down his number?"

Cressida's voice was muffled as she said, "Ian, I need pen and paper."

To Keith, Trina said, "She's with Boyd." Into the phone, she asked, "Cress, is Boyd an ally?"

The pause was too long for Trina's comfort, but it could be the international delay. "Yes."

Of course, the man must be right next to her. Listening. "Okay, answer correctly if he's *not* coercing you..." She closed her eyes and tried to think of something simple but innocuous. "Who hosted the party we went to with Todd last summer?"

There was only one answer that meant Ian Boyd could be trusted. All Cressida had to do was say any other name and they'd know if Boyd was a threat. "Dr. Patrick Hill," Cressida said firmly.

Trina let out the breath she'd been holding. "Okay." She recited the phone number. "Call Sean. He can get you out of Turkey."

"Got it." Cressida said good-bye and hung up.

Trina stood in her living room, staring at her phone. She'd been waiting for that moment for days, and it was over so quickly. Her body shook, and she didn't know if relief or fear caused the tremors.

Keith's arms circled her from behind, and she turned to face him and wrapped her arms around his waist. "I'm scared, Keith."

"If anyone can get her out, it's Sean. He's my best operative."

She nodded. "I just feel...helpless. I wish we knew Boyd. I wish we were certain we could trust him."

"Cressida trusts him, doesn't she?"

"She said she did."

He smiled. "Then we can trust him too."

"What if she's wrong? It's not like she has a great track record."

"Given what we've been able to piece together of their week in Turkey, Cressida *knows* if Boyd is one of the good guys by now."

DISCONNECTING THE CALL with Trina was hard. Hearing a warm, concerned voice, knowing her friends were trying to help her had triggered relief and guilt. She met Ian's gaze. "Keith has already sent a Raptor team to Cizre. Sean Logan is one of the operatives. They want me to call him."

"You have good friends."

She nodded and dialed Sean's number. He answered immediately and said, "Cressida Porter, it's about damn time."

She let out a hard laugh as a rush of emotion hit her for the second time in as many minutes. She was far too emotional these days. "Sean, you have no idea how good it is to hear your voice."

"Same here, Cress. I've been worried. We all have."

She cleared her throat. "Thanks. Listen, I'm handing over the phone to Ian."

"Boyd's a friendly?"

She met and held Ian's gaze as she said, "Yes. I trust him with my life."

Ian's jaw tensed, and his nostrils flared slightly. She wondered what was going on in his mind. It might be best, when this was all over, if she forgot she'd ever met Ian Boyd. She couldn't see how she could maintain contact with him and not want him.

She handed him the phone, then settled down on the dirt floor to listen. He told Sean about Zack, trussed up in the Rover, and described their location. Cressida had been in something of a fog after dealing with Zack, and had lost track of the distance they'd traveled. She hadn't realized quite how close to the Syrian border they were. When Ian estimated their distance from Cizre, she sat upright in shock.

In heading for the nearest cell tower, they'd unintentionally continued on course for the aqueduct.

She glanced around the old stone shack, her mind racing. She leaned toward the wall to inspect the mortar between the stones, then reached for Ian's backpack and pulled out a knife with a sturdy blade. She pressed the edge in a chink between rocks and broke a small chunk of mortar free, then studied her sample in a ray of sunlight that shone through a hole in the rusted roof.

The mortar could be ancient. She'd visited several ancient sites in Istanbul and Antalya to study the concrete so she might be able to identify the ancient Roman variety if the need arose. The mortar in her hands was composed of crushed stone aggregate bound with lime, a combination used for centuries, but the ratio of aggregate to binder had changed over the course of two millennia, and the composition in her hands was consistent with the mix used in antiquity.

She twirled in a slow circle, studying the shed, then zeroed in on the southeast corner. She dropped to her knees and scraped the dirt floor with the knife blade, finding the edges of a massive flat stone. Using her headscarf, she wiped across the surface. The coarse weave worked well to dislodge decades of soil. With the rock exposed she grabbed a flashlight from the pack and laid it flat on the ground, so the light spread across the stone, revealing pits and chinks in the deceptively smooth surface. The mark was there, etched into the flat rock.

"Cressida?" Ian said.

She startled, realizing he was no longer on the phone with Sean. She twisted to face him without leaving her corner.

"We need to head for the rendezvous with Logan's Raptor team."

She shook her head, feeling dazed. "We're here."

His brow furrowed. "What?"

"We made it. This is it. We've found T. E. Lawrence's stone house." She pointed to the exposed flat rock. "That's the entrance to the tunnel. Lawrence etched his initials into the rock, just like he'd marked it on the map."

Chapter Thirty-Two

IAN HAD NEVER imagined they'd be faced with this decision. With Zack tied up not too far away, they were at risk here, but if they'd located a tunnel into Syria and took control of it, preventing it from falling into either the Syrian government's or ISIS's hands...

Forget Raptor, with this intel, he could get the CIA to send in an exfil team. The CIA could get him back inside the US, whereas Raptor might have problems in that area.

This find was...potentially huge. A backdoor into Syria could change the balance of power in their ongoing civil war. The ethnic Kurds of Turkey wanted to join their Kurdish neighbors in Northern Syria and Iraq to form a geopolitically united Kurdistan—a secular, pro-West democracy in the heart of the Middle East. A tunnel like this could bring them one step closer to that goal.

The Kurds in Syria had declared complete autonomy from Assad's regime *and* the separatist rebels. They fought for their own country, their own freedom, using the name People's Protection Units—*Yekîneyên Parastina Gel* in Kurdish, known by the initials YPG—and had been, until the rise of ISIS, in control of northeast Syria, not far from the Turkish city of Cizre. YPG still held the majority of the territory, with skirmishes moving boundaries back and forth on a daily basis.

They should leave. Now. And yet...if Cressida was right...

He looked at her and knew, for the first time in his life, he'd found someone he wasn't willing to risk. At least, not anymore. "We have to go."

"If we find the second entrance, it will confirm this is the tunnel. Maybe we can dig out the other opening with the tools in the Rover. The aqueduct was a series of qanats, just like Gadara. The other entrances are likely to be shafts filled with dirt and rock."

"After we're back in the US, we'll tell the CIA the location of this entrance. It'll be enough."

She frowned. "It may surprise you to know that I wasn't hoping to find this tunnel for its potential espionage and military uses." She shook her head. "It a piece of history. Engineering and construction that was done before the invention of the compass. Before TNT. Do you have any idea how hard it would be to tunnel for miles and stay on course without a compass? If this tunnel is anything like Gadara, it may have taken a hundred years to build. This is an historic wonder. To be studied and learned from."

He could hear her passion for the topic in her voice. "I'm sorry, Cress, but this tunnel *is* strategically important. Two thousand years or two days old, it doesn't matter. What matters is the location is a secret, and it crosses an international border in a heavily disputed region."

"Isn't the strategic value for the Turkish or Syrian people to decide, not the CIA?"

"Would *you* trust the Syrian government with that information right now?"

She frowned and stepped toward him. She cast her gaze back at the corner stone, and her shoulders fell in defeat. "Then we'll tell no one."

He nodded. He could give her that. For now. "Let's head back to the Rover. The Raptor team is only about thirty klicks from here. Logan has a plan for smuggling you over the border into Iraq. They have a jet waiting in Erbil. With luck, you'll be flying out before midnight."

He stepped outside the shack and crouched low behind shrubs that abutted the structure and studied the road. Empty in both directions. The nerves along his neck prickled. Something wasn't right. A moment later, he heard it, the soft whirr of an engine in the distance. With Cressida's hand in a tight grip, he pulled her around to the back side of the shack, which blocked them from view of the road. He gestured for Cressida to take cover under the thick brambles that stretched from hillside to structure and followed her into the vegetative cover.

She cursed the spiky barbs of the dry plants. He gently placed a hand to her lips to silence her as the engine noise drew closer. Tucked low and dressed in desert brown, they blended in, but not well enough to be certain of their safety should someone search the perimeter of the shack.

The engine noise stopped as it drew even with the shack.

Crap.

Ian pulled his gun and nodded to Cressida to do the same.

The sound of three car doors opening and closing followed, then he heard Zack say, "Ganem, check out the shack."

Footsteps approached the shed. Beside him, Cressida's eyes were wide with alarm. She wanted to tell Ian something, but he gave a sharp shake of his head. A whisper now was far too risky.

While Ganem approached the shack, Zack spoke to the third man in broken Turkish. Ian couldn't help but grin at the nasal quality to Zack's voice thanks to his broken nose. He sent the third man to search across the road, then announced he'd climb the hill himself to scan the landscape. From the top of the hill, he might be able to get a glimpse of Ian and Cressida. Ian could only pray the brambles were thick enough to disguise them.

Todros entered the shed. The windows of the old structure lacked glass, making it easy to hear movement inside. The man was on the opposite side of the wall at Ian's back, scraping the flat capstone with something.

He must have seen the cleared stone and was now checking it out himself.

Zack came into Ian's view as he reached the hilltop. He'd have let out a sigh of relief when the man descended, apparently without spotting them, but he still had Todros to worry about inside the shack.

Finally, Todros left the shed and met up with Zack and the other man on the road. "No sign anyone's been inside the shed in months, maybe years."

At hearing the blatant lie, Cressida shifted, shaking a branch. She stilled, her body rigid with alarm, but none of the men in the road seemed to notice.

"Face it, they're long gone," Todros continued. "By my calculations, the tunnel is closer to Cizre."

Zack cursed. "They aren't headed to the tunnel. Ian's gone soft. They planned to call her friend with Raptor ties. There's a team in Cizre waiting to extract them."

"The roads are heavily patrolled in and out of Cizre. They'll never make it."

"They'll go overland." Zack paused. "But the Raptor team won't. Give me your cell. It's time to shut out Raptor—we can have them detained at the next checkpoint."

Dammit. The team could be picked up for any number of

reasons, starting with the simple fact they were in the region working a contract to protect Kurdish government officials in northern Iraq from ISIS. The Turkish government was leery of all things that smacked of Kurdish autonomy and had their own trouble with ISIS. The Raptor team's entry into Turkey could easily be viewed as suspicious.

Zack made his call, instructing whoever was on the other end of the line to push for the Raptor team's detainment. But it was his last demand that made Ian's blood run cold. He wanted an overland search, starting with the area surrounding the nearby village.

CRESSIDA BREATHED A sigh of relief when the black Jeep reached the crest of the hill, then dropped down the other side. Ian watched the vehicle through small binoculars he'd had in his pack. "I caught a quick glimpse of the third man. I think he's the guy with the knife who attacked you by the train."

She shuddered. She'd happily live the rest of her life without coming face-to-face with him again. "Todd lied to Zack about the shack. He saw the scrape marks. He's not stupid. He knows what fresh digging looks like."

"It would be a mistake to rely on him as an ally," Ian said, his voice flat.

She nodded. One lie didn't make up for everything else Todd had done. But it eased the sting a little to know he wasn't one hundred percent complicit with Zack.

"I need to call off the meet with Raptor. They need to return to Iraq. Now. Before they're detained for days."

Dread settled in her gut. They'd been *so* close.

She listened to Ian's side of the conversation with Sean, disheartened and frustrated that their short-lived escape plan was now gone. They'd have to continue overland to the Iraq border to meet with Sean, which would require another crossing of the Tigris. But unfortunately, this close to the Syrian border, there would be patrols all along the river. They'd have to backtrack, go north and around. It would take days. Odds were they'd be caught.

Just as Ian was saying good-bye to Sean, she said, "Wait!"

Ian cocked his head with the phone still pressed to his ear.

"If we can get into Syria, would it be hard to cross the river to get into Iraq?"

He frowned and asked Sean what the river border was like in Iraq. To Cressida, he said, "YPG has control of the river in the north, and for now, ISIS is leaving them alone due to heavier fighting on the western end of the Turkish border. YPG is allied with the Kurds in Northern Iraq, and both groups have used the river to bring in Western reporters into Syria. With the aid of a sympathetic rebel, entering Iraq is doable from Northern Syria, even though it's technically ISIS-controlled territory. It's a route Sean considered if we could find a way to enter Syria, but it's dangerous."

"Tell him we'll meet him on the river—tomorrow."

Ian shook his head. "Cressida, we don't have time to find and dig out one of the openings. It could be twenty feet of dirt and rock, and we'd be in the open. You heard Zack—they're going to start an overland search. Here."

She clenched her hand into a ball to keep from gripping his arm, as if she could physically pull him toward accepting her plan. "We can remove Lawrence's capstone."

"How are we going to do that?"

"Drag it with the winch on the front of the Rover?" she suggested.

Ian's brow furrowed as he considered her idea. "Maybe. We could use the tire iron as a lever. But the cable might not be long enough to reach the house. I don't know how close we could angle the Rover." Then his eyes lit up. "But there is a high-lift jack in the back of the truck. We could lift it." To Sean he said, "We'll give this a try. If we've had no luck in two hours, we'll give up and head north." He hung up. "You know this is insane, right?"

"Everything about this week has been insane. Why should today be any different?"

He let out a strangled laugh. "Fair point." He touched the wall of the stone shack. "Even if we manage to open the tunnel, we might not find an exit at the other end. We'll be proverbial fish in a barrel if Zack returns."

"We'll be caught if we circle back and head to the Iraq border. How much do you want to bet checkpoint guards will shoot us both first, to hell with asking questions?"

Ian's eyes darkened, and his jaw clenched. "That's the only reason I'm willing to try this. I refuse to give anyone the opportunity to take a shot at you again."

The emotion in his words triggered a slight flush.

Who did he think he was fooling with his *"I don't do emotion"* line? Certainly not her.

They waded back through the brambles and headed to the Rover, which was still there, disabled without the distributor cap. They scavenged the vehicle for useable tools, taking the large high-lift jack, a tire iron, and the toolbox containing odds and ends including a wrench, hammer, screwdrivers, and collapsible shovel.

Cressida's breath left her in a sharp, painful whoosh when she found a trowel buried under an old greasy rag.

"What's wrong?" Ian asked.

She studied the carving on the old Marshalltown. Well worn. Sharp as a knife. As familiar as her own. "It's Todd's." She tucked it into the back pocket of her jeans.

"I'm sorry, Cress."

She shrugged. "It's not like we didn't know he's working with Zack." She pursed her lips. "I think..." She hesitated. Ian had a hair trigger when it came to Todd.

"Go ahead. Say it."

"I don't understand why he sent me the text, but I have a feeling Hejan gave me Todd's number because he really believed Todd would help us if he can. And I think that's why Todd lied to Zack."

"I hope you're right. We can use all the help we can get."

They hauled their cache to the stone shed and set to work. Cressida used Todd's trowel while Ian wielded the tire iron. Together they cleared the edges of the stone and dug out a groove in the soil on one side so the lip of the jack could be wedged into position beneath the capstone.

At last, they'd made a deep cut in the dirt floor. Sweat rolled down Cressida's temples as they worked the jack into place. She felt each second, each minute, knowing they could well be wasting precious time when they should be distancing themselves from this place.

Todd knew she'd been here. He and Zack could return at any time.

Even scarier than facing Zack was the knowledge that if they were successful, they could find themselves twenty feet underground and facing a dead end.

She calmed that fear with the reminder T. E. Lawrence had marked the site as a tunnel—and a long one at that. Surely he wouldn't have done that if *he* hadn't explored it. If the passage had been filled with rock and debris, he'd have had no idea about the extent of the shaft. However, the question remained whether there would be an exit at the far end.

Low grunts from both Ian and Cressida were the only sound as they seated the base of the jack in the trough they'd cut into the dirt and wiggled the lip under the ten-inch-thick stone.

Jack in place, Cressida dropped to the floor, panting to recover from the effort of sliding a thick metal bar under what had to be a half-ton stone.

Ian rested his hands on his knees and caught his breath. Thanks to a fine sheen of sweat, his dirt-streaked T-shirt clung to thick muscles. Between that and six days of stubble—now really a beard—he looked rugged and sexy as hell, making her long for a do-over.

Breathing under control, he straightened and pumped the jack handle twice. Rock ground against rock, and the stone shifted, then, ever so slightly, lifted.

Elation shot through her. She couldn't help it and launched herself at him, throwing her arms around his neck. "It works!" Then she pressed her open mouth to his.

Oh *God*. Kissing him felt so damn right. Her fingers threaded through his hair as his hands slid down and cupped her butt.

All too soon, he released her. "It's a shame we don't have time for that," he said, breathing almost as heavily as he had when they positioned the jack.

She nodded. He was right. "Let's get this tunnel open."

He waved to the jack, giving her the honor of pumping the bar next. The jack was old but well oiled, and the mechanism move easily as she worked the handle. The rock slipped on the lip, forcing them to adjust the angle to support the rising stone.

When the rock was three inches above the ground, Ian shined a flashlight into the exposed gap, revealing the edge of a dark hole. Three more inches, and the light caught what appeared to be the first step of a stone staircase.

Ian took over pumping the jack, which strained under the weight of the stone, and finally, they had an opening wide enough for even his broad shoulders to pass through. She shined the flashlight into the depths and counted fifteen steps cut into the earth.

IAN GATHERED THEIR supplies. They would take everything into the tunnel except the jack. They would leave the jack in place, holding up the stone, their only guaranteed exit—but also an invitation for Zack and Todros to follow, which wasn't exactly a minor concern.

They had to drop the supplies down. The opening was too narrow to wear backpacks as they slipped under the precariously perched capstone, but at least the tunnel itself appeared to be tall and wide enough to walk without hunching over or the need to shuffle sideways.

He dropped the toolbox first. The metal container clattered down the lowest of the steps, the sound muted by the depth and angle of the tunnel. Next he tossed the backpacks.

Cressida took a step toward the opening, and his gut clenched. The seconds she'd be under the canted rock, before she was fully in the cavern, were the most dangerous. The slightest bump of the jack or shifting of earth beneath it, and the stone would crush her. He pressed a hard kiss to her lips. He had a thousand words he wanted to say, but he couldn't. Not now. "Be careful," he said, and let her go.

She nodded and slipped through, lithe and sprightly as she disappeared into the dark hole. He took a deep breath once she was cleared of the rock, and another when she called out, "I'm at the bottom." The beam of her flashlight disappeared into the angled corridor. "It's open. At least…as far as the light reaches is passable."

"I'm coming down," he said. He hit Send on the prewritten text message to Sean and waited for confirmation the text was sent before descending into the hole.

He slipped past the jack without a problem, but after clearing it, a whisper of sound alerted him to a subtle shift in air current. He glanced back and saw a narrow stream of dirt drip down from under the base of the tilted, wedged jack. The metal arm bowed slightly, the lip that held the stone straining under the weight.

The minor shift in the soil at the base had redistributed the weight. The jack was about to snap.

"Shit! Cressida! Move!" The words were barely out of his mouth when he leapt forward and down, jumping six steps and rolling when he hit the bottom, catching her and tucking her against him. Above them, metal popped and the boulder slammed down, resealing the hole.

Chapter Thirty-Three

CRESSIDA COUGHED FROM breathing in dirt that had been stirred when the rock slammed across the opening and shook the walls of the tunnel. She lay on her side in the darkness, her eyes watering as she struggled to control the spasms, afraid movement would cause another shift and the two-thousand-year-old tunnel would collapse. Had the bedrock fractured when the boulder fell?

Ian's arms tightened around her. "You okay?" he asked.

Coughing under control, she did a mental check, flexing muscles to make sure everything was fine. "Yes. Just a little freaked."

She felt his lips brush her forehead in the pitch-black darkness. She'd dropped her flashlight when he slammed into her and groped the floor, hoping it hadn't broken.

He flicked on his light, and she spied hers against the wall. She pushed to her knees and reached for it, then let out a soft sigh of relief when the light flickered, then steadied.

Ian shut off his light. "I'll save my batteries. We have no idea how long we'll be down here."

She directed her light upward. The top of the tunnel was about eight inches above her head, clearing Ian's greater height with a scant inch to spare. With his broad shoulders, the narrow cut of the aqueduct—slightly less than a meter at the floor, the opening gradually narrowing to half that size at the arched ceiling—would be a tighter squeeze for him than for her.

She shivered. The length of the tunnel was the only thing that prevented a full-on claustrophobia panic. She couldn't imagine how Ian must feel, with his shoulders scraping the sides. "We're trapped."

He nodded, his mouth tight. "It was one of the risks."

She shined the light on the entrance shaft stairs, then flicked it off. Not even a whisper of sunlight slipped past the edges of the stone. She thumbed on the light again, chilled by the utter darkness of being fifteen feet below ground. "I'm sorry, Ian. This is my fault."

"No, it's mine, Cress. *All* of this is my fault." He gathered her against his chest.

She breathed in his scent. Sweat, dirt, and testosterone. A comfort to have someone solid to hold, another beating heart, in what could well be their tomb.

"We've got food and two days' worth of water if we're careful," she said. "Air could be a problem, but the corridor looks long, and there could be exchange through some of the qanat shafts."

He stroked her cheek. "Your strength amazes me."

She tightened her arms around him. "I'm just borrowing it from you. If you weren't here, I'd be a wreck."

"Same for me." He brushed strands of hair that had escaped the braid from her forehead. "We'll find an exit shaft we can dig through. I *will* get you out of here."

She held his gaze; the dim glow couldn't hide the intensity in his eyes. "Promise?"

He smiled. "Absolutely, beautiful."

It was a ridiculous promise, considering what they were likely facing. Even more ridiculous to take hope from it, but somehow, she did. "Well then, let's go."

He kissed her. "When we get back to the States, I want to whisk you away to a five-star hotel for a week. We'll dine on room service, and I'll devote all my energy to making you come, repeatedly."

Heat unfurled from her core. She licked her lips, her throat dry once again. "Promise?" she repeated.

"It's more than a promise, beautiful. It's my solemn vow."

"Fair warning, I love room service more than almost anything else in the world. It's going to cost you."

"I've got a dozen years' worth of paychecks burning a hole in my pocket. I think I can handle it."

"Can't wait." She wondered if he offered sex or something more, but trapped in a two-thousand-year-old tunnel, she needed hope to cling to and wasn't about to ruin the fantasy by questioning the details.

"Then we should hustle on into Syria and dig our way out."

She laughed. As if it could be that simple.

They donned their packs, and Ian picked up the toolbox and led the way down the dark tunnel. She gave him her flashlight, and he swept the walls and floor with it, ducking and shifting sideways as necessary when the tunnel narrowed too much for his size.

Two-thousand-year-old pick marks evidenced the manual labor that had gone into excavating the passage through solid bedrock. In areas where the tunnel burrowed through dirt instead of rock, the builders had reinforced the walls and ceiling with concrete arches that prevented the loose earth from collapsing the structure.

Ian reached back and took her hand. At first, Cressida thought his goal was to comfort her, but then, the way his fingers shifted and laced through hers, she realized he did it as much for himself, triggering a tightness in her chest. He needed her as much as she needed him.

Reluctantly, she slipped her hand from his to press the button on her dive watch to illuminate the compass. They were heading almost exactly due south and had been for the last six hundred steps. She marveled at the accuracy of the tunnel makers two thousand years ago.

She entwined her fingers with his again and said, "I'm counting steps. I know my pace—twelve steps is ten meters." She stumbled on the uneven ground, and his fingers tightened on hers. He shined the flashlight downward to illuminate the floor. "No. Keep it up. You need to see the ceiling. Better I trip than you hit your head on a low rock."

He raised the light again.

"My guess is the shack was two miles—three at most—from the Syrian border," she said. "We'll be lucky if the tunnel is passable for four miles to get us beyond the border."

He ducked, and she saw the ceiling lowered to the point she had to stoop too. "We're due for some luck about now," he said.

"I don't think luck works that way."

"Yeah, well, I don't think luck works at all." His tone was as dry as the cool tunnel air.

She snorted. "True."

Ahead of him, the beam of light caressed the sloping walls, floor, and ceiling in a slow rotation. He stopped when the light disappeared into a dark hole to the right. "Another entrance shaft."

Her heart pounded with relief at this, the first sign there were, indeed, other exits. They would find a way out. They had to.

She stopped to study the steps cut into rock. Six steps ended abruptly at a wooden barrier. Did T. E. Lawrence place the barrier here a hundred years ago? "This might be the one Lawrence dug out and marked on the map. If we can't find an exit farther south, we may want to come back here." She studied the smooth planks. "If we pull down the boards, we'll probably find a shaft filled with rocks, dirt, and debris, but, from the height of the stairs, my guess is we'd only have a few feet to dig through. Plus, gravity would help—without the planks, the dirt will spill down the stairs."

They *were* going to survive this tunnel. The question was, would they survive what awaited them above?

Ian halted the beam of light on an object resting on the bottom step. At first glance, she'd assumed it was a broken board, but upon closer inspection, it was a small wooden box. Like an old cigar box. Definitely not two thousand years old, but not five or ten years old either. She dropped to her knees and touched the box. Slowly. Reverently.

She'd known when she located the stone with etched initials that T.E. had been here. Even the planks were a telltale sign. But this...this was incontrovertible proof someone had been in this tunnel at least once in the years since the aqueduct had gone out of use and faded from memory.

Ian dropped to his knees beside her. His hand found the small of her back. "Open it, honey. You've earned this moment."

She lifted the lid. A small leather-bound book rested inside. She carefully took it from the box that had housed it for the last hundred years and studied the cover. The letters T-E-L were stamped into the soft hide. She opened the book and scanned the contents. Her heart pounded—this time not due to worry or fear, but excitement. "It's his field journal."

She could work on a thousand sites—digging every day for the rest of her life—but she doubted she'd ever again find anything as interesting as this historical document. Which was funny when she considered that it was just another archaeologist's notes. But it was who the man was, even more than this amazing tunnel he'd found, that made this moment extra special.

In her mind, T. E. Lawrence would always be Peter O'Toole. Tall, handsome. Charismatic. But of course, the real Lawrence was shorter than her by an inch. And historians were divided on his charisma.

She glanced up the tunnel. "We need to leave this here. I can't take it and risk it being lost."

Ian nodded, a sad smile on his face. She guessed he understood what this meant to her. "Read it. Quickly. In case he describes the tunnel ahead—and an exit we should look for."

She settled on the step with Ian by her side and started reading. He opened an energy bar and broke it in half. "Dinner?" he offered.

She smiled and took the paltry meal. "When we're at The Hay-Adams, I'm going to order halibut from room service. With cream sauce. Served over risotto."

He chuckled. "I'll order the salad. I need to watch my figure."

She let out a sharp laugh. His body was perfect—all hard muscle without an ounce of fat. "Don't worry, I'll give you enough of a workout that you'll be able to eat whatever you want and keep your trim shape."

He leaned down and nipped her neck. "Fine. Then I'll order strawberry ice cream with chocolate sauce, paint your body with it, and lick every sweet inch."

Oh. My. She closed her eyes to savor the image he'd planted. Bad timing. She needed to read the book so they could get the hell out of this tunnel and back to the US and into that luxury hotel room.

Ian read over her shoulder. His demeanor toward her had changed, but she wasn't certain when it happened. When she'd cried in his arms? When she took down Zack?

All she knew was something had changed. In a good way. His barriers were… *lower*. He was a hybrid of Ian and John. The sexy, hardened, undercover operative, combined with the charming, gregarious security specialist.

Was this, finally, the real Ian?

"Cress?"

She shook her head and realized she'd been staring at the same page too long as her brain went off on a tangent they didn't have time for. "Sorry." She flipped the page. "Oh, bless you T.E.," she said upon seeing the map the wonderful, brilliant, magnificent man had drawn of the tunnel.

His drawing estimated the tunnel was passable for at least six miles, before crumbling ancient concrete gave way and sealed off the passage. There was a shallow exit near the terminus. If conditions in the tunnel were the same now as they'd been a hundred years ago, they would be well into Syria. And, most importantly, there was a way out.

Chapter Thirty-Four

IAN USED THE cell phone to snap a picture of the map, then took a few more pictures of Lawrence's notes for Cressida. He hoped that somehow she'd be able to use this for a paper of some sort. Someday.

He tucked the phone away as she returned the book to its box and slipped it in a crevasse in the rock wall—a slightly more protected hiding place in case Zack and Todros followed them down the tunnel.

They each took a small sip of water, then resumed their slow progress down the dark, constricted space. Again, Ian took her hand in his, the need to touch her a strange development for a man who'd prided himself on not needing anyone. Ever.

Cressida kept track of their distance, continuing to count her steps. The six-mile trek took longer in the narrow tunnel than it would have on the surface. In several areas, they had to shimmy through tight gaps where concrete reinforcement had given way and the tunnel was partially collapsed. At each constriction, they brushed against loose dirt and rocks that trickled down, threatening to avalanche and close the passage behind them. Finally, several hours after they'd paused to read T. E. Lawrence's field journal, they reached an impassable rockfall.

"By my calculations, we're at the same collapse point that stopped Lawrence," Cressida said. "That last entrance shaft we passed on the east side is the one Lawrence was able to dig through."

"Let's hope he didn't cap this one with a five-hundred-pound stone."

"If he did, we're screwed. So I choose to believe he didn't."

They returned to the exit shaft Lawrence had noted, and sure enough, this one also had wooden planks supporting the dirt and debris that clogged the opening.

Cressida pulled the collapsible shovel from her backpack. She handed him the shovel, then grabbed the tire iron. "I'm going to use this to pry out the keystone holding the barrier in place."

He took the tire iron from her. "That's dangerous, making it my job."

"Which one of us is the professional digger?" she asked, reaching for the iron.

"Which one of us is the professional risk taker who agreed to sacrifice his life for his country if need be?"

"Which one of us is more likely to make it to freedom on the other side? I don't speak the language, Ian. I don't know the rules of the game or even what the game is. If only one of us survives this, it has to be you."

"No. Fucking. Way." He yanked the evil eye pendant from his neck and dropped it over her head. "If only one of us is going to survive, it will be you. Period. No argument. And if we get separated in Syria, if I'm taken and questioned, even tortured, you *will* keep going. No matter what, you will head for the rendezvous point with the Raptor team. You will tell no one—*no one*—about the chip in this pendant until Zack is in custody. Do you understand?"

"Not even the CIA director?"

"Not even him. Zack Barrow is still an agent. *We* know he's playing for the wrong team, but it's doubtful the CIA will believe us. If corruption in the agency goes higher than Zack, and the wrong person gets their hands on the chip, it's game over."

She rose on her toes and kissed him. A soft brush of lips that he wanted to turn into something more. For all they knew, this would be their last chance to be together. But the mission always came first, and his mission was to get Cressida safely into Sean Logan's hands.

Never mind the sharp stab of jealousy he'd felt at hearing the fondness in her voice when she spoke to Logan. Clearly, he had issues when it came to Cressida. They were his to deal with in silence for now and forever. Right now he needed to get her out of this death trap.

He used the tire iron to pry out the boards. The first one popped easily, the old wood splintering under the slightest pressure.

Dirt spilled down onto the stairs where he stood.

"Careful!" Cressida said from her perch on the bottom step.

"Move away from the opening."

"Not until you do the same."

"Dammit, Cress, one of us needs to pry out the wood, and one of us must survive. Stop arguing and move aside."

She let out a low sound he was fairly certain was a growl, but she moved.

Ian popped out the second plank. More rocks and soil tumbled onto the steps, pelting him as gravity was given free rein for the first time in a hundred years. He leaned to the side and placed the tire iron behind the final plank. This one cracked in the middle under the pressure, creating a lip over which dirt and rocks fell like a waterfall.

Cascading soil created a cloud of dust, causing him to cough. Steps above, a pinprick of light grew. And grew. His heart pounded as the truth sank in.

They were close to the surface, without a boulder to block their exit. Syria waited just a few feet above them.

Chapter Thirty-Five

UNSURE OF WHAT they would find at the surface, they agreed to wait until nightfall to dig out an opening wide enough to crawl through. With more than an hour to kill, it was the first break they'd had since Zack interrupted their kiss this morning, and as they settled down in the narrow corridor, facing each other and leaning against opposite walls, Ian fantasized for a moment of picking up where they'd left off, when he'd kissed her without holding back.

But things had changed since this morning. Twelve hours ago, he thought he'd ship her off with Raptor, then head to Cizre and start hunting Zack. Twelve hours ago, he'd figured his odds of surviving this mission and returning to the US were close to nil. Thirty minutes ago, he thought they might die trapped in this tunnel.

But now he'd glimpsed daylight, and he was on an irrevocable course for home, or at least his country—he wasn't quite certain home and the US were one and the same—and faced the very real possibility he would survive. Which changed things as far as Cressida was concerned.

He watched her eat her trail mix. She ate each item in order: first a raisin, then a peanut, cashew, almond, and finally an M&M. Then she started over with a raisin. She was probably the type who ate her vegetables first and dessert last. Ian was a handful-of-trail-mix-all-at-once kind of guy, and he had no problem with dessert first.

He plucked the M&Ms from his ration and dropped them in her hands.

She smiled at him. "I can't take your M&Ms. They're the best part."

"That's why you should have them." He'd give her his entire ration if he thought she could navigate Syria without him. But she needed him, so he would duly eat and drink his share.

"Ian—"

"Just enjoy it, Cress. Please?"

Her brow furrowed, and she set the treat aside. He wasn't sure if she was saving it for last or if she planned to slip the colorful candies back into the mix sack, but at least she didn't protest.

"What are you going to do with your life when you get back to the US?" he asked. It was a question he hadn't dared ask when escaping Turkey seemed improbable.

"I don't know. I can't imagine returning to grad school. Tallahassee isn't home, and Todd is so intertwined with everything that happened there and here. I'll miss Suzanne, though." She leaned her head against the chisel-cut wall, her features soft. "I suppose I could move to DC. Erica talked about a job opening up at NHHC, but with grad school, it wasn't really an option." She let out a bitter laugh. "Silver lining." She cleared her throat. "What about you?"

He reached for the flashlight and flicked the switch, enclosing them in pitch darkness. "We should save the batteries for digging out," he said. Plus he could say what he needed to say without seeing her face. And more importantly, she couldn't see his. "If this op is sorted out, and I'm cleared, I might be able to stay on with the CIA as an analyst."

"So…you'll be in DC, then."

His heart pounded. He knew exactly what she was aiming for. "Probably not. With my language skills, I could work on US bases in the Middle East. With the rise of ISIS, they'll need me here."

"So you won't stay in the US."

"Not if I can avoid it."

"I see." He heard the disappointment in her voice.

It was better this way. Letting her know now. There was no room for her in his life. No matter how he felt about her.

"I won't—" She stopped short. She made a noise, which could have been a sob. Or just a hitch in her breath. "I won't return to the Middle East. Ever."

"I know."

Silence stretched between them. Her clothes rustled as she shifted position. Then he heard a slight crunch as she chewed. A moment later, she said, "Thanks for the M&Ms."

He felt pathetic that five M&Ms was the best he had to offer her.

IT TOOK HOURS to dig in the narrow, confined space. Ian tunneled forward while Cressida rebuilt the backstop behind them, ensuring that filling the opening and hiding the tunnel after they escaped wouldn't be a Herculean task.

Ian crawled through the narrow gap first, emerging onto shrub plain on a cloudless summer night. A quick scan of the area confirmed nothing much had changed since Lawrence penned a description of this exit point—remote and distant from aboveground water sources, this area might see nomads or others passing through, but no one had ever settled on this part of the inhospitable steppe.

He gave silent thanks to any and all higher powers that ISIS hadn't set up camp in this area. ISIS would execute Cressida and him without hesitation, and they'd post the video on the Internet for all the world to see.

He tucked his gun into the holster at the small of his back and reached into the hole to take Cressida's hand as she emerged from the darkness. Feet once again on the surface of the earth, she took a slow deep breath, her chest rising as she threw back her shoulders after hours of constraint in the dark, tight shaft.

Like him, she was coated in a fine layer of dirt. Much of her hair had come loose from the braid and was plastered to her temples as sweat dotted her forehead and formed tracks in the film of dirt.

She'd never looked more beautiful.

Well, maybe twice she had, when he'd held her in his arms and made love to her. Her eyes had met his with revealing emotion and sweat glistened on her brow as he brought her to climax.

They needed to be on guard. They were near ISIS-controlled territory in Northern Syria, of all places, but still, he would have this moment. He cradled her dirt-streaked cheeks in his hands and kissed her fast and hard, then said, "Let's fill the hole, then make tracks so we can call Sean."

She nodded, and they set to work, gathering rocks to fill the opening, their work lit only by the moon and stars. Backfilling took nearly as long as digging their way out had, because this qanat had been tunneled through bedrock, and the wind had scoured the surface of dirt. Cressida located a buildup of soil in the lee of a hill a short distance away.

They emptied their backpacks of supplies, and filled both with dirt from the hillside. The makeshift buckets worked to transport dirt to opening. Finally, hole filled, they covered it with stones large and small to disguise it on the rocky landscape.

Cressida stood back, crossed her arms, and frowned. "It won't pass close inspection, but it's probably the best we can do."

Ian shrugged, not willing to admit the tunnel wouldn't be their secret for long. That argument could wait a few hours.

They set off, using Cressida's dive watch compass and the stars to navigate. After walking over a mile from the tunnel, skirting all roads and places rebels or ISIS were likely to inhabit, Ian checked the cell phone for a signal. No luck. They shifted directions, heading east, toward the Tigris, where towns dotted the landscape and they'd be likely to get a signal, however, they were also more likely to come across an armed group who would shoot them on sight.

Finally, at three in the morning, having thankfully avoided rebel and ISIS encampments, he checked the phone again and a faint bar appeared. He handed it to Cressida and said, "Honey, why don't you call Sean?"

CRESSIDA MERELY SAID hello to Sean, then handed the phone back to Ian, so the spy and the mercenary could discuss options. She listened with interest as Ian outlined his plan, unease filtering through her when he explained that he intended to call an asset within YPG—the Syrian Kurdish rebel group—to aid them in crossing the river into Iraq. YPG controlled the river in the northern part of the country, and fortunately, Ian had connections. Or at least he did before he was burned and publicly accused of being associated with PKK rebels—who, if she had her alphabet straight, were currently at odds with YPG. Even though both groups were Kurdish, the PKK and other Kurdish groups had somewhat allied themselves with an al-Qaeda group that was fighting the Syrian government, while the YPG fought both al-Qaeda and the Assad regime.

One concern Ian didn't voice but had Cressida's throat dry with fear: If Ian's YPG contact believed news reports stating Ian had turned to the PKK, then the YPG also had reason to shoot him on sight.

This war had far too many enemies and victims.

Place and time for a river rendezvous set, Ian clicked off. Without pause, he dialed another number and said something in

Kurdish. Moments later, he chatted in animated Kurdish, and she saw another facet to Ian. This wasn't amiable John Baker with a Kurdish flair, nor was it Ian Boyd, master spy. She guessed this was a hybrid player—the manipulator who trafficked in information.

Ian's gaze met hers, and she saw a flash of remorse. Why? What had he said that triggered guilt?

And then it hit her. He was making a deal. He'd never give up the microchip, which meant the only information he had of value to the YPG was the location of the tunnel entrance.

Chapter Thirty-Six

Logically, she knew it was foolish to be angry with him for giving up the tunnel. He was doing it to save their lives, but still, he must have known all along this would be necessary, yet he'd said nothing.

He'd gone through the motions of burying the entrance—burning precious energy and time, when they were weak with hunger and fatigue. Her arms ached from lifting cobbles and carefully placing them so they wouldn't dislodge the weakened panels she'd managed to replace.

But then, the tunnel was valuable if only one group knew about it, so hiding it had been necessary.

Conversation complete, Ian snapped off the phone, plucked the battery from the back, and shoved both in his pocket. "C'mon. We need to hurry. We're rendezvousing with YPG soldiers in less than an hour."

"You told them. Didn't you?"

"Not yet. If I tell them now, they'll have no reason to keep us alive."

"Dammit, Ian! That tunnel is a piece of history, not a political chip to be played!"

"No, Cressida, that tunnel will change the balance of power between several warring factions. It isn't a damn museum to gawk at, and it sure as hell isn't a pretty relic that tells us about the past. It's a strategic, unmonitored entry and exit point from a war-torn country into a NATO country. It's a way for NATO, the UN, even the European Union to smuggle aid, arms, and supplies to rebels who are fighting the good fight. It's a way for the Kurds in Turkey and the Kurds in Syria to align—instead of fight each other—and maybe, just maybe, join up with the Kurds of Northern Iraq—who are already YPG allies—and form a true Kurdish state."

"How long do you think a tunnel like this can remain secret?"

"How long were the Hamas tunnels a secret? Even if word

gets out after a month, it would be a valuable month for whoever is in control."

His gaze swept across the landscape. "Think about what it could mean, Cressida. A true Kurdish state. We're talking about a pro-Western democracy in the heart of the Middle East. We're talking about having a real US ally—and a Muslim one at that—in al-Qaeda and ISIS's primary breeding ground."

She took a step back. "Is that your agenda? Why you joined the CIA? To create Kurdistan? Do you see yourself as some sort of modern-day Lawrence of Kurdistan?"

"No. I joined the Army to fight for my country and took the job with the CIA to continue that fight, in the best way I could contribute, gathering intel and data to help the US maintain an edge over those who would see our democracy destroyed. I don't have an agenda. I'm just looking out for the US's best interests. And my Middle Eastern studies degree combined with my years of living and working in the Middle East tells me that a true, free Kurdistan is very much in the US's best interests."

Here Cressida faltered. She was supremely outmatched in her knowledge of the issues and players in the Middle East, and she wasn't the type to argue a point she disagreed with only on principle. Especially when she didn't have the facts to back it up. And Ian had more facts on the Middle East in his head than she had in all the research books stacked in her apartment in Tallahassee.

"What was Hejan?" she finally asked, realizing she'd never truly understood the factions they were running from, let alone who they were running toward.

Ian smiled, threaded his fingers through hers, and said, "I'll tell you while we walk."

She left her hand in his and nodded, matching his pace as they set out again.

"Hejan Duhoki first came to me about ten months ago."

"To you? He showed up at your door?" she asked.

"No. That's not how my business works. People put out feelers, the Company responds. In this situation, we learned a member of a PKK splinter group prone to violent acts of rebellion was willing to deal. Since I speak Kurdish, Hejan was assigned to me. We met a few times. My gut said he was the real deal: a man disillusioned with his group—not his cause, mind you, but the tactics of the group—who was looking for a way to make up for his mistakes."

"And what were his mistakes? What did Hejan have to make up for?"

"His cell had received a much sought-after supply of shoulder-fired rocket launchers. They were supposed to be used to aid the rebels in Syria—to fight Assad. And they did, except his group's leader sold them to an al-Qaeda faction that's fighting both Assad *and* the YPG Kurdish rebels.

"The al-Qaeda group used a rocket launcher to attack a YPG stronghold. Hejan's brother, Berzan, had joined the Syrian cause and was one of thirty YPG rebels who died in the attack."

Cressida gasped. "Berzan is *dead?*"

Ian nodded. "When you first told me Berzan was your guide, I knew it was a message from Hejan to me, but I didn't know what it meant—beyond the fact that there was no guide waiting for you in Van. I think Hejan intended for me to be your guide all along."

To her, Hejan had been a translator. An idle young man having fun in the big city. She'd been a shallow academic, enjoying a summer project in sultry Turkey, who valued research and history over the modern issues that shaped the country she visited. Shame and guilt settled low in her belly. She'd been superficial. She'd known about the atrocities being committed in Syria, and the plight of Kurds throughout the region, but she'd turned a blind eye to it as she sought selfish academic glory.

She'd asked Hejan, a devout Muslim, to meet her at a *bar*, of all places. "He must have hated me," she murmured.

"No, Cress. Not hate. He was probably grateful for you. You were his opportunity. Hejan knew simply changing sides and fighting for the YPG—as his brother had—wasn't enough. He wanted revenge against the leader who'd betrayed *all* ethnic Kurds. You made his revenge possible.

"I spent months with Hejan on the small stuff," Ian continued. "Minor information exchanges. There was always a chance I was being played, but his story checked out. At the same time, things were getting tense in Ankara. The Turkish government had been sniffing around. There was speculation that we might have a mole, that I'd been identified as CIA and not a Raptor contractor. My boss considered pulling me. Sending me back to the US. My days in Turkey were likely numbered."

What would that mean for Ian? Did he have a life to return to in the US, or would it have been a form of exile? From his tone, she guessed the prospect of living in the US left him adrift. Was it Turkey he loved or espionage? She was tempted to ask but wanted Hejan's story even more and didn't dare sidetrack the conversation with questions.

"A little more than a month ago, Hejan told me something big was coming, that he'd be the first link in a chain that would lead me to the leader of his group. We're talking the man's name, his location, everything we'd need to remove him from the game. The Turkish government wants the splinter group leader—badly. He's organized several coordinated suicide bombings, killing dozens of people, yet after years, no one even knew the bastard's name."

"Hejan didn't know his name?" she asked.

"He said he didn't." Ian shrugged. "If I could bring down the leader—whoever he is—it would have been a reason for the Turkish government to be quietly grateful to the US, which is something we need right now, as Turkey inches ever closer to a conservative Muslim state wishing to cut all ties with the US."

Cressida's mind swirled with the details. She knew the surface of the story—she'd researched Turkey and the unrest in the eastern part of the country extensively in preparation for her trip—but espionage necessarily went far beyond the headlines.

"Hejan had offered me the one bait that would keep me on the hook—a way to get his leader. Naturally, I bit." Ian's fingers tightened around hers, making her wonder what he thought of his decisions in retrospect. "Hejan made it clear that things could—*would*—get dicey on this mission and said I'd be following the courier to Eastern Turkey, most likely to Batman or Van, and from there we'd go south and could end up along the border somewhere between Cizre and Nusaybin. Being the cautious sort, I set up the safe house in Kurubaş, the apartment in Siirt, and another house in Cizre."

He rolled his shoulders as if bracing himself for her reaction. "I'd planned to get you safely out of the country and then head to the Cizre house so I could regroup and go after Zack."

The idea of him staying behind left her chilled. "And now? Is that what you're planning?"

"No. I refuse to trust your safety with anyone else. I don't care how well you know Sean Logan. I don't trust him to keep you safe."

She found his habit of stopping just short of telling her he cared irritating. But then, did it matter that he cared? He planned to continue on in the Middle East. There was no place for her in his life. "Back to Hejan," she said, her voice harder, maybe, than the conversation warranted.

He glanced sideways at her, his expression unreadable, and she wondered if he knew exactly why she was annoyed.

When in northern Syria with a spy wanted dead or alive en route to a rendezvous with separatists who might shoot them both on sight, it was totally the time to obsess over the fact that he'd all but told her there was no future for them.

Sometimes I'm such a girl.

"Hejan disappeared for a few weeks, and I was concerned. Then, two days before the drop in Antalya, he contacted me. We met, and he told me what was supposed to be on the microchip, as if nabbing the leader of his group wasn't incentive enough."

"Did you believe him?"

"I did."

"Why?"

"Because Hejan was the money guy. He didn't move the weapons that killed his brother, he moved the money that paid for the weapons. And when they were sold to al-Qaeda, he received, for his group, the payment."

"Hejan was a...*banker*? I thought he was a kid. A college student out to make extra money with translation work for the university."

"That's because that's what Hejan wanted you to see. He was young—early twenties—he grew up near Van and moved to the city when he was sixteen, determined to get away from rural farm life. He got a job at a bank there as a teller. He worked his way up from simple transactions and account setups to more complex business accounts and finally to money laundering for the local PKK group. So, you see, when he told me the microchip would contain names, I believed him. He'd spent months tracing back through accounts, connecting names to account numbers. Information that was supposed to be buried."

"Why did he do that—put the list on the chip?"

"I think it was another carrot for me, but he said his leader was hoping to identify who was funding both sides to keep the unrest ongoing. Organizations like Raptor—"

"Alec Ravissant would never—"

"—*used* to be, under Robert Beck. As I said before, Ravissant checked out. So did Hatcher. But the former CEO was dirty as hell and stirring up the Middle East pot with abandon."

She nodded. "Keith spent too many years with the SEALs, putting terrorists down, to have any part in funding them."

"He was a sniper, right?"

"Yes."

Ian's voice dropped, showing a hint of respect. "I look forward to meeting him."

She liked the lack of equivocation. That he *would* meet Keith. Because meeting Keith meant they'd both make it back to the US. And she was having trouble believing this un fairy tale could have a happy ending that included their safe arrival in the US.

She touched the pendant that was once again around her neck. "What do we do with this, then? Do you think the list is on it?"

"I do."

"Is that why Zack and Todd were following us? Even more than wanting the location of the tunnel, they need the microchip?"

"I think Zack is primarily after the chip. According to Hejan's note, Todros is after the tunnel."

"Todd had plenty of time to catch up with us as we were digging our way out. But he never showed."

"A reason to think Hejan was right about Todros. Hejan *knew* him—meaning that fight in the bar wasn't what it seemed to us at the time. Hejan was sent here—in the weeks he'd disappeared—to act as translator for Todros and help find the tunnel."

"I guess I was the perfect patsy," she said. "A clueless American academic, unable to speak even simple Kurdish words, no one would suspect me of carrying a microchip to further a violent insurrection. *I* didn't even suspect me." She frowned. "But Hejan crossed everyone and hid the chip in the necklace instead of storing the information on the USB drive in the digital recorder. He made sure you'd follow me and made me promise not to take off the pendant. Ever."

"Hejan had his own agenda," Ian said. "Revenge for Berzan."

"Why was Todd in Antalya? Did he kill Hejan?"

"I don't think so. My guess is he felt remorse for what was about to happen to you and went to the bar to warn you. To stop you."

"I never would have believed him."

Ian frowned. "But Hejan couldn't take that risk. He couldn't let you talk to Todros, not until after you'd reached Van, so he ejected him from the bar and later convinced you to flee the hotel."

"But then who killed him if not Todd?"

"Hejan double- and triple-crossed so many people that night. Anyone in his cell was capable of killing him."

"He was late meeting me. By over an hour." Movement in the stars above caught her eye. A spy satellite? Never in her life had she considered such a thing when spotting a faint moving light in the sky, but now, she couldn't shake off the idea as nonsense, as she would have done ten days ago.

"That was unusual for him," Ian said. "His evasive route probably took longer than he'd planned. I didn't need to follow him—he'd told me where the drop would take place. And the people who knew you were the intended mule would have known to follow you."

She considered that night as they slowly strolled over dry ground. "The nightclub was my research trip send-off party. Suzanne planned it—everyone on the project was invited. She invited Hejan when he came out to our camp on the island—he was doing translation work for my advisor as well." She inhaled a deep breath of cool night air. "I want to hate Hejan for giving me that chip. For setting me up. But I would have been in danger even if he hadn't given me the pendant, wouldn't I?"

"Todros said you could find the tunnel. You were in danger no matter what. Hejan made sure I'd follow you, and he was confident we'd end up working together—the note was addressed to us both. I think he wanted me by your side to protect and guide you."

"So I'd deliver his damn chip or out of concern for me?"

Ian shrugged. "All I know is Hejan had no intention of you delivering the data to anyone but the CIA."

They reached the top of a rise, and the steppe unfurled before them: miles of nothing, but in the far distance, she thought she saw dark structures dotting the landscape in the early dawn light. The edge of civilization at war.

Ian pulled out his cell, inserted the battery, and dialed. Again he spoke in rapid Kurdish. Call completed, he removed the battery from the phone and handed both to her. "I want you to hide below, in the thick shrubs at the base of the hill. Watch. Wait. If they shoot me, don't move. Don't make a sound. Not until they leave. Then call Logan. Understand?"

Her throat had gone dry, but she nodded.

"Even if they torture me and I beg you to come out of hiding, do not do it. Only come out if you hear me say—" He paused, then said, "Hay-Adams." His jaw tensed. "You got that? Hay-Adams. If I don't say Hay-Adams, stay put."

She gave a sharp nod. If he could be calm and detached, so would she. "How long until they get here?"

"They said thirty minutes—so my guess is ten. You need to get out of sight. They'll have binoculars and will see us long before we see them."

She nodded and pivoted on her heel. He'd just said being shot or tortured were on the short list of possible outcomes, then dismissed her without consulting her first. She was back to feeling helpless and was terrified for his safety.

She'd taken three steps when he said, "Cressida…"

She stopped, her back stiff. She couldn't turn and face him.

Footsteps scraped across the rocky ground. He halted, so close she felt the heat of his body. "I'm not sending you away because you have the pendant." His voice was low, raspy, positively bursting with emotion that pushed up against the dam of his control.

"Then why are you sending me to hide, Ian? Because I really don't relish the idea of watching people torture you and not being able to do anything to stop it."

He let out a harsh growl. "I'm sending you away because if I'm wrong about these people, you could get hurt. And I can't let that happen."

At last she turned. "*Why*, Ian?"

His nostrils flared, then his expression shuttered. "Because getting you to safety is my mission."

The hope that had been building deflated, bouncing around in her chest like an untied balloon that had slipped from her fingers. "Okay, then. If you need me, you know where I'll be." She turned and set off down the hill.

"Hay-Adams, Cressida." The words floated in the air, full of meaning he wouldn't voice.

He'd kissed her, held her, let her know in a dozen ways in the last twenty-four hours that he wanted her, and, more important, he cared about her. But he'd also made it clear his life was here, in the Middle East. She wanted The Hay-Adams, held on to that fantasy like the lifeline it was meant to be, but not if he wasn't offering her more than orgasms. She could have those on her own.

She scanned the low shrubs and spotted a decent hiding place. She took off her backpack and tucked herself down into the thick branches, then pulled the gun from the pack and checked the load. She was ready.

She studied Ian, who stood ever vigilant at the top of the rise. He was different, nothing like any man she'd ever known. And for the first time in her life, she knew without question her instincts about him were solid. He was the one for her, and she wanted all of him. Everything. Love. Commitment. Cohabitating. She hated picket fences, but if he was a fan, it wasn't a deal breaker.

But for that reason, she couldn't show up for a weeklong tryst at The Hay-Adams. It would hurt too much when he walked away.

If he intended to check his emotions at the door, she'd check out altogether.

But before it was time to face everything she couldn't have with him, he had to survive the next ten minutes. She heard the low rumble of a vehicle and was thankful the shrubs were thick and concealing. Not to mention that her top was so coated in dirt, it was now mottled earth tones—a perfect, natural camouflage.

The vehicle, an old Toyota Land Cruiser, approached slowly, and Cressida suspected the two dark bars poking out on both sides were gun barrels of one kind or another. Sure enough, as the Toyota drew closer and turned to go up the hill toward Ian, she got a better view. Machine gun muzzle. Maybe an AK-47? She didn't really know guns.

Her heart went into overdrive as the old Cruiser pulled alongside Ian—who stood as remote and still as a marble statue with his hands in the air.

A door on the Toyota opened, and someone got out. Only bits of the words came down to Cressida, the voice so faint, she wasn't even certain they spoke Kurdish.

She should have chosen a closer shrub.

They spoke for several minutes, Ian never taking his eyes off the muzzle pointed at his chest. Finally, he moved forward and pressed his hands against the vehicle as someone patted him down.

They must have determined he was safe, because he dropped his hands. He never once looked Cressida's way. She marveled at his control and wondered if it was military training or CIA.

Probably both.

One of the YPG soldiers laughed, and the melodic sound carried down to her. A woman? How…surprising. Wasn't this a Muslim group?

After several minutes of conversation, Ian started down the slope toward her. When he was within easy earshot, he said, "Hay-Adams, Cressida." The soldiers waited behind him, but their machine guns were pointed up, not at his back, thank goodness. "Ollie ollie all come free."

She smiled and shook her head. Worst. Hide-and-seek game. *Ever.*

"I thought it was Ollie ollie oxen free?" she said as she extracted herself from the bush.

He chuckled. He seemed lighter somehow. "Now how would that make sense?"

"Well, for starters, who is Ollie?" She brushed brambles from her clothes as she stood up straight. With a glance up the hill, she said, "Are we really free oxen?"

He plucked a twig from her hair. "Yes. They want us to locate the tunnel on a map. They'll send out a team to confirm. If they find it, then an hour after sunset tonight, they'll take us across the river. All we can do is wait and pray for a cloudy night."

She nodded. One day in Syria. Then on to Iraq.

Chapter Thirty-Seven

ALL FOUR SOLDIERS were women, and they were curious about Cressida, wanting to know her relationship with Ian and about her work in the US. But none of them spoke English, so Ian provided the translation for both sides of the conversation, which made it interesting when they asked about Ian.

"He's arrogant and bossy," she answered. "Refuses to voice his emotions and likes to pretend he doesn't have them. He's dedicated to his mission. Being a spy is probably the only thing he really cares about. But he's decent in bed."

Ian choked on a laugh and said something in Kurdish to the soldiers without missing a beat.

Cressida was similarly curious about the women and asked several questions of her own. Ian explained that the Kurds in Syria had no problem with training women for combat. Kurdish views on women's rights were one of the reasons jihadists and al-Qaeda had targeted them.

There was no doubt these women were true soldiers. They moved with the same skill and agility as any man in uniform she'd ever seen, ever alert and ready to lay down bullets to clear their path if need be.

Fortunately, there was no need, and they were taken to a house in the heart of a Kurdish stronghold. Somehow, telling these women fighters the location of the tunnel felt better to Cressida. Not just better, it felt good. Which made no sense, because, regardless of gender, the tunnel would be used strategically. But maybe this wasn't a choice of lesser evils. Maybe they'd allied with the right side.

Cressida couldn't fault what these people—these *women*—were fighting for: freedom from an oppressive government, the right to an education, the right to work, the right to live and make their own choices, and the right not to be subjected to chemical weapons attacks.

Little things she'd taken for granted as an American woman.

After they pinpointed the tunnel based on Cressida's calculations of the distances they'd traveled, she was led to a bathroom, complete with a deep claw-foot tub. *Oh, blessed plumbing.*

She stripped off her dirty, sweat-soaked T-shirt and jeans, noting streaks of blood on the shirt from scrapes earned while digging their way out of a dark, dry tomb. She soaked a long time in the hot water, easing aching muscles while ridding herself of layers of dirt. With closed eyes, she allowed herself to indulge in a fantasy of a shared bath with Ian in a deluxe suite in a luxury hotel, but a glance around her surroundings reminded her that she didn't need luxury to be happy. She figured she'd be content anywhere with Ian.

After the bath, she returned to the living room, which was lined with narrow cots, a makeshift military barrack in what had once been a single-family home. Exhausted from days of walking, digging, and well over twenty-four hours since she'd last slept, she collapsed on a cot, too tired to even wonder where Ian was. Guarded and tense, she couldn't imagine being able to sleep in spite of her exhaustion. She listened to the quiet conversation of soldiers—both male and female—being carried on in the next room. Unable to understand the low, even sounds, her brain morphed them into a soft white noise that offered comfort, a signal that all was fine in the war zone, allowing her to drift into a light sleep.

※

IAN WATCHED CRESSIDA sleep, her dark, damp hair a shimmering halo around her face. It was a relief, almost, to be able to look at her without seeing the fear and hurt in her eyes. Fear he'd triggered. Hurt he'd caused.

He'd known from their first meeting she had a strong need for male approval, and when he'd read her bio later, he'd understood why. Yet even knowing this, he'd pushed and manipulated, finally taking what she offered but giving her none of what she wanted in return.

He wanted her. Unequivocally. He'd meant his vow about the hotel, and if she agreed to it, he'd sure as hell follow through.

He'd lay down his life to get her out of this mess. But could he give her more than his body?

He couldn't imagine that. He'd been in the espionage game too long to have the kind of heart that did anything other than pump blood.

His life was an elaborate poker game. Bluffing, high stakes. He always had to be prepared to fold and wait for the next hand or go all in, because he'd known when he started playing there'd be no walking away from the table.

Ian was an excellent poker player. But then, he loved the game. His boss—and now Cressida—had speculated it was the *only* thing he loved, and they were both probably right. But now the game could end. One card left to draw. His opponent was sitting on an inside straight, while Ian held three jacks. With the right card, it was anyone's hand.

And here he was, staring at Cressida, thinking about the game. She deserved better than a coldhearted bastard whose life was an exercise in deceit. She'd had enough deceit.

One of the soldiers—a woman—sidled up to him and whispered, "You don't look at her like she's an assignment, Ian Boyd."

Thank God the woman spoke Kurdish, as she echoed the words he'd told all the soldiers when they quizzed Cressida with eager enthusiasm because it was rare for them to meet an American woman of like age.

Ian shuttered his expression, turning on the spy with ease. "Did they find the tunnel?" he asked.

She nodded. "We will deliver you across the river, as agreed." She nodded toward the kitchen in the back of the house. "There is food. Wake her?"

He paused, considering. Cressida had to be hungry, but she needed sleep even more. The river crossing would be dangerous, as would be the drive to Erbil. She had to be rested and ready, and they had hours until they set out. "Not yet. I'll make sure she eats before we leave."

With a nod, the soldier left, and Ian stretched out on the cot next to Cressida. He needed to be ready for the crossing too.

He slept for several hours, waking in the early evening. Cressida was up. She sat quietly in the corner, gazing out the window. Lost in thought. He assembled two plates of food and returned to her side. They ate in the gathering darkness. Light created a target, and while this house, this neighborhood was currently safe, everyone knew that could change in a flash, so no lights were lit. Ever.

The lengthening gray shadows reminded Ian of their first meal together, at the restaurant in Van, when he'd introduced her to Kurdish cuisine. She licked her fingers after taking a bite, and that fast, Ian was hard.

Because he had heretofore unknown masochistic tendencies, he slid a bite of *shish taouk* from a skewer and dipped it in a sauce. "Try this," he said, bringing the morsel to her lips.

As he'd hoped, she took a bite. Her beautiful brown eyes closed, a soft smile and relaxed lidded eyes said she savored the flavor. Those heavy lids lifted to a sexy half-mast as she leaned forward and took the rest of the bite. This time she brazenly flicked her tongue against his fingers.

The woman was a sadist. And he her willing victim.

They stared at each other in silence across the shadowy table. Finally, he cleared his throat and said, "Wheels up in thirty."

She rolled her eyes. "Chicken."

When it came to her? Probably. But he owed her the unvarnished truth. "This is my life, Cress. How I feel doesn't matter. I'm a spy."

"Not anymore."

She'd shown her cards too soon. It was a solid move, but spying was too deeply ingrained. After years in the business, he couldn't handle love and the vulnerabilities it invited. But that didn't change the fact that he wanted her. If she let him, next time he'd seduce her properly and wouldn't be a raging ass afterward. "One week," he said.

She raised a brow in question.

"The Hay-Adams or wherever you want to go. I can give you a week."

She shook her head. "I don't want ephemeral. I can get that from a bar pickup seven days a week. That's not what I want from you." She stood and left the room. A moment later, he heard her in the kitchen, offering to help wash using words she must have learned from the women in the nomad camp.

Pain lodged in his gut over the finality in her rejection. He'd expected it. Hell, he deserved it. But it didn't make accepting it any easier.

He occupied himself before their departure with helping the soldiers prep for the river crossing: checking fuel tanks, and rehashing the plan, going over the maps. Busy work, as well as a strange ending to what had been an intense, private journey.

At last they were on the boat, a familiar, simple aluminum

riveted hull propelled with an outboard motor and tiller steering. He could be back in Chicago prepping for a day on Lake Michigan, except this was nothing like that, with everyone on the boat armed with machine guns and the precious cargo to be delivered was the woman he wanted with every beat of his cold heart.

The crossing itself was almost anticlimactic after everything they'd been through.

A large, dark Humvee waited on the rise above the opposite bank. The team of Kurdish soldiers pointed their machine guns at the vehicle with unflinching vigilance. Ian pulled his own gun, and motioned for Cressida to do the same.

They would take no foolish chances.

The skipper steered the boat toward the beach, raising the motor as he did so. They ran aground, and two soldiers in front hopped over the bow onto the truncated beach.

From the shrubs that lined the bank, Ian heard the prearranged bird call. Sean Logan and his team.

Upon hearing the sound, Cressida tucked her gun away and jumped over the gunwale, splashing into the shallow water as she raced up the beach.

"Cressida! Wait."

She ignored him, completely unmindful that she'd just created a target of herself. Ian would be damned before he let anyone take a shot at her. He darted after her, catching her around the waist and pulling her back against his chest. "Wait."

She shoved at him. "Let me go! We know it's Sean."

"Yes, but there could be others. Like Zack. And Todros. They could be waiting to take a shot at you."

She froze. "Damn. I'm sorry! I didn't think—"

"It's okay. This isn't your world. It's mine."

She leaned her forehead on his chest. "Your world sucks."

"Tell me about it."

Their Kurdish escort surrounded them and walked them up the short beach. At the bank, Cressida glanced around for permission to climb. Ian gave a short nod, remaining at her back.

She'd taken two steps up the soft, silty slope, when a black man in fatigues emerged from the foliage, crouched down, and thrust his hand to her. "Hey, Cress. Long time no see."

She let out a soft squeal and took his hand. He pulled her up and dropped her on the bank next to him, moving as he did so to block her from view of the river. As soon as her feet landed, she threw her arms around him.

Jealousy rocked Ian when Logan's arms circled her and crushed her to his chest. Christ, he was pathetic. It was one thing to be jealous of Todros Ganem—the son of a bitch had lived with Cressida for the better part of a year—but he had zero cause to be jealous of Logan, and a million reasons to be grateful she counted the man as one of her friends.

But he couldn't imagine how a man could be her friend and *not* want her. It was illogical, unthinkable. Like Earth without gravity. Impossible.

For the first time he considered how he'd feel someday upon hearing the news Cressida had fallen in love. That she'd gotten married. Or was having another man's child.

How could he live with himself, knowing she could have been his, but he'd pushed her away?

He climbed the bank and was proud of himself for not yanking her from the Raptor operative's arms.

Cressida pulled back. "Damn, you're a sight for sore eyes." She nodded to Ian. "Sean Logan, this is Ian Boyd."

The man offered his hand while giving Ian an assessing perusal. They shook hands. Firm, efficient. Not quite friendly.

That was okay with Ian. And he wouldn't mind at all if the man would take his hand off the small of Cressida's back.

The possessive feeling was probably a residual effect of being responsible for her safety for so long.

Yeah. He couldn't swallow that lie, but if Cressida noticed his reaction, maybe she would.

Logan glanced down at the YPG rebels who waited, and waved to his team. Three men stepped forward, each carrying a large cardboard box, which they passed down into upraised arms.

"What's going on?" she asked.

"We're paying the ransom."

"Ransom?" she asked, her voice pitching higher than usual. "Weapons?"

Logan shook his head. "Food. Aid for families caught in the middle. And we'd have brought the supplies even if they hadn't asked—err, demanded."

She smiled, leaning into Logan, and the man draped his arm around her shoulder and steered her to the Humvee. "Get inside. It's armored. You'll be safe. I need to talk to Boyd." When she started to protest, he added firmly, "Alone."

With a frown, she climbed into the vehicle, and Logan turned to him.

Ian nodded to the last of the boxes as it was handed off. "What's really in the boxes?"

"Like I said, food. Raptor doesn't deal in arms."

"Anymore," Ian couldn't help but add.

Logan nodded. "Not since Rav bought the company."

Ian smiled as the soldiers loaded the boat. "Did they really demand a ransom?"

"They did. They weren't afraid to seize an opportunity. Civil war does that."

Ian silently agreed. If the women who'd picked them up from the steppe had for one moment considered Ian a threat, they'd have shot him in an instant. It didn't take balls to make a soldier. Far from it. All you needed was desperation, and beheadings by ISIS and a chemical weapons attack on civilians launched by their own government made for a highly desperate population.

"Keith wanted me to warn you, odds are when we land at Andrews, you'll be taken into custody. Cressida's word will go a long way toward swaying the attorney general to get involved, but…she doesn't have the best track record, and there's only so much Dominick can do. The CIA and FBI don't always play nice." Logan's gaze flicked to the boat. "This is your chance to disappear quietly. We can say there was a firefight during the crossing. You fell in the Tigris."

Did Logan want him to take this out?

More important, was it what Ian wanted?

If he stayed, he could go after Zack. He had a place in Cizre. He could finish the mission.

Odds were, if he stayed, he'd never clear his name. He'd disappear into the Middle East, never able to return home. The world, his boss, his Delta Force team, they'd all believe him a traitor. But he could still gather intel for his country. It would just be delivered through different channels.

He had no doubt Cressida would try to clear him. With the chip, she might even succeed. But if she didn't, if she couldn't, he'd never see her again.

Stay or go?

"I'm going home," he said firmly. Strange to call it home. He didn't have a clue where home was.

Chapter Thirty-Eight

Erica Scott's unexpected guests set her teeth on edge. But then, she'd always considered Dr. Patrick Hill, the executive director of the MacLeod-Hill Exploration Institute, to be something of a self-aggrandizing braggart, and she was biased against Cressida's friend Suzanne, ever since learning the woman had abandoned Cressida in a bar in Antalya so she could hook up with Hill, right after Todd Ganem appeared.

What kind of friend does that?

The same kind who was now making Cressida's ordeal all about herself—her fear, her worry, her distress over the bestie she'd ignored as soon as Hill was in the picture. Erica wondered if Suzanne was similar to Cressida's mother. As a woman who also had mother issues, Erica *did* understand why Cressida would befriend her.

But still, the woman took drama to a new level, and she wondered how Cressida put up with Suzanne's aggravating narcissism. Erica had no patience for narcissists, and this couple was a dynamic duo of self-absorption. They also weren't hiding their disappointment that they'd been shunted in Erica's direction, rather than visiting with the attorney general, the senator, or even the Raptor CEO.

Frankly, Erica wasn't all that thrilled to be stuck with them either, but someone had to keep these two entertained and away from Keith, who was in constant contact with Sean while the field operative managed an extraction that included passing through ISIS-held territory in Iraq.

Erica shook her head and stepped into the kitchen to grab cheese and crackers for her guests. She was still baffled as to how her life could include spies, mercenaries, and extractions of friends from the Middle East. She was an underwater archaeologist for the US Navy, married to a tech security expert. Their lives should be bureaucratic and normal, maybe even appear a little dull—although life with Lee would never be dull.

The front door opened. Lee was home. *Thank goodness.* Someone to share her misery over having to deal with Hill and morning sickness at the same time. She popped a dry cracker into her mouth before delivering the platter to the living room and greeting Lee with a kiss.

He smiled down at her, but there was something in his eye that sent a shiver of fear up her spine.

"Will you excuse us for a moment?" Lee asked their guests.

Suzanne let out a slight sniff. "If it has to do with Cressida, we have a right to know."

Lee didn't bother to lessen the coldness of his stare. "It's personal and none of your business."

Wow, and here Erica thought *she* had limited patience for Suzanne. Of the two of them, Lee was the diplomat. This must be big. She cast Suzanne an apologetic look she didn't feel and followed Lee into their bedroom.

He pulled her into his arms the moment the door closed. "I'm sorry you've had to deal with them, Shortcake."

She tucked her head against his chest and listened to his firmly beating heart. "Cressida crossed the river? They made it okay?"

"Yes. They're driving to Erbil now."

"Then what's wrong? Is Cressida hurt? Is there a problem with ISIS?"

"Sean says she's fine. Boyd didn't take the out. He's coming back with her."

"That's what we want, right?"

"I think so, but it's a mess. Boyd is wanted for three murders in Turkey, and Curt just learned Turkish authorities intend to charge Cressida with the murder of Hejan Duhoki."

"But…Hejan was alive when Cressida left the hotel room."

"That was according to Boyd, who they think is her accomplice. Apparently, on the day of his death, Duhoki stole a large chunk of money from a relief organization. No one knows where the money is, but he stored the retrieval information on a USB drive. They're saying Cressida killed him, took the drive, and jetted off to Van with Boyd to collect the money."

THE JET WAS the most beautiful hunk of metal and machinery Cressida had ever seen. It was bigger than she expected for a private jet, but then, according to Sean, it had long-range capabilities, and could fly from Erbil to DC without the need to refuel. Plus it was part of the Raptor fleet of jets, so while it was at the highest end of privately owned aircraft, it was outfitted to carry mercenary security teams in and out of war zones. Inside, it was divided into sections: the cockpit; the main cabin with a conference area at the front consisting of a circular table and six seats, followed by three rows of seats to hold nine more passengers; a mini galley on one side behind the rows, and a lavatory that included a separate shower stall on the opposite side; and finally, the entire back quarter of the jet was a plush private cabin for dignitaries taking advantage of Raptor's private security arm.

Trina had flown on the jet with Keith once on a business trip to Rio—as one does when one is dating the CEO—and had told Cressida that after enjoying a private cabin, flying coach would never be the same. Cressida had laughed and called her spoiled, and Trina didn't disagree.

Now that Cressida viewed the luxurious cabin herself, she had to admit, this kind of comfort would be something she wouldn't mind getting used to. She flicked a glance in Ian's direction, well aware that part of what Trina had enjoyed about the flight probably had more to do with Keith's presence than the fact the mattress was made of memory foam.

Well, Cressida had every intention of claiming the cabin—after a week of sleeping on rocky ground, small cots, and hard pallets, a fancy mattress sounded like heaven—but she had no intention of sharing it with Ian. It wasn't that she didn't want him, it was that she didn't want the heartache and regret that would come later.

It didn't take long to prep for the flight once they were all on board. Their group included two pilots, Sean and three Raptor operatives, plus Ian and Cressida. In the main cabin, they took seats around the conference table as they taxied to the runway.

"What's with the door?" she asked. "I've never been on a jet with a door that slides to the side like that."

"It was retrofitted to open in-flight for jumps," Sean said. "An unusual feature for this type of aircraft, but necessary to deposit operatives in hot zones."

She nodded and shivered. Jumping out of an airplane had never been on her to-do list. She glanced at the men seated around the table. All were former military of one branch or another, and she knew Sean had been a SEAL, like Keith. "Am I the only one here who doesn't know how to jump out of a plane?"

The men all glanced around the table, speaking some silent alpha-male language she wasn't privy to, then in unison, all five nodded.

A reminder she wasn't of their ilk.

When sitting inside a private jet fleeing the Middle East in the middle of the night, accompanied by a spy and several mercenaries, one might be prone to reflect upon the choices that had gotten them there.

Choices like Todd. Or the decision not to tell anyone about the map. Or her plan to find the tunnel on her own, when she could have invited Todd or Suzanne or any number of students who would have happily participated in the project.

If she hadn't been so secretive, Hejan wouldn't have been able to set her up. Ian wouldn't have had reason to follow her. She wouldn't have been mugged. She wouldn't have shot a man in the throat.

As the plane reached cruising altitude, the men around her talked shop. Ian offered minimal details to Sean on their activities after they disappeared in Van. For him, the mission was still classified. Burned or not, he couldn't talk about it.

Cressida, under no such restrictions, had already provided her version of events on the long drive to Erbil and had little to add to the conversation. She stood and stretched. "Gentlemen, if you'll excuse me, I'm going to claim the bed, if that's okay?"

Sean nodded. "It's yours. Trina called dibs on it for you." His smile was warm. Friendly. She'd always liked Sean. For a hard-core military man, he wasn't nearly as closed off as *some* former Special Forces men she knew.

In the private cabin, she crawled into the comfy bed but wasn't really tired. She didn't know what she was. After days of being on the run and on edge, she could let her guard down. At last.

She wasn't sure she knew how.

Even when she slept today in the YPG house, her sleep had been light. Guarded.

Back in her old life, when she was too wired to sleep, she'd pick up a book and read until three a.m., enjoying someone else's scary adventure from a safe distance. She glanced at the bookshelf and laughed, seeing Keith's hand at work in the books they offered guests on the plush private jet. True to form, the small library was mostly nonfiction military accounts and arranged according to the Dewey decimal system.

Keith Hatcher, mercenary CEO, closet librarian.

There were a few romances in the fiction section—mostly books by Trina's favorite author, Darcy Burke—interspersed with the political thrillers Keith favored. Cressida was decidedly not in the mood for a thriller, and frankly, the idea of a romance depressed her. Not that she'd be able to focus on a book right now anyway.

She turned off the light and lay down on the bed, determined to try to sleep. But the dark cabin turned into the dark tunnel, and she spent ten minutes trying to banish the feeling before giving up and turning on the bedside light again.

She was too wound up, too haunted by the events of the last days, to rest.

There was a stack of Raptor stationary in the drawer of a mini writing desk. Cressida pulled out a few sheets and grabbed a pen, then settled on the bed with the paper braced on a hardback book.

When she was a girl, she'd kept a journal, until One found it and cruelly mocked her childish hopes and fears. She'd never again been able to commit her innermost thoughts to paper. Hell, One might even be the reason she'd been so secretive with her dissertation research, burying the information on her own computer's hard drive.

She crumpled the paper without writing a word and chucked the pen across the room at the same moment the door opened.

"Ow!" Ian said. "I guess I had that coming."

Her heart pounded at the mere sight of him. It wasn't good how much she wanted him. "Don't you know how to knock?"

"I didn't want to wake you if you were sleeping."

"Liar."

"Yes, I am. A damn good one too. But not this time."

"Then why are you here?"

He stepped into the room and closed the door behind him. "I like watching you sleep."

The statement was so bald. So open. She had to believe it. "You're here to watch me sleep? That's a little creepy." Not really, though. Not after what they'd been through.

"When you're asleep, you aren't glaring at me. You aren't sad. You aren't angry. You're just beautiful. When you're sleeping, I'm not fucking up and pissing you off."

She didn't like the fluttery feeling his words triggered in her belly. Giving in would give him the power to hurt her. "Except for the creepy part about watching me sleep."

His smile lit his eyes. Damn, he was one gorgeous man. He must have shaved in the lavatory while she prowled in the bedroom and tried to sleep, because his beard was gone. She'd liked the rugged beard that scratched against her skin, but now that it was gone, her fingers itched to stroke his smooth cheeks. A fire lit low in her belly as she imagined the soft slide of his bare face against her skin.

He was once again the intensely handsome man she'd glimpsed in a crowded airport terminal, and all the possibilities of that moment, when they'd been complete strangers, came flooding back to her.

Oh damn. Resisting him—if he'd entered the cabin with thoughts of seducing her—would be difficult. Saying no to him now would hurt nearly as much as saying yes, then having him disappear from her life.

He took a step closer, and she held up a hand. "Stop. What are you doing here, Ian?"

"What did you mean when you took down Zack and you said you'd promised yourself you'd never do that again?"

Oh shit. He really knew how to zero in on the weak links in her armor. She cleared her suddenly dry throat. "Will it ease your conscience if you hold me and listen to my sob story? Is that what's in it for you? A chance to rack up bonus points so you can later tell yourself you treated me kindly even as you rejected me? Because I have no interest in sharing my darkest memories with someone who has every intention of walking away from me at the first opportunity."

He took another step toward her. "No. That's not what I want. I want the name of every man who has ever hurt you, so I can hunt each one down and make him pay."

The fluttery feeling in her belly imploded at that, and her breath hitched as she tried to get her traitorous body, that damn traitorous heart, under control.

All she'd ever wanted was for someone to treat her as if she mattered. To have her back. To look at her as Ian did right now, as if he truly, deeply cared about her.

"I will not accept just a week, Ian. I deserve better than that." And she meant it. No more devaluing herself when it came to relationships.

He sat on the bed next to her and reached for her hand. "I know that. And I know you deserve way better than me."

She wanted to interrupt him, to tell him he shouldn't devalue himself either. But she had a feeling he was about to say something far more important and didn't dare derail him. As it was, her heart pounded so hard, it threatened to drown out his words.

"I've never been in a position to offer more than a fling, and I've never met anyone I wanted for more than that even if I could. My life was the Army, and then the CIA. Sure, other men had families. Lives. Wives. But I've never really had anyone except the best friend whose grandmother taught me Turkish when I was a boy. He died in a training accident when we were nineteen. He never even made it out of boot camp. It was a dumb, horrible waste."

She gasped, recognizing he covered a world of pain in those blunt words. "Were you there? Was he in your unit?"

"No. I was already in Afghanistan. He joined a year after me. Between losing my best friend and then losing members of my team in combat, I stopped...*caring* isn't the right word... I'm still human. I care. But I did what I could to cut myself off from caring too much. I would lay down my life for any of the guys on my Delta Force team—they remain my closest friends to this day—but do you want to know how long it's been since I've even emailed any of them?"

She nodded.

"Two...maybe three years." He paused and took a deep breath. "I threw myself into my life as a covert operative. I stopped being a friend or making real friends. You pretty much nailed it when you asked if spies could have friends. I'm sure some do. But I'm not one of them."

He threaded his fingers through hers, staring at their entwined hands, not meeting her gaze. "I'm not a spy anymore. I haven't quite come to grips with that yet. Even when I was in the Army, I was running covert ops for Delta." He shook his head. "But I'm out. I'm leaving the game. Staying in would cost too much. I don't know what's going to happen to me when we land. I could be arrested and disappear into a secret CIA prison, or I may find myself exonerated, but with no job. No prospects. No home. No friends."

She pulled his hand to her chest, placing it over her heart. "Is that what you want from me? Friendship? Because you already have that."

He leaned in and pressed his mouth to hers, slowly. Tentatively. Nothing like the cocksure man who'd kissed her so many times in the last week.

She opened her mouth to deepen the kiss when it became clear he wouldn't. She guessed he wouldn't push her, not now.

She caressed those smooth cheeks with both hands as she slid her tongue against his in a sweet, prolonged kiss that was neither a hello nor a good-bye, and somehow entirely different from all the kisses that had come before.

She pulled back, still cradling his face, and met his intense gaze.

He cleared his throat. "I want you as more than a friend, Cressida. I want to be your lover, your partner, your champion. Because when I think about saying good-bye to you, it hurts already, even when you're right here in front of me." He took both of her hands in his and rubbed his thumbs across her knuckles. "I don't know how to be a boyfriend and am fairly certain I'll be lousy at it, but if you're willing to have me, I'd like to try."

She stared into his gray eyes, taking his words in. He might not have said three particular words, but what he said was even better than M&Ms and blue and red pimpernels.

"You're, uh, sort of leaving me hanging here, Cress." The discomfort in his voice was actually quite charming.

She leaned forward and brushed her lips lightly over his, then said, "One sec." She crawled across the bed and opened the cabinet where she'd stuffed her backpack. She dug through the pack—shoving aside clothes that were so filthy, she'd happily burn them when she got home—and plucked out the one notebook she'd managed to keep when she pared down to the backpack in Siirt. She opened the book to the page where she'd pressed one perfect pimpernel, and showed it to him. "It seems only fair that I give you flowers this time. I'd give you this one, except my plan is to keep it forever. So I'll only give it to you if you're planning to stick around."

His brows drew together. "You kept it? Even after I was an abominable ass to you after?"

"Are you kidding? You gave me pimpernels in a nomad tent. I think it was the most romantic gesture of my life. Of course I kept one."

He chuckled. "That was pretty smooth, wasn't it?"

"You've set the bar high. I'm going to expect my boyfriend to top it in the future."

"Damn. I'm doomed. But still, I'll take this flower." He lifted the notebook from her hands and set it on the side table. "And I'll take you." And then his hands were on her hips, pulling her against him until they were chest to chest. His lips hovered an inch above hers. He lifted the hem of her top and planted a hand on her bare waist. "Now, are we going to join the mile-high club or not?"

He kissed her again, and this time there was no holding back. Her arms circled his neck, and she pressed her body against his hard, muscular form. "We're joining," she murmured against his lips. "Wait!" She pulled away, reaching for the backpack with one groping arm because he hadn't released her waist.

"Why? This was just starting to go in a direction I like."

"Condoms," she said, then kissed him one more time before extricating herself from his arms to dig in the bag. "Get naked while I find them."

"Yes, ma'am." He started with his shirt buttons.

She found the box and tossed it on the bed, then pulled her top over her head and shucked her jeans, all while watching him disrobe with avid interest. They were in a fully lit room, and there was a super-comfortable bed within inches. This was the ultimate do-over.

His body was all corded muscle and smooth skin. A feast for her eyes, and she wanted to lick every inch.

"God, I love it when you look at me like I'm dinner," he said.

"Then finish undressing, because I'm hungry."

His eyes flared with heat. He kicked off his shoes and shucked his pants and briefs in one quick swipe, then sat on the bed to doff his socks. "No fair, Cressida, you aren't stripping for me."

She'd sort of forgotten to move as she took in his sculpted abs and the thin line of hair that trailed down to an erection that was all hers. She reached out to touch him, but, fully naked now, he scooted back on the bed, just out of her reach. "Uh-uh. Strip."

She did as he commanded and in moments stood before him naked, hoping he'd like what he saw even one-tenth as much as she enjoyed his spectacular body. His slow, sexy smile was a good indicator.

He moved to sit at the foot of the bed and pulled her to stand between his thighs. He took her hips in his hands. His tongue flicked across first one nipple, then the other, as his hands slid to her bottom and squeezed. The feel of his tongue and hands made her body clench with anticipation.

He cradled her hips as his mouth explored her breasts. She purred and touched his smooth jaw, enjoying the silky feel of his freshly shaven skin, while watching her nipple disappear into his hot mouth.

He slipped a hand between her thighs and stroked her clit, and she let out a soft moan. This was real. This was Ian. Touching her. And it was only the beginning.

"You can make noise, Cress. The hum of the engine is so loud, the sound won't carry." He brushed a finger over her clit again, fast, hard friction, and she let out a small shriek at the sensation.

She reached down and wrapped a hand around the base of his cock and slowly stroked upward. He lifted his chin and sucked air between his teeth. She loved the power of turning him on. The way his whole body reacted, as if every muscle contracted at once. He was a mass of powerful, perfect manhood, and she could make his entire body respond with just the slightest touch. "Mine," she whispered.

Ian chuckled and slid a finger inside her. He tilted his head back to meet her gaze. "And this is mine."

He was everything she wanted—exceedingly intelligent, alpha, with a protective and possessive streak that fed her needs.

She kissed him, taking his tongue deep into her mouth as she slid her hand up and down his thick length. She loved the feel of his tongue against hers, but she wanted more. Wanted to taste all of him.

She dropped to her knees and licked the head of his hard prick. He let out a low groan. She took the tip into her mouth and sucked as she slid down, taking him deep into her throat.

His fingers threaded through her hair and tilted her head back until she met his hot gaze as she sucked on his cock. She felt his body coil around her, his thighs tighten as his eyes smoldered.

He cradled her cheeks and gently nudged her upward, sliding his cock from her mouth. He pulled her to her feet again, then kissed her deeply. "You are amazing," he said against her lips. He scooted to the side, making room for her on the bed. "And I want to lick you and suck on you, and make you come on my tongue. And then I want to slide deep inside and make you come again."

She lay down beside him and slid a finger between her thighs into her wet center. She groaned at the pleasure of her own touch.

"God, that's hot," he said.

She lifted her damp fingers and slipped them into his mouth. He closed his eyes and sucked. He let out a low growl and placed his hands between her thighs, spreading her wide. She was open and vulnerable and found it hot. Exhilarating.

He dipped his head down and flicked his tongue across her clit. She bucked upward, the touch ten times more intense than fingers had been. He moved his tongue lower, to slip inside her vagina.

"Fuck you taste good." He stroked and teased with his tongue, alternating between her clit and her opening, bringing her so close to orgasm, her whole body shook. But she wanted him inside her when she came. He hadn't said he loved her, but this was still a declaration of sorts, and she wanted to be hip-to-hip, face-to-face as they came together.

She wiggled away from him before he could make her come. "Get a condom on and get inside me, or all deals are off."

He threw back his head and laughed. "Did we make a deal I wasn't aware of?"

"You offered to try being a boyfriend. I might have accepted. But it's a trial run. Starting now, you're on trial."

He let out a loud belly laugh at that and scooted upward until his head rested on her abdomen. "God, Cress, you make me feel so good—lighter—and I'm not talking about sex." He lifted his head and met her gaze over the landscape of her belly and the rise of her breasts. "Just being with you makes me feel…excitement, for something new, different. For you. I haven't let myself feel this way in a long, long time."

Okay, it wasn't *I love you*, but he was getting closer. He was, after all, talking about feelings. "Kiss me," she said.

He slid up the bed, his firm body a sweet pressure on hers as the dark curls on his chest brushed against her skin, setting off tingles along the way. He kissed her, all right…slowly… methodically…passionately. As if every barrier between them had been crushed under the onslaught of a decade worth of banked emotions.

That he'd set his emotions free with *her* only made the moment sweeter. And sexier.

Ohmygod, it was sexier. Heat flooded her. She had to have him, every amazing inch of him, inside her. Pressed up against her.

Touching in every way possible. She needed him. Now.

She groped for the condoms, wondering where the hell they'd left them and why he wasn't in one *now*, because if he didn't get inside her before her next heartbeat…

He somehow produced a condom, and she watched him slide it on, then finally… *Yes!* She gave thanks to whatever higher power made this moment possible. He filled her, his thick cock stroking her with each hot thrust. She'd been on the brink of orgasm since he'd gone down on her, and now she rode that edge, bursts of pleasure threatening to tip her to the other side. With a deep gasp, she clenched around him, and he pulsed into her at a perfect clip. She wanted to melt, to dissolve, to implode, as the pressure built to intense levels.

His mouth found hers, and he kissed her deeply, his tongue a welcome hot intrusion. He lifted his lips from hers and threw back his head as his body rocked between her thighs. The pressure reached the tipping point, and she came with such a hard, sharp intensity, she couldn't hold back a guttural scream.

Ian's back arched, and he laughed as his orgasm followed. She loved watching his face as he came, the handsome lines somehow even sexier as he clenched his jaw and closed his eyes. Unlike her, he was quiet. Instead, she felt his body shudder, and he let out a soft groan.

She caressed his cheeks as he collapsed on her. He slipped his arms around her back and rolled to his side, still inside her, still sending shockwaves of pleasure with the pressure of his cock hitting just the right places.

He must have noticed her reaction, because he thrust his hips forward, and another short wave hit her. "I love making you come," he said. "I love how your face goes soft and dreamy, yet you scream with release."

She tucked her head into his chest. "I hope no one out there heard that."

"And my ego is sort of hoping they did."

She laughed and lightly punched him on the shoulder.

"I could really get used to this. So as your boyfriend, how often do we get to have sex?"

"Every time you seduce me." No point in letting the guy get complacent, after all.

"That much, huh? Sweet." He nuzzled her neck, then met her gaze. "Very sweet." His chin brushed the chain of the evil eye pendant, and she stiffened. This was where everything went wrong the first time.

He shook his head. "Don't worry, honey. I'm going to stick around for the long haul. Promise."

She nodded.

"We should probably get some sleep. We've got a busy day when we land in DC. Or evening. Or night. Honestly, I've lost track."

"Me too. I'm not even certain I could name the day of the week if you asked me."

"Eh, knowing days of the week is overrated."

She smiled and nibbled on his chin, fighting the words *I love you* that burned to be said. She couldn't take the risk, couldn't say them first—not again. What if she did and he didn't say them back to her?

Chapter Thirty-Nine

THEY SLEPT ENTWINED, something Ian had never enjoyed until now. But then, he had a feeling he'd enjoy a lot of things with Cressida that had never been pleasurable before.

He'd probably never know what brought him to the cabin door and gave him the courage to step inside. Maybe it was Sean, calling him an ass for hesitating. Maybe it was talking to the one married operative who somehow made the lifestyle work, or the hardened, lonely operative who gave Ian a glimpse of where he'd be in another ten years. It might have been the thought of Cressida moving on with her life, while he spent the rest of his regretting the decision to let her go.

Regardless of the trigger, entering the cabin had been an impulse, without a clear plan. He just…*wanted*, and was tired of getting in his own way. Tired of denying himself.

She slept soundly in his arms, and once again he watched her. He smiled, knowing she'd accuse him of being creepy, but couldn't help it. This sleep was different from the other times he'd watched. This time she was sated. Tousled. Beautifully fucked.

He was a lucky man.

He toyed with the idea of kissing her awake. He wouldn't mind getting lucky again. But she needed to sleep. They were only a few hours out, and all hell could break loose at the other side.

All the more reason to make love with her again. And again.

She made a soft sound and rolled over, and he gave up on the idea. She hadn't been able to sleep deeply when they were on the run, and she lacked his training.

He pulled Cressida tightly against his side, forced himself to close his eyes and let his guard down. It was time for him to sleep too.

POUNDING WOKE IAN. Sharp, urgent jabs on the door. He bolted up and reached for his gun, as he always did when yanked from sleep. But he didn't have a gun.

Sean had insisted Ian surrender his weapon before he boarded the plane. It had probably been a test of some sort, and Ian had no qualms with passing. It wasn't like he feared a midflight coup. He trusted the Raptor operatives because their mission was the same as his: get Cressida to safety. As long as they had the same mission, they were on the same team.

Cressida was slower to wake but no less alarmed at the pounding when the urgency registered.

"Give us a minute!" he called out as he pulled on his jeans.

Cressida did the same, but without a bra, her nipples were readily apparent through her T-shirt.

He shook his head. "If I catch any of the guys ogling you, I might have to strangle them. So for their safety, put on a bra."

She tossed him a sleepy smile even as she reached for the bra. "None of them would ogle me. To them, I'm just a mission."

"You were my mission, and it didn't stop me." She was clearly clueless as to the ways of men. The operatives would have to be made of stone not to be aroused if she stepped out with pert nipples while looking sex-tousled.

He might be biased, but he didn't think so.

Once she was presentable, Ian opened the door and faced Sean. "What's up?"

"We've got a problem waiting for us at Joint Base Andrews."

***

"How can Zack be in DC? Why hasn't he been arrested?" Cressida asked again. They were all seated around the conference table, and Sean had just finished explaining the situation. Her brain was still foggy from the deepest sleep she'd had in more than a week.

"Zack wasn't burned. He can claim everything he did was following the mission," Ian said.

"Including smoking us out in Kurubaş? Killing the checkpoint guard?"

Ian raked his hands through his hair. "Everyone thinks we—or at least *I*—killed the guard."

"Where is Todd?" Cressida asked.

Sean shrugged. "I don't have info on Ganem." He leaned forward. "Here's the deal. Dominick can help, but he's going to need time. If the CIA takes you into custody on the tarmac, it's already too late. They don't *know* you are on this jet, but they suspect. They'll search this bird top to bottom and there is nothing we can do about it."

"Can Ian put on a Raptor uniform? You guys must have some sort of disguise kit here. Give him a beard, colored contacts. Something?" She could hear the desperation building in her voice. There was no way she would let Ian get railroaded. Not without a fight.

Sean glanced at Ian. "You good with a jump?"

"You've got a 'chute?"

Fear jolted through Cressida's body, making her bolt upright. Ian would...*jump?*

"Enough for all of us if need be," Sean said.

Ian met Cressida's gaze. "No. Only me. Your job is to get Cressida to safety."

"You can't jump," she said in a low croak.

"Don't worry, honey. I got this."

"When was the last time you jumped from a plane?"

He shrugged. "It's like riding a bike."

From the snickers of the other operatives, she had a feeling he was lying.

"This isn't funny! What if...something goes wrong? We can take our chances at Andrews."

"Honey, I can do this. The tricky part is when and where."

"You're good with a water extraction?" Sean asked.

"Sure."

Sean drummed his fingers on the table. "We need a boat. Let me talk to Keith and see what we can arrange."

◉

ERICA AND LEE had returned to Raptor headquarters in the heart of DC after they managed to convince Suzanne and Patrick to return to Patrick's estate in Annapolis with promises to call if they heard anything.

The flight wasn't expected to arrive until just before dawn, so sometime after midnight, Erica settled on a couch in one of the quiet offices for a middle-of-the-night nap. She jolted awake around three a.m., unsure why, but there seemed to be a heightened buzz to the conversation going on in the main room.

She sat up, rubbing her eyes. Well, these short bursts of sleep were good practice for a baby, right? She grabbed a clip from the end table and gathered her hair as she walked into the main room.

Lee stood by a computer station to the right of the conference table, where the others had gathered. She stepped to his side, and he slid an arm around her as she whispered, "What's going on?"

"The CIA agent who we believe outed Boyd returned to the US. His loyalty isn't being questioned—yet. They don't know he was behind Cressida's mugging or the other things Cressida told Sean about."

Sean had debriefed Cressida on the drive from the border to Erbil and then relayed that information to Keith. Ian had not provided a statement, because as a covert CIA operative, even though he'd been burned, he was bound to secrecy. So they only had Cressida's version of events. Which had been chilling, to say the least.

"What will that mean for Ian?"

"He's going to have an uphill battle getting anyone in the CIA to believe him. Zack's story is Ian went rogue. He either kidnapped Cressida or she's his accomplice. Either way, everything that happened backs up his statements, and the agent killed near Gercüş is viewed as further proof Ian is a traitor. The man, Sabal, was supposedly assisting Zack in bringing Ian in."

"And if Ian is taken into custody?"

"He *will* be taken. No question of that. Once he's in custody, Curt will have a hell of a time intervening. If Ian is tried and convicted, Cressida could go down with him."

Erica shuddered to think of what it could mean if Cressida were arrested—*again*.

"So what's the plan?" *Please, let there be a plan.*

"Ian's going to jump from the plane."

"*What?* Can he do that? I mean, does he know how?"

Lee smiled. "Yes. And the plane is equipped. That's not the problem. The problem is, we need a drop location and a boat to pick him up. And we need it in place in less than an hour. I called JT—his boat is moored at the Menanichoch marina—but he said there's an engine problem."

"Ian's going to jump into the Chesapeake?"

"If we can have a boat ready for pickup, yes. Sean estimates he'd need to jump at about five thirty a.m."

Erica smiled. "I hate to say it, but I know the perfect person. He has a giant yacht. On the Chesapeake. He's home right now, and he's sympathetic to our cause."

Lee's eyes lit up. "Shortcake, you're brilliant." To the others he said, "Guys, Erica has a solution: Dr. Patrick Hill."

THE TIME FOR the jump came all too soon for Cressida. It seemed like one moment they were discussing it, and the next, Ian was strapping on the parachute. As soon as they had word there would be a boat in position, the jump was given the thumbs-up, and the pilots adjusted speed and altitude to hit the jump window just right.

These men knew how to do this. The pilots knew what they were doing. And Ian assured her he'd done this many times. It was the only solution, but damn, it scared the hell out of her. She gripped the evil eye pendant through her shirt. A habit that had formed at some point in the last week, but she'd never know if this particular pendant was good or bad luck.

The pendant was also the one thing she hadn't told Sean about. Not that she didn't trust him, but because he was in contact with Keith on the ground, and even though she knew Lee was the best in the business, she couldn't count on the airwaves being secure.

She looked at Ian questioningly, gripping the pendant.

He understood and said, "Keep it. But don't tell the CIA about it. With Zack in the fold, we can't trust anyone there. It's a wild card. Play it last and only in desperation."

She nodded.

They raced ever closer to the jump zone. Every loose item in the cabin was tucked away, and Cressida and the others were all rigged with harnesses and tethers before the jump door was opened.

Sean slid the door to the side. The wind roared as air pressure in and outside the jet equalized. Cressida's hair whipped across her face as she held on to her seat with a white-knuckled grip.

Ian stepped into the opening, his tether hooked to the bar above the door.

Her heart lurched to see him outlined by the dark void of the night sky. She'd had no intention of going near that gaping hole but couldn't stop herself and surged to her feet. She joined him in the opening and felt all the blood drain from her body when she looked down at the dark water far below.

She grabbed the straps of his chute, pulling his chest to hers. "You'd better come back to me. You promised."

"I didn't just promise. I gave you my solemn vow." His kiss was hard and fast. Too fast. Gripping the bar with one hand, he unhooked his tether. "I love you, Cressida."

He released the bar and pitched backward into the night sky.

Chapter Forty

Sean grabbed Cressida's harness and pulled her back from the opening. To the others, he said, "Seal her up. We need to circle for our landing ASAP."

Cressida just stood, dumbfounded as the men around her secured the cabin. She didn't know whether to laugh or to cry. So she did a bit of both, suspecting the tears were happy and the laugh a little bitter.

Not bitter at Ian. Hell, no. He'd pretty much secured her heart forever with that stunt. Good Lord, but the man did know when to play a card. She was angry at fate or whatever had brought them together, only to literally watch him plunge into a ten-thousand-foot abyss.

"He'll be fine, Cress," Sean said. "I've read his service record—the non-redacted parts, anyway—he's jumped plenty of times in far worse conditions."

She nodded and offered a weak smile. "Thanks, Sean."

"One of the things Keith wanted me to gauge was whether or not Boyd could be trusted. To make sure you weren't Stockholming."

She stiffened even while admitting it was a reasonable concern. After all, she'd wondered the same thing on several occasions. "What did you tell him?"

"He's competent, a solid operative, and he refused to break his oath to the Company even after they burned him. But more important was the way he looked at you when you weren't paying attention. That alone told me everything I needed to know."

She cleared her throat. "How long until we land?"

"Twenty minutes or so. Better buckle up."

She dropped into a window seat and leaned her head against the pane, looking down, knowing she'd never see his dark chute against the dark water. She gripped the pendant again and wondered how long until he splashed down.

TRINA STOOD NEXT to Keith on the tarmac at Andrews, feeling both impatient for the jet to land and dreading it at the same time. She didn't like the look of the men in suits who were lined up beside them.

Boyd should have splashed down by now, but she wouldn't find out if Hill had successfully picked him up, not while these men stood by, waiting for someone to slip and reveal their hand.

Keith was here as CEO of the company that had financed and conducted the extraction, Trina as friend of the extracted. Curt waited with the suits, ready to intervene officially on Cressida's behalf. They'd agreed Mara couldn't accompany him, as that would just underscore his personal connection to Cressida.

Erica was with Lee at Raptor headquarters, waiting to hear from Dr. Hill. Alec waited in the wings—AKA his estate in Maryland—with Isabel, ready to jump in if need be, but given the role Raptor had played, it might be best if he sat this one out. The owner of Raptor could face political repercussions if this went badly for Cressida, and his colleagues in the senate suspected he was involved.

The low rumble of a jet engine became a very loud rumble, and Trina's heart picked up speed. *Finally.*

Tires touched pavement with a bump and a squeal, and wind whipped up as the jet shot past them. Flaps dropped on the wings, and the plane slowed, then finally, nearly the length of the runway away, the jet came to a halt.

It circled around, rolling with aching slowness until the jet returned to their end of the tarmac. Moments after coming to a complete stop, the door slid open and steps unfurled. Sean exited first, followed by Cressida.

Trina shot forward, ignoring Keith and the others, who told her to wait. Screw that. She enfolded Cressida in a fierce hug. The younger woman squeezed back and promptly burst into tears.

This was the homecoming Cressida should have. Friends and hugs and tears. Not detainment and interrogation. Not hard questions and fear for the man who'd saved her. Not wondering if Ian would be captured, quietly tried, and executed as a traitor.

Sean had told Keith that Cressida and Ian were involved. All Trina could hope was that this time Cressida had chosen wisely.

Given how volatile and tenuous the situation was, Trina figured it wouldn't hurt to play dumb for the suits. "Let's take Cress back to our place, Keith. She needs a break before being questioned."

"I'm afraid you can't do that, ma'am."

She looked up and realized a new suit had arrived while she'd watched the landing. The CIA director himself had shown up to meet Cressida's flight.

"Ms. Porter, where is Case Officer Boyd?" the director asked.

"Somewhere in the Tigris." She said the words so coldly, so emotionless after the tearful hug, that even though Trina knew it wasn't true, she believed her. "There was a firefight when we crossed the river. He was shot and went overboard. The current took him." She jerked her head toward Sean, as though angry. "He wouldn't go after him, even though I begged. He said his mission was to get me out, not Ian."

"Excuse me, but how is it that I'm just hearing about this so-called firefight now?"

Sean spoke next. "We went radio silent because the firefight was between the YPG rebels who were helping Boyd and Porter and either some of Assad's forces or an al-Qaeda faction. Or possibly ISIS. If we'd radioed in the details and any of the other parties picked up the transmission, they'd know that Raptor had worked in conjunction with YPG—and could assume the CIA was involved as well. Any future alliance would be compromised."

The director's jaw clenched. He clearly didn't buy the story, but it was just plausible enough to make his job more difficult.

Cressida pulled a T-shirt from her bag and thrust it in the man's hands. "I got some of Ian's blood on me when he was shot."

Later, Trina planned to howl with laughter over the look on the director's face as he gazed down at the filthy T-shirt in his hand, but for now she had to keep a straight face. "If Boyd is gone, then the interrogation can wait. Cressida's been through an ordeal and needs a break."

The man met Trina's gaze. "Who the hell are you?"

Beside her, Keith stiffened.

"I'm her friend." She lifted her chin and refused to back down. Better to make this about her rather than about Cressida. Everything that stalled until they were certain Boyd had been picked up was a good thing.

To the suits at his side, the director said, "Search the plane."

"I'm afraid, Leroy, that's my team's job," Curt said softly. He nodded to the FBI agents, who moved forward to carry out his order.

"We really don't want a pissing contest here, *Curt*." The CIA director's emphasis showed he didn't like Curt's casual use of his first name. But then, he probably didn't like it that he wasn't the highest ranking government official present.

"I know you don't, because I will win."

"Boyd is a covert CIA operative who sold out his country—"

"Are we in Turkey right now?"

The director only glared at Curt, refusing to answer.

"Exactly," Curt said. "You have no jurisdiction on US soil. In fact, you are *forbidden* from conducting operations on US soil. So play nice and stand down."

"This isn't an op. This is bringing in one of our own who turned."

"He did not!" The anger in Cressida's voice shocked everyone into silence. "He was betrayed by one of you. *I* was betrayed by one of you." She then linked her arm through Trina's and said, "Sweetie, I'd love to go back to your place and rest."

"You can't do that, Ms. Porter. You're coming with me to Langley."

"Let's compromise. I'll let you question her at the DOJ," Curt said.

"You'll *let* me question her? At your office? No," the CIA director said.

"Sorry, Leroy, but I'm detaining Ms. Porter for questioning," Curt said. "And I'll allow you to question her as a courtesy, because I'm generous that way."

"What's *your* legal standing for detaining her?" the director asked.

Curt smiled like a player about to achieve checkmate and plucked some papers from his breast pocket. He thrust them toward the director, but the man already held Cressida's rancid T-shirt, and didn't take them. "She's a material witness in the case against Todros Ganem, who fled trial and who may have sold classified information to Jordan and possibly Syria."

"Classified information is my field."

"And prosecuting violations is mine." Curt turned to Cressida. "I'm sorry, Ms. Porter, I realize this is a difficult time, but we have important questions about your association with Todros Ganem, and I have the right to detain you if you don't come willingly. Are you willing?"

She nodded. "Certainly, Mr. Dominick. Anything I can do to help you nail Todd will be my pleasure."

Trina met Cressida's gaze and could see the turmoil she held back with iron will.

"Can Trina come with us?" Cressida asked. "I could use a friend."

Curt smiled, and his voice softened. "Sure."

AS THEY DROVE to the DOJ, Cressida kept chanting Ian's final words in her head. Holding on to them for strength. They'd made it through the first hurdle. She wasn't going to Langley. But she was certain the CIA director's interrogation would be difficult, even in Curt's domain. And it wasn't like Curt would go easy on her either. But at least she knew *he* was trustworthy.

She needed to decide if the director could be trusted with the chip or if corruption in the agency went all the way to the top. And even if the director was clean, it didn't mean the people he'd turn the data over to were safe. Ian had said to save it as a last resort, and she intended to do just that.

Plus there were the lies she had to maintain until she knew who all the players were. She wasn't a spy. She didn't know how to play this game. But she'd do it, to save Ian. Who'd said he loved her. Which gave her strength...

They rode in the back of a town car with facing seats. Having a dedicated driver was a perk of being in Curt's position, and Cressida appreciated the fact that she, Trina, and Curt were the only passengers. It gave them a chance to talk in private.

"Mara is sorry she couldn't be there to greet you," Curt said.

"I understand." She paused. "I'm so grateful—for everything."

Curt nodded to Trina. "It was all Keith and Trina. I had no part in your extraction."

Trina, who'd been gripping Cressida's hand like a lifeline, squeezed. "I'm guessing you have one whopper of a story."

She nodded.

Trina's cell phone buzzed, and she dropped Cressida's hand. Tension in the car went up a notch as they all met each other's gazes. Cressida held her breath as Trina glanced at the phone. "It's Erica," she said and answered.

Cressida's mouth went dry. *Please. Please. Please let Ian be okay.*

With a smile, Trina flashed a thumbs-up, and Cressida could

breathe again. And then she was crying, because that seemed to be what she did these days.

Trina said nothing after she tucked away her phone, making Cressida wonder how much Curt knew and how much he wasn't allowed to know. The attorney general was an honest man, and he'd taken oaths he wouldn't violate. Best not to tell him anything he'd have to divulge.

At the Justice Department, the interrogation began with the director asking how they crossed into Syria, forcing Cressida to lie at the start. She didn't feel guilty for lying to a man whose organization trained others to lie, but Curt was another matter. She hoped someday she could tell him about the tunnel and he'd understand why she couldn't give that intel to a CIA that still employed Zack Barrow.

She explained how Zack had detained her and Ian at gunpoint several miles outside of Cizre. Without flinching, she described overpowering him. The director replied Zack had been assigned the task of bringing Ian in, and she could be charged with assault.

She asked how she could be charged in the US for defending herself on Turkish soil, but the director asserted it wasn't self-defense. He viewed her as Ian's accomplice in that she'd abetted his escape from Zack.

He'd already decided Ian's guilt. There was no question in his tone, in his words.

Curt entered the fray, injecting Stockholm syndrome into the line of questioning, and she tensed, wondering if he really believed that. It was possible he'd said it just to muddy the waters. It certainly deflated the director, because he backed off, briefly.

With the allegations that she'd committed crimes in Turkey along with Ian—and she *had* killed a man—it *was* a potential defense. But if she were forced to claim Stockholm to avoid prison, it would mean Ian had already been convicted. And she couldn't live with that.

Finally, hours later, when she was drained, exhausted, and miserable, Curt asked, "Cressida, have you told us everything?"

She looked the attorney general in the eye and lied. "Yes. Everything." Ian must have rubbed off on her, because she felt less guilty this time.

The director suggested Curt provide accommodations at DOJ, so they could resume questioning in the morning, but Curt said he trusted her on her own recognizance and to report back to DOJ the following day for further questioning. For now, she'd given both the CIA and the DOJ enough details for them to begin fact-checking.

She suspected the director agreed because he intended to have her followed, hoping she'd somehow give him a lead on Ian's whereabouts—who he clearly didn't believe was in the Tigris. "Before you go, Ms. Porter, you should know it's a federal crime to reveal the identity of any covert CIA operative, so tread carefully as far as Zack Barrow is concerned. I'd love to have an excuse to bring you in.

She glared at the director. "He's the bastard who betrayed his country and outed Ian. You *might* want to investigate him."

"We've launched a full investigation into who outed Boyd. Right now it looks like it was someone from Hejan Duhoki's cell, but rest assured, Agent Barrow is also being investigated."

She stood. "Good. Make sure he stays away from me."

She found Trina in the front lobby. Because of the classified nature of the questioning, she hadn't been allowed to watch the interrogation, which meant Cressida had a lot of explaining still to do. She took a deep breath, gripped the pendant through her shirt, and said to a friend she now owed her life to, "Take me to Lee. We need a computer and a man who knows how to use it."

Chapter Forty-One

"HE'S LIKE A boy on Christmas morning," Trina said with a laugh as Lee cracked his knuckles and sat before the computer.

Erica rolled her eyes. "Tell me about it."

It felt surreal to Cressida to be sitting in Erica and Lee's Watergate condo again. The last time she'd visited had been for their wedding, the same weekend she'd gone back to NHHC and studied Lawrence's map because the photo she'd been working from was blurred at the edges and some of the notes were unreadable. That was when she'd found his notes about the stone house and capstone he'd placed in the corner.

Finding that little notation had saved her life and Ian's, because even by last April, events had been set in motion that would have led to everything that followed. That one note was the *only* piece of information Cressida had that Todd hadn't been privy to.

And yet Todd hadn't told Zack they'd been in the stone structure.

Erica handed Cressida a glass of red wine, and she hesitated before taking it. She *could* relax and have a glass. It was safe to let her guard down.

But Ian wasn't here. How could she let her guard down without him?

"Cress, tell me what you know about this chip," Lee said after he'd inserted the plastic card into a USB drive and plugged it into his computer.

She sat next to him and relayed the details. As she spoke, Lee's fingers clicked away at the keyboard, and files opened and closed in rapid succession. Some files had Arabic text; others were in English.

"The contents were meant for Ian," Lee said. "Hejan's English notes make that clear, but he ensured a non-Arabic speaker could access the data. Which is good, because my Arabic is rusty." He winked at her.

She gave him a weak smile. "Ian could help you. I wish Hill

would bring him here."

"It's better this way. Hill's known for taking multiday cruises around the Chesapeake and can't break that pattern now. If radar tagged the jet for flying low and circling around, or anyone caught a glimpse of Ian's jump and reports it, everything needs to look routine on Hill's end. Plus you know the CIA is watching everything you do, tracking everywhere you go. Unless we get this cleared up right away, you won't be able to see him for a while."

"I'm that obvious?"

"Um, yeah," Erica said with a laugh. "But don't worry, we get it." She met her husband's gaze and smiled.

"Why can't I call him? You can secure the line, Lee."

"Not on Hill's boat. Too much interference with all the equipment—sonar, radar, all the underwater exploration goodies Hill likes to play with." He studied the computer monitor. "Now this is interesting. This file is encrypted. None of the others were. It looks like I've got three shots at the password, then it wipes the drive clean."

Cressida gasped. They couldn't lose this data.

"Relax," Lee said. "Hejan wasn't sophisticated. He just didn't want an idiot to get the information. I've already backed it up. We're working off a copy." He frowned. "Hejan left a clue for the password. Like a crossword. A six-letter word for revenge."

"Berzan," Cressida said without hesitation. "He wanted revenge for Berzan."

IAN PACED HIS cabin inside the luxurious yacht. It was agonizing being cooped up like this, knowing Cressida was undergoing interrogation. The CIA wouldn't torture her, would they?

He really didn't like the fact that he wasn't certain of the answer.

Surely a woman allied with the US Attorney General was safe? If Dominick had gotten her out of CIA clutches, she'd be protected.

Clutches? This was the organization he'd devoted his life to. And now he was thinking in terms that painted them in rotten shades.

But there *was* something rotten in the state of Denmark. And it started with Zack Barrow.

The doorknob to his cabin twisted, and Ian glared at it, certain he'd locked it. It had better not be Suzanne. The woman was off her meds or something.

But the door opened, and it wasn't Hill, nor was it Suzanne. It was none other than Todros Ganem.

◎

"I'M NOT SURE I understand, Lee. Is this the money Hejan stole from a refugee aid organization?"

Lee frowned as he scrolled down the long list of dates and numbers. "Yes and no. Yes, he stole the money, but no, it appears it was a dummy organization, a front for funneling money into his terrorist group. He took the money just a few hours before meeting you. He cleaned out the account." He pointed to a number on the screen, then opened a spreadsheet with a matching number. "He provided a key. He didn't want anyone to miss what was going on. The money was payment for weapons."

"Ian said his group had gotten into arms dealing."

"It appears that's the *only* thing they were doing. Lots of money transfers in and out. Most of the deposits came from the same place." He frowned as he studied the spreadsheet. "These are payments from the Syrian al-Qaeda group. Hejan took the income from selling weapons to al-Qaeda and hid the money in a numbered password-protected account. Anyone with this data can move the money wherever they want."

Erica sat in a chair on Lee's other side. "How much?" she asked.

"Nine million and change."

Trina let out a low whistle. "When he met you at the bar that night, Cress, he was a walking dead man."

Cressida bit her lip. She'd put the pendant back on after Lee had retrieved the chip, and she gripped it again. "He knew it too. That's why he was so quick to send me off when Todd started pounding on the door. He had to get me out of there with the pendant, or we'd both have ended up dead, and the money would have gone right back to the terrorists."

"Do you think Todd killed him?" Trina asked, taking Cressida's hand in a comforting grip.

Cressida liked the way Trina touched her to let her know she wasn't alone. She needed it. "Actually, I don't." She'd already told them about Todd's lie to Zack. "What will happen to this money if we give this data to the CIA?" she asked.

Lee shrugged. "No idea. My guess is they'll seize it. It's blood money, after all."

"Can you erase the current location of the money? So no one will know where Hejan hid it?"

"Sure."

"And could you drop the money in the account of a *real* relief organization? One that's an open book, which provides aid to Syrian refugees?"

Lee grinned. "Absolutely. It might take me a few days to find the right organization and make the transfer."

They exchanged glances all around. "If we do this, none of us can ever tell. Agreed?" Cressida said.

Trina held up a hand. "Can I tell Keith?"

"Fine. And, of course, I'll tell Ian. But that's it. Agreed?"

Everyone nodded.

Cressida grinned, feeling lighter than she had in…hours? Days? Who knew? But it felt good. "Okay, Lee, where is that list of people who fund terrorism that Ian promised us?"

"Working on that file now. Gimme a sec." Another document opened on the screen. Lee blanched. "*Sonofabitch!*"

Cressida looked at the screen. The list was there, clear as day. Third name from the top: Dr. Patrick Hill.

Chapter Forty-Two

IAN TOOK A swing at Todros, catching him on the chin. As it had in Antalya when Cressida slugged him, Todros's head snapped back, and he went down, but the man didn't make a sound. Ian went after him, grabbing his shirt and hoisting him to his feet.

Todros covered his face with his forearms and shook his head frantically, whispering, "Quiet!" His gaze darted down the corridor. "We need to talk in your cabin."

Ian dragged him inside the stateroom and shut the door. He pulled his gun and pointed it at Cressida's ex. "Give me one good reason not to shoot you."

"Because they'll hear. Then they'll know you've figured out what Hill is. Who he is. He'll seize your gun and slit your throat. Just like he killed Hejan."

Ian kept his gun trained on Todros. "*Hill* killed Hejan?"

"Yes. I was in the bathroom—Hejan shoved me in there just before Hill barged in. I heard everything. Instead of paying off some Russian arms dealers as instructed, Hejan stole the money. He told Hill the account number was on the chip, then Hill killed him so he couldn't talk to you. He bolted out the back door. He had to get back to Suzanne before she noticed he'd been gone too long. Now the organization is desperate to get their hands on the cash before the Russians come calling."

"I CAN GET on the boat. I can claim I want to see Suzanne. He doesn't know I have the chip. Doesn't know I've seen the contents." It was early evening. They'd abandoned Erica and Lee's condo in favor of Raptor's DC headquarters, where Keith had called in every operative on his payroll in the DC area. Cressida paced the main room and tossed out her desperate plan, frantic to convince the mercenaries to help her rescue Ian.

Prior to making the move, Lee had copied the money transfer information along with the money's current location and passwords. He then erased the money's location from the chip and restored the chip to the pendant. A quick call to Mara confirmed Curt was at his office. While Erica, Lee, and Cressida moved to Raptor headquarters, Trina delivered the microchip to the DOJ, placing it directly in Curt's hand as she claimed Cressida had just realized the pendant was from Hejan and might have something inside.

Now here they were, a dozen operatives plus Trina, Erica, Lee, and Cressida. Frantic and feeling ill, Cressida paced as she tossed out ideas for how to free Ian from Hill's boat.

The first question was whether or not they should move in before the FBI got involved. Curt didn't know Ian had jumped from the jet—although he likely suspected—and didn't know Ian was on Hill's boat.

They'd tell him if he showed up at Raptor headquarters, but it had been important to give him the microchip in a way that it could be accepted into evidence in court. Cressida's understanding of the rules for covert evidence was limited, and she prayed the data could be used to convict Hill.

In the corner of the room, Erica looked a little green. Cressida knew she felt guilty for suggesting Hill in the first place, but they'd all thought it was the perfect solution. It wasn't anyone's fault, it was masterful maneuvering on Hill's part, ensuring he'd been in the loop and ready to sweep in and help.

But then, Hill had been masterful from the start.

He'd been in the bar that night with the dual purpose of watching Hejan make the drop *and* hooking up with Suzanne, which had given him an in to ingratiate himself with Cressida's DC friends.

Knowing Cressida's secret about the tunnel, Todd must've turned to Dr. Hill when he was in a desperate legal situation. Of course Todd would contact Hill, the mapping expert Cressida had introduced him to, offering the man a chance for shared glory. Hill would have known immediately exactly how valuable the tunnel could be and must have pulled strings to get Todd out of the US. Todd had been searching for the tunnel for Hill all along.

Did Todd know even then that Hill had his own agenda, or was that something he'd learned along the way? At what point did Todd balk?

She wondered if Todd ever went back to the stone house and saw the jack. If so, did he tell Hill, or did he remove the jack and cover the evidence of recent digging? She suspected he'd done the latter, and wondered if he'd managed to escape Zack and maybe fled to his relatives in Jordan. There, at least, he could start over.

Once upon a time, she'd cared about him very much. She'd never quite understand his motives—whether it was academic jealousy or if he saw the strategic importance of the tunnel—but one thing was certain: After being rash and stupid on his own, he'd then allied himself with the wrong people. Todd wasn't evil, just immoral. He was foolish. Misguided. Childish. There were so many things not to like. But she didn't hate him and hoped he'd escaped the hell he'd created for himself.

"Cressida, why do you think you can get on the boat without getting shot? Hill's got to be jumpy as hell and worried you've got the list. Plus he's got Ian as hostage," Keith said.

"He won't shoot me because I can tell him where the tunnel is—which is what he's been after all along. I can also offer him the chip. Or the money, if he has any part in that end of the organization."

Was Hill simply a man who funded terrorism for his own ends, or was he something more?

Keith drummed his fingers on the table. "All good possibilities. The organization must be desperate to recover the dough. He needs to cover his ass. And the tunnel—he spent months looking for it. But still, the moment he has what he wants, he'll shoot you."

Cressida paced the length of the room. Maybe they were looking at it from the wrong angle. Every approach hinged on getting close enough to take Hill into custody without tipping him off and getting Ian—and Suzanne—shot. "What if we get the FBI to raid the boat, claiming they got a tip that Ian is on board? Hill would have to cooperate with the FBI."

"Admit to Curt you lied and have him send in the FBI to grab Ian?" Keith said.

"I'm no operative, but I like it," Lee said from his position at the side of the room, facing a computer while the others sat at the conference table.

"I am, and I do too," Sean said.

"Simple. Straightforward," Keith said. "But what's to prevent Hill from shooting Boyd and dumping his body overboard?"

The words made her shiver. "I guess it depends on the situation on the boat. If Ian doesn't know Hill's involved, he's safe. But if he knows who and what Hill is, Hill would have to shoot Ian before he could let the FBI take him."

"Lee, have you been able to isolate any calls to or from Hill?"

"It's impossible with the radar interference." Lee frowned. "He's probably sending out a blocking signal. I haven't even been able to pinpoint his GPS location."

Keith's voice took on an edge. "We don't know where the boat is?"

"I've got it narrowed down to a three-mile area."

"What if I call Suzanne?" Cressida asked. "Could you use that to pinpoint the location?"

"It might help," Lee said.

"And it might give us an idea of the situation on the boat," Trina added.

Keith met Cressida's gaze. "Suzanne's a friendly?"

"Yes," Cressida said firmly.

"Sweetie," Erica said, "you should know. She was behaving *very* oddly yesterday. I know she was concerned about you, but it was...*intense*. Alternating between being bitchy and hostile and demanding. She was nothing like the woman you've described."

Dread trickled down Cressida's spine. "Was she a narcissistic diva from hell?"

Erica grimaced. "Um, yeah."

Cressida's heart broke a little. No, a lot. "She's on meds for...something. She doesn't like to talk about it, so I'm not exactly sure. I only know because her doctor changed her prescription once, and she had an...episode. It wasn't pretty, and she was horrified after. She's always really, really careful with her pills."

"Call her," Keith said. "Give us your take on her mental shape."

"No, text her. Send her a phone number. Ask her to call you," Lee said. "That way there will be multiple data points for me to monitor."

"And if she doesn't call me back?" Cressida asked.

"I might be able to tell you if she unlocks her phone and reads the message. Better than rolling into voice mail."

"Do it," Keith said. "I've got a cabinet full of burner phones." He nodded to one of the operatives and slid a key ring across the table. Without a word, the man stood and fetched a phone, while Lee and Keith debated what Cressida's text should say.

After the text was sent, they all waited in silence for a response. Cressida jolted when the phone rang not two minutes later. With a nod from Keith and Lee, she answered the call on speakerphone.

"Cress? Is it really you?" Suzanne said in a soft voice.

"Suz!" Cressida said, giving her voice the excited pitch Suzanne would expect. "Damn, I've had a hell of a week since Antalya."

"Is that how long it's been?" Suzanne's voice was wispy. Faded.

"A little longer. Nine days, I think. Why aren't you in Turkey? The excavation is going for another week."

"Patrick…had to return. He knew how worried…I was…for you. So I came back with him."

"Hey, are you okay? You don't sound right."

"I think…I think I'm not right. I think…I can't seem to think. I saw a ghost."

A ghost? "Suz, could your meds be off?"

"I asked Patrick that this morning. Or yesterday. He gave me a drink. I told him no more. It would mess with my meds, but he said my meds are fine. I think…I think I need to break up with him. He's an ass. Kept pressuring me to talk to your friend Trina. I said no. No."

Was that when he started messing with her medication? So he could manipulate her into reaching out to Trina and Erica? Cressida's heart ached with every rambling word. This wasn't Suzanne. This was a woman whose meds were so far off, she was discombobulated. To top it off, it sounded like Hill had pushed drinks on her, to keep her in an ethereal state.

Suzanne was floating, and Cressida needed to pull her back to earth. "Suz? Can I come see you?"

Beside her, Keith stiffened and glared at her.

"I'll ask Patrick. He's been acting so strange today. I hate this boat. Too many ghosts."

"What do you mean by ghost? Who did you see?"

"He was a shadow. He didn't want me to see him. Begged me not to tell Patrick… He said I'd die if anyone knew I saw him."

"Who, Suz? Who did you see?"

"Todd. He's here. Or his ghost is."

⚜

"THEY DIDN'T TAKE your gun when you got on board because Hill is hoping you'll remain ignorant of who and what he is,"

Todros said.

"Well, you've pretty much fucked that up for me, then, haven't you?" Ian was trying to get a read on the man and was coming up short, but he did believe that in his own messed-up way, Todros was trying to help. "One thing I'm not clear on, Todros, is why you sent the text to lure Cressida to the ferry dock."

The traitor met his gaze without flinching. "Zack was reckless and in a hurry. He said he wouldn't have Cressida mugged while she was on her date with you, but with the money Hejan had stolen, he didn't have the luxury of waiting to collect the chip when she reached the south—not when someone else could get it first. He planned to have Sabal rob her hotel room while she slept that first night. He told me that if she woke, her throat would be slit, just like Hejan's. I told him I could draw her out and provide an opportunity to mug her without killing her."

"But it was an empty threat. Zack wanted her alive to find the tunnel."

"He said he was willing to sacrifice the tunnel to get the disk if need be." He shrugged. "Or maybe he'd figured out that threatening Cressida would secure my cooperation." Todros stiffened his spine. "We're running out of time and options. Are you willing to protect Cressida?"

Ian glared at the selfish prick who'd created this situation because of nothing more than a bruised ego. "I'd die for her."

"You may get that chance, Boyd. But for now, you need to get Suzanne off the boat. Hill messed with her meds to manipulate her, and now he's going to use her to lure Cressida here. After he gets the chip from Cressida, Suzanne is going to drown in what appears to be a booze-and-bad-meds incident, and Hill plans to make it look like Cressida died trying to save her."

Ian's blood ran cold. Hill's name must be on Hejan's list. Add that to the fact that he—according to Todros—owed Russian thugs big bucks, and the man had to be desperate to recover the microchip before his house of cards came tumbling down.

"Where is Suzanne?" Ian asked.

"She's in Hill's stateroom, sleeping off a drugged cocktail. Your options for getting off the boat are two tenders, Hill's two-person submarine, or the helicopter on the deck. Hill has guards on everything."

Ian frowned. He had no clue how to pilot a submarine or helicopter, so he'd have to go for one of the tenders. But the first trick would be getting Suzanne. "Where's Zack?"

"No clue. He probably fled as soon as he heard Cressida made it back—no way would his version of events hold up against hers for very long. I think he planned to betray Hill. I got the impression he was after the chip—and the money—for himself all along."

Ian could believe that. He just wondered how Zack had gotten hooked up with Hill in the first place. He studied Cressida's ex. "What about you, Todros? Why aren't you asking me to get you off the boat?"

The younger man shrugged and opened the stateroom door. "There's only one way this will end for me. I realized that the moment I saw a man I respected and admired slit a Kurdish dissident's throat."

Chapter Forty-Three

"I'M GOING. YOU can't stop me, but you can help me," Cressida said.

"You can't, Cressida," Keith said.

"I'll give him the tunnel location. The money. A copy of the chip. I don't care. I'll do whatever I need to get Suzanne and Ian off that boat." She glared at each person at the table.

"The moment Hill realizes you know what he is, he'll shoot you," Keith reminded her.

"No. He won't, because I can't tell him where the tunnel is if I'm dead, and I'll make sure he knows I *won't* tell him a damn thing if Ian or Suzanne are dead." Her eyes burned with suppressed tears. She couldn't fall apart now. Keith would never agree to take her to the boat if she did.

"He'll kill you after he gets what he wants," Sean said. "He's in too deep. Once he realizes the extent of what you know, he'll go into panicked cover-up mode. You aren't going, Cressida. Period."

The phone on the table in front of her rang, startling everyone. "It's not Suzanne's number," she said.

"Answer it on speaker," Keith instructed.

She did, and Dr. Patrick Hill's ingratiating voice greeted her. "Cressida! I hope you don't mind, but I got your number from Suzanne. She said you'd called."

"Dr. Hill—*P*—*atrick*," she added with an embarrassed laugh, imitating the adoring grad student she used to be. "Yes, I called. I was surprised to hear she's in the area and not in Turkey."

"Yes, well, she was too worried about you to be any good for the excavation. Diving when one is anxious and stressed is dangerous, as I'm sure you know. It wasn't just Suzanne, I'm afraid the whole project had to be shut down."

She caught the censure in his tone, as if it were her fault. "Um…I'm sorry?" She shook her head. She needed to rein in her tongue and be the sycophant grad student he expected her to be. She couldn't hint that she knew who—*what*—he was.

"Well," Hill said with an awkward laugh. "I'm sure you didn't mean to ruin the project."

"Hardly. It was a hell of a research trip." She tagged on her own nervous laugh.

"Listen, I'm calling because you may have guessed from talking to Suzanne that she's not well. I don't know what to do. She refuses to see a doctor, no matter how much I beg. I'm wondering… Would you come out to the boat? Maybe you can talk some sense into her and get her to go to the doctor."

Cressida didn't bother to look toward Keith for approval, because she had no doubt he wouldn't give it. "Of course. I can probably get a boat to give me a ride out there, if you'll tell me where to find you."

"I'll send a tender. Be on the dock at my estate in an hour."

Keith bumped her shoulder, forcing her to meet his gaze. He frowned at her and held up two fingers.

"Better make that two hours, Patrick. I need to borrow a car, and the drive will take some time."

"Of course. I understand."

"See you then." She clicked off the phone and met Keith's angry gaze with her own defiant one. "I'm going. You can't stop me."

"I don't have to give you a car."

"Let's not waste time arguing and start planning. We can assume he invited me because he either wants the chip or the tunnel location. He probably hopes I'm willing to give them up to save Ian and Suzanne. Which I am. If nothing else, I can buy time while you figure out a way to grab Hill. I'm going to need a gun and a wire."

The room fell silent. Finally, Erica cleared her throat. "The best way to approach a boat at night is with scuba."

Lee looked sharply at his wife. "No way, Erica. You aren't an operative."

She smiled and touched his hand. "I wasn't suggesting myself. But what if…Cressida goes to the boat so we can get the GPS location and distracts Hill long enough for the former SEALs here to slip on board?"

Cressida watched Keith's reaction to the suggestion. Her guess was he didn't hate it, but he didn't like it either.

"I hate hate hate the idea of Cressida stepping into the line of fire—of any of you being at risk," Trina said. She met her boyfriend's gaze, then looked away, and Cressida knew she was afraid. "But isn't it simple military strategy to take calculated risks to better your odds of success?"

"We're talking about a coordinated rescue operation. Our goal wouldn't be to take out Hill. It would be to provide an avenue for escape for Suzanne, Ian, and Cressida, then let the FBI swoop in and arrest Hill." Keith met the gazes of the operatives around the table. "You men up for it? We don't have a contract for this, and there could be legal trouble on the back end. Volunteers only."

One by one all the men around the table nodded.

"Okay, then. Sean, you'll drive Cressida to the dock. Try to catch a ride on the tender, but if the skipper balks at taking you, don't put up a fuss."

Sean shook his head. "No way am I sitting this one out on the dock."

"I'll drive her," Trina said.

Keith's eyes flattened. "No."

"I'll stay on the dock. If Hill hears a Raptor operative delivered Cressida to the meet point, he'll *know* something's up. But with me, he'll think the opposite. Because no way would my boyfriend let me anywhere near Hill's boat if we were suspicious of him, right?"

Keith frowned, then gave a sharp nod. "Fine. Josh and I will each lead teams in the water. Sean, I'd have you lead, but you've been on duty more than off in the last week. Your call if you're fit to dive."

"I'm good."

Josh Warner, who Cressida knew had served as a SEAL with Keith, asked, "Do we have intel on how many are on the boat?"

"A minimum of five," Erica said. "Hill generally acts as his own skipper, but he has a small crew he takes out for the multiday trips, so there's always someone at the helm. I know he had to scramble this time, but he told me when he sailed that two men he trusted to keep mum about Ian were on board. He may have lied about the number. The boat houses fifteen crew members, easily."

"Who do we know is on board?"

Erica shrugged. "Ian, Suzanne, two crew members, and Hill."

"Don't forget Todd. Suzanne said he's there," Cressida added.

"There's also a chance Zack Barrow is there," another operative said. "We lost him after he was debriefed at Langley. So we'll plan on fifteen, count on seven, and hope it's only six."

"Erica, you've been on Hill's boat several times," Keith said. "What can you tell us about the layout?"

She smiled. "I can do better than tell you. I've got the plans." She glanced at Lee. "Can you access our home computer from here? I think I have a backup of the proposal there. Otherwise, I'll have to drive to the office."

"Sure thing, Shortcake."

"How'd you manage to get Hill's plans?" Josh asked.

"Several months ago, I put in a proposal to have Hill map a Navy Helldiver wreck that's off the Carolina coast. Because the insurance on the boat, mini sub, and helicopter is insane, the Navy needed full specs before they'd approve it."

"Sweet," Josh said.

For the first time, Cressida thought that maybe, just maybe, this insane operation had a chance. And as long as she didn't think about how horrible Suzanne sounded on the phone, she could breathe.

"We're in luck. I found the plans," Lee said. "Keith, turn on the projector?"

With the flip of a switch, the lights in the room dimmed, and drawings of the luxury sea-exploration yacht filled the screen mounted to the back wall.

Keith stepped to the side of the screen and tapped his upper lip as he studied the projected image. Finally he said, "Okay, this is how we're going to approach…"

◈

IAN STROLLED DOWN the deck alongside the rigging for the tenders, noting that one of the two inflatable boats was in use, as the cables that held it suspended above the water hung empty, flapping in the light breeze that swept across the Chesapeake. A crewmember lounged nearby, seemingly idle. He had to be the guard Todros had mentioned.

Ian needed to grab Suzanne from Hill's stateroom, get her onto the remaining tender, and lower the boat, ideally without alerting the guard.

He leaned his forearms on the rail as if lost in thought, and studied the boat-lowering mechanism. Getting the boat on the water wouldn't be a problem. He could leave right this minute without a hitch, but there was no way he could leave Suzanne behind.

He faced the crewmember. "I'm turned around. Which way to Dr. Hill's stateroom?" Ian knew exactly where the stateroom was. He'd been given the deluxe tour when he was plucked from the water in the predawn hour.

The guard frowned and nodded toward a flight of stairs that led up to the helipad. "It's aft. The deck below the landing pad."

Ian nodded. He moved closer to the man. If this were Turkey, he'd ask him if he had a cigarette and drop him while the man reached in his pocket. But smoking was far less common here, and therefore an obvious ploy. Instead, he said, "What's the deal with Hill's girlfriend? Is she whacked or what?"

The man shrugged. "She's new." He glanced to the side, probably to be certain he wouldn't be overheard. "She's—"

Ian struck, taking him down with one smooth blow. He dragged the guard to the remaining tender and shoved him in the bow of the small inflatable, making sure the unconscious man wasn't visible from the deck. Guard tucked away, he strolled up the stairs and headed toward Hill's stateroom, praying he'd find Suzanne conscious and cooperative.

CRESSIDA SHIVERED AS she waited on the dock with Trina. The wind had kicked up, meaning the ride would be rough and chilly. In the distance, she heard the whirr of a motorboat. Trina called Keith, who was with a team on a Zodiac in the middle of the Chesapeake, nearing the area Lee had identified as the most likely location of the yacht.

"The tender is coming," Trina said and handed the phone to Cressida.

"We'll be moving into position as you do," Keith said. "We'll lock on your coordinates as soon as you hit the panic button on your cell."

"Got it."

"Stay on deck if you can. The helipad deck is the most open, therefore the safest. It shouldn't take us more than five minutes to slip on board. Even if Ian and Suzanne are inside, don't go below deck unless you have no choice."

"I won't."

"Good. See you soon."

"See you. And Keith? Thanks. For everything."

"Sure thing, doll."

She gave Trina back her phone as the boat pulled up to the dock, then pasted a cheerful smile on her face and waved at the skipper.

Just like that, the mission had begun.

Chapter Forty-Four

Suzanne leaned against Ian as they made their way to the tender. "So sorry..." she mumbled. "This isn't..." Her voice faded before she could finish the thought.

He lifted her, placing her in the boat. A quick check of the guard showed the man was still unconscious. He gripped the rail to pull himself into the boat beside Suzanne, when he heard a boat engine in the distance. He glanced at the empty cables for the second tender.

Who was coming?

"Raise your hands and step away from the tender, Boyd."

Ian stiffened but kept his back to the speaker. He recognized the voice: Dr. Patrick Hill.

"Raise your hands," the man repeated.

Ian had no choice and did as instructed. He turned slowly, facing Hill and one of his toadies, whom Ian had met earlier. What was his name? Oh yeah, Carlson. He hadn't caught the guy's first name and frankly didn't care. All that mattered was the guy was as dirty as his boss.

Both Hill and Carlson held guns, which were trained on Ian's chest.

"You really shouldn't take off now, Boyd. Your girl is on her way," Hill said with a snicker. "Things are just about to get interesting."

Shit.

The engine noise grew louder.

"If she gives me the microchip right away, I might be generous and toss you in the bilge together *before* I kill you both, instead of after."

Ian couldn't hold back a growl.

Hill laughed. "And if she won't tell me where the tunnel is, I'll torture her while you watch. One of you is bound to talk."

Ian curled his hands into fists. Cressida wouldn't risk coming to the boat when the CIA was watching her every move. She must have hacked the chip and learned Hill wasn't the good-guy-philanthropist-explorer everyone believed him to be.

Odds were, Hill had guessed that too, but he'd lured her here under a pretense that required her to play clueless. No problem. Ian knew when to call a bluff and when to let the pot build.

Hill had made a reckless bet, because Cressida had Raptor at her back, but dammit, Ian was horrified at the idea of her stepping into the line of fire. If she really did show up on the yacht, when this was over, he and the CEO of Raptor were going to have words.

Ian slammed the lever that controlled the remaining tender. The small boat dropped into the Chesapeake. At least Suzanne was out of the line of fire and couldn't be used against Cressida.

"You'll regret that, Boyd," Hill said. He nodded to his minion. "Take his gun."

Carlson approached slowly. "It's too bad, the things that are going to happen to your girl. I liked Cressida when I met her last summer." The man took Ian's gun from the back holster and pressed it against Ian's forehead. He flashed an ugly grin. "She's got great tits."

Ian would happily rip his face off.

"What do you think, Patrick," Carlson asked, "should I shoot him?"

"Don't be stupid, Perry. Without Suzanne, we need him alive to convince Cressida to talk. I doubt she'll fret much if we torture Ganem." Hill cocked his head, studying Ian. "Ganem tipped you off, didn't he?"

Ian said nothing.

Hill plucked a radio from his belt. "Bring Ganem on deck when I question the girl." He clipped the radio to his hip again and faced Ian. The engine noise had become a low roar. "Sounds like the party is just about to start," Hill said.

The barrel of the gun pressed deeply into Ian's forehead. He could think of no scenario in which he came out of this situation alive.

He had no problem staring death in the face, but fear for Cressida hurt more than any torture Hill could throw his way.

At least he'd told her he loved her. He just wished he'd said it a thousand times in those last hours they had together.

CRESSIDA RECOGNIZED A boat identical to the one she rode in floating in the water not far from the massive yacht. She nodded toward the aimless boat as they neared the docking platform and asked the skipper, "What's going on?"

The man shrugged and eased the boat to the platform. "My job is to drive the boat."

She slipped her hand in her pocket and pressed the panic button. This didn't feel right. But she'd insisted on this plan, so whatever happened from here on out was her own damn fault.

The skipper tied the bow to the platform, and she said a small prayer as she stepped aboard and climbed the ladder to the first deck. Her head popped above the side, giving anyone lying in wait an easy target, but no one was on the lowest deck that ringed the yacht.

She continued upward to the next deck, surprised neither Hill, Suzanne, nor one of Hill's sycophants were there to greet her. Finally she reached the uppermost deck, coming face-to-face with the silent helicopter. Everything was eerily still.

Something was terribly wrong.

"Suz?" she called out. "Dr. Hill?" *Ian?* But his name was her private, silent scream.

Footsteps sounded, and she turned to see Dr. Hill climbing the stairs from a lower forward deck. "I'm afraid Suzanne has left us," he said.

Cressida's heart lurched. What the hell did that mean?

"She took off in one of the tenders. It's just as well," the man continued. "I've been thinking of breaking up with her."

Cressida shrugged, unsure what reaction he wanted from her. "Oh...*kay?*"

Hill crossed the deck and stopped a few feet in front of her. "I have bad news for you. After some thinking, I've decided to deny your grant request."

At that, Cressida let out a sharp laugh. She couldn't help it. "My grant request? You mean the one I haven't even written yet?"

"Yes. I received a similar proposal from Todd Ganem. And I've decided to go with him."

"Yeah, I'll bet you did."

At that moment, a door opened, and Todd was shoved onto the deck. His face was bloody, and he moved slowly, painfully, as if he'd been beaten within an inch of his life.

Dr. Hill's eyes scanned her from head to toe with an assessing gaze. "On second thought, I'm willing to give your proposal another look, on one condition."

She gritted her teeth. He wasn't playing innocent, as they'd all hoped he would. This mission was, as Sean would say, FUBAR squared. She had to buy time until Keith's team could get here. She turned away from Todd, unable to face the obvious hell he'd gone through—an inkling of what she faced if Raptor couldn't save her.

"What's the condition?" she asked.

Hill turned and ever so casually shot Todd in the stomach. "Give me my microchip."

Horror rippled through her, but she maintained enough semblance of sanity to say, "*Your* microchip?"

"Yes. Mine."

Todd groaned, a low grunt of pain that told her he was alive but suffering.

"Hejan told Ian the microchip was intended for the leader of his organization."

"Yes. Exactly. Me."

Chapter Forty-Five

Carlson nudged Ian in the spine with the gun. "Get moving."

No way would Raptor let Cressida board this boat alone. It was only a matter of time before the crew started disappearing like bimbos in a horror flick. Ian needed to get to Cressida's side before all hell broke loose.

He flinched at the sound of the gunshot and hurried up the steps. On the deck above, Cressida faced off with Hill while Todd lay on the deck, slowly bleeding out.

It took all of Ian's willpower to move slowly, not to rush up the last steps. He stepped firmly on the steep metal rungs, catching Cressida's attention. Her eyes widened as she met his gaze.

Damn, she was more beautiful than he remembered. How the hell was that possible? How could he love her more now than he did this morning?

But most important, what would he do if he failed her now?

Cressida returned her gaze to Hill, not sparing a distracted glance for Todd or Ian, and he again saw her tapping into that magnificent iron will, as she had several times on their journey when she was backed into a corner. "If you're the leader, then why didn't Hejan just *hand* the chip to you? In the bar in Antalya?"

"Hejan didn't know who the leader was, and I was hardly about to reveal myself to him. We were following our usual money-transfer protocol—the only difference was I'd picked you to play courier for the first leg. So now we have a happy convergence. You were supposed to deliver the data to the separatist leader, and here we are."

"And my job was to follow the courier and identify the leader," Ian said as he stepped onto the deck with Carlson and his gun at his back. "Isn't it fun when the mission comes full circle?"

Hill met Ian's chill gaze with a cold smile of his own and reached for Cressida as she pulled her own gun. "Pull the trigger, and your boyfriend gets shot in the family jewels."

"Harm him, and I'll never tell you where Hejan hid your nine million dollars."

Ian did a double take. *Nine million?*

Oh, Hejan, you sweet vengeful bastard.

No wonder Hill was in knots, acting without thinking and without a viable plan. He was so far down the rabbit hole, he hadn't realized there was no card he could pull that would save him. He was in the ultimate no-win situation.

When buying arms from former Soviet dealers, a missed payment meant death.

Hill couldn't kill Cressida or Ian without Raptor informing the feds. And if Cressida knew about the nine mil, sure as hell Curt Dominick knew.

Ian caught the exact moment the situation sank in for Hill. With a roar, he backhanded Cressida, knocking her into the side of the helicopter with the force of the blow. Her gun flew from her hand and clattered across the deck.

Watching Hill strike Cressida sort of unhinged Ian, who took down Carlson with a swift strike to the head. He lunged for Hill, but the underwater explorer grabbed Cressida by the hair and pulled her backward. He wrenched open the door of the helicopter and shoved her into the cockpit.

A gun fired, breezing by Ian's ear, and he twisted toward Carlson, kicking outward as he turned. He caught the man's hand, dislodging the gun. More of Hill's men poured from the stairs, heading straight for Ian.

He grappled with Carlson, trying to shake the man off so he could get to Cressida.

The wind whipped up on the deck. Ian took a blow to the jaw and spun to see Hill in the cockpit of the helicopter, at the controls. He'd fired up the engine.

Cressida grappled with the passenger door, trying to get out. Hill punched her in the jaw, then returned his attention to the control panel. The helicopter lifted from the deck.

Ian shoved Carlson back and lunged for the skid, grabbing on as it rose. The copter leaned and shifted, flying out over the cold, dark Chesapeake Bay. Ian clung to the skid, grappling to get his leg over the bar, knowing that if he lost his grip, Hill would escape, and Cressida would be tortured and killed.

The copter soared ever higher into the night sky, as his fingers began to slip.

"ARE YOU INSANE?" Cressida shouted as the helicopter dropped with a stomach-churning lurch.

"That should take care of Boyd," Hill said with smug satisfaction. "Your spy is probably drowning in the bay along with Suzanne."

She gripped the phone in her pocket and again pressed the panic button. It would log GPS coordinates for where Ian fell. If he'd fallen. She couldn't let Hill's words get to her. He wanted to throw her off. Take away all hope. She wouldn't let him win. "I'll never tell you where the money is if Ian and Suzanne die."

"Sweetheart, where I'm taking you, you'll tell me everything I want to know. I've got people in the Middle East who've refined torture to an art form."

The Middle East. He planned to take her back. He was just rich and powerful enough to pull it off. She had no doubt that if he could fly this helicopter to his private jet, he could easily smuggle her onto the plane and fly her back to Turkey or Syria, or wherever his Middle Eastern allies were located.

Unless Curt had read the list and grounded Hill's private jet. She still had hope.

Right now, the only thing that mattered was Ian. Had he survived the drop?

The door beside Hill lurched open, and Ian grabbed him by the throat. The copter pitched sideways and dropped in near free fall. Cressida slammed against her door. The bay loomed just outside her window, then the copter righted moments before crashing into the water.

She reached for Hill, to help Ian as he grappled with the man for the controls. But before she gained purchase, Ian slammed a fist into the release on her door, which flew open. The helicopter tilted sideways again. She slid toward the opening.

She grabbed Ian's arm to stop her fall. He glanced at her hand and met her gaze. "I love you!" he shouted, then he twisted his arm, breaking her grip, and shoved her toward the open door.

She plunged backward, into the abyss, dropping at least two stories into the Chesapeake.

The water was a cold, abrupt shock after the fast fall. At impact, she sucked in seawater and sank into the depths. Disoriented, she forced herself to pause and feel for bubbles that slid along her face, pointing the way to the surface. She twisted to orient herself, then kicked, surging upward. She surfaced and coughed and gasped for breath in the cold water. Above her, the helicopter lurched left, then right. The fast-moving rotors stirred the water, kicking up salt spray and making it hard to see. Hard to breathe.

With a roar of the engine, the bird slanted sideways and flew a short distance, then plunged nose first into the dark water.

Chapter Forty-Six

CRESSIDA WATCHED IN horror as the helicopter broke apart. The bay surged and chopped with the impact. A wave engulfed her. Smothering her.

Ian. She had to get to Ian.

The copter bobbed at the surface, then sank.

She kicked with all her might, swimming with a ferocity she'd never experienced, grateful for her hours of dive time that made her a strong swimmer. She reached the debris field and scanned the water's surface, searching for Ian. He hadn't been harnessed inside. A door floated beside her. It had broken off.

There was hope he wasn't inside the rapidly sinking helicopter.

She located Hill first. He floated facedown in the water. She flipped him over but didn't waste another moment on him as she searched for Ian.

Then she saw him, and her heart stopped. Like Hill, he was facedown. Floating. How long since the impact? Two minutes? Three?

She flipped him upright, turning his face to the night air. A quick check showed he had a pulse but wasn't breathing. They were miles from land. She didn't even have a lifejacket.

She grabbed the nearest floating debris, a panel of some sort, and tried to shove him onto it but couldn't lift his weight without leverage.

She took a deep breath and remembered dive training, which she'd renewed many times during her years of scuba diving. She slipped her body beneath his. She'd be his float. She grabbed the panel with one hand and pulled it under her shoulders. Slowly, she inched it under her until it reached her hips. Then she slid out from beneath Ian, so his upper body rested on the float.

She swiped his mouth, finding no obstruction, and pressed her open mouth to his. A quick puff of breath didn't inflate his chest. She tilted his throat back, opening the passage, and tried again.

She managed to breathe air into his lungs once, twice, three times.

In the distance, she heard a boat engine. Please let it be one of the SEAL teams responding to her panic button call in the helicopter.

She pressed another breath into Ian's lungs. "Don't you dare die on me," she whispered frantically between puffs of air. "You promised." Another breath. "You gave me your solemn vow." Another breath. "I love you. Dammit, I love you."

Ian coughed, a choking gasp that brought tears to her eyes. She tread water and gripped the float all while making sure he didn't slip off the panel as his body shook with the spasms. His eyes popped open, and he vomited seawater.

Before his breathing was under control, a boat pulled up alongside them. "Need a hand, Cress?" Sean Logan asked.

IAN'S COUGHING SUBSIDED as Cressida snuggled against his side. The boat circled so the Raptor team could grab Hill's body from the water, and after the terrorist leader was aboard, Logan announced the man still had a pulse, but barely.

"There's a part of me," Ian said to Cressida, "that wouldn't be bothered if Hill lives and escapes, because the people he's double-crossed in the Middle East will slit his throat without a fuss, whereas he might be rich and connected enough to escape prosecution here. Hejan made sure he was a dead man no matter what."

"Do you think Hejan realized he was the group leader? He was, after all, in the bar that night. And given that Hejan was working with Todd to find the tunnel, there were too many connections for Hill's secret to stay hidden."

"It's possible. He might have figured it all out and then plotted his revenge, knowing the dominos would fall after his death." He held her gaze, knowing this would be hard for her to hear after what she'd witnessed on the boat. "Hill killed Hejan when he discovered Hejan had taken the money. Todd was hiding in your hotel room bathroom and witnessed the whole thing. Tonight, Hill shot Todd because he guessed that Todd tipped me off to what Hill is."

She gave him a sad smile. "You called him Todd."

"Because that's who he is to you. He fucked up a lot. But in the end, it appears he was trying to save you. To right his mistakes."

She nodded. "I hope he recovers. He was in over his head the moment he contacted Hill. He had no idea what the man was—obviously, none of us did—and by the time he found out, it was too late for him." She sighed. "Where's Zack?"

"I don't know. He may have fled, or he may try to claim he was just following orders, but with Hill's capture, I don't think that'll fly."

"And Suzanne? Is she okay?"

Ian turned to Sean, "Did your team find Suzanne?"

Sean nodded. "Good job getting her off the boat. She's safe now. As soon as the FBI takes over on the yacht, we'll get her to a hospital."

"So what happens next?" Cressida asked Ian.

"I'll be taken in for debriefing. You'll get a room at The Hay-Adams and wait for me. We both hope the mess in Turkey is sorted out without me being charged with all sorts of awful things I didn't do."

"Sounds like a plan."

He tightened his arms around her. "I think you said something when we were in the water that I'd like to hear again."

"I was reminding you of your promise to take me to The Hay-Adams."

"Yeah, I'm pretty sure it was after that."

She smiled and stroked his cheek. "I love you, Ian Boyd."

He kissed her, amazed and grateful they were both alive. Together. And in the US. A circumstance he'd seriously doubted would come about. "That's what I thought you said."

The boat surged across the water, and even though Ian knew an interrogation awaited him at the other side, he couldn't wait to reach shore. He was eager to get the debriefing over with, because for the first time in his life, he had a reason to hurry home.

Epilogue

Washington, DC
September

CRESSIDA WAITED OUTSIDE CIA headquarters. A crisp wind brushed her cheeks, making her wonder how the season had turned so quickly. The leaves had yet to change colors, but still, fall was in the air. She glanced at her watch. Today was supposed to be a simple formality, but it was taking too long.

Finally, Ian stepped out of the building, and she caught her breath as she took in the sight of him, always reminded of her first glimpse across the terminal in Antalya. The man was, quite simply, gorgeous, but that was a rather shallow method for judging a person, really. So instead, she chose to judge him on his actions and quickly ran out of fingers and toes to list the ways in which he'd protected her, defended her, and, in the end, loved her.

"It's official. John Baker is dead," he said and dropped a kiss on her lips.

"Long live Ian Boyd." She linked her arm in his. "So, do we have a wake or a party?"

"I'm Scottish. Aren't they the same thing?"

"I thought that was an Irish wake."

"Admittedly, I'm more familiar with Middle Eastern customs."

"Oh, so we get to teach Ian how to be a good Scottish American, do we?" she said in a really bad brogue.

Ian laughed, a full, head-back, facing-the-sun, free laugh, something he did with more and more regularity as they settled into their life together. She loved making him laugh. But then, she pretty much loved everything about him.

"The deputy director asked me to stay on as an analyst again."

"Are you considering it?"

"No. Not even when the director resigns." The director had been the one who'd recruited Patrick Hill—who, they'd learned in the last weeks, had been a CIA informant, which was how his dealings with foreign terrorists and arms dealers had been noted but not investigated over the years. To save face for harboring—and possibly even creating—the biggest US traitor in CIA history, the director had sought a public explanation that exonerated Hill while throwing Ian under a bus.

They'd also learned that when Hill's previous handler retired, Zack—who remained at large—had been tapped as his replacement. Zack was far more astute than his predecessor and caught on to Hill's activities. Instead of turning him in, however, Zack had demanded a cut. So Hill put Zack to work, ensuring the CIA case officer was in too deep to betray him.

Fortunately, the FBI was more interested in the truth than covering for the CIA director, and it was only a matter of time before the director would be forced to step down and Zack would be found and prosecuted.

Hill had survived the helicopter crash and was in custody awaiting trial. Todd had undergone multiple surgeries to repair the damage from the gunshot wound. He was expected to recover and would likely receive a reduced sentence in exchange for testifying against Hill.

"I'm going to tell Keith I'll take the deputy director's offer," Ian continued, "unless Raptor offers me a signing bonus and lets me delay my start date until November."

"Negotiating is a game to you, isn't it?"

He pressed their clasped hands into the small of her back and swung her around to face him. His lips were an inch from hers as he murmured, "Yep." Then he kissed her, holding nothing back even though they were in front of CIA headquarters in the middle of the day.

"Rent a room, Boyd," a man said as he walked past.

Cressida and Ian broke apart in laughter. "Do you know him?" she asked.

Ian glanced at the man's back as he strode toward the entrance. "Nope." Then he kissed her nose and said, "And it's not just because I like yanking Keith's chain. With your job at NHHC delayed until late October, I was thinking we should enjoy the time off together. Maybe go visit your mother."

"Or try to find yours?" she asked softly. It was a suggestion, not a push.

"Not yet, Cress. But someday, yeah."

"Okay." They resumed walking. "I got a call while you were inside. Erica is throwing a going away party for Undine, since she's leaving for the underwater excavation in the Strait of Juan de Fuca next week."

"A dinner party?"

"Yes. I said we'd be there. But if you aren't comfortable, I can go alone. I know it'll be weird, with Keith being your boss and all. And Erica will be mine when I start at NHHC."

"No. It's not that. It's just…I've never been to a dinner party before. I mean, as Ian. John went to many, but he always had an agenda, information he wanted, or a person he wanted to recruit."

"Well, if it's more fun for you, we could pretend the party is a covert op…"

He laughed again, and again she felt a warm buzz. "No. I like having friends and don't want to mess that up."

They reached their car, and instead of unlocking the doors, Ian pressed her against the side of the vehicle and kissed her, slow, long, and deep, then he said against her lips, "But you know what I like even more than having friends?"

"What?" she whispered, staring into his intent warm gray eyes.

"That when I'm with you, I know I've found home."

Author's Note

IN THE LATE nineties, my husband worked for the underwater archaeology branch of Naval History and Heritage Command (then called the Naval Historical Center) at the Washington Navy Yard in Washington, DC. While he was there, he was asked by one of the historians to help move an old armored file cabinet, which had been classified as top secret sometime after World War II. The keys to the cabinet had long since been lost, and no one knew what was inside, nor did anyone really care beyond idle speculation, as the contents were likely to be so outdated as to be irrelevant to today's US Navy. The cabinet was merely a nuisance as it got in the staff's way and was moved from cubicle to cubicle over the years.

To the best of my knowledge, the file cabinet remains locked and forgotten at NHHC; this story is simply my speculation at what treasures could be inside.

Also, while it is true that T. E. Lawrence excavated at Carchemish on the Turkish/Syrian border in 1911 and again in 1914, and he also worked on an expedition on the Sinai Peninsula in 1914 as a cover for British Intelligence, to the best of my knowledge he never conducted archaeological survey or excavation along the border near the Turkish city of Cizre. His role in this story is completely fictional.

THANK YOU FOR reading *Covert Evidence*. I hope you enjoyed it!

If you'd like to know when my next book is available, you can sign up for my new release mailing list at www.Rachel-Grant.net. You can also follow me on Twitter at @rachelsgrant or like my Facebook page at www.facebook.com/RachelGrantAuthor. I'm also on Goodreads at www.goodreads.com/RachelGrantAuthor, where you can see what I'm currently reading.

Reviews help like-minded readers find books. Please consider leaving a review for *Covert Evidence* at your favorite online retailer. All reviews, whether positive or negative, are appreciated.

Books by Rachel Grant

Evidence Series:

Concrete Evidence (#1)

Body of Evidence (#2)

Withholding Evidence (#3)

Incriminating Evidence (#4)

Covert Evidence (#5)

Grave Danger

Midnight Sun

Acknowledgements

THANK YOU TO my agent, Elizabeth Winick Rubinstein, for your untiring enthusiasm and support for this project, and for the insightful feedback that forced me to dig deep and find the emotional core of this story. Working with you makes me a better writer.

Thank you to Elisabeth Naughton and Joan Swan, who originally plotted this story with me in a hotel room in Bellevue. Later I met in another hotel room with Darcy Burke and Elisabeth, for an intensive writing weekend, where I wrote the shower scene and other chapters in that section of the book. That weekend the three of us made a pact to include a certain line of dialogue in our sex scenes, and I can now say I've held up my end of the deal.

Darcy Burke, aside from inspiring the dialogue pact, I have so much to thank you for, but the most important of which is to thank you for being a great and dear friend. I am so lucky to have you not just as a critique partner, but as a person whose friendship goes far beyond our writing world.

Kris Kennedy thank you for your timely and wise critique of an early draft of this manuscript. I would have been lost without you!

Thank you to Gary and Gayle for providing the venue for an amazing retreat where I edited this book in the company of three of the finest authors in the universe: Darcy Woods, Bria Quinlan (AKA Caitie Quinn), and Jenn Stark (AKA Jennifer Chance). Thank you, ladies for sharing that wonderful week with me, and talking me through the rewrites of the final action scene. I need more #MIMayhem and shenanigans!

Jenn Stark, thank you for being available online so I could pester you for immediate feedback when a scene needs help. If you ever block me, I'm doomed.

Thank you to Toni Anderson for the wonderful cover quote and the helpful feedback. And for writing fantastic romantic suspense – I am a total Toni Anderson fangirl!

Thank you to the Northwest Pixies, our annual retreat always refreshes and inspires me, not to mention that thanks to Rebecca Clark's coaching, I always go home with less writing-related backaches than when I arrived. Becky, I need you to move in with me. I will make you chocolate martinis whenever you want.

To my editor, Linda Ingmanson, thank you so much for not only copy editing this book, but for beta reading an earlier draft. I so appreciate the continuity you bring to this series and am thankful for your proofreader's sharp attention to detail. I'll try to work on my commas and dangling modifiers. I promise.

Thank you to my children just for being you.

Lastly, as I end the acknowledgements in every book, thank you to my husband, David Grant. Thank you for telling me about that old file cabinet at NHHC and for everything you do, but mostly thank you for being the love of my life.

Read on for a sneak peek at Rachel Grant's
Paranormal Romance Novella
Midnight Sun

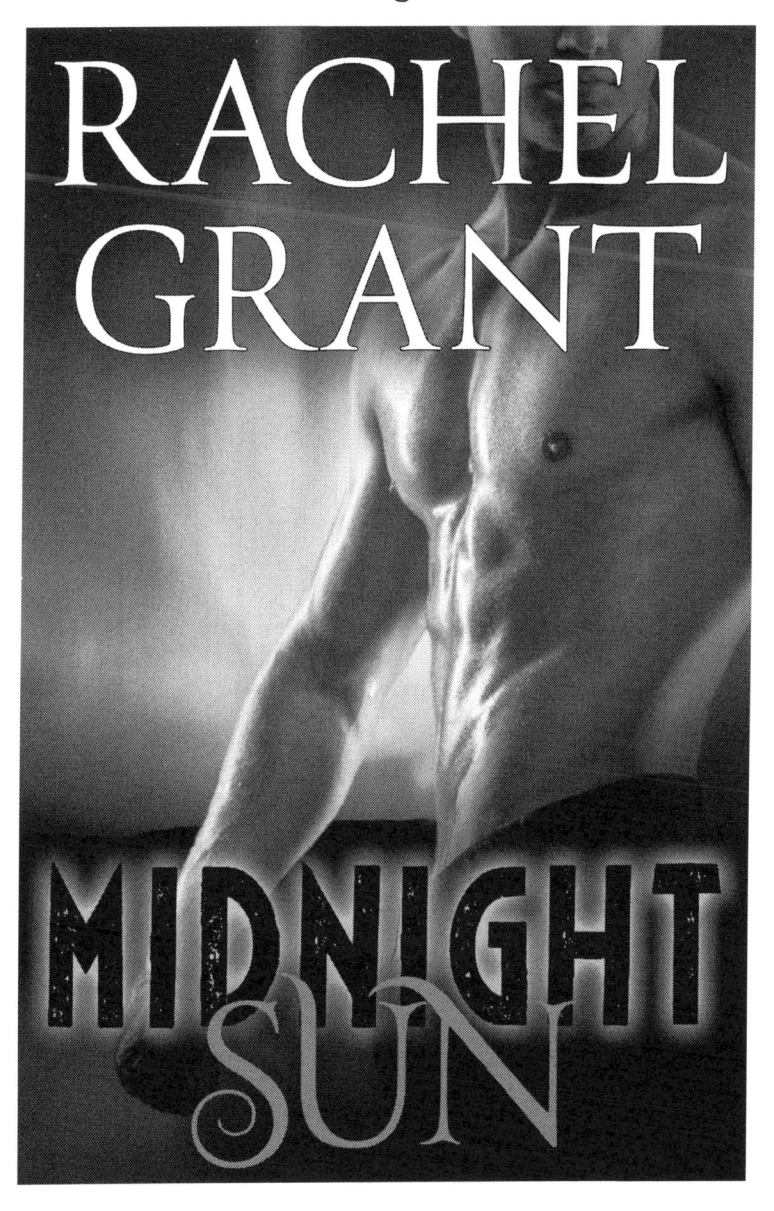

A woman on the edge…

Museum collections specialist Sienna Aubrey is desperate. A prehistoric Iñupiat mask in her client's collection is haunted, and it wants her to return it to Alaska…*now*. Tormented to her breaking point, she steals it. But when she arrives in the remote Alaskan village, the tribal representative refuses to take the troublesome mask off her hands. Even worse, the manipulative artifact pulls the infuriating man into her dream, during which she indulges in her most secret fantasies with him.

A man in search of the truth…

Assistant US Attorney Rhys Vaughan came to the Arctic Circle to prove someone tried to murder his cousin. When Sienna shows up at his cousin's office with the local tribe's most sacred artifact, she becomes his prime suspect. Then the mask delivers him into Sienna's hot, fantasy-laden dream, and his desire to investigate her takes an entirely different turn.

An artifact seeking justice…

But the mask has an agenda, and it's not to play matchmaker. If Sienna doesn't do what the artifact wants, she may pay the ultimate price, and only Rhys can save her.

Chapter One

Itqaklut, Alaska
June

"This is the most insane thing I've ever done," Sienna Aubrey muttered as she stared at the cold metal door. She balanced the heavy cedar box containing the stolen artifact on her hip, held her breath, and reached for the knob, silently asking the universe to make this one task easy.

As if anything about this reckless errand could be easy. Her flight had been late and her checked bag lost before she'd reached her layover in Anchorage. The rental car got a flat two miles from the airport, and the lug nuts had been machine tightened, making it nearly impossible to change the tire herself.

Now here she was, arriving at the tribal headquarters office long after close of business, and wonder of wonders, the knob turned. The door was unlocked. *At last.* Something had gone her way. It was crazy to hope the tribal cultural resources manager would still be in the office, but since she'd gone off the deep end and stolen the artifact from her client and flown to Alaska to return it to the tribe, hope was just one more slice of crazy on her overloaded plate.

The freight-elevator-size lobby was fitting for a small tribal headquarters in a tiny town in a massive state. She again wished this tribe were part of a larger corporation with offices in Anchorage or Juneau, but no such luck. This offshoot of the

Iñupiat was hardly convenient. The Itqaklut Tribal Corporation, located on the remote north end of the Bering Straits, was as far off the beaten path as Sienna had ever traveled.

The lobby might be small, but it still had a directory, posted right next to a photo of the chief executive of the tribal corporation. Fourth on the list was the man she wanted to see: Tribal Cultural Resources Manager Chuck Vaughan, Suite 204. She climbed the narrow switchback staircase, her steps echoing in the silent building.

It was hard to imagine anyone was here. Why was the door unlocked? Maybe in Nowhere, Alaska, locks were unnecessary?

Halfway up the stairs, the cedar box seemed to… lighten. As if it could float from her hands. No. Not float away from her. It was *pulling* her, as it had been doing for the last two months, but this time the feeling didn't have a malicious bent. The mask was happy.

I will make an appointment with a therapist as soon as I get back home to Washington. No excuses.

It would be easier if she truly thought she'd lost her grip on reality, but she didn't. If she didn't believe the mask had been communicating with her, she wouldn't be here.

There were really only two options: either she was crazy, or the mask was possessed. Maybe haunted was the right word. All she knew was that if she stopped having nightmares, premonitions, and strange sensations after she handed off the artifact to Chuck Vaughan, then she, Sienna Aubrey, wasn't crazy. Of course, proving her sanity meant she was a criminal who'd just tanked her career, but it was a small price to pay for a clean bill of mental health. Right?

A light shone behind the opaque glass door of suite 204. *Thank God.* She balanced the box on her hip again and turned the knob. The door slid open on silent hinges. No one sat at the front desk—not surprising given the lateness of the hour, but still disappointing.

"Hello?" she called out as she entered the vestibule.

No answer, but the suite lights were on, so she ventured down the short hall with doors on either side. Name plates marked each office, and she spotted Chuck Vaughan's on the door at the end of the corridor—the corner office, as befitted the head of the department. The door was ajar, and a sliver of light spilled out.

"Mr. Vaughan?"

A thump sounded in the office, then the door opened wider, and a man peered out. "Yes?"

"Thank goodness you're still here. I'm Sienna Aubrey. I emailed you last week?"

Confusion flashed on the man's face, but he opened the door wider and waved his arm toward the opening, inviting her to enter. She stepped inside, ignoring the urge to shove the box into his hands as she passed him in the doorway.

She dropped into the visitor's chair, holding the large box—which had barely fit in the overhead compartment on the plane—on her knees. He took the seat on the opposite side of the desk, saying nothing.

It was disconcerting, this silence, this utter lack of warmth as the man studied her with Paul Newman–blue eyes. Vaughan was a tribal member, but his light hair, vivid eyes, and the arch of his cheekbones reflected his Euro-American rather than Iñupiat ancestors.

He raised a brow in silent question. A man of few words.

She cleared her dry throat. "As I mentioned in my email, this mask,"—she tapped the box on her lap—"belongs to the Itqaklut tribe—*bal* corporation." She stumbled, reminding herself that in Alaska, the legal entity was a corporation, not a tribe. "As a NAGPRA specialist, it's my job to return it." Forget the fact that she was skipping every protocol required by her profession, that Alaska Native Corporations no longer had standing under NAGPRA, and that she could never explain how she'd determined the mask belonged to *this specific* Bering Coast corporation. It was enough that the artwork was specific to the region. That, and the shaman who wore the mask hundreds of years ago had invaded her dreams and demanded she return it to the Itqaklut village. Repeatedly.

Sometimes the mask was even nice to her when it pummeled her with demands.

"NAGPRA?" the tribal cultural resources manager asked.

She furrowed her brow. What CRM officer didn't know NAGPRA? He was the equivalent of a Tribal Historic Preservation Officer in the lower forty-eight. "The Native American Graves Protection and Repatriation Act—one of the primary US laws that drives your work and funds your office and my contracts?"

"Oh. *NAGPRA.* I thought you said NPR."

Her jaw dropped. She didn't believe him for a moment. Was he messing with her? She glanced at the dark streaks on her hands—from changing the tire—and wondered if she had similar streaks on her cheeks. She probably should have checked her appearance in the mirror before entering the building. Maybe she looked like a lunatic. Which, of course, she might be. But she really didn't think so.

Good lord, she hoped she wasn't crazy.

"No. Not National Public Radio." She frowned. It was time to start over. "Did you receive my email?"

"Last week was rough. Refresh my memory?"

"My client is a small museum in Washington State, near Tacoma. I'm auditing their collection to identify artifacts subject to repatriation through NAGPRA and came across this mask." She set the cedar box on the floor and unhooked the latch, then lifted out the heavy carved wooden Iñupiat mask. An orca motif, it represented both human and orca spirit, and had been painted with earth pigments including ochre and burnt sienna. She'd wondered more than once if her name had something to do with her strange connection to the artifact.

"There was some confusion as to its provenance," she continued, "but my research indicates it belongs to your tribe. I mean, corporation. Er, village." She shook her head to brush off the verbal stumble, thankful, at least, that her voice wasn't shaking. No way could she let Chuck Vaughan see her nervousness. "As such, it's my duty to return it."

She set the mask on the man's clear desktop, more than eager to let it go. Her fingers tingled every time she touched it. Not an unpleasant sensation, but still, unsettling. The cedar box was the only vessel she'd found that blocked the feeling.

From inside the box, she plucked the handwritten delivery receipt she'd drawn up during the flight and set it on the desk before the cultural resources manager. "If you'll just sign here that you've received the mask, I'll be on my way."

He leaned back in his chair, a slow smile spreading across his face. For the first time, his eyes showed a hint of life, no longer an icy blue. It occurred to her that he was rather hot, something she hadn't noticed in her flustered, eager-to-unload-the-artifact state.

"No," he said.

The force of her heartbeat increased as her body flushed with adrenaline. He *had* to take the artifact. She'd risked her career for this, not to mention her sanity. If he didn't take it, how would she get the nightmares to stop? She couldn't go on like this. She doubted she'd last another day. "No?"

"No."

The man conserved words like they were a finite resource. She found the trait irritating. "Why not?" Admittedly, the receipt was a cheap ploy to defend herself from prosecution should the museum claim she stole the artifact—*which she had*—and tried to sell it—*which she would never, ever do*. The cultural resource manager's signature would at least show she'd returned the artifact to its rightful owner, and that no money had changed hands.

"You can't just walk in here, drop off a priceless artifact, ask me to sign a release for it, and leave."

Priceless? Since when did tribal cultural resource managers think in terms of worth when it came to artifacts? Usually they assiduously avoided all references to monetary value when it came to artifacts of cultural heritage—*especially* artifacts subject to NAGPRA. And this mask almost certainly had been grave goods. Odds were, it had been buried with a powerful tribal leader—a shaman, who, Sienna believed, still inhabited the annoying relic. "Are you..." She wanted to say *kidding me?* but stopped herself and instead said, "Mr. Vaughan?" managing to erase all snark from her tone.

"Yes."

The single word sat alone in the air as she waited for him to offer some sort of explanation for his refusal. What Tribal Historic Preservation Officer—or rather, THPO equivalent—didn't want to receive an obviously old and dear piece of his tribe's cultural history?

But, true to form, the man said nothing. He merely stared at her, waiting for her to hang herself. She had a feeling he visualized handing her the rope. Which made her wonder if he knew exactly what she'd risked in bringing the mask home, and why he refused to help her.

She stood, slowly, feeling an ache in her belly and in her heart as she realized how badly she'd miscalculated. If he wouldn't take the mask, she really had stolen it. She'd already lost her client, but now she might lose her business. She could even go to jail. But the worst part was her sister—co-owner of Aubrey Sisters Heritage Preservation—was going to kill her.

But Larkspur had been in Hawaii for the last two months and

didn't know what was going on with Sienna and their museum client. Larkspur had no idea the mask had taken over. Or that maybe Sienna had gone insane. One or the other.

But the mask being possessed by a spirit was the preferred option.

"The mask is yours. Why refuse it? I've never met a tribal cultural resources manager who wasn't eager to reclaim a piece of their tribe's cultural heritage."

"You show up here after hours, drop an ancient mask on the desk, and expect me to sign a scribbled delivery receipt when you haven't even shown me so much as a business card? We may be out in the Alaskan boonies, Ms. Aubrey, but that doesn't make me ignorant. I recognize when something is off. And *you* are definitely off."

She stiffened her spine, hating that he was right but ready to defend herself anyway. "I was supposed to arrive much earlier, but my flight from Seattle was late into Anchorage, plus they lost my bag, so I missed the ten thirty flight to Itqaklut and had to catch the four o'clock. Then I got a flat tire on the way here. It took me almost forty-five minutes to get the bolts off. I had a seat on the nine o'clock flight back to Anchorage tonight. Without the flat, I might have made it."

The man cocked his head. "What if I hadn't been here? Was your plan to dump the mask on the front steps and leave?"

"Heavens, no! I would never be so negligent with an artifact! I'm a curation specialist." She sighed and sat back in her seat. "I didn't expect you to be here, but it was worth a shot. I don't exactly have anywhere else to go. With the Midnight Sun Festival this week, there isn't a hotel room or bed and breakfast with a bed available—which was why I'd booked a flight back to Anchorage tonight. So it was either drive here and see if I could catch you, and maybe even catch the return flight, or sit in the airport until morning and then drive here."

If she were less desperate, she'd never have risked getting on the flight from Anchorage in the first place. She'd known the odds of catching the return flight were slim, but the idea of spending even one more night with the demon mask was too much. She'd had to try to get rid of it.

She dug around in her purse and pulled out a business card. "Here's my card. I'm legit. Please, sign the release so I can get to one of the restaurants in Itqaklut before they close. I haven't eaten since before my six a.m. flight from Seattle this morning. I'm exhausted, hungry, and I've got a long night ahead of me without a bed in my future."

Vaughan stared at her, his face blank and those blue, blue eyes unreadable. Finally he said, "I won't sign the release, but I can offer you dinner and a bed."

WANT TO READ more? You can find links to purchase *Midnight Sun* on my website at www.Rachel-Grant.net.

About the Author

Four-time Golden Heart® finalist Rachel Grant worked for over a decade as a professional archaeologist and mines her experiences for storylines and settings, which are as diverse as excavating a cemetery underneath an historic art museum in San Francisco, survey and excavation of many prehistoric Native American sites in the Pacific Northwest, researching an historic concrete house in Virginia, and mapping a seventeenth century Spanish and Dutch fort on the island of Sint Maarten in the Netherlands Antilles.

She lives in the Pacific Northwest with her husband and children and can be found on the web at Rachel-Grant.net.

Printed in Great Britain
by Amazon